The Silk Road

Also by Kathryn Davis

The Silk Road

A Novel

Kathryn Davis

Graywolf Press

This publication is made possible, in part, by the voters of Minnesota through a Minnesota State Arts Board Operating Support grant, thanks to a legislative appropriation from the arts and cultural heritage fund, and a grant from the Wells Fargo Foundation. Significant support has also been provided by Target, the McKnight Foundation, the Lannan Foundation, the Amazon Literary Partnership, and other generous contributions from foundations, corporations, and individuals. To these organizations and individuals we offer our heartfelt thanks.

Published by Graywolf Press
250 Third Avenue North, Suite 600
Minneapolis, Minnesota 55401

www.graywolfpress.org

Published in the United States of America
Printed in Canada

ISBN 978-1-55597-829-7

2 4 6 8 9 7 5 3 1
First Graywolf Printing, 2019

Library of Congress Control Number: 2018947090

Cover design: Kyle G. Hunter

Cover art: Shutterstock

For Eric

The Silk Road

We were in the labyrinth. Afterward, no one could agree on the time. Jee Moon was tucking someone's right hand in under their blanket, having first tucked in the left. She did this tenderly but firmly, as if to suggest we could be doing it for ourselves. Next she took someone's head and lifted it like it wasn't part of a human body, a cabbage or a planet or the repository of all good thoughts and evil, which, when you think about it, is exactly what a human head is. Everyone could smell the gas the permafrost gave off as it melted; we could feel the labyrinth floor sinking under our mats. Lower, lower, going down, deeper down than Paradise. Department stores used to have elevators and the elevators had operators who told you what you were going to find when you stepped through the slowly opening door. There would be a white torso without a head or arms; there would be people you knew you'd never meet again.

The smell of gas in the labyrinth mixed with the smell of incense and, though no one could see it—Jee Moon having covered our dark, restless eyes with eye pillows—we could picture smoke emerging from the incense burner in a coil that continued to hold its shape even after lifting into the air. Like the goddess Dhumavati, she who represents ultimate annihilation, the smoke that's going to be what's left of the universe after everything else has been destroyed.

At some point someone started snoring, a surprisingly gentle noise. You weren't supposed to pay attention to things like that but it was hard not to, the world—all fourteen of them, of which ours was the lowest of the low if Jee Moon was to be believed—being too much with us. Sometimes she would move on quickly from blanket to blanket, but today she lingered, pressing her fingers into the soft tissue at the base of each skull.

You can't pretend to be relaxed. You can't pretend the smoky one isn't right there in the room with you, with her winnowing basket and her crow.

Though in the north the crow would have to be a raven.

I am breathing in, I am breathing out; I am hearing someone snore, I am hearing someone think.

There is more organic carbon in northern peat than in all other living things combined.

Man is the knot and bond of the universe.

You are my sweetheart. My darling.

So the gods take their seats.

We couldn't hear each other's thoughts distinctly, nor could we hear them all at once. Jee Moon was a mystery to us, shrouded in something aqueous, something radiant and endlessly shifting, the impenetrable deep blue of a newborn's eyes. The winnowing basket used to separate the husk from the grain, the outer illusory form from the inner reality.

The practice that day had been strenuous, involving arm balances, and you didn't have to be a mind reader to know everyone was relieved to be lying on their mat for Savasana. Time to relax, let everything go, lie there like a corpse. This was the most challenging of the poses if you took into account the fact that the room was filled with people who knew the world was coming to an end and that if we worked at it hard enough we would never die.

Sometimes it happened that an image was not supplied and that what before was a woman turned out to have changed into a man, a different age and face succeeding the first. The deer, the fire worm, the black bee, the fish—each of us had made the same mistake at least once, thrown off by shifting leaves or the smell of sex, by a flickering candle or a worm on a hook. The Astronomer, the Archivist, the Botanist, the Keeper, the Topologist, the Geographer, the Iceman. The Cook was in the kitchen; he always had an excuse.

There were two doors in the room. One door led back into the labyrinth's tunnel system through an anteroom with hooks to hang things on, cubbyholes for shoes and personal belongings such as eyeglasses or notebooks. The second door led to a small lavatory in which, on a shelf above the toilet, Ganesh reclined, his belly rising and falling, composed of the dirt of Shakti's body. The five-headed snake ferried Lord Krishna across the water.

Chariot, chariot, si tu veux de moi . . .

Moreover in the sum of all things there is no one thing that is begotten single.

This was the way it happened in this room: thoughts swarmed from our heads and—not being solely the province of the brain— from other parts of our bodies, and rose to link themselves with other thoughts in a molecular action not unlike that of the incense with the air, giving rise to new entities and worlds, pasts, presents, and futures. The Chariot rode the stars, five of them driven by the five celestial emperors in the constellation *wuche* or tucked inside the constellation Ursa Major, *arktos* for north, *bear* in Greek, number seven in the Major Arcana, and rendered "I will follow him" by Little Peggy March, the song's English translation being so much less frightening than "Under the last star I will leave with you across the plain, the plain, the plain with no ending . . ."

The danger, as always, was incontestable, we knew that. It was intent on breaking up the first beginnings of things, on stopping our vital motions entirely until we ended up untying from our bodies the fastenings of the soul, forcing it out through the pores.

The danger was everywhere, but we didn't know where to look for it, only that it was gathering strength, getting ready to send a foot out at a sudden angle like an amoeba preparing to move, tripping whoever was trying to make their way to the bathroom without being noticed. Later the question would arise as to whether this was done on purpose—whether someone had looked out from under their eye pillow at the exact moment whoever it was who was heading to the bathroom began to move, though everyone swore they hadn't seen a thing.

What happened wasn't exactly like karma—it was more like we couldn't imagine any other way for things to happen. Even if we believed in past lives or in being reborn as something different from ourselves, whoever each of us was could never imagine having come from a previous life or to be entering into a new one totally unlike the lives we were living now. The cars of the train needed to at least be cars, if not from the same railroad, or the same kind of cars, sleepers, dining cars, freight, engine, caboose. Not all things that befell us from the heavenly bodies were inevitable.

The door to the bathroom opened and shut almost noiselessly. Once a person was inside it was impossible to do anything without being overheard. First came the sound of water, in a rush or a protracted trickle, followed sometimes by the rattle of the paper dispenser. The quiet intensified as everyone waited, trying not to laugh. The toilet flushed; the door to the tunnel slammed.

What was *that*? someone whispered.

The answer was obvious but even so someone whispered back, the *bath*room.

Carefully, trying not to attract Jee Moon's attention, we stole a look. The bathroom door was still shut but the door to the tunnel was ajar, and beyond all our blanket-wrapped forms the anteroom's shadowy interior was just barely visible. Had the door to the tunnel been open the whole time we'd been inside? Jee Moon's habit was to close it once we were settled on our mats, seated in easy pose and starting to pay attention to our breathing. The idea was to keep everything in the room *in* the room, to stifle the temptation to think past the door and into the anteroom, down the unlit pathways of the labyrinth we'd all learned to traverse blind like ideas navigating the neural pathways of the brain, moving as far from the settlement as we could to arrive finally in the outspread blue air at the cove's edge. This was late spring, the season of candle ice. The caribou were on the move. You didn't want your mind slipping through along with that first cloven hoof.

Slowly now, Jee Moon was saying. Roll onto your side. Slowly, slowly. Take your time. Curl yourself in a ball like a baby.

At first you couldn't hear the sounds everyone was making, you were so tuned to the sound of your own breath. Gradually it was a pleasure to hear the ripping sound of skin lifting from a rubber mat, a sigh, a blown nose, outerwear being zipped. By the time you found yourself back in easy pose and had opened your eyes it was as if you didn't know where you'd been for the last hour. It could have been more than that; it could have been an instant. Without windows or a clock it was impossible to tell.

We didn't realize what was going on right away. Hey, sleepyhead, Jee Moon said, approaching the back of the room.

Later we couldn't remember which one of us it was who asked if anybody had a mirror to check for breath. The Iceman thought it was the Topologist who provided a compact but it was the Keeper who turned out to have one. From the old days, she explained, accessory to a bad habit.

Each of us came with a past attached, like a wagon or a bindle or a hump.

The town of Le Puy-en-Velay is cupped inside what was once the core of an ancient volcano; high pointed peaks stick up everywhere. For over a thousand years pilgrims have been walking the trail leading out of it to a place where the world comes to an end on the Spanish coast.

Upon her arrival in Le Puy the Topologist located the hostel she'd found circled in the guidebook; for almost no money at all she was allotted a cubicle containing a narrow bed and a lumpy bolster over which she spread the blue silk sleep sack that was to protect her from bedbugs. The trip and the guidebook describing it had been a retirement present from her department, the sleep sack from the department secretary, who cried when she left.

Les punaises, the Geographer said. *Punaise* was French for *bedbug*. She was fluent in the language, having spent a year as an exchange student in France. By this date in history most people in the civilized world had sustained a bite or two, if not a full-blown infestation.

Le Puy is also the lentil capital of the world, the Cook informed us.

It was still light out when the Topologist left the hostel to explore; the sun wouldn't set until ten. She climbed the steps—267 of them—to the chapel set atop the "Needle," a magma plug from which vantage point she could look down on the town as it lost definition at her feet. Soon it would be nothing more than a twinkling of lights—this was probably how God came up with his idea for the night sky.

Back home it was still afternoon; back home nothing had changed. The department secretary would be sitting at her desk, sharing the postcard the Topologist had sent from Paris with some of her colleagues. If it weren't for them, she wouldn't have been in Le Puy in the first place.

Of course there had never been an alternative for any of us; we were linked in ways we could only begin to dream of imagining.

Think of it, Jee Moon said. We were, all of us, dark-eyed. We had, all of us, experienced childhood as a storm of black pebbles, of dazzling brocade and hail, our sixteenth birthday a carpet rolled like a shadowed pathway to an ever-receding vanishing point.

Was this true? The Topologist prided herself on her imperfect memory of the past in contrast to her ability to name the countable ordinals. Her eyes were brown, not particularly dark. She seemed to recall a fight, a bad one, the night she turned sixteen. But as for who was fighting and with whom, she had no recollection, only of heavy footfalls down the front hall, the unfamiliar smell of a wet thing cracked open.

You might come around a bend, open a door, turn a corner, and there it would be, the very thing you thought you'd lost, restored to life. That was why we had, all of us, accumulated so many black pebbles.

It would be best if we prepared ourselves to move on, Jee Moon said.

Get ready to go swiftly on the black path!

Even though the volcano that had exploded where she now stood had been asleep for centuries, the Topologist could feel the fury of the earth's molten core coming up from the bottom of her feet and out the top of her head. Before it had been a Christian chapel this had been a shrine to Mercury, god of messages and poetry, commerce and thieves. He was also charged with conveying the souls of the newly dead to the Underworld. Little green lizards appeared from between crevices in the stonework and just as suddenly disappeared back into them, their pink tongues poking in and out of their grinning mouths.

The Topologist didn't sleep well that first night, surrounded on all sides by the intimate sound of people sleeping. "You snore," the Swede in the adjacent cubicle cheerfully informed her when they emerged from their beds at the same time the next morning.

"You do too," the Topologist replied, even though he hadn't.

The Swede had a wide-open face and a cap of white-blond hair. "Are you going to get blessed?" he asked. After the bishop blessed you, you were given a free rosary.

It was hard to resist the kind of prize a person got for doing something for which you'd normally get nothing. On the other hand, if the Topologist left with the Swede to be blessed by the bishop they'd have to walk together on the trail.

"I don't think so," she said.

"It's no big deal," the Swede said. "They're made of plastic."

The morning was beautiful, Le Puy's streets empty of all but a few clerics in long black cassocks, sliding up and down the steep pathways like chessmen. Dew had fallen on everything, leaving behind the smell of wet stone and, as the sun rose, the smell of water evaporating into thin air. Evaporation could happen to anyone—there hadn't always been blazes to guide an errant pilgrim. In the Middle Ages pilgrims got lost, never to be seen again. Nowadays all a pilgrim had to do was follow the blazes. These were a white stripe above a red stripe; if the stripes made an X it meant you'd taken a wrong turn. Sometimes there were stretches of trail where the blazes were hard to see. In the Savage Domain, known for its terrible weather, its hail and lightning and impenetrable fog, its monstrous dog-headed beast—when you were in the Savage Domain and you couldn't see the blazes, you had the bell. All you had to do to escape the beast was to follow the sound of the bell.

The bell had a girl's name. Surely one of us remembered?

But there were things we'd decided to forget and this was one of them.

The Topologist lifted her hands to her ears. What if the part of her that was capable of hearing vanished first? She was experiencing the uncanny effect of Le Puy. A person could feel her own embodiment shrink in contrast with all the stone. And what about the smell of food? What about that? The space here wasn't foldable or stretchable the way she was used to it behaving in a controlled environment. In Le Puy the idea of eating—of trying to insert one solid object inside another, an apple into a human body, say, or even something as small as a lentil—was impossible.

She started walking. Downhill, downhill, into the cool dark bottom of the volcano. The sun kept rising; the sky was the color of the Swede's eyes. When she was a girl the plan had been simple: she would tether herself to another person. It had been a fine plan; more than once it had saved her life. Even now, years later, she was capable of feeling the tug. But did it keep her safe or was it more like a noose?

The Archivist objected. The noose was *his*, he pointed out. It was *his* scourge, not hers.

As if a person could own a means of execution.

At length the Topologist hit bottom and began ascending the rue des Capucins. The ascent was even steeper than the descent, and there were benches at intervals along the road, on one of which sat a heavyset woman wearing a red rain poncho. "Courage!" the woman said, giving the word its French pronunciation while lifting her hand in a fist. The poncho made it hard to see her face.

"Courage!" the Topologist echoed, though what she wanted to say was "It's not raining."

Courage, courage. It wasn't like it took courage to do what she was doing. At the top of the hill, as the guidebook predicted, there was a modern factory building, a wide gravel lane along a high stone wall. Up, then down again. This was what volcanoes did to a landscape! For a while she walked above the gorge of the Gazelle on a path strewn with mossy boulders. Her plan was to stop at the first village she came to and buy bread and cheese and sausage for lunch. She saw cows and donkeys, cats and chickens.

What kind of moss? the Iceman asked, though we all knew he didn't expect an answer.

The Cook awoke from his nap with a start. Don't forget the wine, he said. The wine there is the best in the world.

So you walked, said the Archivist. There were cows. There were walls. No one's interested in a travelogue.

It was obvious he was still angry about the noose. In any case, we knew where the story was headed. According to the lore of the trail, a day or so out of Le Puy a person was going to appear and advise the Topologist to ignore the red and white blazes in favor of a shortcut they would describe in detail. The consequences of taking this advice were various. She might end up back where she started. She might find herself spending a lonely night in a dark wood. She might never be seen again.

The dark wood, of course. The dark wood was the clue.

Jee Moon was looking off into space in that way of hers, narrowing her eyes.

Midway on our life's journey, the Iceman said.

It was a large person, the Topologist said. There were so many wayside crosses it was confusing. She glanced around the room and we all became self-conscious about our size.

Was it a man or a woman? The Geographer was taking out her tablet.

I don't know, the Topologist replied.

You don't know? the Keeper said, laughing. You scholars! It's a miracle you ever reproduce.

The person was *back*lit, the Topologist explained. Whoever they were, they stepped out from behind a cross. They had on a bandana, pirate style. It must have been late in the day because the sun was shining in the Topologist's eyes as it made its way to the horizon. Soon night would fall and the section of trail between where she stood and the next village was steep and rocky. The trail here was treacherous under the best of conditions but now that a light rain had started falling, the moss-covered rocks were going to be slippery.

It was on the third day. Aside from the Swede, the Topologist had encountered very few fellow pilgrims, the fast pilgrims who strode past her as if late for important appointments, the tired pilgrims propped against the trunks of trees. She was lonely, a condition she failed to recognize. Back home she spent a lot of time alone and so she thought she never got lonely; she forgot that someone was usually there even if she couldn't see them, in the department kitchen making coffee, at the copy machine, or mailing a package.

Sometimes her office mate was sitting right beside her in the same room and still she couldn't see him. That would be when she was busy traversing the infinity of points that were going to end up describing a perfect model of the unsolvable continuum hypothesis.

There turned out to be a shortcut skirting the Lake of the Egg. The Topologist liked the sound of that. She could bypass the steep section and get to Monistrol in time for dinner. If she decided to avoid the hostel, Monistrol boasted a three-star hotel. All she needed to do was ignore the blazes and follow a series of cairns marked with the letter *M*.

"For Monistrol," the Topologist guessed.

"If you like," the figure in the bandana said. It had a deep voice, but then so did some women.

The rain was coming down harder now. The first cairn was just visible off to the left in a thicket of yellow broom.

One foot in front of the other. This is how a person walks. We all knew this fact perfectly well. Voluntary action arises from within, from the unpredictable movement of a single atom. A trail was unfolding just ahead of each footstep, and then, faintly visible through the rain and gathering dark, another cairn. How is it possible for the solid objects around us to melt away into the past, and for a new order of objects to emerge mysteriously from the future? As promised, the trail didn't descend sharply, nor was it rock-strewn. If anything, it was resilient underfoot, a moist web of vegetation, pale green and translucent like a luna moth's wings. While she walked, the Topologist felt herself becoming aroused. It was as if whatever lay beneath her had its attention fixed amorously on the cleft between her legs. She felt like she was naked from the waist down, hungrily observed and getting wet, her breath coming faster and faster.

Walking can do that, said the Keeper. It's perfectly normal. She was trying to be reassuring, like a mother.

Sphagnum subnitens, said the Iceman. Glittering sphagnum. All it thinks about is sex.

Two cairns, three cairns, four cairns. By now the rain was coming down so hard the Topologist could barely see a thing. Eventually she lost count, her mind's aching avenues of thought set loose through every part of her. There was a sound emerging from the back of her throat and her eyes had stopped seeing anything except in her mind's eye those moist green funicles, glittering— yes! that's what they were doing!—glittering and teasing. Touch me, she thought, please, oh please, the slightest touch . . .

She came violently, lying on her back at the threshold of a low stone building that appeared to be a shrine to Saint Roch. A small brown dog, some kind of hound with long ears and pleading eyes, sat off to one side of the building, violently trying to scratch itself in a place it couldn't reach. "Here boy," the Topologist said, putting out her hand, but of course she was forgetting. The dog spoke French.

Saint Roch, said the Archivist. That one's mine, too.

You can't *own* a saint, said the Keeper. A saint's day can be yours, but that's it.

I'm not trying to take anything away from you, said the Topologist. I'm just saying where I was. I thought that's what we were supposed to be doing. To figure out what happened to one of us back there in the labyrinth.

She looked at Jee Moon, who was looking at the Archivist with a severe expression on her face.

Stop it, Jee Moon said to him, and everyone drew a breath, momentarily shocked.

Where was I? the Topologist asked. I certainly wasn't anywhere near the Lake of the Egg, if there even is such a place.

Blazing a trail through pathless tracts, said the Iceman.

There was a plastic bag caught in the underbrush. A scrap of something held trembling there. Am I the only one who remembers? said the Botanist.

It happened that the Topologist was on the threshold of a very old shrine to the saint known in France as Saint Roch, in Germany as Rochus, Rocco in Italy, Rock in England. The trail guide listed many shrines to Saint Roch but this wasn't one of them. Like the other shrines it was Romanesque in style, the windows mere slits in the walls, the ceiling low, the only light coming from a handful of votive candles of varying length, burning in two small racks near the altar. Who had lit them? the Topologist wondered—it seemed like she had ventured a great distance from the trail, though the presence of the dog suggested she might not be as far from human habitation as she thought.

The saint was in the shrine. He was a good-looking young man clad in a brown tunic printed with gold *fleurs-de-lys*, the hem of which he was in the process of lifting flirtatiously above his left knee.

Flirtatious! said the Archivist. You've got to be kidding. The saint isn't *flirting*! The saint is lifting his hem to show the plague sores on his thigh. The Archivist had learned this from the sisters at Saint Roch parochial school. The saint was born to rich parents who died when he was twenty years old, at which point he gave away his worldly possessions and set out on a pilgrimage. Somewhere in Italy he encountered an epidemic of the plague and for a while he tended the sick, effecting many miraculous cures by the power of prayer and the touch of his hand. Eventually, though, he contracted the disease and was expelled from town by the very people he'd been helping. He went into the forest where he lived in a hut made of tree limbs and leaves; he would have died if it weren't for the little dog that brought him bread and licked his wounds to heal them.

You mean an icon, right? The Botanist had come to sit beside the Topologist; she was sitting very close, closer than the Topologist liked. It wasn't the saint himself in the shrine with you, the Botanist said. She didn't mean this as a question.

But that was such a long time ago! The Topologist could feel the Botanist scrutinizing her for a sign of whatever it was that had turned her from a stern-faced girl with dark brows and thin brown hair and a long upper lip, a string bean of a girl wearing pale blue cat's-eye glasses, into what she was now, a tube of skin that could be stretched into a torus to contain an entire universe. Soon there would be nothing left, the walls of the tube getting thinner and thinner, the skin powdering off, powdering, powdering, like the snow that wouldn't stop falling, the uncountable realm of stars.

I don't know, the Topologist said. Maybe it was just an icon.

But if so, why was he warm to the touch? And what about the little dog?

The Botanist was petting the Topologist's forearm, a gesture we remembered from our school days, sitting in assembly singing songs about the seasons, about the bluebirds gaily singing, the autumn leaves falling, the ash grove how peaceful, the sleigh on the roof. A light stroke from the crook of the elbow to the wrist—the girl who invented it called it tickling and she was especially good at it. She was a poet but our mother called her P, for Pest. P for Perfect. P for Poisonous. Everyone wanted to sit next to her.

All I know is, we are very lucky to be here, the Botanist said. We should count our lucky stars.

That's right, said Jee Moon. You should.

We should count carefully, said the Topologist. It's easy to make a mistake.

Lucky stars! The Astronomer was laughing.

I don't see what's so funny, said the Botanist.

But everyone knew the Botanist didn't have a sense of humor.

The settlement was here before we arrived. Though it appeared uninhabited there was a sense in the place of a room you've walked into that's been recently vacated, that feeling of a stir in the air we associated with entering what we used to call the Morning Room, due to the fact that the sun streamed through its tall front windows every morning and then went away before noon, leaving the room dark and cold and more empty than before, Father's paper still unfolding itself on the piecrust table, the stems of his reading glasses folding themselves back in place, the leather wings of the daemon that had only recently left the room spreading for flight.

There had been no trail guide any of us could remember. The Geographer had been mapping the retreating hem of the glacier, the Astronomer the wandering stars of Boötes. At some point the Topologist remembered having owned a guidebook but she thought she left it on a café table somewhere in the Aubrac. She'd been preoccupied, having just noticed the nice-looking blond man across the road, pausing to upturn a pebble from his hiking shoe.

The Swede! said the Botanist. He was waiting for you—don't tell me it wasn't the Swede!

The Archivist expelled a breath. Love and marriage, he said. Is that all you girls think about?

When pressed to give an explanation for how he got here all he could remember was an overwhelming need to keep a long-standing appointment.

Like in a dream, said the Cook. The train is leaving the station. There's so much steam you can't see a thing. And where is your bag? And where is your sweetheart?

With a trail guide you have the illusion of control, the Geographer conceded. The way you do with a map. The sense of space as a controlled substance is overpowering, except you don't know where it's going to take you.

You don't! agreed the Keeper. One minute you're hallucinating, the next minute here you are. She tossed her head and a shudder ran through her magnificent burnished flesh.

When you arrive at the edge of the world you stop remembering things like how you got there. Your attention keeps pouring over the edge, out and away from the footprints left behind you in the snow, unable to focus on anything except the cove of sparkling light there at the foot of the escarpment. It was either a real pool full of something like water—we were in agreement on that if nothing else—or just a gathering of attention, all of it in one place, as solid and bright-surfaced as a jewel but otherwise beside the point.

Meanwhile the sky had lifted so far above us that we could hardly see it. It was white the way everything in the place was white, only strangely contained as if soffitted, as if in lifting itself it had become part of an immense architectural plan, the ceiling of a house that had been there from the beginning. I am so small, each of us thought, stirring the air while we walked along in a way we experienced as a need to speak, something inside ourselves opening. That's when Nanny would appear from out of nowhere, a pile of fresh, warm towels in her arms. Bath time proceeded according to age, youngest to oldest. There would be some tears and then, in the little yard behind the scullery, a shared cigarette or two.

The land the settlement was built on belonged to our ancestor who had been a famous explorer. It was a wild, tilting tract high above the sea, at its foot the cove where the floatplane landed. His journals were kept behind locked doors in the glass-fronted bookcase in the library, along with family treasures like the big egg with maroon spots and the meteorite. From the distaff side, our mother told us. All of it. You won't find a single explorer on your father's side. They're meek as lambs, the lot of them.

Of course to say that the land belonged to our ancestor is a falsehood. He never paid for it and even if he'd wanted to, the original inhabitants of the place didn't consider it their property. The money we came from was old money, our ancestors having hauled it with them first across land and then across sea, planting it where they landed, cultivating whatever grew there until its taproot was too deep to disturb. Human beings have always moved from place to place, whether by design or due to the unforeseen, droughts and wars, pestilence and persecution, the Silk Road they traveled on a conduit not merely for precious commodities, for spices and jewels, mirrors and honey, but for everything strange or unknown, a variety of alien gods and ideas, an unbounded universe with nothing outside it, the dung-covered eggs of the silkworm. This was our birthright, this easy assurance that whatever we wanted was ours, both to have and to bestow. We knew nothing about privation and adventure, as Jee Moon liked to remind us. It was common knowledge Nanny had spoiled us rotten.

According to our ancestor's journal, he fell in love with the place at first sight, having traversed the interior plateau in a canoe with his new bride. After weeks navigating rapids in a seething cloud of bugs, the occult emptiness of the scene before him was like hearing from someone he thought had died. He rested his paddle athwart his knees. He shivered, sharply aware of his carnal self, the sea extending everywhere he looked as darkly bright as outer space.

Back then there was nothing to interpose between the young couple and eternity. There was no greenhouse, no kennel, no labyrinth, and whatever grew was stunted in the way of Arctic vegetation, whole trees no bigger than a person's little finger. They erected their tent on the site of what would eventually become the Great Hall, and because they were tenting on bare rock in a high wind they had to weight the pegs with deadmen. It was a boundless night, the compass needle quivering, unable to fix on a single point. At some moment near dawn a child was conceived. Our mother told us the rest was history, her intention, as usual, misleading.

By the time we got here the settlement was firmly established, with the Great Hall at its center and the labyrinth beneath it, though none of this was apparent from the beach. The first snow had fallen, leaving the face of the bedrock shining through like a postulant's from behind a veil. The black flies and mosquitoes were long gone and the sea was so clear you could see all the way to the gas fields on the bottom.

I need to take a sounding, said the Geographer. Could you give me room? She removed from her pack a thing that looked like an icicle and held it out in front of her, heading down the beach to where the Iceman sat eating a sandwich with his back leaned up against a large cairn. The cairn stood alone, suggesting it might not be a trail marker but a monument of some kind, possibly a cenotaph or an actual gravestone with a dead person lying beneath it. No matter what it was, we were cheered to discover it, its presence suggesting that we had actually arrived somewhere.

Do you think you should be doing that? asked the Archivist, and the Iceman laughed, snapping the top off a bottle of beer.

Relax, he said, holding out his sandwich. Have a bite.

The Keeper hugged herself, pulling her hands up into her sleeves. You're right, she said to the Archivist. We don't want to be disrespectful. She glanced back over her shoulder at the rim of the escarpment where the white sky was being overrun by thick, churning clouds.

The sense of being watched was overpowering: we were all aware of it, even if we pretended not to be. Such regard created an illusion of intimacy between us, a sense that whatever was watching could feel each breath as it took visible shape in the air, could register each passing thought each time we moved our eyes, as well as the moistness of our eyes, the dryness of our chapped lips.

Like that depressing magazine in the pediatrician's office. This is a watchbird watching a person doing something they shouldn't be doing. This is a watchbird watching *you*.

An immense angle of sunlight had erected itself where we stood on the beach, illuminating us and the pile of stones around which we were gathered. Someone had been fastidious when assembling these stones, limiting their selection to beach cobble, quartzite, and chert. There was no way of knowing how long ago this had happened.

The things that got left behind were left here because no one was in any condition to take them away, or because the people who left them wanted to make sure they'd return. Whalers left behind baleen carvings and floor tiles, fishermen left behind fish skeletons and little leeks called hives. The Moravian missionaries thought they were never going to leave; thousands of years before them the first mammal hunters, appeasing a different god, left behind the body of a young girl, wrapped in bark and painted with red ocher.

The Place of the Watchbird, the Geographer wrote in her tablet, naming it, and the icicle meter began clicking like a cat when it sees a mouse.

It had been the same for all of us: we left in a hurry, without the proper maps. We forgot things, a purse, a ticket, a kiss goodbye. The water faucet wasn't shut off all the way and the lights were still on, or at least they were when we turned the key in the lock. What was the use of locking up? There was no way to keep the water from escaping once it filled every room, to keep it from rising to the ceiling where it would short the lights. Not to mention the bodies of the fleas, borne on the flood, gleaming like jet beadwork. Did fleas even know how to swim?

Water is the flea's enemy, said the Keeper.

Several of us had been under the impression that fleas were the ones who were going to survive Armageddon, but it turned out that was cockroaches.

The Geographer said it was like she wasn't even there and we all knew what she meant. Except for the bites it was like we didn't exist. This was the first time in her life the Geographer had no idea where she was, and it wasn't going to be the last.

In the distance she heard a bell toll, an old bell with a crack in it, once, twice, three times. Meanwhile the river continued to bend and the road to bend with it. There wasn't any other traffic, the tire tracks visible for a moment before filling with white. There was nothing, really.

The Angelus, the Archivist said. That's what you were hearing. Three strokes. Hail Mary full of grace.

Maybe it had just turned three o'clock, said the Cook.

The bell, though—the bell was to be expected. No one needed to point this out.

The Geographer and her husband had just come over the bridge when she saw a pair of eyes—a pair of yellow eyes suspended in a thicket. "What's that?" she asked. Visibility was poor, her husband's vision not so good. He was older than she was and he drove too fast. The planet moved on its axis; morning approached. With one hand the Geographer was scratching bites, with the other she was trying to bring something besides static in on the radio. The bell continued to ring; in the headlights she saw a faint suggestion of a face, a terrible combination of one thing and another, maybe a dog with a human hairdo or a person with a pointed snout.

"Watch out!" the Geographer screamed. Her husband applied the brakes, pressing his foot down hard.

A pair of eyes—they were the brightest thing they'd seen for hours. A pair of eyes. Paradise. It was as dark there as in the deepest well.

It was even darker than that, said the Iceman. It was as if the darkness filled all the openings and blocked all the passages.

The Geographer and her husband must have been on Portal Road. That was the road a person had to take to get to the Garden of Paradise. You had to keep going—wrap yourself in your cloak!— just like in the story the principal used to tell us in assembly. The sun was burning but a step farther on it was icy cold. The bird that flew past had one wing in the heat of summer, the other in the cold of winter.

How fast had they been traveling? We would never know, though it had to have been extremely fast, given the evidence of the impact. The car was headed north on Portal Road, the Geographer's husband braking just before reaching the foot of the steep driveway that led to the hospital. At this point the road curved right and the car continued straight ahead, eventually crashing into the pillar marking the foot of the drive with sufficient force to knock it over, detaching the statue of the angel that had roosted there back when the hospital used to be a convent.

The snow kept falling, the flakes wider spread, bigger, signifying the storm's flagging energy. The world outside was silent; in the hospital atop the hill someone was swabbing a dying person's mouth. Neither person heard the crash—they were too far away and even if they hadn't been the snow acted like soundproofing.

A cotton washcloth, said the Botanist. That's what you use for the dying. You dip the washcloth in a basin of warm water infused with mint. The dying person's eyes don't slide shut the way they do in the movies.

What about the thing they hit? asked the Keeper. Did they kill it or what?

Still we all knew that whenever a thing quit its proper limits, this change of state would mark the death of that which went before.

The Geographer and her husband had left the city after dark. That's when it began, the Geographer turning the key in the door of their apartment and dropping it in the mailbox in case their daughter showed up. They both assumed they weren't going back, though to admit it would be to include the other in a private nightmare, like the drunk at the frat party who suggests everyone climb into his car while he drives into town for pizza. They didn't know where their daughter was, hadn't heard from her except for a postcard, its postmark smeared and illegible.

That was what was surprising—even though we presented as

27

childless, almost all of us had children, or were going to have them, or had had them, some of the children no longer alive, having ventured into the interstices, the infinity of gaps between the infinity of points on the line that was the continuum from A to Z, all those dying villages along the Silk Road where we stopped to ply our trade.

The subject of children was a subject we didn't tend to talk about. It emerged gradually, like a bad habit.

Like a genetic trait, said the Botanist. A birthmark.

Or like a solar system, said the Astronomer.

Like the identity of a murderer in a mystery, said the Archivist.

It had been a sweet, mild evening, the sidewalks wet from the latest storm, the smell of decomposing leaves and rain-damp concrete in the air. The Geographer had just returned to the apartment carrying a bag of groceries. She knew the power was off but she hit the wall switch with her elbow, anyway. That was when she felt the fleas.

Even if she hadn't heard the announcement the Geographer would have known what they were. She and her husband used to have a dog. They lost him around the same time they lost contact with their daughter. The Geographer had been walking him when he slipped his collar and took off around the corner, vanishing into the back alleyways where the marketeers and sexgirls plied their trade.

The apartment was lightless and quiet, the windows black. The drapes had yet to be drawn; the Geographer hated drapes. They made it look like the windows were wearing dresses. She set down the groceries and began feeling around in the bachelor chest for candles and a book of matches.

The chest stood just inside the front door, the same location our mother chose for it in the house on Fairmount Avenue. It was made of the same dark wood every other piece of furniture in the house was made of.

Candles? said the Topologist. Don't you mean candle ends? There were never any unburned candles in the chest. The chest was a mess. Someone kept the drawer pulls polished, though. Wasn't there a cleaning lady?

No, said the Cook. It was Great Aunt Somebody. She had big bosoms and a tinkling voice like a fairy.

There was a little silver shoe, said the Keeper. There was a little silver hat. There were decks of playing cards with cards missing. Single gloves and single mittens. Dog licenses. Jacks. Besides, unburned candles are bad luck.

The truth is, when we were young the future was like a dream.

From somewhere—outside, inside, the street below, the heavens—came the sound of wind, a rustling noise like a horse pawing snow, clearing space to graze. The Geographer's husband turned his key in the lock and opened the door, letting in a pool of shadows, a trickle of water.

Like anything with an exoskeleton, fleas are hard to kill. They've been endowed with extraordinarily long legs, for jumping. It was as if no time at all had passed. The fleas had been carried along the Silk Road in the traders' garments and in the silk itself, hidden among the spices and jewels and perfumes, on the bodies of the slaves. There hadn't been as many people coming and going then, though in most respects the situation wasn't very different. The Geographer's husband, for example—the pool of shadows surged around him. He had been bringing the fleas into the house with him for a while now, she knew this. The slaves' bodies were the only currency they had.

The weather, too, had changed for the worse. Everyone was heading north, the sickness not having arrived there yet. Everyone knew it was a physical condition—they were that knowledgeable—but the extent of what they knew was compromised by exposure to a glut of information and rumor, making it difficult to predict anything. Some people claimed mortality didn't come through Saturn and Jupiter but rather through Mars. Others said the work of the planets could not be avoided but there were things it was possible to avoid. Transmutation was easiest between bodies that had matching qualities. No one knew where the sickness came from or where it was going. No one knew which hospitals had medicine or empty beds or doctors or nurses. There were robbers abroad in the land. There were wild beasts.

Whatever the Geographer's husband had tried not to hit, he'd hit it anyway—the blood wasn't just inside the car but also on the snow outside it, big red drops leading to the river. The Geographer followed the trail of blood across the road and down a steep embankment. There were tracks of some kind as well, but the snow and wind and the fact that an appendage had been broken and dragged along behind, obliterating everything that preceded it, made them hard to read. They were big, though, bigger than you'd expect from the animals that usually get hit crossing a road. Deer mainly, and squirrels, the occasional large cat.

Black willow grew along the river, a tangle of fetters cased in ice. The Geographer drew back a branch and looked through the opening at the frozen water, a white expanse with a scrawl across it, some pale crouching thing just barely visible as it disappeared into the trees on the opposite bank. It seemed to have a large plumed tail and even at a distance it gave off an odor both repulsive and affecting, like the breath of a beloved old person with rotten teeth.

The Geographer tucked her coat tighter around herself and returned to the car. "You're going to be all right," she told her husband, though she had no idea whether this was true. She took his hand and felt the beat of his heart latent in the tip of each finger. It was as if she were holding onto a leash with some unpredictable thing hitched to the end of it. Like that time with their dog when it got away from her. Of course she couldn't control him—he was so much bigger and ruled by desires about which she knew absolutely nothing.

Some things were easier to remember than others. This was true for all of us. One thing we remembered was that there were always fresh flowers in the Morning Room. Our mother saw to it despite her allergies. She had terrible allergies, liquid running from her eyes and nose—also she sneezed constantly. She would arrange the stems in the vase Father bought for her on their honeymoon in France. She had been a virgin when she married— women were, then. She had asthma, too. We had to buy medicine for her from a short man standing behind a counter on a platform that made him look tall. Do you remember? Jee Moon was tracing the Geographer's inner forearm with the tip of her index finger and a thrill ran all the way from the Geographer's present self to her child self and back again.

Some of us wondered how Jee Moon knew about tickling, though she seemed to know about a lot of things, what had gone on in the elementary school auditorium, for example, the principal standing in front of us, hands clasped behind her back, waiting for us to be perfectly quiet so she could tell her depressing fairy tale. The Garden of Paradise. There was once a king's son. Was he handsome? Was he smart? He was certainly obsessed. Fresh flowers were always everywhere in the house, the Botanist said, but the most exotic blooms ended up in the Morning Room. Acacia. It smelled like girlhood.

And what did *that* smell like? The Cook, as usual, had a vulgar idea. He liked women though, he genuinely liked them—unlike the Archivist who claimed to be a ladies' man and wasn't.

We all had our love stories. This was true even for the Archivist, whose misfortune it had been to fall in love as a child with a girl who grew up to be a famous poet. Like most humans, she had a single heart, and that heart had room in it for only one person—that person being herself. The spirit of the age was compounded of arrogance and inattention, the predominant humor begotten of the *chylus*, cold and moist.

To our surprise, shortly after our arrival at the settlement we learned that one of us had two hearts, like an egg with two yolks. Supposedly there was a test that could tell us who it was. Even if you were pure as the driven snow it could happen. A shade, a shade that crept into the mind while the eyes were busy looking elsewhere. To have two hearts meant watch out!

The thing is, something happened in the labyrinth. Most of us had been alive and one of us was dead. If we remembered nothing else, surely we could remember that.

Don't look at me, said the Botanist. Why is everyone looking at me? Why are you looking at me like that?

In the labyrinth the Botanist was the one who yelled Wake up! Even though she was the nearest thing we had to a doctor, it felt weird to turn the body over to her for examination. How could she be impartial? the Archivist wanted to know—he was the first to mention foul play.

Still, we all knew there was something we were forgetting. Something obvious like the flowers or the principal or a wish made for something we'd been told we couldn't have, something taken away from us like the Garden of Paradise shining far off like a tiny twinkling star. Once a bee flew out of an acacia blossom as it opened and it flew around the Morning Room for a while until we forgot it was there. Don't you remember? the Keeper said. It landed on the edge of the love seat and when our mother took a nap the bee stung her on the foot. The Keeper made a paste of baking soda and water to draw out the stinger. She knew how to do things like this.

That was because she liked to go barefoot, the Geographer reminded us. The Geographer could be sentimental, something we tended to forget, but then the Iceman reminded us about the bunions.

By the time the Cook came to find us we were still standing around trying to decide what to do. Dinner was getting cold, he told us. He was angry, we could tell—even after he noticed the body lying there under a blanket he remained visibly annoyed. What makes you think it was murder? the Cook asked. People die. He pulled off the blanket.

It left in its stinger, the Keeper said. There was swelling.

What the fuck are you talking about? asked the Cook.

That, said the Keeper, and she pointed at the foot.

The Archivist warned her not to touch. Until the Botanist concluded her examination, he said, better assume anything was possible.

We let him play detective even though he wasn't very good at it.

Think back, the Archivist said; despite a psyche beset with thorns, he had a beautiful baritone voice.

The past, he reminded us, and all at once we felt it slithering through our ears and throats like a bolt of silk, Mother on her way out the door and the smell of her perfume, the man leaning against the hood of the town car, smoking a cigarette.

Maybe it was poison, said the Keeper.

Maybe there were other people involved, said the Iceman. People besides us.

The thing is, we hadn't been loved equally. Those nights when our mother left us alone with Nanny she would kiss each of us goodnight, but the kisses weren't the same. She used to pretend they were but we could tell the difference—once we were old enough to compare notes, that is. Some of us got the lightest touch of her lips on the hardest part of our head. Some of us got a little squeeze and a kiss in the air near our cheek. Some of us got our name, whispered. Some of us got a pat on the rear end. The ones who refused to talk about it were the ones who got the best kisses. We knew this, just as we knew that when each of us came out of her we could have been anything. We could have been a caterpillar or an acorn, fashioned of cloth or hammered tin. We could have been like paper money or silver like a coin. We could have been silverfish. We could have fallen to the floor, slid between the tiles, never to be seen again.

The Keeper was pointing at a spot on the foot just below the ankle. It's possible the skin was punctured by a needle, she said. An ordinary needle like a woman would use to hem a dress, with an eye too small to thread.

We were all presbyopic, even the Botanist, our deteriorating eyesight the way we knew time was moving in a forward direction.

The needle was the vehicle, said the Keeper. She knew about needles because she had a sewing basket; whenever we needed a button replaced or a seam repaired we'd go to her.

The greenhouse is full of poisonous plants, said the Cook.

They're food plants, said the Botanist.

Food if you want to *die* from it, the Cook replied.

Maybe the Archivist really was a good detective. When everyone else was saying the first thing that came into their head, he held back.

We needed to sever the ties of attachment, that much was clear. Our bodies were going to be snatched away, even though we cherished them, our life spans shorter than our memory of what just happened.

Like the king's son in the fairy tale, Jee Moon said softly. One day he went walking into the woods. He went alone, for that was his greatest pleasure. She was looking into space in that unfocused way of hers and we all knew what it was she was seeing, because we could see it too. There was the principal standing in front of us, her black hair wound around and around her nutlike skull in braids, her hands folded behind her back. She wore the same shoes the fathers wore but a dark-colored dress with a lace collar like the mothers. There were windows in the assembly room only they were so high we couldn't see out of them except for the sky and every now and then a little bird.

Evening came on, the principal recited, clouds gathered, and it rained as if the whole heaven had become a sluice from which the water poured in sheets. Winding through us, the trackless wood.

It is true, we went alone, each of us.

In the beginning we lived on Fairmount Avenue. Our house was in a row of houses, all of them once grand. Even now you could tell how grand they'd been from the size of the windows, too big for the curtains people on the side streets put up, as well as from the fact that the houses had names. Berpark or Berdale or Berland. Our house had been grand when our father was a boy—he was born in the bed he slept in with our mother. Nanny was the one who raised him. She'd been young then, not much more than a girl. According to our mother everything that was wrong with our father could be pinned to Nanny; why our mother had kept her on, allowing her to work her magic on us, is anybody's guess. She looked like a regular person but recognizing her for what she was would prove useful, though we didn't know that then. One day the black winds of past actions would prove useful!

There was a prison in the neighborhood not far from our house and when we lived there it had prisoners in it. Only later did the prison get turned into a haunted house at Halloween with people paying money to be scared to death; the rest of the time it was empty. When we were children we used to go out where the prisoners could see us. Father made a smile for each of our faces with a melon slice and he made one for himself even though he wasn't happy. After they locked the prisoners up they threw away the key, Mother said, and she showed us a key in a gold cigarette case. Poor things, she said. They need something pretty. She would put on her pearl necklace and stand in the Morning Room window, smoking.

Back then we had no idea where we were headed. We were children, some of us good as angels and some of us bad, but none of us really bad, none of us evil devils like the men we'd see lined up in the prison yard in their striped garb, chained together at the ankle. Maybe we got that from the movies. It wasn't until later that we became things with names, a Geographer, a Cook, an Astronomer, etc., though people were always asking what we wanted to be when we grew up, as if what we already were was meaningless. We would never have said Murderer.

Mother went out in the evenings; every morning Father went to work. The entire neighborhood consisted mostly of grand houses not unlike our own, houses three stories tall with a back entrance and a set of back stairs for the servants, though the only servant we had was Nanny. The prison had always been there; it was, in its own way, a grand edifice of red brick with turrets and crenellations, designed by the same famous architect who designed the university buildings. Usually the prisoners were kept under strict control, but Father remembered a stone coming through the Morning Room window one day; he had been a little boy then. What's the big idea? he remembered Nanny saying.

That was the question, really. The thing is, we were all caught in the flood of time but without a back-pool or sluggish eddy or swamp root or *any*thing to catch on, to get a grip on, to stop long enough to have a look at what we were becoming or had become.

As for the excursion, it's unclear whose idea it was, only that it was unusual—without precedent or recurrence—for all of us to go out together at the same time. The town car wasn't big enough and it belonged to Mother: she didn't want us spilling food in it or, worse, throwing up. Several of us suffered from carsickness and her cigarette smoke didn't help.

No, it was decided. We would take the train. We would take it to the end of the line and then we'd get out and walk.

Where we were going was to be a surprise.

Naturally, years later, we didn't all remember it the same way. The day wasn't fine, the train practically empty, the station we got off at made of stone. One of us couldn't find the bathroom and wet their pants. Aside from these details, though, there was little agreement. The woman hanging laundry who waved her rail-thin arms at us frantically as we sped past—it had to have been an emergency for her to wave her arms like that, but most of us didn't remember her at all. Were we given jelly omelets in the dining car? Going through a tunnel, the train blew its whistle and someone touched someone inappropriately. The hill we climbed after leaving the station—was it so steep Mother decided to stay in the restaurant at the foot of it rather than accompany us to the top? Father was furious; he drove his fist through the powder room door. There was no powder room. Mother got to the top before any of us. The view from the top was of a lake so wide it might have been the ocean. The view from the top was of our city. The view from the top was shrouded in mist. The rain was driving down.

Something was always driving down though it wasn't always the same thing. Rain, sleet, snow, hail.

Think of the prisoners, Mother said. She was agitated—we all remembered that.

At least they're not standing in the pouring rain, said Father, removing his hat to wring it out.

There were piles of stone atop the hill, trail markers, spaced equidistant from one another and leading across the summit and down the other side, which we couldn't see. We walked in pairs, holding hands, so as not to get lost.

Two by two, like onto the ark, said the Keeper.

Like in our favorite book, *Madeline*. The girls' favorite book, that is. The boys loved a comic called "Prince Valiant" which was about a Nordic prince from Thule who seemed able to travel with equal ease through space and time.

The Astronomer hadn't been paired with anyone that day; this was because someone always had to walk with Mother. Two by two onto the ark except for poor, lonely Monoceros, he said. He was referring to the constellation on the celestial equator whose name is Greek for *unicorn*, its three largest stars forming a seemingly fixed triangle barely visible to the naked eye. The most beautiful sight in the heavens, according to the man who discovered it. Like all the constellations, it doesn't look a bit like the thing it was named for.

But I was *with* you, Jee Moon said to him. I've always been with you.

The Topologist drew a shape in the air with her finger. What the coordinates describe is an abstraction, she said. Say you're in a spaceship and you start going in one direction for a very long period of time. You could hit a wall. You could keep going forever. Or you could end up back where you started but you wouldn't know it.

Exactly, said Jee Moon.

The day of the excursion the Botanist was still a baby and had to be nursed; until we got to the restaurant this constituted a hindrance. The fad for breast-feeding was a fairly recent one. Most of us had been bottle-fed and, as Nanny was quick to point out, none the worse for it. They used to have special nursing rooms for mothers with babies—often these rooms were attached to the lavatory. The boys were roughhousing and the place was fancy, damask tablecloths, real silverware, and waiters dressed in black waistcoats and trousers, wearing sneers on their faces and their aprons low on their hips. Why our mother decided to take us to a place like that is a mystery.

But it was Mother's birthday!

We had escargots. *Escargots* meant *snails*, if only we knew what was going on.

We could die from happiness, if only we knew.

Father's vexation of spirit notwithstanding, Mother was humming, the buttons of her blouse unevenly buttoned.

That's when Father put his fist through the powder room door, said the Geographer. Not earlier.

If he ever did such a thing. The Archivist was Father's champion, both of them Virgos, not that easy to get along with though delicate, a delicate nature stretched and then suspended above the fathomless abyss.

We dipped them in butter, said the Cook. Snails are delicious dipped in butter.

Anything is delicious dipped in butter, said the Botanist.

When she was a little girl, she used to bring garden slugs in from the backyard and feed them saltines. Remember? That was how it worked, the Geographer said, the kindest acts spawning disastrous outcomes.

Still, how did she get there? Our mother, that is. Did she climb the hill in her designer high heels? The ones that gave her bunions? Did she even know a trail marker when she saw one? It's almost impossible to imagine. Conversely, how did *we* get there, back to her? The whole point of the excursion was to celebrate her birthday, after all. Not everyone remembered the hill, though those who did remembered it vividly. The trail was slippery from the rain. The Topologist lost her footing on the way down, breaking her fall with her right hand, abrading the palm and spraining her wrist. She cried through most of the birthday meal. Remember? The Archivist pretended to wipe tears from his eyes, sniffling.

Only I never fell, replied the Topologist. *You* were the one who fell.

Tensions always ran high between those two, the one dedicated to the preservation of *materia mundi*, the other to proving its immateriality, the Topologist's painstaking arrangement of game pieces on the hearthstone neatly swept up by the Archivist and stored in the wooden box in the middle drawer of the bachelor chest where they belonged.

We had rack of lamb, said the Cook. Overdone. With mint jelly, he added, and smiled at the Botanist, who loved sweets. You weren't a vegetarian back then, he reminded her. Back then you ate like a horse.

A baby horse, she said. Remember?

Mealtimes were always the happiest times we spent together, Mother and Father seated at opposite ends of a table, making contention between them difficult if not impossible. Dear Heart, she called him at such moments. It was a restaurant, though— not everyone ate the same thing. Mother ordered *confit de canard*, Father prime rib au jus.

Was it a French restaurant?

What difference would that make?

All the difference in the world, said the Cook.

As long as it wasn't in France, said the Archivist.

And why is that, Mr. Smartypants? The Botanist loved to bait him, and we liked watching his reaction.

We need to know where everyone was, the Archivist said. All those times when we were on our own, in other places with other people.

For his own part, he'd been at the university. It had just started raining and the only place he could find to park was on the wrong side of campus. Rain hadn't been predicted; the sky was clear when he left his apartment, the spring constellations clustering brightly overhead. They wouldn't be visible until he emerged from under the trees, though. The Archivist's street was lined with ash trees but he didn't know that's what they were. The living world didn't interest him.

Hydra, Canis Minor, Lyra. We could see them if we went outside, said the Astronomer. Not Boötes, though.

It's too cold to go out, said Jee Moon. She sighed and left the banquet table to stand at the window. A full moon had recently risen over the sea, hung like a lamp above the cove's heaving, boreal waves.

There was an ash tree behind the house, said the Geographer. Remember?

Gone, said the Botanist. Dead and gone. Eaten by cutworms.

Do you always have to be so melodramatic? The Keeper was scraping our plates for the dogs. I remember when you got stuck at the top, she said, and Nanny had to call the fire department.

The Black Death, said the Botanist. *That's* what I remember.

It's the ash that draws the flash, said the Iceman.

The university parking spaces were divided into color-coded areas and came with stickers to match. The red stickers were the most expensive, allowing you to park close to the most important buildings; next came the green stickers, followed by the blue, and finally the yellow. The Archivist never paid for a sticker; he usually walked to work. Tonight was a special occasion, though. P had donated her papers to the university and she was to give a reading in the rare books room.

The Archivist had little admiration for the work. *The Lonely Thoroughfares*, P's first book, had appeared at a difficult time in his life, and he felt she showed an astounding lack of sympathy for her subject. "Little thing, little sniveling thing . . ." Reading his personally inscribed copy, the Archivist thought it was almost as if she wanted to make fun of the lonely, of the sorry spectacle they presented traversing the vast, empty thoroughfares of their loneliness. Often in these poems, tracks of some kind could be discerned leading into the distance; there would be a leafless tree, an indistinct sound, a choked cry.

Obviously she was stealing from Hadrian. Only it wasn't called stealing, it was called appropriation, and what you were left with was called a debt.

Such a shame, our mother used to say of P. As a girl she hadn't been what you'd call pretty, but at some point that changed. If the recent author photo was to be believed, even now with age making inroads around the eyes and mouth, she remained quite attractive. The photographer had posed her in a straight-backed chair, which seemed appropriate, given her unyielding nature.

The Archivist had allowed himself more than enough time to get to campus and park, but the places where a sticker wasn't necessary were already taken. The rain had begun to fall in earnest; every time a car came toward him he couldn't see a thing. Twice he got honked at, once he almost hit a woman he recognized from the political science department. She darted in front of him in a white, ankle-length raincoat, only to be pulled back at the last minute by her husband, who shook his fist.

Time was running out. The energetic level of conversation that preceded these events would have begun its decrescendo into silence. The Chancellor would be scanning the room, checking his watch. P would be seated in the front row, her head bent over her manuscript, the white stalk of her neck just begging to be slipped in a noose. XOXOXO. What kind of inscription was that? Meanwhile the first weed whacker of the season would have begun tidying the edges of the flower beds. Like the undead, the university groundskeepers never slept.

The space the Archivist finally found was at the edge of the blue section, so far from the center of campus as to be practically yellow, near Fraternity Row, a fanciful assortment of structures whose high Gothic style married uneasily with the immense gas grills and piles of athletic equipment filling their courtyards. Though it seemed impossible, the rain was coming down harder than ever, as if it were being hurled at his car in fistfuls. Naturally he hadn't brought an umbrella—he was going to get drenched. He was going to look pathetic, not unlike Hadrian's soul.

As if a soul could be said to have a *look*, said the Cook. He was studying the table scraps, ready to take offense at anything we hadn't eaten. P always had it easy, he said.

You don't know what you're talking about, said Jee Moon. Nothing was easy for her.

We all knew what Jee Moon meant. We had all seen P throw away positive actions like dirt. She seized upon negative actions.

Worst of all she wasted the highly meaningful human body that had been so difficult to obtain in the first place.

Upon parking his car the Archivist had been relieved to see, off to one side, the apse-shaped back end of January Hall, a large Romanesque edifice housing several all-but-obsolete departments. There was a tunnel that connected the building with the basement level of the library—the January Tunnel was legendary in the neighborhood, a favorite haunt of teen lovers and drug dealers. A few of us had spent more than a little time there, whereas the Archivist wasn't even sure the tunnel existed. The only thing to do was make a run for it—though if there was no tunnel he was going to get soaked and the light wool suit he'd bought for the occasion would end up clinging unbecomingly to his sticklike figure. That man on the gallows looks like you, P had told him merrily, the first time she got him to play a game of Hangman. She hadn't been a famous poet then—she'd just been an aloof child waiting her turn at the water fountain outside Saint Roch Elementary. When she lowered her lips to drink, he could hear her braces hit the bubbler.

The Archivist dove into the downpour. He couldn't tell where he was going; one moment he couldn't see a thing, the next moment a door marked January Tunnel appeared in front of him. Once inside, he paused to shake the water from his hair and to wipe his glasses on the hem of his dress shirt. The tunnel was well lit; it extended ahead of him a great distance, its brightness devolving into dimness. There was the sound of machinery, a low thrumming coming from either side of him as well as overhead, and while there were no machines in view the Archivist wasn't troubled by the noise. It took an enormous amount of energy to keep a university running smoothly.

Against the wall just inside the door someone had arranged several brooms, a bucket with a mop in it, a pile of rags, but otherwise the tunnel was empty. The walls had been painted with the green paint beloved of institutions, applied in what seemed like a spirit of gay abandon. The concrete floor was splashed with it and it depended in hardened drips from a series of pipes running lengthwise along the ceiling.

The Archivist's glasses were steaming up—luckily he hadn't bothered to tuck his shirt back in. Ever since her cataract surgery, P no longer needed corrective lenses and at night her gray eyes were said to refract light like an animal's. She was known for her beautiful eyes, eyes that had looked small and beady to us throughout her girlhood due to the unusual thickness of her glasses. For a time she wore plaid frames, the plaid of the rims not matching that of the stems. She'd been one of the unpopular girls, a condition that hadn't bothered her the way being one of the unpopular boys bothered the Archivist. She took pride in the fact that no one wanted to dance with her at Mrs. Chaliffe's ballroom dance class.

At some point the Archivist realized he was beginning to hear a second sound insinuating itself under the thrumming of the machinery—a fainter sound, more personal really, in that it seemed meant for his ears alone. Faint and precise, a lightly repeated *thwap thwap thwap* punctuated with tiny clicks, it suggested the presence of a creature with soft footpads and delicate claws, either running away from him or coaxing him forward. Ahead on the left he could see a break in the otherwise unbroken wall that turned out to be a short dark hallway ending with a door that no doubt led to one of the windowless basement-level offices assigned to adjuncts or teaching assistants. How long had it taken him to make his way up from just such an office to one with two large windows facing a graceful colonnade? Longer than it should have, that was for sure.

Based on the sound of the footfalls it seemed like whatever it was he'd been following had ducked into that hallway—but when the Archivist looked, the only thing he saw was a wadded-up ball of paper on the floor near the door, a piece of university letterhead on which someone had drawn ten dashes, penciling in an *O* above the seventh dash, an *X* above the eighth. XOXOXO, P wrote in her sloppy mannish handwriting across the title page of her first book. This says it all, she said, giving it to him, and he knew she didn't mean hugs and kisses but the pattern around the base of the dome in the concert hall he'd taken her to for her sixteenth birthday. He smoothed the sheet of paper and folded it in half carefully before tucking it in his breast pocket.

You were collecting evidence! said the Geographer.

Collecting evidence? said the Cook. More like collecting trash.

The Botanist did that thing of hers, leaning across the banquet table with her head resting on her upper arm, looking up at the Cook coquettishly. Those hallways, she said with a sigh. You never knew what you'd find there.

Don't be silly, said the Keeper. How could that be evidence?

He's an Archivist. He keeps everything, said the Astronomer.

I read *The Lonely Thoroughfares*, said the Topologist. I had to read it for a class. I thought it was pretty good.

The further the Archivist walked into the tunnel, the more muffled the sound of the machinery; short hallways continued to materialize off to the left, each one culminating in a door with a name card taped to the window. Professor This, Professor That, though clearly no one down here ever came close to making full professor. The Archivist recognized some of the names—Professor Bunting had been a noisy feminist. Professor Liu had been dead for years. All these offices were dark and the tunnel itself seemed to be growing darker, the light fixtures stationed at greater and greater intervals. Occasionally a door would have been left open, revealing a room that looked like it had been abandoned under emergency evacuation orders.

A period ensued during which the Archivist thought he was merely imagining the sound of an animal padding along ahead of him; in its place all he could hear was the sound of his stomach. He'd been prone to anxiety attacks for as long as he could remember and he hadn't had a thing to eat all day. Meanwhile the tunnel floor was showing signs of increasingly bad drainage. The Archivist had to watch where he put his feet in order to protect his new shoes and to keep from slipping—at first he could step over or around the puddles, though eventually there was no way to avoid stepping right into pools of standing water. The quality of the light, too, seemed to be decaying, though ironically enough, the dimmer the tunnel got the farther ahead in it he could see. At last he thought he could make out the shadowy shape of what certainly looked like an animal, low slung and with a tail that was surprisingly full, resplendent even. The animal was slinking along the left-hand side of the tunnel, disappearing from time to time into one or another of the secondary hallways, only to emerge once again farther ahead. It was difficult to tell what color she was: sometimes her coat seemed spectral and gray, at other times russet, vulpine. Despite what his eyes told him, though, his sense of the creature—the image her coat created in his mind—was pure white.

P would be upset that the Archivist wasn't there to hear her. She planned to read from her latest collection, the title of which she refused to reveal to anyone, though her editor must know it. The publication date was a week off.

She used to like it when the Archivist brushed her hair, which was surprisingly thick for being so straight, and which she wore long, though often wrenched into a small, tight knob at the back of her head. That was one aspect of their relationship that always went smoothly—P liked to be groomed, though not for too long, and not with any sense of personal involvement on the part of the groomer. If the Archivist made it clear that the act of grooming her was arousing him, she would bat the brush from his hand. How many letters? she would ask, leaning in, her gray eyes sparkling. She would pick up a pad of paper and draw a gallows.

The first bite, when it came, was more like a playful nip; the second tore through the light wool of his pant leg and sank deep, drawing blood.

The main axis of the campus, as the Archivist knew, ran east to west, in homage to the Trail of Tears. The January Tunnel, on the other hand, ran south to north, in homage to the Suspension of Misrule, also known as Thule.

False Foxes, said Jee Moon. That's the name of the new book.

How do you know? asked the Archivist.

We were best friends, Jee Moon said. Since we were little girls.

I thought she was partners with me, said the Botanist. I thought you were off somewhere else.

We smiled at the good and frowned at the bad, Jee Moon said. And sometimes we were very sad. I can't believe you don't remember.

Of course the question is: Was she there when we arrived or did she arrive after? Like the place in the dream where you always get lost, a well-traveled, well-known road shaking you loose into fear and confusion, propelling you toward that house just around the bend but there is no toward, there is no house, there is no bend. Because, finally, none of us could remember a time when she wasn't with us, Jee Moon, just as it was never determined which of us saw her first, a red speck approaching from each of the cardinal directions, her red parka coming closer from outside the circumference of the known world.

Whoever saw her first must have had the best eyesight. Who would that have been?

Not the Topologist. Hers was the worst.

It had to be me, the Astronomer said. I was the one who told everyone she was coming.

Like that's even important, *guys*, Jee Moon said.

It was extremely cold and she had been wearing a red felt parka embroidered with scenes showing seals pierced by harpoons, the cuffs and hood trimmed with the fur of a fox whose paws crossed decorously under her chin. Red was a good color on Jee Moon, given her pitch-black hair and spectral skin.

With the exception of the Cook, who was indoors cooking dinner, all of us had been outdoors on skis. The dogs were outside with us too; there were enough of them for a team, though we were just figuring out how to attach a harness. In northern lands the power of frost and the falls of snow are generally so severe, and the weather with its thick, sudden mists that darken the air so dreadful, that a person can't tell whether a traveler they meet at close quarters is friend or foe. In any case, Jee Moon was impervious to routine displays of etiquette.

She had a nice smile, though. We all agreed.

She extended her hand knuckles first, the way everyone knows to approach an unfamiliar dog. The lead male licked her as did the gray. The Astronomer was obviously smitten—we could see this from the initial encounter. He got as close as he could, ski tips permitting, a besotted expression on his long, flat face. Also an attractive face—handsome even, if you went for that kind of look. Though he'd tried to keep it a secret, we knew the Astronomer had already broken several hearts.

But do you expect heartbreak once you're past a certain age? Does anyone? Our heartbreak had all happened such a long time ago: a pair of eyes in a thicket, a saint in a shrine. We knew marriage didn't betoken true love. Romantic heartbreak was nothing compared with what came later.

Maybe it wasn't until we were gathering for cocktails that we noticed her—a slim woman standing alone by the fireplace, nursing a shot of the single malt whiskey we had discovered in the cellar not long after our arrival. She'd tucked her hair behind her ears and she was smiling at something no one else could see out one of the great mullioned windows facing the interior. Standing there smiling in the teeth of the "gray cold" as it approached with the lengthening night.

They're babies now but just wait, Jee Moon told the Cook. The father's off getting dinner. That's what fathers do, Jee Moon said, looking across the room at the Astronomer.

The Cook, yes, it had to have been him, wiping his thick, freckled fingers on his blood-stained apron. The Cook was definitely the first to approach her, before the Astronomer, before everyone.

They never had such a supper in their life, the Cook sang, and the little ones chewed on the bones-oh. He had a pleasant voice, sweeter than you'd expect given his manly physique. The song was about a fox stealing a goose for his family. Do you have any dietary restrictions? the Cook asked.

I restrict my diet to ingredients, Jee Moon replied. She was looking at him from over the rim of her glass, from under her thick eyelashes.

The Cook was a widower, his heart already broken. Reduced to dust, really. He had adored his wife from the beginning to the end, from A to Z—an eternal transit. He had adored his wife without cease, and that is why his story was the shortest.

Jee Moon had on a heavy white pullover, black leather pants, and felt boot liners, at some point having discarded her outdoor gear. The hooks were in the entryway, on either side of the door to the cellar; she must have opened the door and gone downstairs without anyone noticing. She was a curious woman, despite her strangely fixed aura, like a reliquary or a carapace, something designed to hide something better left unseen. When you went into the cellar you needed a flashlight since there wasn't any electricity. The oak casks containing the whiskey were lined up against the south wall. There were lots of them, more than enough to keep us in good spirits for a long time, the Iceman's heroic thirst notwithstanding. The cellar ran the length of the hall and was deep enough for the tallest of us—i.e., the Iceman, whose self-appointed job it was to retrieve the evening's libation—to walk around in without having to stoop. It must have required a prodigious amount of work to carve away the permafrost.

But the Iceman hadn't been down there yet. He was still outside, playing with the dogs while the rest of us, Jee Moon excepted, had come inside and impatiently awaited our cocktails. The Iceman was like a dog, rolling on his back in the recently fallen snow while the dogs licked his face. Unlike the rest of us he thrived on the cold—it used to get hot in the summer on Fairmount Avenue and he hated heat. The colder it was, the better. He was big like an oven.

Jee Moon's coming coincided with the coming of the gray cold. The gray cold burned the eyes of animals and stiffened their hairs. It deprived all creatures living near the pole of their eyesight. The gray cold made them gather in packs to hunt their food. It caused the pelts of all creatures to be thicker and handsomer. Gray cold turned white the crests of cocks and the beaks and feet of geese. It made hares, foxes, and ermines change color. Gray cold made the skin peel off human lips, fingers, and nostrils. It caused lips that touched other lips to stick as if held by indissoluble pitch. It opened up all pathless territories to travelers and hunters.

Meanwhile the Cook was leading Jee Moon around the room as if to introduce her to the rest of us. Soon enough, of course, she came to assume knowledge of our names, just as each of us had done upon arrival, our presence unheralded yet inevitable.

This was the force of the space. It intruded on our bodies, which is how we originally had come into being. At first there wasn't sky or earth or skin or house or anything to separate us one from another. It was not *nothing* though! At first there was something that was everywhere and everything. You might call it space and it was, truly, intrusive, full of folds and pockets, thickenings and spheres, taking up the places where our bodies needed to be. Some of us had been kept in the labyrinth and fed there; others felt the ice crack beneath us as if we had hooves instead of feet. Such was the force of the space that it could summon to its grasp a faraway thing visible to it alone, however intricate a string of knots the thing had been tied with.

We all watched with interest as the Iceman approached the window where Jee Moon and the Cook were standing. A chill smell clung to his clothes from his time in the cellar, as well as multiple cobwebs. Bottoms up, he said, downing his drink in one swallow and cocking an eyebrow in Jee Moon's direction. The Iceman was always most cheerful drink in hand.

Yes, please, Jee Moon said, holding out her glass.

The Cook excused himself and returned to the kitchen, at which point the rest of us approached, eager to have our drinks freshened and to get a closer look at the stranger.

Me too? said the Geographer. Usually she dressed native-style in caribou leggings and sealskin boots—tonight for some reason she'd put on an evening dress of crushed dark green velvet.

Say when, said the Iceman.

The Geographer explained that tomorrow an expedition had been planned into the interior. Snow was forecast, she said, which might complicate our mission. Once the snow fell it obscured everything, a cairn no longer distinguishable from any other element in the landscape. Heavy snow, she added, and then she apologized— being a theoretical meteorologist, Jee Moon no doubt knew this already. We were always respectful of each other's area of expertise. It was the realm in which our sensitivity to someone else's feelings was most evident. Otherwise, with the possible exception of the Botanist, we often acted as if none of us had feelings.

The thing is, though—we did. We loved one another. That was

the arrangement, after all. We were so feral, so damp, so swift to bolt. We might have been the silverfish Nanny shook from the bedclothes every morning. She considered them household pests, eating book bindings and carpet, coffee and glue, photographs, linen, plaster and sugar. Nocturnal, silverfish, and wingless— their complex mating ritual lasts well over half an hour, the male and female standing face to face, antennae shivering and touching, both parties repeatedly backing off before returning to their former position, the male running away and the female chasing him until, at long last, they stand side by side, head to tail, and the male produces the elegant gossamer-covered sperm capsule that the female invites into her body.

An expedition? asked the Iceman. I seem to recall an excursion. But where to and for what purpose?

Maybe that's not the right word. The Geographer looked into the fire and straightened her shoulders. If we leave early there shouldn't be a problem. We can use the sleds.

You still haven't said where we're going. The Iceman poured himself another drink.

Away from the edge, I hope, Jee Moon said, leaning up against him, laughing.

The smell and thickness of him—it was like sinking into peat.

Jee Moon could never hold her liquor. That first night she had too much to drink and went to bed early, pleading exhaustion. Her room was in Dormitory Number Two; it took her forever to fall asleep. Outside, the landscape extended itself in all directions. It looked the way the moon looked to the early astronauts, milk-white and serrated peaks rising above bone-white craters.

Our dormitory rooms were perfect squares. According to the Topologist, squares were spaces in which completeness made sense, their many points separated by what are called neighborhoods.

There was a hallway, long and thin, running down the center of each dormitory. The hallway was a slack space, incomplete, a place where things went to settle. The minute we opened our doors and left our rooms to enter that space we belonged nowhere. Thoughts flew over us like birds, their eyes seeking the narrow straits. If we hadn't been used to swerving we would have fallen down like drops of rain through the deep void, and nothing would have been begotten.

Jee Moon lay in her bed, her face lit by snow light, the light that is more beautiful than any other, a collaboration of heaven and earth, star and ice crystal, like the empty place inside a body where the life resides. She woke and saw the Astronomer standing in her doorway.

It wasn't love at first sight—they'd already met, remember? In the Aubrac. We came up the long hill that went on forever. For once Mother wasn't watching us like a hawk.

Or maybe they never met—they'd just known one another forever.

It was always so exhausting to find a mate, said the Geographer.

It's exhausting to survive, said the Keeper, when you're raised by Darwinists.

The hill was the longest hill any of us had ever seen. Even though there were trail markers we got lost. The paths crisscrossed, split apart, wandered off to die.

Cattle tracks, said the Keeper. Those were cattle tracks, not trails.

Soon enough we developed the tendency common to lost travelers to go in circles. Queenly clouds dragged long trains of rain-shower behind themselves and over us. Roaring blackness up above and all around and underfoot and two birds flying over the lake, linked by a chain of gold. Who was it said, How I wish I could have those birds, one of them upon each of my two shoulders? My little birds from the Palace, my little lambs, welcome!

The shrine presented itself as a welcome shelter from the rain; in our dark cloaks we huddled together just inside the door. Most of us wore the rosaries we'd been given by the Bishop. There were a lot of people in the shrine besides us, some of them lighting candles, some of them praying, some chatting or looking for romance. A bell was ringing. Danger was abroad in the land.

Plus the Swede was there! the Botanist said to Jee Moon. And you were too! You were kneeling at the altar.

That wouldn't have been me, Jee Moon said. Not kneeling.

No one wanted to get too close to anyone else. Everyone had discarded their little moons and chains, their necklaces and bracelets, their jewels hanging on the forehead and the crisping pins and looking glasses. Instead of a girdle, there would be a cord. Instead of a stomacher, haircloth.

The Geographer glared across the banquet table at the Botanist. I kept the windows of the car *closed*, she said. Everyone knows what gets loose when you open a window. After the crash my husband took the medicine, she said. He *took* it. She sounded upset.

If you say so, said the Botanist.

In the hospital, the Geographer added. In case you've forgotten. She gave the Botanist a look.

The rosaries were pale blue plastic. They were junk but even so they were powerful, more powerful than the rosaries some of us were wearing when we ran into the shrine to escape the rain.

I still have mine, said the Geographer. The cross is gold and the beads are semiprecious stones. They're garnets, to ward off plague.

How did that work out for you? said the Iceman. His rosary had gotten lost somewhere but he hadn't noticed it was missing until recently.

In fact the rosaries didn't make sense, since we weren't religious. Apart from the Cook, that is, though in his case it was to honor the memory of his wife, who had been Catholic. He lit a candle for her and left his rosary in the shrine, in the pile of blue plastic rosaries at the saint's feet.

The shrine was small but still it was difficult to tell who was in there. The pilgrims' faces were hard to see under the enormous rain ponchos. For those of us who wore glasses it was even worse, the heat of all the bodies making our lenses fog over, rain and perspiration dripping down our foreheads and cheeks, off the tips of our noses. Likewise distracting was the smell, compounded of wet primeval stone and candle wax, unwashed human flesh and foul undergarments. Despite what we came to learn later, the place seemed to be bursting at the seams with human beings and their manifold effects—about as far from empty as a space could be.

You were supposed to pay for those candles, the Keeper told the Cook. They weren't giving them away.

The Botanist reached into the neck of her sweater and drew forth her rosary, still warm from where it had lain nestled in the cleft between her breasts. The rosary was strung with opals, milky white and limpid as her skin. I wear it all the time, she said. Even to bed.

A person wore garnets to ward off plague, amethysts to cure drunkenness, opals to confer invisibility—we were all perfectly aware of the applications.

Of course you wear it all the time, said the Archivist. Even for yoga.

Hey! said the Cook. Are you suggesting what I think you are?

I never know what you think, said the Archivist. Your mind is as impenetrable to me as a brick.

I was in the *bath*room, said the Botanist.

If you say so, said the Geographer. She was mimicking the Botanist—we could all tell she was doing this because she was a good mimic.

She *was*, said the Astronomer. I watched her walk in.

The Archivist reached across the table to tap the Geographer sharply on the wrist. You're supposed to be taking notes, he said.

What about your eye pillow? said the Keeper.

He peeked, said Jee Moon. I was looking.

Jee Moon! If only we could agree when we first saw her. The shrine was what the Topologist called an étale space, meaning slack like a slack tide, the stand of the tide, the time when everyone is waiting to take up the slack. In an étale space it's always difficult to recognize who or what isn't in it.

The thing is, she wasn't one of us.

Like everyone with us in the shrine, she was something else. Like P or the Swede, like the saint or the principal. All of us were one thing and everyone else was another. Our mother and father had been one thing along with us but they'd reverted at some point to whatever they'd been before we existed. Those of us who'd had husbands or wives remained undecided about their status. Nanny was a special case but we couldn't agree about her, either.

Besides, the Keeper said to the Cook, it's true. Opals make a person invisible. Where do you think your chocolate disappears to at night?

Good question, said the Botanist. Every single night. Who do you think brushes the sleep from your eyes? Gives you your dreams? Sweet dreams, every single night.

The cairn we found on the beach had so much vitality we could almost see eyes on it, a nose, a mouth.

Whatever the thing was, we could tell it was alive, even though it was made of stone, a pile of stones but animate, with a girl who died long ago buried underneath. It is said that living worms spring out of stinking dung.

The girl who lay buried under the cairn was flat on her back, wrapped in bark and painted with red ocher, her arms at her sides, a large stone placed atop her sternum to keep her from getting up. She could do that—get up. The pared-down shape of her could arise and float anywhere she wanted. Her eyes were missing. Of course they were, after all this time. Back when she was alive, everyone had brown eyes, unlike the way it is now with blue and violet and hazel. She was a sacrifice; the people who killed her lit fires on both sides of her body. She was sixteen years old when she died.

A virgin sacrifice, said the Cook. She must have been a virgin.

The Keeper disagreed. Sixteen was all about sex, she said.

The brownness of the Keeper's eyes had faded to a color harder to describe, still brown though glassy like the marbles in the bachelor chest. As far as we knew, no one ever played with them. No one ever used anything in that chest, except maybe our mother—we all remembered seeing her rummaging around in it, her eyes perfectly round the way they got when she was hysterical about something or excited. I know it's in here, she was saying.

Like maybe when she lost her marbles, the Keeper said. But it wasn't her marbles she lost—we all knew that.

When P was sixteen, the Archivist said, her idea of having sex involved two chairs facing one another with a basin between them on the floor. Not that they executed this plan. As he recalled he tried kissing her but it didn't go well. They were walking past the Grand Basin after the birthday concert. All the fountains had been lit from below and were unfurling sparkling umbrellas of water. I need to sit, P said impatiently, as if the Archivist had been preventing her from doing this. They sat on a stone bench facing the water. She removed a shoe and shook out a pebble and we all found ourselves thinking of the Swede, the time the Topologist watched him shaking the pebble from his hiking shoe in the Aubrac. Is that better? the Archivist asked and when P turned to him to answer and he leaned in to give her a kiss, a stretch limo pulled up filled with beautifully dressed and hilarious prom-goers.

Ha ha, the Geographer said sourly. First kiss.

Hers was with a French boy, she said. He *French* kissed her and his tongue felt like a snail in her mouth, though snails tended to inertia and the French boy's tongue was busy. It felt thick, full of sand, like what a person would put out to kill snails in the garden. It felt like the gray sand at Omaha Beach where the French boy took her to kiss her instead of showing her the bank of shingle she'd asked him to take her to see.

Plus no one puts out sand to kill snails, said the Botanist.

Escargots! said the Cook. But what happened at sixteen if it wasn't sex?

There was a game, said the Archivist, and when the Cook laughed the Archivist said, No, I thought I was going to die.

That kind of game, said the Botanist. Life or death, she said, and we knew she was thinking of the boy who died, the one she told us she loved more than anything who supposedly died in her arms.

Sixteen, said the Topologist. Sixteen is a centered pentagonal number. The matrix of *Y, N, X, I, I, t, n, u* has sixteen dyads.

Also it's an even number, said the Keeper.

She wasn't good at math but she was good with animals and tarot cards. We weren't allowed pets, due to Mother's allergies, but Father had arranged for the Keeper to have horseback riding lessons. For an animal there is no difference between the future and the present, the Keeper explained. The tarot was the next best thing to a pet. Where did you find those? the Archivist asked the first time we saw the Keeper laying out cards for a reading. You'd better not let Mother see you doing that.

The whole idea is to open one thing up for another thing to get inside it, said the Iceman.

Inasmuch as the eggs of fowls change into living chicks, and worms burst forth from the earth after excessive rain.

Turning sixteen, though—it's true, as Jee Moon reminded us. Some moments in a life are like that. Time stops flying by. Something *happens*. All of us did something we would rather not remember but we didn't want to talk about it. The girl under the cairn—she had just been a girl. The lives people lived were different then but they were *lives* and they were lived in bodies like ours, with what felt like a beginning and a middle and an end. Maybe she never had sex but she had teeth. She bit into things and ate them. What she ate made its way through her body; it went in one end and came out the other.

It's worse not to talk about it, the Keeper said. People imagine the worst. They imagine things are much worse than what you actually did.

That day on the train the Keeper was sitting in the dining car with her tarot cards arranged on the table in front of her, exactly the same way she sat at the banquet table in the Great Hall, shuffling and reshuffling the deck as if it were possible to alter fate.

Whose cards had she been reading? It could have been practically any one of us—aside from the Archivist, who claimed only to care about the past, we were always pestering her to predict our future. But then why did some of us remember seeing him standing there, shifting his weight from foot to foot, attempting to maintain balance as the train went around a curve? We remembered seeing him and we remembered seeing Mother—Mother leaning forward, desperate not to miss a word. Who is that? Who is *that*? she kept asking, pointing at a card that showed a tall man in a cloak surrounded by five cups, looking down sadly at the three cups that had spilled on the ground.

It's a card of marriage, said the Keeper. Marriage, but not without bitterness or frustration. The five of any suit is always bad news, she said. Even the five of Wands, even though wands are made of ash.

That doesn't look like your father, Mother said. Your father is short.

It's not supposed to be a person, the Keeper said. It stands for something else. The way one card leads to another, like trail markers.

We knew what she was talking about. We had all been on the train that day, watching the snarl of gray leafless branches fly past and the thing we ended up remembering, the piece of trash caught trembling in them like a mind trying to compose itself.

Listen to me! said the Archivist, and we could hear it, the way his voice was shaking. There was the gallows above, the blank spaces below. That's the way the game was played, he said.

By the time you see the black spot on your groin you know you're doomed. It doesn't matter whether you take good care of yourself, eat wholesome food, and avoid unwholesome behavior. You could be a saint, he said, and he gave the Topologist a scornful look. His eyes were extremely dark, unusually so, given his pale complexion—Saxon blood, as he had often explained. By the time the bubo forms there's nothing you can do.

We often see a man pass away gradually limb by limb, said the Iceman. First the toes of his feet and the nails, then the feet and shanks, then the steps of chilly death creep with slow pace over all the other members.

Even without saying it we knew we were thinking the same thing. All those winters and summers of our lives lived together, every step we were making and had made before and would make again until, at last, we'd find ourselves coming upon the unexpected sight like a piece of trash caught in a snarl of leafless branches that made a sound and suddenly moved, slightly, on its own.

You would reach for it if only you thought it mattered.

P lived one block over in the Highgate Apartments; from the living room balcony you could see the prison and the bell tower at the university as well as the back entrance to our house. It was as if she lived there by herself—her parents both had important teaching jobs and were never home, even though their bedroom had air-conditioning. One thing all of us remembered was P lying on her stomach on her mother's bed, drawing a row of ten dashes along the bottom of a sheet of university letterhead.

The whole world was too hot. The sloth of the shepherds left the flocks straying and cuckoos intruded into every poor bird's nest. Men preferred fur to hair shirts, stuffing themselves with dainties. Charity had grown cold. Truth and faith were lukewarm but spite and harshness blazed up everywhere.

As for us, we were overwhelmed by the heat, though some of us handled it better than others. The Botanist loved the way sweat felt running between her shoulder blades. The Iceman thought he was going to die.

X, said the Archivist, who didn't care about the weather one way or the other. He was sitting with his back against the padded headboard of P's mother's bed.

X? said the Topologist. What kind of guess is that? You're supposed to start with the twelve most commonly occurring letters in the English language.

And what would those be? asked the Keeper.

F U, said the Cook. He had slid beneath P's father's bed and was sticking his head out from under the dust ruffle.

You look like Little Bo Peep, said the Topologist. She pointed her finger and laughed.

We all waited for P to draw the first element of the hanged man stick figure, the line perpendicular to the crossbeam indicating the noose. Instead she put an *X* in the eighth slot.

Of course it was entirely possible her word didn't have an *X* in it. That was what we were thinking: she put the *X* in to give the Archivist an advantage. However mean she was—and P could be very mean—she favored him. It was no secret the way she nested the back of her head within the curve of his thigh, making numerous small adjustments to get the position right.

The venetian blind slats were closed. The room was dark, the wallpaper printed with dark birds and vines, the bedspreads quilted sateen, a shade of maroon so dark as to be almost black. Even though we were too young to understand such things, we'd been trained to recognize the room's erotic implications, if only on a subconscious level.

Another letter, said P.

She snapped her fingers and looked over to where someone we would realize later looked a lot like Jee Moon had arrayed herself upon the *petit point* vanity bench, staring intently at something in the mirror that wasn't her own face.

You're mighty quiet over there, P said.

E, said the Topologist.

P ignored her. Really, she said. What do you think you're doing?

There are two of them, the person on the vanity bench said. Two *E*s. Am I right?

This was way before Jee Moon and the Astronomer fell in love. He was just a boy then, lying on the floor by the windows, involved in a childish punching match with the Iceman. Every now and then they bumped against the wall hard enough to jostle the blinds, letting fall a slat of sunlight on the Astronomer's face. Some of us were so close we could see his eyelashes wave at us, great semicircles of sweat emerge at the Iceman's groin and armpits, the exact places where the symptoms would first appear.

It was very hot out. It was so hot that certain trees had started catching fire, the ones with leaves shaped more or less like hands, horse chestnuts and maples and sycamores, though it remained forever a mystery why this should have been the case. At some point the sirens started up.

Naturally we wondered what they signified. Often it was fire or a weather event. According to Nanny things were preparing to drop down on us from above, bombs or meteorites. People, too, people could prove hazardous, especially given the ills our flesh was heir to. Father had warned us about opening the door to just anyone; even the slightest touch could prove fatal. It remained unclear why one place was affected more than another, one house more than another. Not all streets were affected in the same way, or both sides of one street, or neighboring houses, the impact of the heavens not affecting all things equally. We knew this. We knew about neighborhoods. The effect of a lunar eclipse lasted as many months as there were hours of darkness. A greater number of the dead were carried to the grave after dinner than before it.

Oh dear what can the matter be, sang the Botanist. When she was a girl she was possessed of a sweet singing voice. Mother had an idea the Botanist should go on the stage, but eventually her voice grew husky and, pretty as she was, she ceased to enjoy being looked at.

Oh dear what can the matter be
Oh dear what can the matter be
Oh dear what can the matter be, the Botanist sang.

This time it was a prison break, though how were we to know? The prison wasn't especially secure and the prisoners escaped regularly. The prison siren went off all the time. Besides, every siren sounded the same.

The Iceman got up and pried apart the blind slats. Someone was running around the corner, he told us, so fast they were nothing more than a blur, though maybe it was the heat that was making them blur, making everything out there waver and blow apart into ashes. It was definitely a *he*—the Iceman could tell by the breadth of the shoulders and the narrowness of the hips. This was definitely a male configuration, he claimed, despite the Keeper's reminder that there were women built that way too, athletic women, girls like the Geographer who could outrun a boy any day of the week.

She was napping now, the Geographer, having slept through the sirens. As we all knew, she would sleep through Armageddon, curled there at the foot of P's father's bed, her hands folded under her cheek, her lips parted, snoring.

Some nations wax while others wane, the Iceman said, and in a brief space the race of things is changed and, like runners, they hand over the lamp of life.

Meanwhile P's nose had begun to bleed, dark red spots landing on her mother's bedspread. She seemed unconcerned though—amused even—by the mess she was making.

Let me through, said the Keeper; she'd grabbed a handful of tissues from the velveteen-covered box on the vanity table and was trying to step over and around the outspread arms and legs of the Astronomer who was still lying on the floor in front of the window.

He's going in our house! said the Iceman.

Who is? asked the Astronomer.

He turned to look, not out the window but at the face in the mirror above the vanity, and we could see him positioning himself at the start of a journey that we, ourselves, couldn't begin to name, even though inside each of us there was a little knob of becoming, and inside each of those knobs, a lifetime. P lifted herself from her mother's bed, her bloody nose lulling us into inattention as, at the same time, the sun concluded its slow circuit over the apartment building, making way for the moon and the stars.

It was New Year's Eve. Lots of people had already set up blankets on the lawn surrounding the Vocational School. They came, as they did every year, to see the fireworks. For a while the Cook had been enrolled in the school and when he was, we got the best seats, on a flat section of roof near the exhaust fan. Our father used to be the one to bring us, for as much as our mother claimed to adore beautiful, transitory things, she also hated noise and crowds.

The yellow acacia petals on the mahogany tabletop, she loved them.

Her children—until we got big, that is.

The Astronomer was on his bicycle. He'd ridden a great distance to get away from everything and yet here he was, back at the Vocational School; his knees were stiff and his back ached. Since the last time he'd been here he'd devoted himself to studying the spherical vastness of the Boötes Void, a part of outer space into which particles entered and, millions of years later, out of which they exited, looking exactly the same. As he explained, there hadn't been enough time since the universe began for the void to empty itself the way it seemed to have done.

Sometimes the Astronomer wandered on foot, sometimes he

went via bus or train. He never owned a car and he almost never flew, aside from that one time landing at the cove in the floatplane. He was especially partial to his bicycle and he rode it everywhere.

Everywhere, that's a big place. The Geographer made a shape with her hands.

Or you could say that's all there is, said the Topologist.

The sky had only just gotten dark enough for the fireworks to start. The sky was dark but the darkness still had a sheet of light inside, the way a philosophic tenet is backed by intuition. The Astronomer wheeled his bike between the blankets, scanning faces—of course no one looked familiar after all that time.

He had decided to try his luck getting into the school building and climbing to the roof when a woman wearing a fur cloak and sitting on a plaid blanket called out to him as he wheeled past.

"Hello there, handsome," she said. At first he thought she was alone, until he noticed the bearded man stretched out beside her on the blanket, his eyes wide open, looking at the sky.

The cloak was made of squirrel fur and it was hooded; all the Astronomer could see of the woman was the disk of her face and one hand, ungloved, lifting a flute of champagne to her mouth. "Sit," she said, patting the blanket.

There was enough room for him if he sat very close to her; otherwise he would have ended up sitting on some part of the bearded man, who was steadying the champagne bottle between his feet.

"Your poor mother would be so proud of you if only she could see you now," the woman said. She tipped back her head to take a swallow and the hood slid onto her shoulders, giving him a better look. "Do you need a hint?" she asked, and she began to hum. "Slow slow quick quick? Does that ring a bell?"

The Astronomer peered closer. He had the best eyesight of us all, but the worst memory for faces.

"The first token," the woman said. "The first token is when there's a sudden change in the weather."

As she spoke, an umbrella of stars came raining down from above, making the night brighter, followed by a loud bang and a scattering of applause.

"Oh," the Astronomer said. "Mrs. Chaliffe."

At some point we had all been subjected to Mrs. Chaliffe's ballroom dance class. Some of us had wept or broken out in hives. It made no sense, really, how unalike we were despite our best efforts. But the Astronomer—the Astronomer had truly shone. That he spent a lot of time looking at the sky while not watching where he put his feet had led us to believe he was clumsy, when in fact there was no one more graceful. He danced like a dream; he won prizes. With light step, as if earth and its trammels had little power to restrain him, the Keeper said. The number of his tarot card was zero for the Fool; it showed a young man in tights and a doublet getting ready to walk off a cliff.

When she wanted to demonstrate a step, Mrs. Chaliffe always picked him as her partner, even though Mr. Chaliffe was supposed to fulfill that need. He didn't have a beard back then but he was short and plump, whereas the Astronomer had always been tall and looked good in a suit.

Jee Moon used to have to dance with him, Mr. Chaliffe.

There was the Cinderella dance where each girl put a shoe in the middle of the floor and each prince chose a shoe and went to find its mate. Even though she was small P had big feet and to have big feet was a liability; we knew this from the fairy tale. If you had big feet you were going to have to cut all your toes off or both your heels.

Nor had it been a glass slipper Cinderella wore but a slipper made of squirrel fur, a commodity with which everyone on the

Silk Road was well acquainted. Squirrel fur was called *vair*, like the French word for *glass*, which is where the idea of a glass slipper came from.

"I was so sorry to hear about your poor mother," said Mrs. Chaliffe. "It sounds like it came as a complete shock to everyone. That's what happens when you let strangers into your house."

The Astronomer had no idea what she was talking about. Then again, he often was oblivious to what happened on the earthly plane. He remembered sirens, circles of blood on a pillowcase. A circle of violet stars swelling to swallow a circle of purple that a red tongue shot out of, accompanied by admiring murmurings, but that was the fireworks.

"The fourth token is when the stars seem to fall," he said, "and the air fills with a venomous vapor."

We knew the tokens, every one of them. The weather, the darkness, the flies, the stars, the lightning and thunder, the winds. We knew them and could recite them on command.

"Mr. Chaliffe and I would be honored if you would come back to the house with us." Mrs. Chaliffe handed her champagne flute to the Astronomer and nodded encouragingly to make him take a sip.

The Astronomer was never much of a drinker, but before Jee Moon he didn't drink at all. With that first sip of champagne he felt nostalgic as he never had before. He remembered the polished floor of the ballroom, the blue exit sign in the far corner and the row of coat hooks as you entered off the street, Mr. Chaliffe attentive to the record player and the large flying saucer–shaped light fixtures hanging from the ceiling. Mrs. Chaliffe was quite tiny, decked out in a sea-green tea gown. She had a permanent wave, which meant she was older than everyone, but she had a beautiful face.

The fifth token is when a blazing star appears, the Cook said. He seemed meditative, looking toward the window, though it had gotten too dark to see anything except the strange glow emitted by the snow cover. We knew he was thinking about his wife. It took her years to hit the bottom of the bottomless well of her illness, and when she finally did she opened her mouth to say something to him and whatever she had to say sank deeper still, sucked back into the primal soup of whatever she'd been to begin with.

There were seven of them: the seven tokens of Infirmity and the Great Sickness called the Pestilence.

But why number them? Why call them tokens?

Tokens were things we used to carry in our pockets. To get to school we dropped them in a box on the trolley car. Nanny made sure we had plenty of them even when we got old enough to do this for ourselves. A token in the pocket and a tuna sandwich in a brown paper bag. Why try to make a system out of something like life? The sickness came no matter what the stars were doing, whether falling or staying put.

The fireworks ended with the usual violent display of multiple, overlapping colors and loud noises; everyone began gathering their things, heading in a slow-moving mass toward the main thoroughfare. The trolleys were still running but they were few and far between; some people had parked their cars on a side street, others didn't have far to walk. The Chaliffes lived nearby in a semidetached stone house on one of the side streets. The Astronomer was surprised to see how modest the house was, given the opulence of the ballroom.

Even though it was very late, Mrs. Chaliffe put a record on the turntable and stood in the middle of the living room floor, her hands on her hips, swaying from side to side.

The Cook rolled his eyes. Who came up with that music? he said, and the Keeper let out a sigh. Maybe I didn't have the smallest feet, she said to the Astronomer, but I wasn't the worst dancer. I always hoped you'd pick me but you were already taken.

The Topologist was the worst even though her feet were small.

Besides which, the Astronomer had no choice. It wasn't as if he could refuse Mrs. Chaliffe.

That was the thing when we were children. Whereas now we were old enough to refuse anything, only refusal no longer worked.

What was that song? The one they used to play to get things going? The Iceman was humming a tune that sounded familiar. He put out his hand and invited the Botanist to dance. I hope you don't expect me to dip, he said.

Almost immediately the rest of us took up the tune, and the next thing we knew we were dancing, filling the darkness of the Great Hall with the darker shapes of our conjoined bodies, four-legged and with two heads like creatures in a myth. The Astronomer had his fingers pressed into Jee Moon's back, and despite her belly's growing convexity, their bodies were perfectly aligned as they moved across the floor. He had always been trying to get away from us—we just hadn't realized it.

Remember what it was like? the Keeper said. You could look out the window and see all the way to where we are now, dancing at the edge of the world.

Above us the sky extended its fluid, heaving hide, punctured with stars, though of course that isn't what stars are.

Looking back at us looking back at us—this was called a "closed walk." The choice of starting point wasn't important; the important thing was to cycle through the same sequence of edges. The eyes, searching. The black spot on the skin. The stowaway in the knapsack. The little biting thing. A topologist had figured this system out a long time ago while walking over the seven bridges of his native city.

The second floor of the Chaliffes' house consisted of three bedrooms off a narrow hallway; there was a small pink-tiled bathroom at the head of the stairs. Mrs. Chaliffe gave the Astronomer the room directly next to the master bedroom. The first time he went to use the bathroom he knocked discreetly on the door and, when there was no response, he opened it to find Mrs. Chaliffe seated on the toilet. "Don't give it another thought," she said.

The dog, on the other hand, came as something of a surprise. One morning, after the Astronomer had been living in the house for about a week, he walked into the kitchen and there it was, a medium-sized dog with a rough coat of blond fur, whining at the back door to be let in. Mrs. Chaliffe was in her bathrobe making a pot of coffee and pretending not to notice. "Oh him," she said, when the Astronomer asked. "Ignore him and he'll go away." When he asked what the dog's name was she looked at him in disbelief; when he looked back at the door the dog was gone and Mr. Chaliffe was there in its stead, morning paper in hand.

There were four modes of rebirth—we knew this, all four of them a means of letting something in.

The first indication was that when you looked into water you couldn't see your reflection. Your body didn't cast a shadow. You needed to concentrate harder than ever. You had to concentrate your mind with singularity of intent, like a horse being controlled by a bridle. Otherwise you might open your eyes and emerge as a puppy, the lowest order of being.

There had been dogs in the neighborhood where we grew up, but they didn't resemble one another the way the dogs at the settlement did. Many of the dogs in our neighborhood had sorrowful expressions even when they were busy humping our legs, whereas the dogs in the settlement looked uniformly joyful, especially when they were running. They could run forever—that was what they liked to do best. Unlike us, they had no sense of destination aside from a wish for food. Even as they slept their legs kept moving, traversing in advance the landscape we'd be covering the next day. They would be speaking, too, making small soft noises, yips of excitement.

Didn't P used to have a dog? asked the Topologist.

I remember they had it put to sleep, said the Iceman.

It bit a child, said the Keeper. Or so the parents said. In the Highgate Apartments, the next floor down.

P loved that dog, the Archivist said.

She loved it more than anything, said the Cook. Us included. But I thought the child it bit was *you*.

The Chaliffes' dog never bit anyone, as far as the Astronomer could tell. It merely registered its dislike of him whenever it had a chance, letting out a very low, almost inaudible sound that, being almost inaudible, was all the more menacing. Mrs. Chaliffe seemed distressed the first time he offered to take it for a walk. "You don't know what you're getting yourself in for," she told him. They were busy practicing. The Annual Ballroom Challenge was coming up. Their tango was without flaw; they excelled at floorcraft but were weak on expression. Usually it was just the two of them, though every now and then the dog would appear and when he was watching, Mrs. Chaliffe seemed to have trouble keeping the beat.

It was impossible to tell whether it was very late or very early. The windows were open—a pale green moth flew straight at the Astronomer's face, its wings like gossamer and its body dense and throbbing. Eventually the rising sun spread its light across the eastern sky like an enormous gold eyeball.

That was me, Jee Moon said.

What was you? asked the Astronomer.

The moth, she said. Couldn't you tell? I came from my home in the Purple Forbidden Enclosure, she said, pointing in the direction of the sky. In Boötes. Where you came from too, remember?

The great cosmic void. If I hadn't flown at you at that exact moment who knows what would have become of us.

How could you have been a moth? the Iceman asked.

A luna moth, said Jee Moon.

A luna moth only lives for a week, said the Botanist. Its whole purpose is reproduction. It doesn't even have a mouth.

So? said Jee Moon.

She took the Botanist's hand and ran it over the curve of her belly.

And truly, when we looked at her we had to admit that while she seemed delicate to the point of insubstantiality, she also exuded a force as obvious and incontestable as gravity. Her skin, too, had the slightest green tint to it, not unlike the Qingbai porcelain water dropper that had traveled with us the length of the Silk Road, only to end its days in the top drawer of the bachelor chest among the marbles. It was a treasure, the water dropper. It was a souvenir, a memento of our grueling transit. It was evidence of our birthright, plus it could be used to moisten ink.

This wasn't the first excursion we went on together. We always prepared for every eventuality, packing adequate provisions even if we knew there would be a café or market, a welcoming host or unattended cornfield in our future. There weren't as many pilgrims on the road then as there once had been, but we had a good explanation for this, including the curfew, which was new, and the weather. It was a matter of dreadful foreboding to contemplate a winter without storms, a spring without mild weather, a summer without heat. News of the prison break hadn't reached us yet, but undoubtedly that, too, was having an effect on travel. It's almost certain our mother knew about it but we didn't know that, only that she lagged behind while the rest of us plunged ahead.

According to the Iceman, who usually brought up the rear, polishing off leftover sausage or the remains of a bottle of wine, she was doing something to the cairns. Adding a stone, taking a stone away, taking all the stones away—he couldn't tell, just that she was doing something to them. Nothing behaves as it does without a cause and the universe is not entangled in causal accidents.

The farther we got from home, the darker the sky. The wind

was from the south, slackening our muscles and bringing disorder to our bodies, moistening and exhausting our brains. Earlier, many of us had eaten too much, heavy foods we weren't accustomed to, dark pottage ladled from an iron kettle. It wasn't as if we were ever actually starving. We always ate like kings. Well, maybe not always. Maybe not there at the end. The little house, the little knives and forks and spoons. But that hadn't happened yet.

There were robbers abroad in the land, said the Geographer. Wild beasts. I wanted to stop to take a sounding but no one would let me.

Oh, a *sound*ing, said the Keeper. It's true, she found everything the Geographer said adorable. The Keeper was older than the rest of us, more like a mother than our mother. She was heavyset in a confidential way, and had a smell like risen dough mixed with rain-soaked dirt. Her hair was long and gray and she wore it, often, in braids.

Our mother, on the other hand, smelled like perfume, the kind of dense yet hollow smell a body cavity exudes after pleasure. Her perfume was expensive; we were forbidden to touch the bottle. The one time one of us poured some on our scalp to smell like her, the rest of us had to, too. We weren't equal, though, we knew that. She came to kiss us goodnight and we could tell. Our mother had sharp elbows. Even so she was well endowed, bending to give each of us a goodnight kiss with her bright red lips.

I remember hearing the saleslady say she had an excellent bust line, said the Botanist.

From behind you could see up her skirt, said the Cook. You could see where the tops of her stockings attached to the garter belt.

Her dresses were short and formfitting. They were usually red or black. Very *à la chinoise*, said the Geographer.

He put his hand up there, said the Archivist. She let him.

He could fit his whole hand inside her, said the Cook.

We had to pick our way carefully. At some point we left behind the sandy track we'd been following and entered into a wood. Our eyes took a moment to adjust to the shifting darkness, the other watchful eyes. We went through a little gate and shortly thereafter another. A preponderance of beech trees, the old kind, the trunks smooth and seamless and gray like elephant hide. There were also ash trees, though not enough to be of any use. The thing is, we had to apprehend of what kind and how widely differing in their forms were the beginnings of things, how varied by manifold diversities of shape. We were new, too, the skin beneath our cloaks just acquiring density. Only recently had we learned to tell ourselves apart. The trail ascended steeply between two houses and some chickens came to greet us, speckled black and white. From the smaller of the two houses someone called out to us. Wait! they called. They had news: someone, something that had escaped was . . . We didn't stop; we kept climbing.

She would have known, said the Botanist. She always stuck up for Mother, but this was because the Botanist was physically attractive and our mother preferred things that looked good. She would never have led us into danger, the Botanist said, and the Topologist rolled her eyes. Oh, come on! she said.

Like when the flavor of a wine is gone or the aroma of a perfume has been dispersed into the air or the savor has left the body.

Okay, said the Cook. Maybe she didn't lead us. But she left the door unlocked and threw away the key.

Of course we remembered our mother saying this about the prison a long time ago, except there, the door was locked.

It was a memory we all shared. Probably because it was the opposite of the way she felt about us.

She wanted us to try our wings, said the Botanist.

She wanted us to crash land, said the Topologist.

At last we arrived on the plateau. We couldn't see where we were because of the rain and the wind. The rain and the hail and the howling wind. And the snow, said the Archivist. Don't forget the snow. At some point we heard the bell. We all heard it; it kept ringing and ringing, ringing without stop.

It wasn't the Angelus; by now we knew how to recognize the Angelus.

It's marking a death, said the Archivist. One stroke for every year of the deceased's life.

No one could live to be that old, said the Keeper.

You don't know what you're talking about, the Topologist said. The bell is Maria. The Dômerie must be nearby.

When she told us it was a hospital we all felt the same relief.

Maria was the Bell of the Lost, forged in the thirteenth century. Evidently bells could have names. A wealthy pilgrim had the Dômerie built in gratitude after he survived a fierce attack by an unknown assailant when he went astray in the Aubrac. According to the words written on it, the bell was made to praise God, cast out demons, call home the lost.

That's us all right, said the Cook.

It would have helped if one of us had thought to bring a compass. It would have helped if one of us had been paying attention to what we were doing. The expedition was Mother's idea. She was the one we'd been counting on to tell us what to do. We couldn't go back; our tracks were obliterated as fast as we made them by whatever was falling from the sky. Besides, said the Iceman, where would we go back to? A thing never returns to nothing, but all things after disruption go back into the first bodies of matter.

It would be great if you spoke English, said the Keeper.

The Topologist was the one we were counting on now. She was

the one who could remember leaving her guidebook on a café table somewhere in the Aubrac. The saint had his shrines everywhere along the route but we hadn't seen one in a while. We hadn't seen *anything* in a while. We were ill equipped to travel, every one of us, our fingers unable to perform the simplest task, wiping our eyeglasses dry, buttoning our cloaks. The bell continued ringing but the closer we got to the sound, the dimmer the sound grew. Meanwhile the sound of howling that we thought was the wind was growing louder.

This is exactly what I've been trying to tell you, said the Archivist. The dog-headed beast is on the loose. He lifted his pant leg to show us the bite marks. No one ever listens to me, he said.

I'm listening, said the Geographer, and she crouched down to get a better look.

The Topologist held the Archivist's hands in hers and stared him in the eye. Calm down, she said. Breathe in and breathe out. The way Jee Moon taught us.

Of course the idea of being nowhere was easier for her, as a Topologist, as well as the idea of being in a neighborhood that didn't exist. She had been sitting in a nonexistent neighborhood the time she noticed the Swede shaking the stone loose from his shoe and invited him to come join her. The way the Topologist saw it, she and the Swede were distinct points separated by their respective nonexistent neighborhoods. Luckily it had been late enough in the day that they decided to share a bottle of wine. A festival was under way; all the cows of the Aubrac had been set free onto the plateau to graze and multiply. Soon enough the Topologist and the Swede were surrounded by luminous golden cows, their heads decorated with flowers. Spring had been late that year. A cow came close to stare at them and they could see its breath.

Animals dwell upon the moment, Jee Moon said. They have that in common, even the beast.

The thing about the dog-headed beast was that it dwelt in so many different moments it had begun to seem like it didn't exist.

We kept closer to the Topologist than usual. We were careful, having been warned time and again that she didn't like to be touched. At some point we realized we were following the contour of a small lively stream feeding into an almost perfectly round lake. Even though we couldn't see the lake, we knew the Dômerie was right there on the other side of it. The bell continued its muffled tolling, more a feeling than a sound, as if our blood were pulsing outside our bodies or we were back inside our mother, waiting to be born.

The Topologist didn't like to talk about what happened to her after she left the shrine. Most of us assumed that whatever it was the Swede had been involved, though there was a lot of disagreement about whether he'd been in the shrine with us that day or she had met up with him after. Some of us thought we remembered seeing someone who might have been him, a good-looking man in a dark green rain poncho, lighting a candle for Saint Roch. But did this mean that by then the Swede was already sick?

Really, it could have been any one of us. We had all experienced the agonizing sensation of the skull shrinking around the soft mass of the brain, driving out thoughts the way seawater boils with the mastering might of the winds.

I thought I could help him, the Topologist said, if only I could get him to the hospital.

Right, said the Geographer. The hospital.

We all had the same idea, for whatever good it did.

While we're on the subject, the Archivist said, again lifting his pant leg.

The Botanist bent down to see what he was talking about. I don't like the looks of that, she said.

Me neither, said the Cook, but it was obvious he was making a joke.

Under the circumstances it was difficult to see anything, the night saturated with water and without a moon, the wind causing the heavy fabric of our cloaks to spread and fold like wings.

We had to be careful, traversing the lip of the lake. From the start the ground had been slippery underfoot, but now, given this most recent precipitation, the way was fraught with danger. The Keeper was the least agile among us and needed to hang onto the Geographer's arm. If she hadn't, the Geographer might have raced ahead, being the swiftest and eager to run. If it weren't for the Keeper who knows where the Geographer would be by now?

Meanwhile the Dômerie began assembling itself in large wavering blocks, some of the blocks advancing toward us more aggressively than others, piling side by side and one atop the other over and over and over again into an impossibly tall tower with a pointed turret, alongside of which a low building extended itself alluringly, stretching to its full length like an animal. Everything was wet, dark; even without moon or stars the stones glistened. There it was, the hospital, right there in front of us. All we needed to do was enter it.

The Topologist followed along the hospital wall, trailing her fingers across the stone. There must be a door here somewhere, she said. From the beginning, small things have figured out how to get through impossibly small openings. This was one of the advantages of being small, the Geographer said. Something practically invisible to the naked eye like a flea could change the course of history.

Remember Nanny and the mice? said the Botanist.

She thought there was just the one, said the Cook. She gave it a name. Something upper crust. Miles.

And then Miles had babies in the hamper.

Nanny always wondered how he got in, said the Topologist.

My question exactly, said the Cook, pointing at the hospital.

But the Topologist either couldn't remember or didn't want to say. The little dog, though! There had been a little dog that followed them from the shrine, attracted by the meat the Swede had stowed in his pack, and when they got to the hospital the little dog ran up to what turned out to be a door and barked at it.

I think the door is hard to see, the Topologist said. It blends in with the stone. You have to push on it to make it open, she said. Like an ashtray in a car. Push *down*.

The next thing we all knew, the Botanist had disappeared.

We were used to people disappearing. Our mother for example: one minute she was right there, so close we could see the fine colorless hair on her upper lip and smell the egg on her breath. The next minute she was gone. She was quick moving; we could hear the click of her heels along the hallway. There was nothing magical about it, the Iceman said. She never wanted children. We cramped her style. I saw her with that man, he said. Her thighs like wings—she wanted to fly, remember? She even took lessons. The Iceman said it was so dark when he went into the Morning Room he couldn't tell if he was floating or falling. He'd been having the dream about the daemon with the howling mouth we'd all grown tired of hearing; for such a substantial person his psyche was surprisingly delicate. It was easy to hurt his feelings. We tried to watch what we said around him. The Botanist was his favorite and now she was gone.

How did she do that? The Archivist was pushing on stones, one after another, to no avail.

Like when we used to play Sardines, said the Keeper. You'd think someone was there with you and all of a sudden they weren't.

You'd feel more alone than ever, said the Geographer.

Remember running up the stairs to Nanny's room? the Keeper asked.

The back staircase was dimly lit and smelled like damp varnish and baby powder; its wallpaper was coming loose and there were lion faces in the roses. We weren't supposed to play on that staircase— the staircase was for Nanny's use, just as we weren't supposed to go into her room even though she could come into our rooms whenever she felt like it. Nanny's room didn't smell like the rest of the house and the things she kept there weren't like our things. When the Cook put her brassiere on over his shirt it was frightening.

Nanny's room was small. It didn't seem possible that all of us could fit into it at once, let alone find a place to hide in it.

Her things weren't as good as ours, the Archivist said. She bought her things in a box store.

She kept hard candies in a dish shaped like a woman's shoe, said the Cook. Also she believed in God.

When we'd been least expecting it the sky cleared, like a curtain sweeping open on a new act. The moon, too, was in a new phase, one we'd never seen before. It was *our* moon though, not some other heavenly body. It shone its light down onto the hospital and the lake and we were amazed to see the beauty of the landscape, whereas before all had seemed hideous, treacherous, even the stones' shimmering designed to trick us.

The Keeper reached out to steady herself on the Geographer's arm but the Geographer was no longer there. Hey! she said. What's going on?

With the Botanist we'd grown used to this, due to the opals. The opal wasn't the Botanist's birthstone, though, and we also knew that to wear an opal if you hadn't been born in October was bad luck.

Hello? Hello? The Keeper looked down the length of the hospital wall and around the foot of the tower. It took her a while to realize that everyone except for her had found the door and gone inside. Hello? she said again, but she knew there was nobody out there with her. She had the moon and the stars and the planets, the stones and the lake. She tuned her ears to the low frequencies, the muffled voices of bottom dwellers, the sharp whispers of gnats. Nothing.

Eventually from off in the distance came a faint thrumming noise as the hydroelectric plant awakened, while close at hand she could hear us talking and laughing on the other side of the wall— the same way she heard us when we were hiding under Nanny's bed in a game of Sardines. Usually we were busy making fun of Nanny, having located the copy of *Bonjour Tristesse* she kept hidden between her mattress and a bed slat.

The Keeper used to be thin, tall, and purposeful like an arrow, but that was before, back when she was a tomboy. Now she was overweight, her ankles tending to swell if she stayed on her feet too long.

We worried about her. She was in worse shape than the Iceman and, if that wasn't bad enough, she was a smoker. At some point we'd all been smokers—even the Archivist when he was trying to impress P—but we'd managed to quit, each of us enduring the loss in his or her own fashion. For some of us it proved trifling, a mere annoyance, while for others it proved unbearable, a feeling akin to grief.

The Keeper never even tried to quit; she loved to smoke. She was the kind of person whose destiny seemed as inevitable to her as it was opaque. Now, in the moonlight outside the hospital, she was surprised to discover a practically full pack of cigarettes in her pants pocket. The Cook must have put them there, she figured, along with the little Zippo that used to be kept in the cloisonné stamp box atop the bachelor chest. It had to have been him, since the rest of us were continually trying everything we could think of to make her stop.

The Keeper flicked the lighter's wheel and a flame burst out. The cigarette was damp but she managed to get it going, its round orange eye looking this way and that.

What's she up to out there do you think? asked the Topologist.

Who the hell knows, said the Iceman.

Shhh, said Jee Moon, putting her hand over his mouth. This is a hospital.

The Iceman's eyes opened wide in surprise—it was the first and only time she had touched him.

We often heard conversations go on, even through closed doors. This was because a voice can pass uninjured through the winding openings of things, whereas eidola refuse to pass: they're torn to shreds, especially if the openings through which they try gliding aren't straight.

Up ahead was the Botanist, floating in the dark. No matter how she'd managed to get inside the hospital, now that she was an eidolon there was no way she could get out. We could see her bare feet hovering above the floor, her blond hair floating around her head as if darkness were water. The closer we drew, the smaller the Botanist became, the outermost surface streaming off her. She was facing us but moving away.

It's not her, though, is it? said the Cook.

He thought he was seeing his wife's ghost, the light cast by the Botanist leading him on. As so often happened when we came face to face with the unexpected, our thoughts got loose from our brainpans, sending us straightaway to the place we thought we'd left behind forever. The Cook's wife made him promise not to go seeking her ghost in mirrors or in pools. When I'm dead I'll be dead, she said. That will be the end of me. Some people became ghosts, she told him; they were the ones with a spare soul. Others, well. Who could say what the others became? The little fox with

91

the goose in its mouth, the Astronomer recalled with a start. It was his favorite constellation. As for the sound of machinery, the Archivist didn't realize it was coming from a hydroelectric plant. He would be late, he was thinking. An X suture is what that bite calls for. X X X X X.

Thoughts were the one thing we couldn't control, the seeds of the mind possessing a power of moving in proportion to the seeds' smallness and smoothness.

At the end of the hall, right before the place where a thick length of rope hung down from the bell tower, a low, narrow passageway like the January tunnel extended off to the right. I'm not going in there, said the Iceman. If I go in there I'll never get out. When the Geographer took her tablet from her pack and tried to check the coordinates it was so dark she couldn't see a thing. None of us could, aside from the light the Botanist made as she passed.

Meanwhile the Keeper was on the other side of the wall, all by herself in the Savage Domain with only a cigarette for company.

Most of us came to the settlement on the floatplane; we had no trouble fitting inside it, just as we'd all managed to fit inside our mother and the doctor had no trouble getting us out. The Iceman, on the other hand, always turned out to be too big for every place in which he found himself. The desks at school were a torment, a challenge posed by having to pour his form into an impossibly small opening between two immovable parts, the heavy wooden chair attached to the desktop belonging to the child sitting behind him, and the heavy wooden lid with its pencil tray and inkwell attached to the seatback of the child sitting in front of him, a skinny little girl with a birthmark on her neck.

We knew about this even though he thought he was keeping it a secret. For one thing, he said the girl's name in his sleep. For another, we'd all had the same experience: a sudden vision of the tender blade of the girl's neck as it bent in the breeze of our rapt regard, the delicate brown hair and the café au lait birthmark shaped like something familiar, something along the lines of a mop at the entrance to a tunnel, a leaping flea, a little green lizard. A cairn too, of course.

I was the one sitting behind him, said the Geographer. I couldn't see the chalkboard. My view of the world always had an obstruction.

We weren't seated alphabetically, said the Keeper.

It was more like he was teacher's pet, said the Geographer. He wasn't a very good student, though.

He thought "Prince Valiant" was beneath him, said the Cook. Even though the prince spent his childhood in a bog.

Well, yes, the Iceman said, when one of us mentioned the birthmark.

Pictures of things and the thin shapes of them are emitted off the surfaces of things: these are like films or rinds, the image bearing an appearance and form resembling the thing, whatever it was, from whose body the picture was shed and wandered forth.

The day of the Iceman's arrival the weather was bad; the plane couldn't fly. Even if it could, how could it land? the woman on the phone wanted to know. She threw the question at the Iceman like a challenge. "It needs to land on *wa*ter," she said. Meanwhile he was stuck in a motel room barely bigger than he was, with the same framed print of a sailing vessel above the bed we all remembered from when we, too, had been stuck there, waiting. The sky opened and let loose everything it had at its disposal. There was an election going on somewhere and the candidates stood behind podia and held forth, hatefully. Sweetness, the Iceman thought. Where did it go? Even the mosses, sweetest things on earth, were dying. Who knew what would be left of them by the time he found a pilot willing to take him up the coast?

Of course he was right: the mosses *were* the sweetest things on earth and they *were* dying. So many people on the move, all sorts of things were getting trampled. It would be difficult to isolate any one of them. The Silk Road began in the east and headed west—that was the original orientation. When did it veer north? How did word travel?

There would be a town or village, a church tower with a bell or bells in it, and then the tongues of the bells would lash out, the sound they made expanding the dark blue air. Did we breathe better when the bells were ringing? It seemed, truly, like there was a greater quantity of air—better, fresher air—when the bells rang, though that may only have been their sound. The Silk Road made allowances for quarantines, the piled bodies of the dead. The outfits we wore were outlandish. There was a garment of silk called a *paltok*. There was particolored and striped hose that we tied with laces to our *paltoks*, which were called *harlottes*. There were shoes with pointed toes as long as our fingers, called *crakowes*. Some of us went about with our loins uncovered. Some of us wore belts studded with gold and silver. We would approach a village and the only person to come out to meet us would be the village idiot.

Back then we were way too young and inexperienced to understand what it was we were being asked to contend with.

Once the weather cleared the Iceman made his way to the dock. The floatplane was red and the pilot a girl, strong and rawboned and with a flat black braid down her back. "Watch the dog," she said, for there was a large one draped courtesan-like across the rear seat. "You have to sit up here," she said, pointing at the seat beside her. The next thing the Iceman knew, they were taking off.

For an instant it seemed like the plane was headed back into the water. Then a fish jumped. We'd all been there. A person might fall into the abyss and see stars. They might climb into heaven and, being too high above everything, see nothing. Since we came from the past we knew how to look forward, but it was possible one of us came from the future, too, and when that happens it's possible to see what it was like before there was anything, anything at all.

Not the one with two hearts, though—not that one. It's possible the one who came from the future didn't have a heart.

"Sure you'll fit," the pilot said to the Iceman, who stood hunched in the open door. "Right here," she said, patting the seat beside her. The Iceman wasn't the only one of us she brought to the settlement, but he was the only one she let sit beside her that way in the cockpit.

We'd grown used to this with him. The corner grocer slipped him chocolate-covered pretzels when we stopped to buy comic books. The goodwives called off the dogs; the nuns blessed him and gave him bowls of *aligot* to eat. The teenage girl behind the soda fountain fed him maraschino cherries while we waited to pick up our mother's asthma medicine. Once, on the road, a trader gave him a bag of salt and a lambskin cloak.

The Astronomer may have been handsome but the Iceman was lovable. He kept a terrarium in the Morning Room with different kinds of moss in it, a sexual generation of mosses including male and female sex organs alike, living things in some cases so little their sex parts could not be seen at all. Of what size were we to suppose the sex parts of such creatures to be? Or the ball of the heart or the eyes? Not to mention the first beginnings out of which the soul and the nature of the mind were formed?

It had been the same for all of us. From the air the world looked like a hive of bees. Then the plane landed and everything divided into individual parts, each of which grew big again, the cove, the escarpment, the raised beach. Landing, for all of us, was a dream come true and a disappointment. The floatplane unfolded wings of water cold enough to kill. The girl at the controls turned to the Iceman and smiled. She told him the dock had floated away during the night but he didn't need to worry. Someone wearing oilskins was approaching in a trap boat. Welcome, the person said.

That was *me*, said the Geographer. Remember? She mimed a hat.

The Iceman didn't remember, but he didn't want to say so.

We were all remembering, then.

The pilot cut the engines and dropped anchor. She was serious but she could be made to laugh. She had a sense of humor, several of us remembered that. When the Cook told her one of those jokes of his, she laughed.

Wit is the hallmark of intelligence, said the Archivist, by which he meant to disagree.

He remembered the bush pilot differently, the look on her face as she guided the plane across treacherous mountain terrain. There was something in her expression that made him think of our mother. But when and under what circumstances? A long time ago, that was for sure, our mother's face coming closer—maybe the time she showed him how to tie a necktie. The necktie had white stars on a blue background, he remembered. He remembered the tip of our mother's tongue caught between her teeth like she was going to bite it off, her eyes all but crossed in fierce concentration.

He won a prize at school, it must have been then. A spelling bee? He was the only one of us who was good at spelling. Or maybe it was for penmanship. On the report card the quality of a person's cursive was judged to be more important than everything else, including health habits. We were made to practice our cursive until it was perfect; there was no room for improvisation or originality.

Maybe the prize was for that essay you wrote, said the Geographer. About Hadrian. She didn't say it, but we were all thinking the same thing: he'd only written the essay to impress P.

A duel to the death, said the Topologist. Plus wasn't it her essay that won the prize?

The day the Iceman arrived at the settlement it was just the Geographer and the Topologist in the boat, leaving him plenty of room. The Geographer was driving the boat; the Topologist gave the Iceman a set of oilskins to wear and told him to hold on tight. She was the one who understood him best, space having been her lifelong companion, the place that she dwelt in and that she loved more than anything. Tightness was a necessary criterion she knew, especially when a measure had infinite dimensions. She told the Iceman they didn't have far to go, and pointed ahead to the escarpment.

What's that? he asked.

Over near the shore to the left of them an animal was lifting its head from the water, bracing itself on the rocks as it kept rising, lifting its hindquarters and shaking the water from its surprisingly long and not quite snow-white body in one endless ripple, beginning to turn casually as if it had all the time in the world, its black nose pulsating to take in the smell of them.

It had a beautiful shape, that nose! A shape like the drawer pulls on the bachelor chest that stood in the entry hall near the front door. Bear noses, the Botanist used to call them. But not everyone found her adorable.

For example the Botanist used to force the Geographer to be the baby when they played family, even though it was the Botanist who was the youngest. Eventually the Botanist grew to be very tall, whereas the Geographer remained short. The Iceman would be the father, the Botanist the mother. She would put a shower cap on the Geographer's head and get the Iceman to pull her around the block in a wagon.

The Geographer remembered the prisoners making fun of her, calling her names. One of them in particular, the one we called the Cute Prisoner because of his shining hair and the scar on his cheek the Archivist told us he'd gotten in a duel.

Breaking and entering, said the Iceman. That's how he got it. We saw him, remember? That time we were playing Hangman.

Except the Cute Prisoner didn't have to break and enter; it was our mother who let him in. She let him in the front door like he was a regular visitor. He pushed her against the bachelor chest and then he pushed his knee between her legs to open them, raising his knee slowly, pressing the kneecap up until it couldn't go any further. Each one of us remembered—at night, upstairs, feigning sleep when Nanny came patrolling with her flashlight, or consigned to our beds in the settlement, with the snow falling thick around us.

We thought we were being taken to the isolation ward; we thought we were being taken *somewhere*, maybe to our mother who had been known to volunteer as a Gray Lady despite her horror of human infirmity, especially anything involving blood. The outfit she got to wear as a Gray Lady suited her, narrow at the waist and with a red cross atop her right breast, as did the image she carried in her mind's eye of her lovely self ministering to those less fortunate.

This was probably how the Prisoner got his toe in the door, said the Iceman.

Well, more than his toe, said the Topologist.

But if she was here in the Dômerie, said the Cook, wouldn't we be smelling that perfume?

The thing is, we had no way of knowing where the Botanist was taking us. Her eyes, usually the warmest brown of all our eyes, gold and shining like honey, seemed less like eyes than holes in her skull and her pretty mouth hung open trailing a low sound like spoor. Still, we followed her avidly, down the long hall and around the corner past the bell tower, down another corridor and up a flight of stairs. Alone among us, the Geographer kept looking back over her shoulder.

We shouldn't have left her out there like that, she said; we knew she meant the Keeper. It was cold inside but not as cold as it had been outside—we were glad to have our cloaks and heavy boots.

The staircase seemed endless. Now we could see cool bluish light ahead of us, flickering the way light does from a fluorescent tube when it's about to go out. We could hear, too, the sounds of a working hospital, the rumbling of the wheels of gurneys along the hallway, liquid spilling from basins. Someone screaming, someone moaning, someone telling someone to lie still.

You need to be taken to the station for processing, said the Botanist. She looked like she'd gone back to being her regular self, standing there before us at the head of the stairs, her eyes bright, her blond hair bound in a coil at the nape of her neck. Unlike her regular self, though, she didn't seem to register who we were. Proper names, surnames first, she said, consulting a clipboard. This was puzzling, since the Botanist had always been best at remembering everyone's name. Under her cloak she was wearing a white doctor's gown, goatskin boots, and gauntlets.

For heaven's sake! the Topologist said, pushing her way past. She was trying to get to the elevator we could see opening and closing its doors on the other side of the nurses' station. Opening, closing, opening, closing—it was like watching a mind trying to make itself up.

Don't waste your time, said the Geographer. I've been here, remember? She was looking at the Botanist. If I remember correctly, only a very few people are allowed to use the elevator. Isn't that so?

It's a good thing you came inside when you did, the Botanist said, looking the other way, ignoring her. She made her hands into claws. Don't worry about *her*, the Botanist said, and we knew she meant the Keeper. The only dangerous thing out there is a *beast*.

Processing involved having our scalps checked for bald spots, being told to spit into a metal pan, and being bled. The Iceman, bald already, had to submit to examination of his pubic hair, but the nurse was young and attractive and so he didn't mind. Eventually we were allowed to proceed, though it was never clear in what capacity, whether as visitor or patient. We were given theriac; we were told to keep our voices down. Maybe it wasn't the same for all of us. Some of us were made to wear an identification bracelet. Some of us were made to wear a mask. The Cook was tasked with bringing along a large pot of soup.

The higher we went in the building, the warmer it got. The isolation ward was on the third floor. At one time it had occupied its own separate building next to the stables, back when coal was plentiful. A little table stood between the white hospital bed where a sick person lay motionless and the straight-backed chair where the Botanist sat reading aloud from an old copy of *Life* magazine. She appeared deeply engrossed in what she was reading, as if she'd been at it for hours, even though we knew she couldn't have been sitting there for more than a few minutes before we arrived.

". . . very little time to do what needed to be done . . ." The Botanist was turning pages and scowling. ". . . an epidemic of this proportion had never been seen before and never would be again . . ."

To help retain heat, some of which was coming through a register cut in the floor, and some of which was coming from a poorly ventilated woodstove, the whole room and everything in it had been draped in animal skin. The head of the skin on the patient's bed was looking down over the foot of it at something on the floor. It was a bear, we were pretty sure of that, though the animals to whom the skins on the walls had once belonged were harder to identify, being headless.

Don't touch! the Botanist warned when the Topologist approached the patient.

I wasn't going to, the Topologist replied. It was obvious she thought it might be the Swede. At some point they'd lost contact with one another.

The person lying in the bed seemed to be doing something with its fingers. It was impossible to tell what sex the person was, though if it was a man he wasn't a very big one. The person was small-boned, like Father—it had been such a long time since we'd seen him; people shrank as they got older.

He'd always been noticeably smaller than Mother. Looking at the wedding picture, you found yourself thinking of something small and dark in contention with something large and white. An alpinist on the Matterhorn. An ant on a wedding cake. Not that Mother was particularly big, just sweeping like a generalization. Father, on the other hand, required a certain degree of vigilance to take in, not unlike that scrap we saw from the train, caught in a tangle of branches, the one that presaged everything.

No wonder we kept trying to duplicate our first excursion.

Though of course you can't go back. We all knew this. You can't!

The Geographer hung her cloak in the closet. She saw where the closet was without being told. The Astronomer opened the window and looked out; he was checking for signs of planetary conjunction. There was to be driving rain, the regular kind and the kind composed of dead birds. People were going to get in bed healthy and wake up dead. The Astronomer was humming; everything that happened in the heavens made him happy. The Cook put the soup pot on the little table. He took off the lid and made a face. Did something die in here? he asked.

The smell was, indeed, repulsive; we found ourselves thinking of Nanny's room the time the mice ate the poison she put out for them and went behind the lathe to decompose. Mother insisted our house was a celebration of life but we all knew what she meant by that was that our house was a good place to have sex. Even though she never went so far as to make fun of those of us who weren't interested in sex, we knew the force of her disdain. We were the ones who weren't invited to sit with her in the first class carriage; it was as if we had a character flaw. Nor did we bond with one another. We hated one another.

When the Topologist was running up and down the train from car to car, looking for a bathroom, we didn't help. When the porter gave her a brown paper bag to put her wet underpants in, we laughed. We laughed at the wet spot the underpants made on the bag and we laughed at the thought of the Topologist with nothing on under her skirt. Besides, everyone's days with Mother in the first class carriage were numbered, we knew that. It was just that not all of us were humiliated in the same way. Mostly our mother favored boys. She didn't have to worry about who was prettiest.

It had gotten to be very late, so late it was almost early. The wind was coming from the west, rattling the windowpanes; we could see the Keeper buffeted by it as she made her way along the path to the stables. Soon it would be dawn, the planet tipping away from the universe and toward the bright center of its own system. Soon it would be time to feed the animals.

The walkway was slippery; the Keeper was trying to watch where she put her feet, the beam of her flashlight guiding her past the stone angel and the dead flower stalks. She had to know we were watching her. To her we were blobs in a window casing, whereas to us she was a clearly defined figure, the beam of her flashlight darting here and there. To us she looked like a child— that was how we all looked from above, like children and then, the higher we went, like mice, like fleas, nothing.

The stables lay north of the Dômerie. They had been built of the same stone as the hospital and were set into the side of the same hill, only they faced away from the lake, toward the river and Portal Road. Though the door stood slightly open there were no tracks leading up to it. Often the Keeper found rats inside, sometimes a raptor eating a rat.

Which do you think will be gone first, people or animals? she asked. This was before she ran off, leaving us behind with the Botanist.

Today, instead of a horse in the box stall the Keeper found an old man and woman lying in limp embrace on the straw, their glands swollen and dark as plums. Maybe they weren't that old; maybe the disease had gotten there first, filling their bodies with its unbearable din like that of a door being smashed down. "Begone!" the old woman exclaimed.

They seemed unable to get enough of one another, nor did they seem to care that they had an audience. "Cover your eyes!" the old man said as they went at it again, cheerfully pumping like sex-starved youngsters. In point of fact they needed to procreate; everyone did. "Don't look at us," the old woman said, and the two of them broke into mocking laughter.

The Keeper wasn't worried that they might communicate the sickness to her; everyone who spent time around horses turned out to be immune, the disease rendered impotent by their smell.

Ordinarily she didn't set out for town until after breakfast but today was going to be an exception. She was going to have to walk; besides which, something had killed the hens that supplied the breakfast eggs. How could she have neglected to latch the stable door? Our mother would sooner overlook a mortal sin than forgive mere negligence, especially if it involved loss of property. She had never gotten over the time the Botanist borrowed her fur piece without asking, and left it on the bus.

Beyond the Dômerie there was nothing much to see aside from

bare trees and underbrush, outcroppings of rock and flashes of river. The wish to fill the empty space between one place and the next was overwhelming. It was an impulse having less to do with wanting to *see* things, what was next, around the bend, than with trying to make time contiguous. The sun brightened, releasing mist from the road, smells of sweat and damp wool.

The Keeper disliked walking but she loved to ride. She always had and, unlike the rest of us, she was good at it. Nanny always made sure there was an abundance of hot water waiting for her afterward, a cake of black soap from Spain, a pile of fresh towels. The Keeper would remove her boots, her velvet riding hat and dark green jacket, her matching jodhpurs. She would undress completely and step into the tub. She knew the Cook had made a peephole above the toothbrush holder but she didn't care. She liked thinking of him watching her wet body.

Past the fallen pillar where the accident happened, the ash tree, the stone mileage marker, the drinking trough, the sharp curve before the railroad underpass. The Keeper had been reading our mother's fortune while the train was headed across the bridge. Make your mind as blank as possible when shuffling. Five of wands, strenuous competition. The greedy four of pentacles. The page of the same suit, reversed. Carelessness. Could any future be more boring?

Everyone knew it was dangerous for a woman to travel alone. It was dangerous for men, too, and a traveling companion didn't assure safety unless you were lucky enough to be traveling with an armed mercenary. The town appeared deserted but the Keeper knew it wasn't; everyone was holed up indoors, peering out from between blinds or behind curtains. The houses were old and crammed together in a row the way the prisoners used to stand chained together on Fairmount Avenue, waiting to follow one another wherever the road took them, in this case into the river, which was beginning to freeze over. After it froze solid the washer-women could no longer drive up and down it in their gaily painted barges to take in laundry, taking in laundry being another way of saying they were prepared to offer their services to lonely men along the route.

One day a laundry basket appeared on the Keeper's front stoop with a baby inside, wrapped in a pink blanket. At first, because of the blanket, she took the baby for a girl. He was a quiet child, so quiet the Keeper found it hard to remember he was in the house. Sometimes he cried—a soughing of wind in the trees, woodnotes in the gloaming. But she was used to being by herself and, un-like a real mother's, her breasts had never had milk in them to let down and serve as a reminder.

The Keeper approached the house cautiously; she wasn't sur-prised to see that the horse had arrived before her, and that it was standing in the front yard, pawing at the frozen grass. Hello, the Keeper called past the open front door. Once inside she could hear the sound of keys tapping, paper rustling, a drawer being slammed shut. She fed the stove and put on the kettle. The baby had grown to be a skinny little thing, but whether he was sneaky or merely timid, she'd never been able to tell. Lately he spent most of his time in his room, and when he came out it seemed like she never actually saw him, just felt him wrapping himself around her legs the way a cat does. When he wasn't in the house he played rough. He would come home with blood on his shirt. His clothes always needed fixing—that was something she could do for him.

Of course we knew this about the Keeper—more than any of us, she was meant to be a mother. Given who our mother was, she was meant to be *our* mother, and on this account it was diffi-cult for us not to resent the boy, especially when the Keeper asked us to help pay for the shoes he needed because of his clubfoot.

It wasn't a bad one. By the time he was half-grown you'd never know he'd had a problem. He was going to end up tall and attractive, we could see.

The Keeper had everything a mother is supposed to have. She had a teakettle and a hearth. She had a stand mixer and a wide lap. She had a blurred soft side and a raptor-like watchful side. She had a sewing basket.

Needles, she had needles.

Inside the boy's room it was dark; the sun stayed outside along with the horse and the river and the town, borne like a shield between two arms of water. The dog-headed beast was out there too; sometimes the boy thought he could see its face looking in his window. Its fur had a white tinge to it and it emitted a terrible odor. If only he could get the sequence right, the boy thought, tapping keys. The beast had torn out the throats of shepherdesses celebrated for their beauty; it had drained the blood from the bodies of little children. In his room the boy slid his finger across an image; there was something he was supposed to destroy, if he could get the sequence right. The devil had appeared close at hand; often it emerged as *pokkes* on the bodies of men and animals.

Meanwhile the Keeper was looking through her kitchen cabinets to see if she had the ingredients to make a One-Two-Three-Four Cake, so named because it was made with one cup of butter, two cups of sugar, three cups of flour, four eggs. A cake made this way is slightly dull and not a little heavy but otherwise foolproof, unless one of the eggs is rotten or someone, somewhere slams a door.

Whether we liked this kind of cake or not, it was what we got for our birthdays, a yellow cake with white buttercream frosting and pink or blue candles, depending. Today might as well have been the boy's birthday, the Keeper thought. She didn't have any sugar but the market hadn't closed yet.

In his dark room the boy continued tapping on his keys. Tap tap tap. Tea was steeping in the Keeper's yellow pot. The boy was tapping on his keys, moving the dog-headed beast from place to place. He slid his finger across an image: a tree, a house like a drawing of a house, a door in the middle with a window on either side of it and three above.

Tap tap tap. A horse. It happened in an instant, the moment the Keeper stepped outside. In the channel branch at the eastern gate of her heart, an expanse of light, the sage of the anguished spirits. Compare the black and white pebbles of past actions. If you are to be reborn as an animal, you will see rocky caverns, empty hollows, and straw sheds shrouded by mist.

What were we supposed to do? Time was, as they say, slipping through our fingers—how long would it take before others of our number disappeared forever, leaving the rest of us weeping into our hands? The hike from the hospital was arduous; the footpath rock-strewn and flooded, descending steadily and steeply, like walking down a stream.

Like walking in a dream, someone said, merrily merrily merrily. Maybe there was a rainbow, a shrub with livid purple fruit. Whatever you do, don't eat it, said the Botanist. But the Geographer and the Topologist were too distraught to pay attention, the Geographer because she couldn't stop worrying about the Keeper, the Topologist because she had seen the Swede's rosary lying on the path. She pocketed it, we saw her do this; then she kept playing with it in her pocket, continuing to do so as we passed under an electric pylon and entered a small, walled lane.

Watch out for live wires, said the Astronomer, but the line was dead.

The day had dawned clear and bright, the sky rising above us, deep blue and streaming with clouds, like the garment of a deity.

Eventually the lane brought us to a large tall house with a steep slate roof. We could see a face looking down at us from a third-floor window—a small, wan face that seemed familiar, the face of someone we once knew well, maybe even loved.

Hello! the Botanist called up to it, but whoever it was in the window continued to look down, making no response.

We could tell the Botanist wanted us to help her remember who the person was, but as far as we were concerned, she was on her own. None of us had the least interest in digging up the past except insofar as we played a starring role in it.

Greedily held in the chains of Venus, said the Iceman. In her sea-colored dress and her beautiful Sicyonian shoes. The Botanist's tale was a love story. How could it be otherwise, given who she was?

Though it wasn't the Botanist's lover up there; her lover, as we seemed to remember, had died in her arms. He hadn't been sickly like the person looking down at us, either, but he had been dead and this person was alive. Nor did the person up there actually seem to be looking down at us but at the deep gorge into which we were about to descend, the Allier so far away it might have been a single strand of hair, shining and silver, lost and fallen from one of our heads.

The face in the window was such a small face to strike fear in our hearts. But this was the way it always happened, the wedge driving us asunder so slender as to be practically invisible.

We had all been lying on our backs. It was like Savasana only there were roses in the wallpaper. There were mouths. Those of us who couldn't sleep heard everyone else breathe the deep breaths of sleeping people. Those of us who slept, slept lightly, always on the verge of being awakened by those of us who couldn't. The light fixture looked like a dog face. The light fixture looked like a breast. The Geographer walked in her sleep; we called her Miss Bit on account of her strong white teeth, the scalloped mark they left in more than one forearm. Had anyone shared a bed with her? Maybe we had separate bedrooms. Truly, bedtime had been a time of terror for all of us and our mother's kisses didn't help. If you tried to read under the covers with a flashlight Nanny would swoop down on you. Tomorrow is another day, she always said, to which someone would reply, Duh, and someone else would say, Maybe not. The Archivist talked in his sleep. In his sleep he was genial, conversational. How many of them were there? we heard him say, and then he started to laugh. The Keeper tossed and turned and threw off her blankets. Sleeping with her was like sleeping with a horse. Run slowly, slowly, horses of the night. According to Nanny, if you had a bad dream it was a good idea to examine it in the light of day, letting the sun lap into its corners and reveal the terror for what it was, something as ordinary as a pearl button or a glass of milk.

But the terror was real. It was a by-product of having been born.

In every nightmare there was a place you were not supposed to enter. No matter how hard you tried to stop yourself, it was where you ended up. It was the end of you, and if you tried to scream, something that started out endearing like a puppy turned to wind, a howling wind, the tongue in your mouth thick and blue at the root as you swallowed yourself up.

For whatever reason, we didn't want to linger on the lane in front of the large tall house. The sun was behind it, casting its shadow over us. We could see where the trail bent sharply to the left, becoming once again a narrow footpath before continuing its descent into the gorge.

Come on, the Cook said to the Botanist. Being a cook, he usually had better luck with her than the rest of us. He said that once we got to the river there would be food, good food. We could smell it cooking all the way up here, he said, but when he took the Botanist's hand, teasingly, and tried to pull her toward the footpath, she pulled in the opposite direction. She looked the way she always had, her feet planted firmly and her eyes honey-gold and gleaming, yet it was as if she'd gone back to being the person she'd been in the hospital, hovering above the ground, only a fraction of an inch this time, a distance too insignificant to be visible and yet unsettling. At last she started waving her arms around like someone who has walked into a cloud of midges, and we took it as dismissal.

The hillside was so steep that to begin walking down it felt like stepping off a cliff. Luckily the footpath had been designed with switchbacks; it was also quite narrow, forcing us to walk single file. Because of this quite a lot of time elapsed before we realized the Botanist wasn't with us, maybe not even until we got to the river. There was a sizeable crowd gathered on the riverbank, some people bundled up against the weather, some stripped naked to swim. To everyone's amazement the Archivist materialized among the swimmers, his small wet head appearing and disappearing within the wings and limbs of the current, winsomely, like the head of the Keeper's pet river otter that lived for a while in the cellar washbasin. What had the Archivist done with his clothing, his spectacles? Our mother warned us about swimming with other people. Until we were told otherwise, it was better to stay out of the water.

As the Cook had promised, the concession stand was open. A sweet child of indeterminate sex, clad in a faded green pinafore and bog shoes, sold wine to those of us who would drink it. Meanwhile, a short distance away, a man who seemed much too old to be the child's father roasted a medium-sized animal over a fire, turning the spit, then dozing off, then starting awake and turning the spit once more.

He should have been basting the animal, we knew that much, even without being instructed by the Cook. The Archivist should have been mindful of the force of the current, we knew that much as well.

We were growing careless. If we didn't watch what we were doing there would be no one left. Inside each of us there were red and white drops, in each heart a drop the size of a pea with a white top and a red bottom. It was called the indestructible drop; our life-bearing wind dwelt inside it.

At length we found a place to sit in the shade of a large beech tree. The little brown dog lay curled up fast asleep in the hollow between two roots. Was it possible the Swede was still alive and close at hand? The Topologist went off to see if she could find him while the rest of us stayed put. The theriac was having its effect, leaving us sluggish and irritable and without ambition. The Geographer's stomach swelled, the Iceman bled from his mucous membrane. You were supposed to relax the bones of your ear; you were supposed to let your nostrils flare. At some point we saw the Astronomer wade into the water with a fishing pole and cast a line into a deep hole near the bank. He was fishing for grayling; people around here called it the shadow of the river. If he managed to catch any fish it would be advisable for us to eat them. What we needed to do now was to fortify our systems with elements native to the region, whereas theriac was a foreign substance that had made its way to us from town to town along the Silk Road. It was compounded of sweet liqueur and opium and the flesh of vipers. After taking theriac you got the feeling of a lump in the throat that could not be swallowed. Your stools passed with difficulty. The theriac might possess properties capable of prolonging life. On the other hand, it might be making things worse.

We sat on the grass drinking wine and eating roast meat. If the Keeper were with us, she would be laying out her cards. Even though we pretended to be above such things, we counted on her to tell us who we were, what crowned or crossed us, what the future had in store. In the same way we had come to count on the Botanist's sweetness, her idle flirtations, her complete lack of a sense of humor.

The day had been windy. It seemed like it was windy all the time those days, and the wind didn't seem to originate in one of the cardinal directions nor did it seem to emerge from all of them at once but instead to be a function of the air itself, something akin to the restlessness in our bodies that made us keep moving, as if all a person had to do to escape the sickness was to outrun it.

The mysterious horseman moves slowly, according to the thirteenth card in the Greater Arcana. Of course the Keeper wasn't there to say it, but we could hear her saying it clearly just the same, just as we could see the card, a handsome skeleton astride a snow-white horse.

Death is nothing, the Iceman said, since the nature of the mind has proved to be mortal. When the body dies the soul does too. To link a mortal thing with an everlasting one and suppose they have something in common, weathering the same furious storms, is folly.

At death, all the winds undergo dissolution and get channeled into the heart. Our limbs become smaller, our sight darkens, inside us there is the appearance of smoke, of fireflies, of a butter lamp going out.

The moment she could no longer see us the Botanist opened the door to the tall house with the steep roof and went in. Mostly, she needed to put it all behind her, and by "all" she meant all of us, as well as the events of her life, what people call memories. Right away it was as if she had never been inside a house before; even the noise the door made closing behind her seemed not to have been made by wood sliding against wood with an accompanying burst of air, but instead signaled the presence nearby of something previously unknown or imagined, something large and shifting around in a space too small for it, breathing heavily through the mouth.

Little bug, little scrub, little bead, little need. The Botanist knew she was being summoned. She was floating again, that much was for sure.

Up a long staircase and onto a landing. The windows were shut tight yet if she looked back she could see smoke seeping from the crevices, as well as from hundreds of small objects on shelves along the walls, unrecognizable, glinting as if in the light of a fire but there was no fire, no stove, no candle, no light at all. Meanwhile the smell of smoke occurred to her like the image of a small girl in a smocked dress playing jacks, *not* a memory but an idea.

It was exactly the way it happened when she was working: there would be the smell of hyacinth and there would be an old lady reaching for something just out of reach. There would be the taste of a cranberry bean and there would be a young man sharpening a pencil. You couldn't interrupt these operations of reaching, of sharpening—they were each, in their own way, eternal.

The thing is, we couldn't save one another. The Botanist was in danger but there was nothing we could do. Ditto the Archivist, borne on the increasingly powerful current, headed for the rapids where the Rock That Cries had ended many a life. We hadn't heard about this yet but we were going to. There was nothing we could do. Once you were in the Savage Domain there was no escaping the dog-headed beast. Meanwhile we sat on our cloaks under the capacious beech tree, eating meat and drinking wine and planning what to do next, as if the operation we were involved in, however it might be described—*déjeuner sur l'herbe*, maybe, or fiddling while Rome burns—were not, likewise, eternal. As if we could have any say about the outcome. As if we couldn't see the little brown dog curled on the grass at our feet.

The Botanist floated along the second-floor hallway and up the final flight of stairs to the third floor. Was it true, what they said? Once you went up you never came down? Little bug, little bud, little hug, little judge, little mug, little rug, little BUD. LITTLE BUD! On and on she drifted along the hallway, her obedience ferrying her past many doors, all of them closed tight, all of them with smoke seeping through the cracks. It is true that smoke is often used to create a barrier of aromatic vapor through which the air that carries sickness is unable to penetrate. Get out quickly, go a long way away, and don't be in a hurry to come back: that was what the doctors were prescribing—the ones who hadn't run away themselves, that is.

The family who used to live here had been beset by *X. cheopis* or rat fleas, pests known to be happiest (if pests can be said to be happy) during unseasonably mild, damp winters, which this one certainly seemed to have been. The family consisted of a mother and father and a boy, but when the boy got sick from sleeping in the bedclothes his father acquired in trade for a rooster, they left him behind. They left him behind for dead—that was the spirit of the age. The Silk Road ran in front of their house; everyone was using it, for commerce or as a means of escape. Some travelers relied on word of mouth, some on cairns or blazes. What everyone had in common was lack of destination.

The boy wasn't dead though. When he awakened the place he was in was as dark as the deepest well. There seemed to be a log fire burning in the middle of the floor—though how could that have been? He was still inside his house, wasn't he? Inside the house where he'd been born and suckled and weaned? The bedclothes, too, seemed to be arranging themselves without assistance. The trader had stuffed them with rat flea–infested feathers and hair; as the boy watched, the stuffing reassembled itself into a large creature that glistened like a pearl.

"Come to me," the creature said, but it wasn't talking to him.

The sun went down and for just one moment the sky was bathed in golden light. Then the Botanist opened the door and came floating across the threshold.

Inside she saw the boy sitting by the window, though he wasn't exactly a boy. The person sitting by the window was older than he'd looked from below, older and bigger, and because he had wrapped himself in his cloak she couldn't see the swellings on his body, but she could smell the sickness on him. What the Botanist saw, smelling it, was the Fairy beckoning the Prince to join her in the Garden of Paradise, even though she'd told him it was the one thing he was forbidden to do. The Fairy said if he joined her there and kissed her, Paradise would sink deep into the earth, which is where it was located in the first place.

In assembly, if you so much as thought of talking to your neighbor while the principal was telling the story of the Garden of Paradise, you would be turned to stone. The Prince drew back the branches and saw tears welling in the Botanist's eyelashes. "I have not sinned yet," he insisted. Even if everlasting night were to descend on him like the lid of his own casket, a moment like this would be worth it. He kissed the tears away from the Botanist's eyes and then he kissed her lips, whereupon there came a sound like thunder, louder and more dreadful than any sound any living thing on earth had ever heard before. The chill of death crept over his limbs. The cold rain fell on his face, and the sharp wind blew around his head.

Down by the river we all heard it.

The man behind the concession stand doused the fire while the child in the faded green pinafore began closing up shop. Both of them looked around nervously, as if they were being followed.

What lightning bolt devoured everyone? What earthquake? There had been a crowd of us but now we were almost one.

In the river the Archivist felt raindrops hit the side of his face each time he turned his head to breathe; at length he stopped turning his head, no longer feeling the need to do so. P used to make fun of how afraid he was of everything but she never understood what a good swimmer he was; at Saint Roch he had been captain of the swim team.

Now, in the water, he was naked, his flutter kick more muscular than ever.

The river charged over rocks and around fallen logs; it surged and eddied and funneled; it leapt into the air and then dropped a great distance in a waterfall, spangled and unfettered, foaming and loud, into a moss-lined pool. The Archivist's eyes were wet and he could see perfectly without his spectacles. Or, more accurately, he could see perfectly except for a spot in the middle that was nothing. Of course that's where P was, in that spot, monitoring his arrival. That's where she always was and always had been, in the spot he couldn't see.

The thing is, he wasn't himself or what he thought of as himself, just as the farther we walked along the trail the less we knew of what we thought of as ourselves. It was disconcerting, our titles having been so deeply imprinted in us as to become identities. The Cook hadn't cooked anything in a long time; the Iceman had abandoned his quest for permafrost. If the Archivist was going to turn into something like a fish, no one was going to find it strange. It was all right, as long as he eluded the lure.

Meanwhile the beech tree provided us with protection from whatever was falling from the sky; beech trees allow very little light or much of anything else to reach the ground, appropriating it all for themselves. The tree was being imperial but we didn't know that, its imperial behavior limited to other trees and not people. In this way we could be certain that we were people and not plant life, though as was the case with the Archivist, it wasn't always possible to register a transformation as it happened. Some of us were putting forth branches we couldn't see called fear branches, like a tree whose space is being commandeered by a beech.

If the Botanist were here she could have explained what was going on. But that was how she'd always been, drifting away in pursuit of something better than anything we could offer, a keg party or a rare mushroom, a doomed boyfriend or a clump of lady's slippers. Besides, we never paid attention to scientific explanation—none of us did, aside from the person providing it.

The Astronomer walked up from the riverbank with an armload of fish, their tall dorsal fins shedding water like stars. The fish constellation isn't very bright, he told us; it's hard to see with the naked eye. As might be expected, we weren't interested. The Astronomer said we should use what was left of the concession-aire's fire to roast the fish if that infernal child would let us, and this was a side of him we hadn't been aware of—a side of him that, unlike the scientific information he was quick to dispense, actually caught our interest.

The Cook was sound asleep on his back, grinding his teeth.

We don't have that much time, someone said.

Our sense of urgency was strong, even though we didn't know where we had to be, or when we had to be there.

In the third-floor bedroom in the tall, narrow house, the Botanist was lifting the person from the floor and putting him into bed. He weighed almost nothing. He was as light as a feather, almost as if he was already dead and gone and what she was lifting wasn't his body but his soul. He looked at her beseechingly and she shook her head *No*. Brushing the hair back from the forehead, drawing the eyelids down over the eyeballs. They don't know my story, she was thinking, I got taken away too soon so they can't put their fingers into it and ruin it the way they've done to all the other stories. Except for the Cook, whose story was the shortest—as he had reminded us repeatedly—everyone had already told their tale.

Now she would suck the air from the sac. Extract the lights on their string of silk. The Silk Trail was far shorter than the Silk Road but the distance it covered was far greater, the compass of a human life.

We were to proceed into the interior, over the snow. We were to proceed across the plain, the plain with no ending. Someone in the labyrinth had been singing about the plain with no ending but we couldn't remember who or when. How far we were to go and in what direction remained a mystery, too, though the Geographer took a sounding at the foot of the cairn. Our dogs knew little or no fear. Once in their traces they were obedient; they were loyal first to each other, only as an afterthought to us. We knew better than to get between a dog and its food or a dog and its mate. The dogs would eat their traces if we let them, also the whips and the boots. They would eat us if there were nothing else. Not me, though, said the Iceman, but he was a romantic.

Snow was falling, the kind that comes late in the season, big flakes that land on the eyeballs and melt, making everything bright and insanely clear, snow in pieces falling from above and one unbroken bolt of snow beneath the runners of the sleds and the landscape unrolling endlessly as if moving forward meant there was a future, drifts of snow filling the crevices of the black cliffs that began rearing up on either side of us the farther we got from the coast.

Our lips were cold, making speech difficult. From time to time the Geographer urged us to remember how happy it had made us to find the next cairn that time we were crossing the top of the hill. It was the pleasure of finding something you knew was there, even when you didn't know where it was or when you would find it.

Like finding your sweetheart, said the Cook. He was thinking of his wife—we could tell. His story was the shortest because it began and ended with true love, an appetite that ended in a trail of crumbs. Meanwhile we stood watching the approach of Jee Moon, upright on her sled in her bright red parka, maintaining balance while spurring her dogs on through curtains of snow.

When was the last time we'd seen her? That day in the hospital when she put her hand over the Iceman's mouth? Without realizing it we had missed her, and now here she was.

Should she be doing that? we wondered. But the Astronomer seemed unconcerned.

There was a trail, said the Archivist. We were following a trail across the top of the hill. Of course there would have been trail markers. Some of us remembered that our mother had been messing around with them.

Listen to me, said the Topologist. It's a matter of simple geometry. There can't be a line from point A if there isn't a point B.

If she was trying to reassure us, it wasn't working. What she meant was that if we succeeded in our mission and located the cairn that was the next one after the one on the beach, the cairn that led to the next one after that, everything would be different. What she meant was that to locate the next cairn would mean there was a future.

It's like that game we used to play, said the Topologist. What was it called? Sardines?

When we thought of the game, the smell of the house came back to us. The smell of varnish and acacia blossoms, boiled marrowbones and cloves, of cold air from an open window, damp wool and sweat.

Someone would be selected to be "it." We would stand in the front hallway near the bachelor chest, hiding our eyes while the person who was "it" ran off into the house and hid. Meanwhile above our heads our ancestor, the one who got here first, without whom we would be somewhere else no doubt, somewhere warm and sun-dappled possibly, or maybe here but without a sense of why here and not elsewhere, stared meditatively out of his gilt frame at the front door.

The Botanist used to say he was handsome, like Sir Walter Scott in the Authors card game; the Keeper said he was cross-eyed. The Cook said he'd been put there to scare off salesmen.

Sardines was the worst game in the world for people striving to get away from one another. It left no room for strangers; it left no room to be alone. The person who was "it" got to dwell briefly in the luxury of an otherwise empty hiding place, but the whole point of the game was to find a place that everyone, ultimately, could jam into. The truth is, the game replicated so perfectly the condition of our lives together it's a wonder we ever chose to play it.

There would be the moment you thought you were the only one left. The sound of running feet, of doors opening and closing, of muffled laughter, of bodies bumping against bodies and surprised delight—there would be the moment all these sounds stopped and in their stead silence would open its mouth, the huge black yawning hole you were about to fall into.

We had each experienced this, each of us alone and in different ways. Nanny half inside the linen closet, pressed against the shelves with her head tilted back and her mouth hanging open and her hand up and moving under her dress. Did she see us or was she too involved to notice? It was more exciting to think about being watched than it was to be the watcher. The watch-bird! Mother at the kitchen door, standing very close to someone we couldn't see, laughing and leaning into an embrace, gasping for breath. Father setting aside his newspaper before putting his face in his hands. We saw him do this, but whether he was laughing or weeping was impossible to know for certain.

A broad body of water appeared alongside us, an arm of the sea, bending at the elbow up ahead. Some of us thought it had been there from the start; we could tell we were going to have to cross it sooner or later in order to continue. Either that or change direction, which the Geographer said would be a mistake. The water looked frozen but the Iceman warned about places where the internal current moved quickly and you could fall through—these places were called rattles, it happened all the time. The snow was falling harder; we saw something white moving across it, something white across something white, a bird maybe, flying above the snow, a bear, loping toward us. It could have been the snow itself, gathering itself into a living being. It could have been a fox.

The process was called sublimation, the Iceman said. Most solid bodies of matter flew about unvanquished through all time.

We had no plans for dealing with whatever we might encounter. At some point we stopped to let the dogs rest. It was a pleasure to watch them cock their heads, listening for mice. The lead dogs, the swing dogs, the wheelers—they jumped stiff-legged into the air and then pounced. They never chewed what they caught.

And, truly, this was the way it always was: we were, as always, together, some of us shivering, some of us holding hands, linked by our chain of tracks in the snow. We could see one another's breath; we could hear the sound of someone crying. Someone was homesick, though for where, that was a good question. It was like spending the night at the Highgate Apartments, not being able to sleep and hearing the clock strike the hours and a stale corn muffin the only thing to eat. Time had truly slipped through our fingers! See how our great band of friends had dwindled!

Why don't you go back? someone said. You're never going to find anything out here.

Who was that? asked the Geographer. Did everyone hear that?

It would be a bad idea to lie down in the snow and go to sleep, the person said.

By now we'd all recognized the voice. It was the Botanist.

Those corn muffins were worse than nothing, the Botanist said. I'd rather eat mice.

It was just like her to show up this way, drifting in and out of our brains the very moment we'd abandoned hope of seeing her again. So ill-equipped to travel o'er the snow at the globe's tip, she said, if a globe can be said to have a tip. Her voice was singsong; she sounded like she was mocking us.

The dogs' hackles were raised, surprisingly—the Botanist had always been their favorite, after the Keeper.

You saw everything, remember? she said. We all did. When you were playing Sardines, you could sneak around. There would be the dog-headed beast on its hands and knees on the floor beside the bachelor chest. There would be Father. Everyone saw. There would be the enemy laid low with a mortal wound. There would be the country teeming with creatures unfamiliar elsewhere, its many rivers thundering and foaming and swirling along their courses.

There would be Nanny with her black stones. We should have made new friends—but how, when the human race was almost wiped out? And why? Why pretend? How shallow the foundations on which we reared our towers!

When the Botanist talked this way we knew what she was doing, hauling the past into the present so we would feel comforted.

126

Then you dug the hole, she said. Don't say you didn't. The thing is, it didn't work. You thought you could save yourselves but it didn't work.

And it is true: the bachelor chest survived many dislocations and upheavals. Even after it had undergone its final transformation to pulp and then to nothing, it didn't serve as a reminder of the past. It *was* the past. Our mother brought the bachelor chest with her into the marriage; it was quite old, and had come down to her from her father's side of the family. You could tell the chest was old because it was made of black walnut and had bun feet and two retractable runners called lopers that were used to support the hinged leaf on which the bachelor penned his letters. Most Esteemed Mistress So-and-so. How fiercely I burn. No. How fiercely I miss you. Our mother told one of us about this but we couldn't remember who. Furniture was important to people who cared about the surfaces of things, she said. Like bachelors? said the Geographer. As if *she's* so deep, said the Topologist.

The sleds had come to a halt at a rattle, the ground falling away in a deep crevasse through which water ran, colorless as midnight. The dogs were lying down now, curled together in a pile with the snow landing on their fur. Soon all we could see of them was a pile of snow that sometimes moved or uttered a cry, threw out a paw here, a paw there.

We knew we ought to keep going. The snow kept falling from the sky, onto our arms and legs, the firm outline of a nose erod-ing. It was very cold and still the Botanist wouldn't stop talking.

The great green and white ice pans arrived as expected, she told us. The ice wasn't gone, she said. The ice was everywhere.

It was jewel time! the Botanist said. I was there! The ice wasn't gone!

Someone passed a stone down into the hole, remember? It was so heavy. Death was near. You could tell because the hair on her neck was growing upward, the limbs jerking, scaling the mountain of the elements, the tears flowing uncontrollably and the ears lying flat against the head, blocking the stairway. The energy of water dissolved into fire; the throat and the tongue became dry.

All lice and nits left the body.

The red generative essence derived from the mother rose upward.

The white generative essence derived from the father fell downward.

A single drop of blood formed at the heart center.

The exhaled breath extended from the body by a cubit.

The exhaled breath extended from the body by an arrow length. The blood in the heart formed two drops.

It's always darkest before the dawn is something our father used to say. He would say it at a time when it didn't make sense and then, later, when it would have helped to hear a cheery word, when, being the nearer, the air of darkness had first entered and taken possession of our open eyes, when we'd lost even the cheeriest among us (by which most of us meant the Botanist though even the Cook would have been a welcome sight, toiling toward us up that wet, grassy hill with an armload of stolen provisions), our father was nowhere to be found. It wasn't a surprise. It was the way it had been on Fairmount Avenue, one of us in tears after having fallen down the stairs, our knee bleeding and our heart broken, having been denied a piece of candy from the dish shaped like a shoe Nanny kept on her dresser beside the postcard of Niagara Falls, and the whole time we could hear our father whistling a tune from a popular show but we could never figure out what room he was in.

We could always tell where our mother was, even though she acted like she wanted to keep everything she did secret, whereas we could never tell where our father was, even though he acted like he didn't care. Our mother wanted to be watched; it's amazing how much of our time was spent watching her.

We were trained to be vigilant. The thing is, *we* were what we had become accustomed to watching, all of us, all those winters and summers of our lives together, every step we were taking and had taken before and would take again. But we were so busy being vigilant we failed to notice one another's comings and goings, the modest lapses, the entrances, the exits.

The towns were empty for the most part. The little dog continued on with us, biting at our ankles as if in play though we knew he had to be hungry. He had saved someone's life; it was hard now to remember the story but it had changed everything and so, despite the bites and the smell, we knew we owed him fealty. The Swede had either succumbed to the sickness or been eaten by the beast or joined the marketeers.

At last we found a roadside table with enough chairs for all of us to sit down around it. The sun had come out; a dark blue awning was spread above us, fluttering and waving and dyeing the seated assembly below with its color. A man emerged from behind a potted shrub, a white apron low on his hips. He ran his hand through his thinning hair. If he was there to take our order he gave no sign of it.

Two French doors led into the hostelry, painted dark green, one of them slightly ajar. We knew they were going to be there: this is where we had been headed from the first intake of breath and the first expulsion of breath, the table set as it had been from the start, the knives and forks and spoons. The napkins, folded in triangles. The white plates with a blue stripe around the rim. The table could have been set for a party, except then you'd have known who the guests were. A party often serves as a kind of explanation. It's the least interesting part of a life, really. We already knew all we needed to know or thought we did.

This is no place for a baby, the man with the apron said. We could tell he was disapproving, scornful even, though of what, we were unsure. He had seen everything that had attained a human body come through here. Alas! The human body ages day by day! The relatives and friends surrounding us in this life are like a gathering of shoppers at a market. When the market closes, the shoppers disperse. Likewise this illusory aggregate of form.

One of us had failed to obstruct the womb entrance and thus was forced to suffer in a dog kennel or a pigsty or an anthill or a worm hill for the rest of this temporal existence. There was to be no way back.

One of us appeared filleted on a platter, drenched in lemon, a sprig of parsley in his mouth.

One of us lay like a fallen cairn at the top of a pass, severed of all flesh and bone.

One of us remained in the kitchen, seeing to the food.

On Fairmount Avenue we hadn't had a cook. There were so many of us you'd think we would have, but our mother liked to say she did the cooking herself. She gave us jobs in the kitchen—chopping, stirring, pounding, beating, folding, washing, slicing—we never knew what we were involved in making and then, amazingly, there would be a dish to carry to the table, following the presentation of which our father would heap praise upon our mother and we would start to eat. The Cook wasn't interested in cooking; back then he had a chemistry set. The Botanist used to sneak into the kitchen in the middle of the night and eat all the maraschino cherries out of the jar on the back of the refrigerator door, leaving our father with nothing but stems for his cocktails. The Topologist used to sneak into the kitchen, too; she was attracted to pots and pans and mixing bowls, anything that could be used to contain something else. The Iceman went for the freezer, the Archivist, the trash can. The Keeper, though—the Keeper liked to bake, but mostly because she liked to eat.

In through the French doors went the man with the apron. Out came the dough effigy made with seven kinds of grain. Out came the seed syllables of the four elements, as well as other pastel-colored delicacies. When the serving utensils made contact with one another they caused an unpleasant chiming sound.

The Astronomer sat with his baby on his lap. Already it was quite self-possessed, like its mother, who was nowhere to be seen. One of us slipped the baby some food; this was how Nanny had done it with us, to win us over. You think Nanny is so great, our mother used to say. You don't know the half of it. There there, darling, we heard someone say—it sounded like Jee Moon but we couldn't be sure, the voice pale green, folding in on itself like wings. Even as she spoke we were slipping away like shadows.

Don't feed the dog from the table! the man with the apron commanded.

The year of feeding in the human realm had come to an end. When we ate, it seemed tasty. But did it taste so good now? Even the gods with their terrific stature couldn't stop the effect of our actions, the greatest of which was our journey from one place to another, the smallest of which was the killing of fleas.

You think any of it belongs to you? the man with the apron said.

This is what we were asked, and, really, already we could see our eyes weren't there, the way pieces of us were disappearing, hair, black eyebrows, a smile, a crown of gold.

Acknowledgments

Portions of this novel were originally published, in slightly different form, as "*La Bête du Gévaudan*," in the *Cincinnati Review*, "The Botanist's House," in *Conjunctions*, "The Excursion," in *Fairy Tale Review*, an untitled excerpt in *Fence*, "The January Tunnel," in the *Harvard Advocate*, and an untitled excerpt in the *Review of Contemporary Fiction*.

I want to thank Louise Glück and Polly Young-Eisendrath, who together with Olaus Magnus, Lucretius, and *The Tibetan Book of the Dead*, are among the animating spirits of my book.

Kathryn Davis is the author of seven previous novels, the most recent of which is *Duplex*. She has received the Kafka Prize for fiction by an American woman, both the Morton Dauwen Zabel Award and the Katherine Anne Porter Award from the American Academy of Arts and Letters, a Guggenheim Fellowship, and the Lannan Foundation Literary Award. She teaches at Washington University in St. Louis and lives in Vermont.

The text of *The Silk Road* is set in Adobe Garamond Pro. Book design by Rachel Holscher. Composition by Bookmobile Design and Digital Publisher Services, Minneapolis, Minnesota. Manufactured by Friesens on acid-free, 100 percent postconsumer wastepaper.

Gustave Flaubert

MADAME BOVARY

A STORY OF PROVINCIAL LIFE

TRANSLATED BY ALAN RUSSELL

ILLUSTRATED WITH ETCHINGS BY
ALBERT FOURIÉ

Greenwich House Classics Library

Greenwich House
Distributed by Crown Publishers, Inc.
New York

This 1982 edition is published by Greenwich House,
a division of Arlington House, Inc.,
distributed by Crown Publishers, Inc., by arrangement with
Penguin Books, Ltd.

The illustrations have been reproduced from the French
edition of *Madame Bovary* published in 1885 by A. Quantin,
courtesy of the New York Public Library Astor, Lenox and Tilden
Foundations.

Manufactured in the United States of America

h g f e d c b a

Library of Congress Cataloging in Publication Data

Flaubert, Gustave, 1821–1880.
Madame Bovary: a story of provincial life.
(Greenwich House classics library)
Reprint. Originally published: Penguin Books.
I. Russell, A.K. (Alan Keith) II. Title.
PQ2246.M2E5   1982b   843'.8   82-11792
ISBN: 0-517-385880

INTRODUCTION

In France, as in England, it was during the nineteenth century that the novel rose to its present position as the most popular literary form. The seventeenth and eighteenth centuries had produced tales of aristocratic intrigue such as *The Princess of Cleves* and *Dangerous Liaisons*; the eighteenth had originated the custom of mixing sociology and philosophy with fiction. In the 1830s, the more realistic novels of Stendhal and Balzac began to challenge the Romantic poets for the attention of a growing reading public. It is for the decisive advance he made along this road of 'realism' that Gustave Flaubert is famous. *Madame Bovary* is generally recognized as a landmark in French literature.

Flaubert was born at Rouen in 1821, a doctor's son. His early years may best be summed up in a remark he wrote to a friend as early as the age of thirteen, that he would be 'quite disgusted with life' were he not engaged upon a novel. Like many young men of his day he reacted with violence to the stupidity and vulgarity of the middle-class, or 'bourgeois', society into which he had been born. He was a truculent rebel, a Byronic, a Rabelaisian, a 'red romantic'; the sordidness of his surroundings sent him off on heady excursions into the remote, the historical and the extraordinary.

Yet he was also severely critical of 'artificial' romanticism, or what might nowadays be called 'escapism'; alongside that flamboyant rebelliousness went a strong sense of fact. In 1849 he made a journey to the Middle East, which sufficed to cure him of his longing for remote places by showing him their actuality. He had also written a novel, *The Temptation of St Anthony*, an exotic, rhetorical work – inspired by the famous surrealistic painting by Breughel – which was coldly received

5

by the two friends to whom he read it; in particular by his boon companion Louis Bouilhet, who acted as a selfless sort of literary conscience to Flaubert. Bouilhet told him bluntly that this was not the 'thunderclap' which Flaubert had always insisted that his first publication must be — and went on to mention a certain local occurrence that would make an excellent theme for a cool, realistic novel.

This was the 'Bovary' story. It was a plain enough tale to commend itself to Flaubert's severer side. In his version it runs as follows: a young woman, married to a dull country doctor and possessed of worldly and sensual-romantic longings, takes a lover and is deserted by him; takes a second lover, falls hopelessly into debt, and finally resorts to arsenic: a simple tragedy, to be enacted within the constricting limits of a Norman 'bourg' or small market-town, with its priest and its chemist, its Agricultural Show and its incurable 'bourgeoisdom'.

For such 'ordinary people' as Flaubert here set out to portray he had always had an ungovernable contempt that amounted to a phobia. The bourgeois — that dull, graceless animal, petty, materialistic, cliché-ridden — could make him feel physically ill; he took a twisted, satanic delight in discovering all the enormities of which it was capable. He had been wont to solace his outraged sensitivity in ceaseless attack. But now he was undertaking to paint an objective portrait, and even a sympathetic one.

Flaubert's general rampageousness on the subject of his fellow-beings has seemed to some readers to be a somewhat facile attitude in one who was saved, by the possession of a private income, from the coarsening necessity of earning his own living. He has been castigated for a 'defect of character', patronized as a man with an inflated demand upon life howling over its inevitable disappointment. Whether one calls such a discontent divine or infantile, however, one can only sympathize with the extraordinary, exhausting struggle it cost him to write about what he most hated. He knew, though he often found it difficult to remember, that 'any man who sets up to judge his fellows thereby makes himself ridiculous as they'. And he knew that he was himself a bourgeois; in fact, that was really the trouble – *all* life was a bourgeois phenomenon, a grotesque automatism that started every morning in his own shaving-mirror.

Flaubert was born literary, and literature remained a defence against disgust as well as becoming, in *Madame Bovary*, the occasion of it. Caught between the one squalor of reality and the other squalor of pretence, he lashed himself to a scrupulous objectivity. Instead of sticking on emotive labels, instead of indulging in overt satire, he forced himself to show people talking, thinking and acting as people do talk, think and act. He tried to eliminate himself entirely from his work; and it is to be noted that he specifically disclaimed all direct moral intention.

There was one part of that work that involved no descent into the mud, though it was equally exhausting, and that is what is loosely termed 'style'. He devoted more care than any novelist, even any French novelist, had done before him to the actual writing of his sentences. It was his ambition to make them rhythmical, euphonious and expressive in a way that would lift prose to the level of poetry. The labour which went to the pursuit of this object quickly became a legend; it introduced a new conception of the literary life as a vocation demanding a saint-like single-mindedness. For five years Flaubert sat in his room by the Seine at Croisset, drumming out his sentences on the table and reducing his manuscript to a tangle of corrections. 'One week – two pages!' Such cries recur in his letters. The insistence he laid on rhythm can be judged from a remark he made when he was nearing the end of the book, that he had all the rest mapped out, he could *hear* the 'fall of the phrases' for pages ahead, before he actually had the words.

The result of all this is a prose that is easy to read because it was so hard to write. But the 'style' is no mere decoration, neither is it a strait-jacket; it does not (despite certain incautious utterances of his) become his master. 'The form of a thought is its very flesh': such sayings by no means indicate that form has usurped the place of matter, but that Flaubert's thoughts were so subtly poised as to demand each its own particular form and no other. In the larger aspects of form he was not, in fact, consistently successful; he relied on 'style' to neutralize certain faults of construction he knew to be present, such as the shift of emphasis from Charles to Emma or the obtrusion of the club-foot incident. (But life, he said, was a bit like that.)

He saw himself as 'exorcizing the romantic demons that hover about literature'. It would be truer to say that he resolved, or by-passed, the conflict, which much exercised his age, between the claims of romanticism and those of realism. He had the Romantics' awareness of personality and mood, but he sank it into a naturalistic narrative that is at once objective and intimate. His attention to style did not represent a return to that barren intellectualism to which the great classical tradition in France had dwindled. Careful composition is matched by discernment of typical reality and exact choice of detail. With both the people and the material background of *Madame Bovary*, he was thoroughly conversant. Flaubert's artistry was pre-eminently of the 'ivory-tower' type, yet it did not involve a divorce from life, difficult as his relations with life undoubtedly were.

After making a rigorous effort to observe his rule of self-elimination, he came to realize that in describing the sick longings of Emma Bovary he was, in fact, bodying forth his own inner self. Consequently he was wont to reply, when questioned as to the original of Emma, that it was he himself — 'Madame Bovary, c'est moi!' At some level he ceased to be the objective artist observing from the margin. Not that all of

Emma's qualities were his, or vice versa. For one thing, he gave her no saving positive such as he found in writing about her. But the romantic malaise, the need to live in dreams, the failure to accept life, the longing for colour, for miraculous loves in distant lands – all this had its place in his own history; Emma is drawn from the inside.

She is one of the great individuals of fiction. Self-centred, self-dramatizing, envious, improvident, impulsive, aspiring above either her 'station' or her capabilities, 'sensitive' in the egoistic sense, and desperate with the raging of unsatisfied desire – of such a character her name (or, to be accurate, the name of Bovary, which, as Rodolphe reminds her, is really someone else's) has become the symbol; as such it has passed into the French language.

The second great character in the book, Homais the chemist, is, as the repository of flashy intellectuality, the foil to Emma's emotionality: he is Technical Man, Apostle of Progress, up-and-coming committee-member, imitation Voltaire.

In any estimate of the character of Emma, it must be remembered that Flaubert, throughout his five years' ordeal, exhausted as he was by his labours of style and by the sheer struggle of will that it cost him to keep at his distasteful subject, invariably spoke of Emma with tenderness. His other characters sometimes made him so angry that he scribbled down whole scenes that were not intended for inclusion in the book, simply to relieve his feelings.

He had another safety-valve in his correspondence with his mistress Louise Colet, to whom he poured out all the personal trenchancy, the uncompromising and sometimes perverse self-expression – and, incidentally, the free flow of metaphor – which he kept out of the novel. These letters form a unique record of literary composition, and a fascinating commentary on art and life as each affects the other. From them we learn of the extraordinary intensity with which Flaubert felt himself into everything he wrote – how he 'became' not only the lovers in the wood but 'the leaves, the wind, the horses'. We are told what he read during these years – the chief item is *Don Quixote*, that masterpiece of the tragic in the ridiculous. And we see him at the moment when he realizes that his *Bovary* will be 'more extraordinary than *St Anthony*, without appearing so'. There are also times of bitterness and despair; the book seems to him to be over-calculated, an exercise that he must, nevertheless, finish in order to go on with perfected equipment to less restricting themes. Yet it was while he saw himself as 'learning his fingering' that he was, in fact, producing his finest work.

When the book was eventually published, in serial form, in the *Revue de Paris*, its realism was such that all the young women in Normandy saw themselves as Emma, and all the chemists in Normandy took exception to Homais.

Now, there were certain scenes in the book which shocked some of the magazine's (bourgeois) subscribers, who raised an outcry. It happened that the repressive administration of Napoleon III had for some time been anxious to liquidate the *Revue*, and Flaubert seemed to have provided an excellent opportunity for doing so. Accordingly a case was brought against the author and the magazine for 'outrage to public morals and religion'. It could not be established, and Flaubert was acquitted.

Whatever the outcome of the trial, he had said, his reputation was made. However that may be, the book sold handsomely, despite a not too favourable press. The influential Ste-Beuve approved and Baudelaire appreciated. Other reviewers annoyed him either by bracketing him with the so-called 'Realist' school of Champfleury or by insisting on his 'debt to Balzac', a writer whom he admired (but did not largely read) for a careless vigour that was the antithesis of his own talent.

The trial was the only instance of persecution suffered by

Flaubert. Later in life, he was even awarded the Legion of Honour, and a pension. After *Madame Bovary* had made him famous, he was more to be seen in Paris, where he met the leading literary figures of the day. But he always remained a provincial to whom the superficial, semi-intimate, cultural chatter of the metropolis was no less antipathetic than the bourgeois chatter he could hear any day in Rouen.

Flaubert's life was singularly uneventful in any but a literary sense. The greater part of it from the age of twenty-five onwards – when his father died – was spent in comparative seclusion at the little village of Croisset, near Rouen, in the society of his mother and small niece, with visits from Louis Bouilhet at week-ends. The reverse of precocious at school, where he had been overshadowed by a technically brilliant elder brother, he went up to Paris at the age of eighteen to study law; but when, one day in 1843, he was suddenly prostrated by a mysterious kind of nervous attack, he found ample consolation for his debility in the opportunity it afforded him of giving up his studies and spending all his time reading and writing at Croisset. Though he was of a large physique, tall and striking in appearance, his nervous trouble recurred at intervals throughout his life, his literary torments doing nothing to mitigate it. In the final stages of *Bovary* he became a mass of minor ailments, to such an extent had his health been sapped by the sedentary life he led.

His mistress, Louise Colet, was a poetess, some years his senior, and he preserved with her only a sporadic, indeed a largely postal, relationship. Any deeper intimacy with a woman was unthinkable to him; it would have taken him too far out of himself, out of the solitude that was indispensable to him as air. 'Let us love one another in Art, as the old mystics loved one another in God!' he writes to her. Louise, after unwittingly posing for something of Emma Bovary, eventually became so importunate in her demands for attention that Flaubert turned her away with some harshness. But though capable of cruelty under provocation, he was capable also of great kindness, particularly in assisting his friends and true 'fellows' in their fight against the world. Proud and timid, he remained all his life curiously in subjection to his bourgeois mother, while for his bourgeois father he preserved all his life an enthusiastic admiration. Not the least surprising aspect of him is the savage contempt with which he came to regard the success of his masterpiece. It is not a comfortable book to live with, still less to be responsible for; there are those who would deny its claim to 'realism' on the ground that it contains not one character of positive virtue. The fact remains that Flaubert devoted five of the best years of his life to writing it. It had perhaps cost him too much.

In 1851, when he began on it, he already had a pile of manuscripts in his drawer. They were either romantically and morbidly autobiographical, like *November*, or exotic and magniloquent in the style of *The Temptation of St Anthony*. His next publication after *Madame Bovary* was *Salammbo, or The Maid of Carthage*, in 1862; then in 1869 the *Sentimental Education*, which alone has rivalled *Bovary* in popularity. The *Temptation* eventually came out in 1874, and the highly successful *Three Tales* in 1877. At the end of his life he was working on the unfinished *Bouvard and Pécuchet*. It is not a large body of work; but Flaubert was inordinately conscientious, not only in the perfecting of his style, but also in getting his facts right; the amount of preparatory reading he did for the historical novel *Salammbo* was prodigious.

Later in life, he derived much interest and solace from friendship and correspondence with George Sand.

He died in his fifty-ninth year, of an apoplectic stroke.

July 1949   ALAN RUSSELL

The translator would like to record his gratitude to his wife, Teresa Russell, who read the translation in manuscript and made many valuable suggestions.

PART ONE

I

WE were at preparation, when the headmaster came in, followed by a new boy dressed in 'civvies' and a school servant carrying a big desk. Those who were asleep woke up, and everyone got to his feet with an air of being interrupted at work.

Motioning us to sit down, the Head turned to speak to the form-master.

'Here is a boy for you, Monsieur Roger,' he said in a quiet voice. 'I'm putting him in the Second for a start, but if his work and conduct are satisfactory he can go up higher, where he belongs by age.'

In the corner behind the door, only just visible, stood a country lad of about fifteen, taller than any of us, with hair cut square on his forehead like a village chorister; sensible-looking and extremely ill at ease. He had on a short green jacket with black buttons, which must have pinched him under the arms although he was not broad-shouldered, and which revealed at the cuffs a glimpse of red wrists that were used to going bare. His breeches were fawn-coloured and braced up tight, his legs were clad in blue stockings, and on his feet he wore a pair of sturdy, unpolished hobnail boots.

We began going over the lesson. He was all ears, he listened as if it were the sermon in church, not daring even to cross his legs or to lean on his elbow; and when the bell rang at two o'clock, the master was obliged to tell him that he could go along with the rest of us.

It was our habit, on returning into class, to fling our caps under the bench as we came in at the door, so that they hit up against the wall, raising a cloud of dust; this was the thing to do.

The new boy had perhaps not noticed our procedure, or if he had he felt too scared to attempt it himself, for he was still holding his cap on his knees when prayers were over. His was one of those composite pieces of headgear in which you may trace features of bearskin, lancer-cap and bowler, night-cap and otterskin: one of those pathetic objects that are deeply expressive in their dumb ugliness, like an idiot's face. An oval splayed out with whale-bone, it started off with three pompons; these were followed by lozenges of velvet and rabbit's fur alternately, separated by a red band, and after that came a kind of bag ending in a polygon of cardboard with intricate braiding on it; and from this there hung down like a tassel, at the end of a long, too slender cord, a little sheaf of gold threads. It was a new cap, with a shiny peak.

'Stand up!' said the master.

He stood up, his cap fell down, and the whole class tittered.

He bent down to retrieve it. His neighbour put out an elbow and knocked it out of his hand again. Again he picked it up.

'Disburden yourself of your helmet,' said the master, who was a wit.

A roar of laughter from the class made the poor boy so uncomfortable that he didn't know whether to keep his cap in his hand, or put it on the floor or on his head. He sat down and deposited it on his knees.

'Stand up and tell me your name.'

The boy stammered out some unintelligible noise.

'Again!'

The same halting syllables, smothered by hoots from the class.

'Louder! louder!'

This time the new boy plucked up his courage, opened his mouth to an enormous width, and brought out at the top of his voice, as if he were hailing someone, the word *Charbovari.*

Pandemonium was let loose: a rising crescendo of shrieking and howling and stamping of feet, of shrill voices bursting out repeatedly: 'Charbovari! ... Charbovari!' It broke into a succession of distinct notes, subsided slowly, then started up again, sweeping along a whole row, as a splutter of suppressed laughter went off here and there like a damp squib.

Under a hail of impositions, order was eventually restored. By having it pronounced and spelt and said over, the master succeeded in getting the name 'Charles Bovary'. He at once ordered the unfortunate boy to go and sit on the dunce's seat just under his own desk.

The boy made a movement, then stood still, hesitating.

'What are you looking for?' the master asked.

'M-my c-cap ... ' faltered the timid voice, and he glanced nervously about him.

'Five hundred lines the whole class!' Rapped out in a rage, the words quelled a fresh outbreak as if they had been Neptune's 'Quos ego ...'

'Now will you be quiet!' And taking a handkerchief from his cap, the angry master mopped his brow.

'You, boy – you'll write me out twenty times the phrase *ridiculus sum.*'

More gently he added:

'You shall have your cap back. It hasn't been stolen.'

Everything was quiet again. Heads bowed over desks, and for two hours the new boy's behaviour was exemplary. Spattered now and then by a paper pellet flicked from a pennib, he only wiped his face with his hand and kept quite still, without raising his eyes.

At evening prep he took his cuffs from his desk, set out his little belongings and ruled his paper with care. We saw him working conscientiously, looking up every word in the dictionary, taking the utmost pains. He doubtless owed it to this evident willingness that he was not put down into the class below; for though his knowledge of grammar may have been passable, his renderings had but little elegance. He had been started on Latin by the priest in his village, his parents having postponed sending him to school as long as they possibly could, for reasons of economy.

His father, Monsieur Charles Denis Bartholomé Bovary, ex-assistant-surgeon-major, after being implicated in some matter of conscription round about 1812, and forced to resign the service, had exploited his personal attractions to collect a dowry of two thousand five hundred pounds which came along in the person of a hosier's daughter, who had fallen in love with his smart figure. He was a handsome braggart in clattering spurs, with whiskers that met his moustache, flamboyant clothes and fingers always ringed; with the build of a guardsman, and the hail-fellow-well-met of a commercial traveller. Once he was married, he lived on his wife's money for two or three years, dining well and rising late, smoking big porcelain pipes, never coming home at night until the theatre finished, and almost living in the pubs. His father-in-law died, leaving practically nothing. Outraged by this, he plunged into business, lost some money at it, and then withdrew to the country, to try his luck there. But as he knew no more about farming than he did about calico, as he rode his horses instead of sending them to plough, drank his cider by the bottle instead of selling it by the barrel, ate the finest poultry in his yard and greased his hunting-boots with the lard from his pigs, he soon perceived that he had better give up all idea of making money.

In a village on the borders of Caux and Picardy he found, for ten pounds a year, a place something between a farm and a private house; and there, consumed with vexation and regret, blaspheming Heaven and envying all the world, he shut himself up at the age of forty-five, in disgust with men, he said, and determined on a quiet life.

His wife had loved him to distraction, lavishing on him a thousand servilities which had the more estranged him from her. Her once lively, open, affectionate nature had changed with age – like uncorked wine that turns to vinegar – to ill temper and querulous irritability. She had suffered so much at first without complaining, when she saw him running after all the village trollops, when a score of bawdy-houses had sent him back to her at night, surfeited, stinking with drink. But her pride had revolted. Finally, she shut her mouth and swallowed her fury in a stoic silence which she preserved till the day of her death. She was always out and about, seeing the lawyers or the magistrate, remembering when bills fell due, and getting them renewed; and at home she ironed and sewed and washed, looked after the workmen and settled the accounts, while the master of the house sat smoking by the fire and spitting in the ashes, deaf to everything, sunk in a perpetual sullen torpor from which he never roused himself but to say something disagreeable to her.

A baby came, and had to be put out to nurse. Fetched home again, the youngster was utterly spoilt by his mother, who fed him on sweetmeats. His father let him run about barefoot, and even asserted, with a high philosophical air, that it would do him no harm to go quite naked, like a young animal. In opposition to the maternal influence, he had in his head a certain manly ideal of boyhood, according to which he tried to fashion his son. He wanted him brought up the Spartan way, to give him a good constitution. He sent him to bed without a fire, taught him to drain down great swigs of rum, and to jeer at church processions. Being of a peaceable disposition, the child responded poorly to these efforts. His mother kept him tied to her apron strings; she cut out cardboard figures for him, told him stories and regaled him with endless monologues full of melancholy gaiety and playful chatter. In her loneliness she gathered up all the fragments of her ambition and centred them upon his young head. She had visions of greatness – already seeing him as a grown man, handsome and intelligent, with a settled position in the Highways Department or the Law. She taught him to read, and even to sing two or three little ballads, to the accompaniment of an old piano that she had. All of which was pronounced by Monsieur Bovary, who had little use for culture, to be so much waste of time. How would they ever be able to keep the boy at a national school, to buy him a post, or set him up in business? And anyhow, with a bit of cheek a man can always get on in the world ... Madame Bovary bit her lip, and the boy ran wild in the village.

He followed the ploughmen, scaring away the crows with clods of earth; went blackberrying along the hedges; minded the turkeys, switch in hand; helped at haymaking, roamed the woods, played hopscotch in the church porch when it rained, and on Saints' days begged the verger to let him ring the bells, so that he could hang on the great rope with all his weight and feel it swing him up through the air.

And so he grew like an oak-tree, and acquired a strong pair of hands and a fresh colour.

At twelve, his mother getting her way, he began his studies under the supervision of the *curé*. But the lessons were so short and so haphazard that they could be of little use. They were given at odd moments, in the vestry, standing up, between a baptism and a burial. Or if he had nothing to go out for, the priest might send for his pupil after the Angelus. They went up to his room, where gnats and moths were wheeling round the candle, and settled themselves down. It was stuffy. The boy fell asleep. And with his hands folded upon his belly, the reverend gentleman would soon grow drowsy and start snoring, open-mouthed. At other times the good *curé* caught sight of Charles scampering about in the fields as he made his way back from administering the last sacrament to some sick parishioner. He called out to him, gave him a quarter of an hour's lecture, and seized the opportunity to hear him conjugate his verbs at the foot of a tree. They would be interrupted by rain or a passing acquaintance. But he was always pleased with the young fellow, and even said he had a good memory.

Charles could not be allowed to rest on those laurels. Mamma was determined; and Papa was either too ashamed to refuse, or too inert. They waited a year for the boy to make his first communion; another six months went by, and in the following year Charles was finally put to school in Rouen. He was brought by his father himself, about the end of October, at the time of St Romain's Fair.

It would be impossible for any of us to remember the least thing about him now. He was a youth of even temperament, who played in play-time and worked in school-time, attended in class, slept well in the dormitory and ate well in the dining-hall. For his temporary guardian he had a wholesale iron-monger in the Rue Ganterie, who called for him once a month on Sundays after shutting up shop, sent him for a walk along the quayside to look at the boats, and brought him back to school in time for supper at seven. Every Thursday evening he wrote a long letter to his mother, with red ink and three sealing-wafers; after which he went over his history notes or picked up an old volume of the *Travels of Anacharsis* that was lying about in the school-room. On school walks he talked to the servant, who came from the country like himself.

By dint of steady work he always kept about the middle of the class. Once he even got a second place in natural history. But at the end of his third year he was taken away from school to study medicine, his parents being convinced that he could reach degree standard by himself.

His mother found lodgings for him with a dyer of her ac-quaintance – a room on the fourth floor, overlooking the Eau de Robec. She made arrangements for his board, got together some furniture – two chairs and a table – and had an old cherrywood bedstead sent from home. In addition, she bought a small cast-iron stove and a load of firewood to keep her poor child warm; and at the end of the week she went, after repeated injunctions to him to be good, now that he was going to be left to himself.

The syllabus he saw on the notice-board stunned him. Lectures on anatomy, lectures on pathology, lectures on physiology, lectures on pharmacy, on chemistry and botany, on diagnosis and therapy, not to mention hygiene and materia medica – all names of unknown import to him: doors into so many sanctuaries filled with an august obscurity.

He didn't understand a word of it; couldn't grasp it, however hard he listened. Nevertheless he worked, he possessed bound note-books, he attended all the lectures and never missed a round at the hospital. He performed his daily little task like a mill-horse tramping round blindfold, grinding away at he knows not what.

To spare him expense, his mother sent him a piece of baked veal each week by the carrier; and on this he lunched when he returned from the hospital in the morning, drumming his feet against the wall as he ate. Afterwards he had to hurry off to his lessons, to the operating-theatre or the hospital, finding his way back again all across the town. At night, after a meagre dinner with his landlord, he went up to his room and started work once more, his wet clothes steaming in front of the red-hot stove.

On fine summer evenings, at the hour when the warm streets are empty and the maids play shuttlecock in doorways, he would open his window and lean out on the sill. The river, which turns this part of Rouen into a sort of shabby little Venice, flowed by beneath him, yellow, violet or blue between its bridges and its railings. Some workmen were crouched down on the bank, washing their arms in the water. On poles projecting from the lofts up above, skeins of cotton hung out to dry. In front, away beyond the roof-tops, was a pure expanse of sky with a red sun setting. How good it would be over yonder, now! How cool under the beeches! He opened his nostrils to breathe in the wholesome country smells – which failed to reach him here.

He grew lean and lanky, and his face took on a doleful sort of expression that made it almost interesting.

Devoid of enthusiasm, he came naturally to absolve himself from all the good resolutions he had made. One day he cut the hospital round, the next his lectures. Savouring the joys of idleness, he gradually dropped the whole thing.

He acquired a habit of going to the pubs and a passion for dominoes. To shut himself up every evening in a dirty public bar and to rattle the little black-dotted bones over the marble table-top seemed to him a precious declaration of his freedom, that raised him in his own esteem. It was an initiation into the great world, an attaining to forbidden pleasures; as he went in he put his hand on the door-knob with an almost sensual delight. Much that had been repressed within him now blossomed forth. He learnt rhymes by ear and sang them to his female companions; enthused about Béranger; took lessons in making punch, and finally in making love.

Thanks to his attention to these subjects, he failed miserably to get his diploma. And he was expected home on the very night of the examination, to celebrate his success!

He set off on foot. Outside the village he stopped and sent to fetch his mother; he told her everything. She made excuses for him, attributed his failure to the unfairness of the examiners, cheered him up a bit, and undertook to put things right at home. Not till five years later did Monsieur Bovary know the truth, and he accepted it then as it was past history. In any case, he could never have imagined that a son of his could be a fool.

Charles accordingly set to work once more, and this time

he studied assiduously, learning up all the questions by heart. He passed pretty well. What a proud day it was for his mother! They gave a big dinner-party.

Now, where should he go to practise his art? To Tostes. The only doctor there was an old man; Madame Bovary had long been on the lookout for his death, and now, even before the old fellow had finally packed his traps, Charles was installed across the way as his successor.

It was not enough, however, to have brought up a son, given him a medical training and then discovered Tostes for his practice. He must have a wife as well. She found him one: a bailiff's widow from Dieppe, forty-five years of age, fifty pounds of income.

Though she was ugly, thin as a lath, with as many pimples as the spring has buds, yet Madame Dubuc had, undeniably, no lack of suitors. To attain her ends, Madame Bovary was obliged to cut them all out, foiling with particular ingenuity the designs of a pork-butcher backed by the clergy.

Charles had seen in marriage the promise of a happier lot, fancying that he would be free, free to do what he liked with himself and his money. But his wife was master. He had to say this, and not that, in company. He must eat fish on Fridays, must dress as she decided, and harass at her bidding the patients who didn't pay. She opened his letters, kept a watch on his movements, and listened behind the partition when he had women in the consulting-room.

She had to have her cup of chocolate every morning, and endless other attentions. She was always complaining of her nerves, her chest or her moods. The sound of a footfall upset her. Leave her alone — solitude grew hateful to her. Return to her — it was doubtless 'to see her die'. When Charles came home at night she drew her long thin arms from under the sheet and put them around his neck; then sat him down on the edge of the bed and began the tale of her woes. He was neglecting her, he was in love with another! — yes, she had been told she would be unhappy ... And she ended by asking him for a dose of medicine and a little more love.

2

ABOUT eleven o'clock one night they were awakened by the sound of a horse pulling up just outside. The maid opened the attic window and parleyed for a while with a man in the street below. He had come for the doctor, and he had a letter. Nastasie went downstairs shivering, unlocked the door and drew the bolts one by one. The man left his horse standing, followed the maid upstairs and strode into the room behind her. From his grey woollen cap he produced a letter wrapped in a piece of cloth, and carefully handed it to Charles, who propped himself up on the pillow to read it. Nastasie held the light over the bed; Madame remained modestly facing the wall, her back turned to them.

The letter, sealed with a small blue seal, begged Monsieur Bovary to go immediately to a farm called Les Bertaux, to set a broken leg. Now, from Tostes to Les Bertaux is a good eighteen miles across country, by way of Longueville and St Victor. It was a dark night, and Bovary's bride was afraid of accidents. So they decided that the man from the farm should go on ahead, and Charles would follow three hours later, at moonrise. A boy would be sent to meet him, to show him the way and open the gates.

At about four in the morning Charles, well wrapped up in his cloak, started out for Les Bertaux. He was still sleepy from the warmth of his bed, and let himself be lulled by his horse's gentle trot. When the animal stopped of its own accord at one of those holes, surrounded by thorn-bushes, that are dug beside the furrows, Charles woke with a start, suddenly bethought him of the broken leg, and searched his memory for all the fractures he had studied. The rain had stopped; it was beginning to grow light. On the leafless branches of the apple-trees birds sat motionless, their little feathers ruffling in the cold morning wind. The flat countryside stretched as far as the eye could see; clumps of trees round the farmhouses made patches of dark violet at distant intervals on that vast grey surface which merged at the horizon into the sombre tones of the sky. From time to time Charles opened his eyes. But then, his senses growing weary and sleepiness automatically returning, he soon went off into a kind of doze, wherein recent sensations were mixed up with memories, and he saw himself as two selves, student and husband at once – lying in bed as he had been an hour ago, and going through a wardful of patients as in the old days. A warm smell of poultices mingled in his consciousness with the sharp tang of the dew, the sound of iron rings running along the curtain-rods over the beds ... with his wife sleeping. Going through Vassonville he saw a small boy sitting on the grass at the edge of a ditch.

'Are you the doctor?' the child asked. And when Charles said he was, he picked up his wooden shoes and started running along in front of him.

On the way the Officer of Health gathered from his guide's discourse that Monsieur Rouault must be one of the more prosperous farmers. He had broken his leg the night before, on his way back from keeping Twelfth Night at a neighbour's. Madame Rouault had died two years ago. There was no one else but the 'young lady', who kept house for him.

The ruts grew deeper; they were approaching Les Bertaux. The youngster slipped through a hole in the hedge, to reappear at the entrance to the farmyard and open the gate. The horse slipped on the wet grass, and Charles ducked down to avoid the branches. The watch-dogs barked in their kennels, tugging at their chains. As he entered Les Bertaux, his horse took fright and went down on all fours.

It looked a good sort of farm. Over the open stable-doors you saw great plough-horses feeding tranquilly at new racks.

A large, steaming dunghill stretched the length of the out-houses, and on top of it, along with the chickens and turkeys, about half a dozen peacocks – the pride of the Caux farmyard – were foraging. The sheepfold was a long one, the barn lofty, with walls as smooth as your hand. In the shed stood two large carts and four ploughs, with whips and collars and harness all complete, and some blue-dyed fleeces which were getting covered by the fine dust that fell from the lofts. The yard sloped upwards, planted with trees symmetrically spaced, and beside the pond a flock of geese cackled merrily.

A young woman, clad in a blue merino dress with three flounces, appeared in the doorway to welcome Monsieur Bovary, and asked him into the kitchen. A big fire was blazing there. Around it the farm-hands' breakfast was cooking in an assortment of little pots. Wet clothes were drying in the chimney corner. The shovel, the tongs, the nozzle of the bellows, were all of colossal size and shone like polished steel, while along the walls hung an array of kitchen utensils, fit-fully reflecting the bright flames in the fireplace and the first gleams of sunshine entering at the window.

Charles went upstairs to see the patient. He found him in bed, sweating under the clothes, his cotton night-cap hurled into a far corner. He was a stout little man of fifty with fair skin and blue eyes, bald in front and wearing ear-rings. On a chair beside him stood a large flask of brandy, from which he helped himself at intervals, to 'put some guts into him'. When he saw the doctor, however, his spirits subsided, and instead of swearing as he had been doing for the past twelve hours, he began to whimper.

The fracture was a simple one, with no complication of any kind. Charles could not have hoped for anything easier. Remembering his instructors' bedside manner, he comforted the injured man with a variety of bright remarks – the sur-geon's blandishments, oil for his lancet, as it were. For splints, they fetched a bundle of laths from the cart-shed. Charles selected one, cut it into sections and smoothed it down with a piece of broken glass, while the maidservant tore up some sheets for bandages and Mademoiselle Emma tried to sew some pads. She was so long finding her work-box that her father lost patience with her. She made no answer; but as she sewed she pricked her fingers, and then she put them to her mouth and sucked them.

Charles was astonished at the whiteness of her nails. They were shiny and tapering, scrubbed cleaner than Dieppe ivory, and cut almond-shape. Yet her hands were not beautiful, not pale enough perhaps, and somewhat hard at the knuckles; too long, as well, with no soft, curving contours. Her beauty was in her eyes – brown eyes, but made to look black by their dark lashes: eyes that came to meet yours openly, with a bold candour.

The bandaging finished, the doctor was invited by the patient to 'take a bite' before leaving.

Charles went down into the living-room. Two places were laid, with silver drinking-mugs, at the foot of a big four-poster bed draped with a figured calico depicting some Turks. From the tall oak wardrobe facing the window came an odour of iris and damp sheets. Some sacks of wheat stood in the corners – the overflow from the granary, which led out of the room up three stone steps. In the middle of the wall, whose green paint was flaking off with the saltpetre, the room was adorned with a head of Minerva drawn in black pencil, hung up on a nail, in a gilt frame, with underneath it in Gothic lettering, the words 'To dear Papa'.

First they discussed the patient; then the weather, the severe cold, the wolves that roamed the countryside at night. It wasn't very exciting for Mademoiselle Rouault living in the country, especially now that she had to look after the farm practically single-handed. The room was chilly, and she shivered as she ate, revealing then something of her full lips, which she had a habit of biting in her silent moments.

Round her neck was a white turn-down collar. Her hair, so smooth that its two black braids seemed each a single piece, was parted in the middle with a fine line that dipped slightly with the curve of her head, and was swept together in a thick bun at the back, leaving the tips of her ears just visible; at the temples was a wavy effect that the country doctor had never seen in his life before. Her cheeks were like rosy apples; and she carried a pair of tortoise-shell eye-glasses attached, in masculine fashion, to two buttonholes of her bodice.

Charles went up to say good-bye to her father. Before leaving, he came down into the living-room again, and found her standing with her forehead against the window, looking out into the garden, where the bean-sticks had been blown down by the wind. She turned round.

'Are you looking for anything?' she asked.

'My whip, if you please,' he answered.

He started ferreting about on the bed, behind the doors, under the chairs. It had slipped down between the wheat-sacks and the wall. Mademoiselle Emma saw it and reached over for it. Charles sprang to her aid, and as he stretched out his arm in a like movement, he felt his chest brush against the girl's back, bending beneath him. She got up red in the face, and looked at him over her shoulder as she handed him the lash.

Instead of returning three days later as he had promised, he went back to Les Bertaux the very next day, and twice a week regularly after that, besides the unexpected visits he made now and then in a casual sort of way.

All went well: the patient made an exemplary recovery and when at the end of forty-six days Rouault was seen attempting to walk round the yard unaided, Monsieur Bovary began to be considered a most capable man. Rouault said he couldn't have been treated more successfully by the leading doctors in Yvetot, or even in Rouen.

As for Charles, he never asked himself why he liked going

to Les Bertaux. Had he thought about it, he would doubtless have ascribed his zeal to the gravity of the case, or perhaps to the fees he hoped to obtain from it. Yet was that really what made his visits to the farm such a delightful change from the dull round of duty? On those days he got up early and set off at the gallop, urging his horse hard; then dismounted to wipe his boots on the grass and put on his black gloves before going in.

He liked to find himself riding into the farmyard and to feel the gate turning against his shoulder. He liked the cock crowing on the wall and the boys running to meet him. He liked the barn and the stables, he liked old Rouault, who patted him on the hand and called him his saviour. And he liked Mademoiselle Emma's little clogs on the scrubbed stones of the kitchen floor. Her high heels made her taller, and as she walked in front of him the wooden soles sprang up with a smart clack against the leather of her boots.

She always came to the top of the steps to see him off. If his horse was not yet there, she waited with him. Having said good-bye, they would speak no further. The fresh air played around her, ruffling up stray wisps of hair at the nape of her neck, setting the strings of her apron dancing and fluttering like streamers at her hips. Once when the thaw had set in, and the bark of the trees was running with water and the snow melting on the roofs of the farm buildings, she turned back at the door and went to fetch her parasol. She opened it out; it was of shot silk, and the sun shining through it cast flickering lights over the white skin of her face. She smiled in the moist warmth beneath it, and they heard the drops of water dripping on to the taut silk one by one.

When Charles first went to Les Bertaux, his wife invariably asked about the patient, and had even allotted Monsieur Rouault a clean new page in her account-book, which she kept in double-entry. But when she was told he had a daughter, she started making inquiries, and discovered that Mademoiselle Rouault had been brought up at an Ursuline convent and been what is called 'well educated'; in consequence of which she was expert at dancing, geography, drawing, fancy needlework and the piano. It was too much!

So that's why he beams all over his face when he goes to see her – she said to herself – and puts on his new waistcoat and risks getting it spoilt in the rain! The hussy!

Instinctively she hated her. At first she sought consolation in dropping hints, which were lost on Charles; then in more pointed remarks which he ignored for fear of a scene; and finally in direct harangue to which he had no answer. Why did he keep on going to Les Bertaux now that Monsieur Rouault was better – and the bill still unpaid? Why? Because there was a *certain person* there, who could talk, and embroider, and be clever! That was what he wanted – young ladies from the town!

'From the town!' she repeated. 'Old Rouault's girl! I don't think! Why, their grandfather was a shepherd, and they've got a cousin who was nearly had up in court for knocking a man down in a quarrel. *She* needn't go making such a how-d'ye-do, and showing off in a silk dress at church on Sundays, like a countess. Why, if it hadn't been for the cabbage crop last year, the poor old fellow'd have had a job to keep his head above water!'

From very weariness Charles left off going to Les Bertaux. After much sobbing and kissing, in a mighty surge of love, Héloise had made him lay his hand on the prayer-book and swear he wouldn't go again. He had given in; but the boldness of his desire protested against the servility of his conduct, and with a sort of naïve hypocrisy he reckoned that this injunction against seeing her gave him a virtual right to love her. So did the widow's lean frame and long teeth, and the little black shawl she wore all the year round with the end hanging down between her shoulder-blades. Her bony figure was encased in dresses like sheaths, which were too short for her and showed her ankles with the laces of her large shoes crossed over her grey stockings.

Charles' mother came to see them now and again. But after a few days the daughter-in-law seemed to sharpen her on her own sharp edge, and they would both be at him like a pair of knives, scarifying him with their comments and criticisms. He oughtn't to eat so much! Why offer drinks to anyone and everyone? Sheer pigheadedness, refusing to wear flannel!

It happened at the beginning of spring that a solicitor at Ingouville, who had had charge of the widow Dubuc's investments, sailed off one fine day with all the money in his office. True, Héloïse still owned her house in the Rue St François and an interest in a boat valued at two hundred and fifty pounds. Yet, for all that fortune that had been cried so high, there was nothing to show in the house, except perhaps a few personal possessions and some bits of clothing. The thing had to be gone into thoroughly. The house at Dieppe was discovered to be eaten away with mortgages to its very foundations; how much she had placed with the solicitor, God alone knew; the share in the boat came to no more than a hundred and twenty-five pounds. So the good lady had lied! In his annoyance, Monsieur Bovary senior smashed a chair on the floor and accused his wife of ruining their son by hooking him up to an old harridan whose harness was no better than her hide. They came to Tostes. There were explanations. There were scenes. Héloïse, in tears, threw herself into her husband's arms and bade him protect her from his parents. Charles tried to speak up for her; the old people were offended, and went.

But the damage had been done. A week later, as she was hanging out the washing in the yard, she had a spasm, and spat blood; and on the following day, as Charles was drawing the curtains, his back turned to her, she exclaimed: 'Oh, God!' heaved a sigh and fell unconscious. She was dead! It was incredible!

When all was over at the cemetery, Charles returned home.

Finding no one downstairs, he went up into the bedroom and saw her dress still hanging at the foot of the alcove. Then, leaning against the writing-desk, he remained till nightfall lost in a sorrowful reverie. She had loved him, after all.

3

ONE morning Monsieur Rouault came to pay Charles for setting his leg – seventy-five francs in forty-sou pieces, and a turkey. He had heard of his misfortune, and gave him what consolation he could.

'I know what it is,' he said, clapping Charles on the shoulder. 'I've been through it too. When I lost my poor wife, I went out into the fields to be alone, and threw myself down at the foot of a tree, and cried, called on Almighty God, raved at Him. I wished I had been like the moles I saw hanging on the branches, with worms crawling over their bellies – I wished I were dead. And when I thought that other men were at that moment with their dear little wives, holding them in their arms, I banged hard on the ground with my stick. I nearly went crazy; I couldn't eat. It made me sick to think of going to the café even: you wouldn't believe it. Well: quite gently, as one day followed another, as winter ran into spring and autumn came round after summer, it wore away bit by bit, crumb by crumb. It vanished, it went! Went *down*, I should say, for there's always something left deep down inside, a weight here on your chest, as you might say ... But we all come to it sooner or later. We mustn't give way and want to die because others have died ... You must shake yourself out of it, my dear Bovary. It will pass! Come and see us some time. My daughter thinks of you, don't you know – says you've forgotten her, she does. Spring will soon be here now. You must come and shoot a rabbit with us in the warren. That'll take your mind off things.'

Charles took his advice and went to Les Bertaux again. He found everything just as it had been last time – five months ago. The pear-trees were already in blossom, and the good Rouault went in and out, on his own legs again now, which made things more lively at the farm.

Thinking it incumbent upon him to lavish every possible attention on the doctor in his painful circumstances, he begged him to keep his cap on, talked to him in hushed tones as if he were ill, and even pretended to get annoyed because they hadn't prepared something a little lighter for him – some jugs of cream, say, or some stewed pears. He started telling stories, and Charles found himself laughing, but then suddenly remembered his wife and grew grave again. Coffee was brought in; he thought no more about her.

He thought about her less and less as he became used to living by himself. The novel charm of independence soon lightened the burden of his solitude. He could change his meal times now, come in and out unquestioned and, when he was very tired, stretch his arms and legs all over the bed. So he pampered and coddled himself, and accepted the consolation that people offered him. Professionally, his wife's death had done him no ill service. For a whole month people had been saying: 'Poor young man! What a misfortune!' His name had got about and his practice had grown. Then, too, he could go to Les Bertaux whenever he liked. He felt vaguely hopeful and happy. Brushing his whiskers in the mirror, he thought he had got better-looking.

One day he arrived at the farm about three o'clock. Everybody was out in the fields. He went into the kitchen, and at first failed to notice Emma; the shutters were closed. Through the chinks in the wood the sunshine came streaking across the floor in long slender lines that broke on the corners of the furniture and flickered on the ceiling. Flies were crawling over the dirty glasses on the table, buzzing as they drowned themselves in the dregs of the cider. Daylight came down the chimney, laying a velvet sheen on the soot in the fireplace and tinging the cold ashes with blue. Emma sat between the window and the hearth, sewing. She had nothing round her neck, and little drops of perspiration stood on her bare shoulders.

In accordance with country custom, she offered him a drink. He declined. She pressed him. Finally she suggested with a laugh that they should take a liqueur together. She fetched a bottle of curaçao from the cupboard, reached down two small glasses, filled one to the brim, poured the merest drop into the other and, after clinking glasses, raised hers to her lips. As there was practically nothing in it, she tilted her head right back to drink. With her head back and her lips rounded and the skin of her neck stretched tight, she laughed at her own vain efforts, and slid the tip of her tongue between her fine teeth to lick, drop by drop, the bottom of the glass.

She sat down again and resumed her work, a white cotton stocking that she was darning. She worked with her head lowered. She did not speak, neither did Charles. The draught beneath the door blew a little dust over the flagstones, and he watched it creep along. He could hear nothing but the throbbing inside his head and the cackle of a laying hen somewhere away in the farmyard. From time to time Emma put the palms of her hands to her cheeks to cool them, then cooled her hands on the knobs of the big fire-dogs.

Since the turn of the season, she had been complaining of attacks of dizziness, and she asked whether sea-bathing would do her any good. She started talking about her convent, Charles about his school; their tongues loosened. They went up to her room. She showed him her old music-books, the little volumes she had been given for prizes, and the oak-leaf crowns, all stowed away at the bottom of a cupboard. She spoke of her mother, and the cemetery where she was buried, even showing him the bed in the garden where she picked flowers on the first Friday of every month to lay on her grave.

...But the gardener they had was no good at all. Servants were so unsatisfactory! She would have liked very much to live in town, at any rate during the winter – though perhaps the long days made the country still *more* boring in the summer ... As she talked, she suited her voice to her words: now clear, now shrill, now suddenly laden with languor, with drawling intonations as she started talking to herself: merry the next minute, while her eyes opened wide and innocent, then half closed, submerged in boredom, thoughts wandering.

On his way home that night Charles went over the things she had said, trying to remember all of them, to fill out their meaning and so piece the rest of her life together. But he could not visualize her other than as she had been at their first meeting or when he had left her just now. He wondered what would happen to her. Would she marry? Whom would she marry? Alas, her father was rich, and she ... so beautiful! But Emma's face kept coming back before his eyes, and in his ears was a perpetual buzzing monotone like the humming of a top – *Suppose you married, suppose you married!* That night he couldn't sleep, he had a tight feeling in his throat, he felt thirsty. He got out to have a drink from his water-jug and opened the window. The sky was thick with stars, a warm breeze was blowing, dogs barked in the distance. He turned his head in the direction of Les Bertaux.

Thinking that, after all, he had nothing to lose, Charles resolved to put the question when the occasion offered. But whenever occasion did offer, he was tongue-tied with fear of saying the wrong thing.

Old Rouault would not have been sorry to get rid of his daughter, who was of little use to him about the place. He excused her in his own mind, as being too clever for farming – a calling under the curse of Heaven, for it had never made anyone's fortune. Far from its having made his, the good man lost money every year. Though he excelled at marketing, where he was in his element, for the actual job of farming and the internal management of his property there could be no one less suited. He never willingly took his hands from his pockets; and he spared no expense where his own comfort was concerned, being fond of good food, a good fire and a good bed. He liked old cider, an underdone leg of mutton, a well-mixed coffee-and-brandy. He took his meals by himself in the kitchen, facing the fire, at a little table brought to him ready served, as at the theatre.

So when he saw that his daughter's presence brought a flush to Charles' cheek – which meant that one of these days he would be asking her hand in marriage – he pondered the whole affair beforehand. He thought Charles rather a wisp of a man, to be sure, not quite the son-in-law he could have wished for. But he was said to be steady and thrifty, and well-educated. Most likely he wouldn't haggle too much over the dowry. So, as the farmer was just then having to sell twenty-two acres of his land, and owed a lot of money to the mason and a lot of money to the saddler, and as the shaft of the cider-press needed repairing, he said to himself: 'If he asks for her, he shall have her.'

At Michaelmas Charles went to spend three days at Les Bertaux. He let the last day slip by like the rest, putting it off from one quarter of an hour to the next. When he left, Monsieur Rouault came to set him on his way. They were going along a sunken lane; they were about to part; the moment had come. Charles gave himself to the corner of the hedge; they passed it, and at last he mumbled:

'Maître Rouault, there's something I want to tell you.'

They stopped. Charles was silent.

'Well, well, out with it, then! ... As if I didn't know all about it already!' said Rouault, chuckling.

'Monsieur Rouault ... Monsieur Rouault,' Charles stammered.

'For my part, there's nothing I'd like better, and though I expect the little girl will be of the same mind, still we must put it to her and see. Now then – I'll say good-bye to you and get back home. If it's "Yes" – you get me – there's no need for you to come back, what with everyone about, and, anyhow, it would be too much for her. But so as you won't fret yourself, I'll push the shutter flat against the wall – you'll see it from the back here if you lean over the hedge.'

And he went off.

Charles tethered his horse to a tree, ran back on to the path, and waited. Half an hour passed. Then he counted another nineteen minutes by his watch. Suddenly there was a clatter against the wall. The shutter had been folded back, the hook was still rattling.

Next morning he was at the farm by nine o'clock. Emma blushed as he entered, but tried to carry it off with a little laugh. Her father embraced his future son-in-law. The matter of the settlement was shelved for the time being; they had time enough before them, for the wedding could not decently take place until Charles was out of mourning, which would be some time next spring.

They looked forward to it all through the winter. Mademoiselle Rouault attended to her trousseau, ordering part of it in Rouen, and herself making up some underclothes and nightcaps, from borrowed patterns. Whenever Charles went to visit them they discussed the preparations, wondering in which room to hold the wedding-breakfast, how many dishes would be needed, and what the main ones should be.

Emma would have preferred a midnight wedding with torches, but her father couldn't understand that idea at all. So there was a great wedding-party, at which they sat down forty-three to table and remained there sixteen hours; it was resumed next day, and in a lesser degree on the following days.

4

THE guests arrived early, in carriages, one-horse traps, two-wheeled wagonettes, old cabs minus their hoods, or spring-vans with leather curtains. The young people from the neighbouring villages came in farm-carts, standing up in rows, with their hands on the rails to prevent themselves from falling: trotting along and getting severely shaken up. Some people came from thirty miles away, from Goderville, Normanville and Cany. All the relatives on both sides had been invited. Old estrangements had been patched up and letters sent to long-forgotten acquaintances.

Every now and then the crack of a whip would be heard behind the hedge. Another moment, and the gate opened, a trap drove in. It galloped up to the foot of the steps, pulled up sharp and emptied its load. They tumbled out on all sides, with a rubbing of knees and a stretching of arms. The ladies were in bonnets, and wore town-style dresses, with gold watch-chains, and capes with the ends tucked inside their sashes, or little coloured neckerchiefs pinned down at the back, leaving their necks bare. The boys were dressed like their papas, and looked uncomfortable in their new clothes. Many, indeed, were that day sampling the first pair of boots they had ever had. Beside them went a big girl of fourteen to sixteen, cousin or elder sister no doubt, all red and flustered and speechless in her white first-communion dress (let down for the occasion), with a rose pomade smarmed over her hair, and gloves that she was terrified of getting dirty. As there were not enough stablemen to unharness all the carriages, the gentlemen pulled up their sleeves and went to work themselves. According to the difference in their social status, they wore dress-coats, frock-coats, jackets or waistcoats. Fine dress-coats, invested with all a family's esteem, that only came out of the wardrobe on special occasions. Frock-coats with long skirts flapping in the breeze, cylindrical collars and baggy pockets. Jackets of coarse cloth, usually accompanied by a cap with a rim of brass round the peak. Waistcoats, very short, with two buttons set close together at the back like a pair of eyes, and flaps that looked as if they had been cut out of a single block by the carpenter's axe. Some again (but these, you may be sure, were to sit at the bottom end of the table) wore their best smocks – smocks with the collar turned down over the shoulders, the back gathered in little pleats, the waist fastened very low with a stitched belt.

And the shirts bulged out like breastplates! Heads were all freshly cropped, with ears sticking out and faces close-shaven. Some who had got up before it was light enough to shave properly showed diagonal slashes under the nose or cuts along the jaw as far across as a three-franc piece. The fresh air had inflamed their wounds on the way, and so set mottled patches of pink on all those great white beaming faces.

The mayor's office being within a mile and a half of the farm, they made their way there on foot, and returned in the same manner after the church ceremony was over. At first the procession was compact, a single band of colour billowing across the fields, all along the narrow path that wound through the green corn; but soon it lengthened out and split up into several groups, which dawdled to gossip. The fiddler led the way, his violin adorned with rosettes and streamers of ribbon. After him came the bride and bridegroom, then the relatives, then the friends, in any order; and the children kept at the back, amusing themselves by plucking the bell-flowers from among the oat-stalks, or playing among themselves without being seen. Emma's dress was too long and dragged on the ground slightly. Now and again she stopped to pull it up, and then with her gloved fingers she daintily removed the coarse grasses and thistle burrs, while Charles waited, empty-handed, until she had finished. Rouault, with a new silk hat on his head and coat cuffs that came right down to his finger-tips, had

The fiddler led the way.

given his arm to the bridegroom's mother. Monsieur Bovary senior, who, utterly despising the lot of them, had put on a plain frock-coat of military cut with one row of buttons, was addressing tavern gallantries to a fair-haired peasant-girl. She bobbed and blushed and didn't know what to say. The remainder of the guests were talking business or playing tricks behind one another's backs, warming up for the party. And whenever they cocked an ear they could hear the fiddler still scraping away as he went on ahead through the fields. When he discovered that he had left them all far behind, he stopped to draw breath, and thoroughly rosined his bow to give the strings a better squeak. Then he set off again, moving the neck of his violin up and down to mark the time to himself. The sound of the instrument scattered the little birds far in front of him.

The wedding-feast had been laid in the cart-shed. On the table were four sirloins, six dishes of hashed chicken, some stewed veal, three legs of mutton, and in the middle a nice roast sucking-pig flanked by four pork sausages with sorrel. Flasks of brandy stood at the corners. A rich foam had frothed out round the corks of the cider-bottles. Every glass had already been filled to the brim with wine. Yellow custard stood in big dishes, shaking at the slightest jog of the table, with the initials of the newly wedded couple traced on its smooth surface in arabesques of sugared almond. For the tarts and confectioneries they had hired a pastry-cook from Yvetot. He was new to the district, and so had taken great pains with his work. At dessert he brought in with his own hands a tiered cake that made them all cry out. It started off at the base with a square of blue cardboard representing a temple with porticoes and colonnades, with stucco statuettes all round it in recesses studded with gilt-paper stars; on the second layer was a castle-keep in Savoy cake, surrounded by tiny fortifications in angelica, almonds, raisins and quarters of orange; and finally, on the uppermost platform, which was a green meadow with rocks, pools of jam and boats of nutshell, stood a little Cupid, poised on a chocolate swing whose uprights had two real rose-buds for knobs at the top.

The meal went on till dusk. When they got tired of sitting, they went for a stroll round the farm, or played a game of 'corks' in the granary, after which they returned to their seats. Towards the end some of the guests were asleep and snoring. But with the coffee there was a general revival. They struck up a song, performed party-tricks, lifted weights, went 'under your thumb', tried hoisting the carts up on their shoulders, joked broadly and kissed the ladies. The horses, gorged to the nostrils with oats, could hardly be got into the shafts to go home at night. They kicked and reared and broke their har-ness, their masters swore or laughed; and all through the night by the light of the moon there were runaway carriages galloping along country roads, plunging into ditches, career-ing over stone-heaps, bumping into the banks, while women leaned out of the doors trying to catch hold of the reins.

Those who stayed behind at Les Bertaux spent the night drinking in the kitchen. The children had dropped off to sleep under the seats.

The bride had begged her father to be spared the custom-ary pleasantries. However, a fishmonger cousin – the same who had brought a pair of soles for his wedding-present – was about to squirt some water out of his mouth through the key-hole of their room, when Rouault came up just in time to prevent him and explain that his son-in-law's position in the world forbade such improprieties. Only with reluctance did the cousin yield to that argument. Inwardly he accused old Rouault of being proud, and went into a corner with four or five other guests who, having chanced several times in suc-cession to get the last helpings of meat at table, likewise felt that they had been shabbily treated, and were muttering against their host, expressing in guarded terms their desire for his downfall.

The elder Madame Bovary had not opened her lips all day. She had not been consulted about the bride's dress, nor about the feast. She went to bed early. Instead of following her, her husband sent to St Victor for cigars and smoked till daybreak, drinking rum and kirsch, a mixture unknown to the company, which raised him yet higher in their esteem.

Charles had no facetious side, and hadn't shone at his wedding. He responded feebly to the puns and quips and innuendoes, the compliments and ribaldries, which it was considered necessary to let fly at him as soon as the soup appeared.

Next morning, however, he seemed a different man. He was the one you would have taken for yesterday's virgin. Whereas the bride gave nothing away. The slyest among them were nonplussed. They surveyed her as she approached with the liveliest curiosity. But Charles made no pretences. He called her 'my wife', addressed her affectionately, kept asking everyone where she was, looked for her everywhere, and frequently led her out into the yard, where he was seen, away among the trees, putting his arm round her waist, leaning over her as they walked, and burying his face in the frills of her bodice.

Two days after the wedding, husband and wife departed. Charles could not be away from his patients any longer. Rouault let them have his trap for the journey, and accompanied them himself as far as Vassonville. There he kissed his daughter for the last time, then got down and started back homewards. When he had gone about a hundred yards, he halted; and the sight of the trap going farther and farther into the distance, its wheels turning in the dust, drew from him a deep sigh. He remembered his own wedding, his early married life, his wife's first pregnancy. He had been pretty happy himself, that day he took her from her father and brought her home mounted behind him, trotting over the snow. For it had been round about Christmas-time, and the country was all white. She held on to him with one arm, her basket hung from the other; the wind lifted the long lace ribbons of her Caux headdress, so that sometimes they flapped over his mouth; and when he turned his head, he saw, close beside him against his shoulder, her rosy little face quietly smiling beneath the gold crown of her bonnet. From time to time she put her fingers in the front of his coat, to warm them ... How long ago it was, all that. Their boy would have been thirty by now ... He looked back, and there was nothing to be seen along the road. He felt dreary as an empty house. In his brain, still clouded with the fumes of the feast, dark thoughts and tender memories mingled. He felt a momentary inclination to go round by the church. But he was afraid the sight of it would only make him sadder still, and he went straight home.

Monsieur and Madame Charles arrived at Tostes at about six o'clock. The neighbours stationed themselves at the windows to see their doctor's new wife.

The old servant stepped forward to pay her respects, apologized for not having dinner ready, and suggested that in the meantime Madame might like to look over her house.

5

THE brick front ran flush with the street, or rather road. Behind the door hung a cloak with a small cape, a bridle and a black leather cap, and in a corner on the floor stood a pair of leggings with the mud dried on them. To the right was the parlour, that is to say the room where they ate and lived. Canary-yellow wallpaper, relieved at the top by a chain of pale flowers, flapped all over the badly hung canvas. White calico curtains with a red border were arranged crosswise along the windows, and on the narrow mantelpiece, between two silver-plated candlesticks with oval shades, a clock with a head of Hippocrates shone resplendent. On the other side of the passage was Charles' consulting-room, a little place about six yards across, with a table, an office-chair and three ordinary chairs. The half-dozen shelves of the deal bookcase were stocked with practically nothing but the *Dictionary of Medical Science*, its volumes uncut, though the bindings looked somewhat the worse for the successive sales they had been through. The smell of melted butter seeped in through the partition during surgery hours, while conversely anyone in the kitchen could hear the patients coughing and reciting their history. Next, opening straight on to the stable-yard, came a big dilapidated room containing an oven, used now as woodshed, cellar and store-room, full of old junk, empty barrels, worn-out gardening implements and a host of dust-covered objects whose function could not be guessed.

The garden, longer than it was broad, ran between two clay-walls with apricot-trees growing along them, down to a thorn hedge which divided it off from the fields. In the centre was a slate sun-dial on a stone pedestal. Four flower-beds, planted with scraggy dog-roses, were laid out symmetrically around the more serviceable square of kitchen-garden. Right at the bottom, under the spruce-trees, stood a plaster priest reading his breviary.

Emma went upstairs. There was no furniture in the first room, but the second, which was the bridal chamber, had a mahogany bed in an alcove, with red hangings. A box worked in shells adorned the chest of drawers; and on the writing-desk by the window stood a water-bottle containing a bouquet of orange-blossom, tied with white satin ribbon. It was a bride's bouquet – the first one's! She stared at it. Charles noticed, and took it out and up to the attic, while Emma sat down in an armchair, watching her belongings being set down around her, thinking of her own bouquet packed away in a bandbox and wondering what would happen to it if she were to die.

The first few days she spent planning alterations in the house. She removed the shades from the candlesticks, had the walls repapered, the staircase repainted and benches put all round the sun-dial in the garden; and asked how one could get a fish-pond made, with a fountain. And finally her husband, knowing how fond she was of driving out, picked up a second-hand dog-cart which, given new lamps and a splash-board of mottled leather, looked almost as good as a Tilbury.

So he was happy, without a care in the world. A meal together, a walk along the highroad in the evening, a way she had of putting her hand to her hair, the sight of her straw hat hanging on the window latch, and a great many things besides in which Charles had never thought to find pleasure, now made up the even tenor of his happiness. In bed in the morning, their heads side by side on the pillow, he would watch the sunlight glinting on the down of her fair cheeks, half-hidden by the scalloped ribbons of her nightcap. Seen so close, her eyes appeared enlarged, especially when she blinked them open several times in succession on waking. Black in the shadow, and a rich blue in broad daylight, they seemed to hold successive layers of colour, darkest at the depths and growing brighter and brighter towards the surface. His own eyes would lose themselves in those depths. He saw himself reflected there in miniature, down to the shoulders, with his silk handkerchief over his head and his nightshirt open at the neck. ... He got up. She came to the window to see him off, leaning on the sill between two geranium-pots, with her dressing-gown wrapped loosely around her.

Down below, Charles buckled on his spurs, resting his foot on the mounting-block. She went on talking to him from up above, biting off a fragment of flower or leaf and blowing it down to him. It fluttered and floated and turned semicircles in the air like a bird, and before it reached the ground got caught up in the bedraggled mane of the old white mare standing stockstill at the door. Charles, mounted, blew her a kiss. She waved in answer and shut the window. He set off. Along the highroad stretching away before him in an endless ribbon of dust, through sunken lanes of overhanging trees, down paths knee-deep in springing corn, with the sun on his back and the morning air in his nostrils, his heart full of the joys of the night, he rode along in peace of mind and bodily content, ruminating on his good fortune, like one who continues to savour the taste of the truffles while he digests his dinner.

When, till now, had life been good to him? In his school-days? – shut away behind high walls, alone among school-fellows who had more money than he or were cleverer in class, who laughed at his accent and made fun of his clothes, and whose mothers came to the visitors' room with cakes in-side their muffs? Or later, when he had been studying medi-cine, and never had a full enough purse to take out a little working-girl who might have become his mistress? And then for fourteen months he had lived with the widow, whose feet were like blocks of ice in bed. But now, this pretty woman he adored was his for life. The universe, for him, was contracted to the silken compass of her petticoat. He used to reproach himself for not loving her enough, he couldn't bear to be away from her; so he hurried back, and mounted the stairs with a beating heart. Emma was sitting at her dressing-table. He stole up on tiptoe and kissed her on the back. She gave a little scream.

He couldn't keep from constantly touching her comb, her rings, her neckerchief. Sometimes he gave her great smacking kisses on the cheek, sometimes a chain of little ones all the way up her arm from finger-tip to shoulder. And she pushed him away with a weary half-smile, as you do a child that hangs on to you.

Before the wedding, she had believed herself in love. But not having obtained the happiness that should have resulted from that love, she now fancied that she must have been mis-taken. And Emma wondered exactly what was meant in life by the words 'bliss', 'passion', 'ecstasy', which had looked so beautiful in books.

6

SHE had read *Paul and Virginia*, and seen in her dreams the little bamboo hut, Domingo the nigger and Faithful the dog, and, above all, the dear little brother, gentle and loving, who fetches down red fruits for you from great trees taller than church steeples, or comes running barefoot along the sands to bring you a bird's nest.

When she was thirteen her father had taken her into the town and entered her at the convent. They stopped at an inn in the St Gervais quarter, where their supper was served on painted plates depicting the story of Mademoiselle de la Vallière. The explanatory wording, worn away here and there by the scratch of cutlery, all glorified religion, the tender heart and Court ceremony.

At first, far from being bored at the convent, she enjoyed the society of the nuns, who entertained her by taking her into the chapel, which one reached down a long corridor from the refectory. She played very little at play-time. She knew her catechism well, and it was always she who answered the curate's harder questions. Living among those white-faced women with their rosaries and copper crosses, never getting away from the stuffy schoolroom atmosphere, she gradually succumbed to the mystic languor exhaled by the perfumes of the altar, the coolness of the holy-water fonts and the radiance of the tapers. Instead of following the Mass, she used to gaze at the azure-bordered religious drawings in her book. She loved the sick lamb, the Sacred Heart pierced with sharp arrows, and poor Jesus falling beneath His cross. To mortify the flesh, she tried to go a whole day without food; and she puzzled her head for some vow to accomplish.

When she went to confession, she invented small sins in order to stay there longer, kneeling in the shadows with her hands together and her face against the grating, beneath the whisperings of the priest. The metaphors of betrothed, spouse, heavenly lover, marriage everlasting, that recur in sermons, awoke in the depths of her soul an unlooked-for delight.

In the evening, before prayers, they had a religious reading in the schoolroom. During the week it would be a Bible story or an extract from the Lectures of the Abbé Frayssinous, on Sundays something lighter out of the *Christian Spirit*. How she listened, those first evenings, to the sonorous lamentations of romantic melancholy re-echoing through Earth and Eternity! If she had passed her childhood in the back room of a shop somewhere in the middle of a town, she might now have awakened to the lyric call of Nature, which usually reaches us only through the medium of books. But she was too familiar with the country: with the bleating of the flocks, with the dairy and the plough. Accustomed to the peaceful, she turned in reaction to the picturesque. She loved the sea only for its storms, green foliage only when it was scattered amid ruins. It was necessary for her to derive a sort of personal profit from things, she rejected as useless whatever did not minister to her heart's immediate fulfilment – being of a sentimental rather than an artistic temperament, in search of emotions, not of scenery.

There was an old maid who came to the convent one week in every month to mend the linen. Being under the Archbishop's protection as coming of an old family of gentlefolk ruined in the Revolution, she took her meals in the refectory along with the holy sisters, and afterwards joined them in a little chat before resuming her work. The girls often slipped out of preparation to go and see her. She sang half to herself as she plied her needle some romantic ballads of the last century, which she knew by heart. She told you stories, brought news, and did little errands for you in the town. In the pocket of her apron she always kept some novel or other, which she would lend to the bigger girls on the sly, and which the maiden lady herself devoured, whole chapters at a time, in the intervals of her task. They were all about love and lovers, damsels in distress swooning in lonely lodges, postillions slaughtered all along the road, horses ridden to death on every page, gloomy forests, troubles of the heart, vows, sobs, tears, kisses, rowing-boats in the moonlight, nightingales in the grove, gentlemen brave as lions and gentle as lambs, too virtuous to be true, invariably well-dressed, and weeping like fountains. And so for six months of her sixteenth year, Emma soiled her hands with this refuse of old lending libraries. Coming later to Sir Walter Scott, she conceived a passion for the historical, and dreamed about oak chests, guardrooms, minstrels. She would have liked to live in some old manor house, like those deep-bosomed châtelaines who spend their days beneath pointed arches, leaning on the parapet, chin in hand, watching a cavalier with a white plume galloping up out of the distant countryside on a black charger. She was at this time a worshipper of Mary Queen of Scots, and had an enthusiastic veneration for all illustrious or ill-fated women. Joan of Arc, Héloïse, Agnès Sorel, 'La Belle Ferronnière', Clémence Isaure, stood out for her like comets upon the dark immensity of history, along with certain more shadowy and mutually unrelated phenomena such as St Louis and his oak-tree, the dying Bayard, some atrocities of Louis XI, something about St Bartholomew's Day, the crest of the Béarnais, and that enduring memory of the painted plates glorifying Louis XIV.

The songs she learnt in the music lesson were all about madonnas, lagoons, gondoliers and little angels with golden wings: placid pieces that afforded her a glimpse, through verbal silliness and musical solecism, of the alluring phantasmagoria of real feeling. Some of her companions brought back keepsakes presented to them at the New Year, and there was a great business of hiding them away and reading them in the dormitory. Delicately fingering their lovely satin bindings, Emma gazed in wonder at the unknown signatures beneath the contributions – mostly Counts and Viscounts.

She thrilled as she blew back the tissue paper over the prints. It rose in a half-fold and sank gently down on the opposite page. Behind a balcony railing a young man in a short cloak would be pressing to his heart a girl in white with an alms-purse at her waist. Or it would be an unnamed portrait of an English milady with golden curls, looking at you with her big bright eyes from under a round straw hat. Other ladies lolled in carriages, gliding through the park with a greyhound leaping in front of the horses and two little postillions driving them along at a trot. Others lay on sofas, with an opened letter beside them, gazing dreamily at the moon through an open window half-veiled by a black curtain. Artless creatures with a tear on their cheek would be cooing at a dove through the bars of a Gothic cage, or smiling with head on one side as, with tapering fingers curled up at the tips like pointed shoes, they plucked the petals from a daisy ... And the Sultans, with their long pipes, swooning in arbours in the arms of dancing-girls! The Giaours, the Turkish sabres, the Greek fezzes! And all those pallid landscapes of dithyrambic regions, depicting often palms and pines together, with tigers on the right and a lion on the left, Tartar minarets on the horizon, Roman ruins in the foreground, and some kneeling camels in between: the whole framed by a well-kept virgin forest, with a great perpendicular sunbeam quivering on the water, and, at isolated points on its steel-grey surface, a few white scratches to represent swans floating.

The argand lamp fixed in the wall above Emma's head shone down on this 'world in pictures' as it passed before her. In the dormitory all was silent, in the distance some belated hackney-cab would still be rattling along the boulevards.

When her mother died, she wept a great deal for a few days. She had a lock of the dead woman's hair mounted on a memorial card, and in a letter she wrote home, full of sorrowful reflections on life, she asked that when her time came she might be buried in the same grave. Her father thought she

must be ill, and came to see her. Emma was inwardly gratified
to feel she had attained at the outset to that rare ideal of sensitive beings to which the common soul cannot aspire. And so
she drifted off down the meandering ways of Lamartine,
listened to harps on lakes, to all the songs of dying swans, all
the falling of leaves, the pure virgins rising to Heaven and the
voice of the Eternal speaking in the valleys. It palled on her,
she refused to admit the fact, and kept on at first from force of
habit, then from vanity: until quite suddenly she was surprised to feel herself at peace, with no more sadness in her
heart than wrinkles on her brow.

The good nuns, who had felt so sure of her vocation, perceived to their astonishment that Mademoiselle Rouault seemed
to be slipping through their fingers. They had lavished on
her so many offices and retreats, novenas and sermons, had
preached so much about the reverence due to the saints and
martyrs, given her so much good advice on the modesty of her
person and the salvation of her soul, that she did what horses
do when you rein them in too tight – pulled up sharp and
dropped the bit from beneath her teeth. Practically minded
in the midst of all her enthusiasm, she loved the church for its
flowers, music for the words of the songs, literature for its
passionate excitements, and she rebelled against the mysteries
of the faith as she grew the more irritated with discipline, a
thing repugnant to her nature. When her father took her
away, no one was sorry to see her go. Indeed, the Mother
Superior had lately found in her a want of reverence towards
their community.

Home once more, Emma at first enjoyed managing the
servants; then sickened of the country and longed for the
convent again. At the time of Charles' first appearance at Les
Bertaux she regarded herself as being utterly disillusioned,
with nothing more to learn and nothing more to feel.

Then, the anxiety occasioned by her change of state, or
perhaps a certain agitation caused by the presence of this man

had sufficed to make her believe herself possessed at last of that wonderful passion which hitherto had hovered above her like a great bird of rosy plumage in the splendour of a poetic heaven ... But she could hardly persuade herself that the quietness of her present life was the happiness of her dreams.

7

AND yet sometimes it occurred to her that this was the finest time of her life, the so-called honeymoon. To savour all its sweetness, it would doubtless have been necessary to sail away to lands with musical names where wedding nights leave behind them a more delicious indolence. In a post-chaise, behind blue silk blinds, you climb at a foot-pace up precipitous roads, listening to the postillion's song echoing across the mountain, amid the tinkling of goat-bells and the muffled noise of waterfalls. At sunset you breathe the scent of lemon trees on the shore of a bay. At night, together on the terrace of your villa, with fingers intertwined, you gaze at the stars and make plans for the future. It seemed to her that certain parts of the world must produce happiness, as they produce peculiar plants which will flourish nowhere else. Why could she not now be leaning on the balcony of a Swiss chalet, or immuring her sadness in a Scotch cottage, with a husband in a black velvet coat with long flaps, and soft boots, and peaked hat, and ruffles!

She would have been glad of someone in whom to confide all this; but how describe an intangible unease, that shifts like the clouds and eddies like the wind? Lacking the words, she had neither the opportunity nor the courage.

Nevertheless, had Charles so wished, had he guessed, had his eyes once read her thoughts, it would instantly have delivered her heart of a rich load, as a single touch will bring the ripe fruit falling from the tree. But as their outward familiarity grew, she began to be inwardly detached, to hold herself more aloof from him.

Charles' conversation was as flat as a street pavement, on which everybody's ideas trudged past, in their workaday dress, provoking no emotion, no laughter, no dreams. At Rouen, he said, he had never had any desire to go and see a Paris company at the theatre. He couldn't swim, or fence, or fire a pistol, and was unable to explain a riding term she came across in a novel one day.

Whereas a man, surely, should know about everything; excel in a multitude of activities, introduce you to passion in all its force, to life in all its grace, initiate you into all mysteries! But this one had nothing to teach; knew nothing, wanted nothing. He thought she was happy; and she hated him for that placid immobility, that stolid serenity of his, for that very happiness which she herself brought him.

She used to sketch; and it was great sport for Charles to stand there, bolt upright, watching her as she bent over her drawing-block, half-closing her eyes to see her work better, or rolling little bread-crumb pellets between finger and thumb. Then there was the piano: the faster her fingers flew over the keys, the more he marvelled. She had a confident touch, and would run right down the key-board from top to bottom without a break. Shaken up, like this, the aged instrument, with its warped chords, could be heard all through the village when the window was open, and the bailiff's clerk would often pause as he went by bareheaded along the highroad and stand there in his felt slippers, his sheet of paper in his hand, listening.

Emma knew how to run the house, as well. She sent out the accounts to the patients, in well-phrased letters devoid of all commercial flavour. When they had one of the neighbours to dinner on a Sunday she always managed to put some dainty dish on the table. She was expert at building a pyramid of greengages on a base of vine-leaves, could turn preserves out of the jar on to a plate, and even spoke of getting finger-bowls for use at dessert. All this reflected considerable glory on Bovary.

Possessing such a wife, Charles came to have an increased respect for himself. In the living-room he would point with pride to two little pencil drawings of hers, which he had had mounted in very large frames and hung up on the wall with long green cords. As you came out of Mass you could see him at his door wearing a handsome pair of embroidered slippers.

Sometimes he came home late, at ten or even twelve o'clock. He would want something to eat, and as the maid had gone to bed, Emma looked after him. He took off his frock-coat to eat his meal in comfort, and told her all the people he had met, the villages he had been to, the prescriptions he had written. Then, well pleased with himself, he finished up the onion stew, pared the rind from his cheese, munched an apple, emptied the decanter, and took himself off to bed, where he lay down on his back and started snoring.

Having long been used to a night-cap, he couldn't make his new silk handkerchief stay on, and in the morning his hair would be flopping down all over his face, white with feathers from the pillow, which came untied during the night. Every day he wore heavy boots, which had two deep creases at the instep slanting up to the ankle, while the remainder of the upper went quite straight as though stretched on a shoe-tree. He said they were 'quite good enough for the country'; and his mother approved his thrift. She still came to see him whenever there was an outbreak of some violence at home. The elder Madame Bovary seemed, however, to be prejudiced against her daughter-in-law, who had 'ideas above her station in life', and ran away with 'enough firewood and sugar and candles for a mansion' – Why, the amount of coal burning in the kitchen would have done to cook dinner for twenty-five! She tidied the linen in the cupboards, and taught Emma to keep a check on the butcher when he brought the meat. Emma bowed to her wisdom; Madame Bovary was lavish with it. And all day long the words 'Mother' and 'Daughter' went to and fro, accompanied by little quiverings of the lips, as each of them delivered soft speeches in a voice that trembled with anger.

In Madame Dubuc's day the older woman had felt herself still the favourite. But now she saw in Charles' love for Emma a kind of defection from her own love, an encroaching on something that was hers, and she observed her son's happiness in gloomy silence, like a ruined man gazing through the windows at people dining in his old home. In reminiscent fashion, she recounted her troubles and sacrifices in the past, compared them with Emma's thoughtlessness, and concluded that to worship her so exclusively as he did was contrary to reason.

Charles didn't know what to say. He respected his mother; and he utterly adored his wife. The one he regarded as having an infallible judgement, yet he could find nothing to reproach in the other. When the elder Madame Bovary left, he timidly ventured to pass on, in the very words she used, one or two of her more innocuous criticisms. Emma quickly showed him his mistake and packed him off to his patients.

Despite everything, she tried, according to theories she considered sound, to make herself in love. By moonlight in the garden she used to recite to him all the love poetry she knew, or to sing with a sigh slow melancholy songs. It left her as unmoved as before, neither did it appear to make Charles more loving or more emotional.

Having thus plied the flint for a while without striking a single spark from her heart; being, moreover, as incapable of understanding what she had not experienced as she was of believing in anything that did not present itself in the accepted forms, she had no difficulty in persuading herself that there was nothing very startling now about Charles' passion for her. His ardours had lapsed into a routine, his embraces kept fixed hours; it was just one more habit, a sort of dessert he looked forward to after the monotony of dinner.

A game-keeper, whom he had cured of inflammation of the lungs, had given the doctor's wife a young Italian greyhound, which she used to take out for walks with her; for she did go out sometimes, to get a moment's solitude away from the eternal garden and the dusty road. She went to the beech-copse at Banneville, where the derelict summer-house stands at the turn of the wall facing the fields, and among the grasses in the ditch are some long rushes with knife-edged leaves.

First she cast a glance all round to see if there were any change since last she was there. She found the foxgloves and wallflowers in their places, the nettles still growing round the big stones, and the patches of lichen spreading along the three windows, whose shutters, always closed, were rotting away on their rusty iron bars. At first her mind roved aimlessly hither and thither, like her greyhound, which went circling over the grass, yapping after the yellow butterflies, giving chase to the field-mice or nibbling the poppies on the edge of a cornfield. Then gradually her thoughts took focus. Sitting on the grass, poking at the turf with the point of her sunshade, Emma said over and over again: 'O God, O God, why did I get married?'

If matters had fallen out differently, she wondered, might she not have met some other man? She tried to picture to herself the things that might have been – that different life, that unknown husband. For they weren't all like this one. He might have been handsome, intelligent, distinguished, attractive, as were no doubt the men her old school friends had married. ... What would *they* be doing now? Living in town, amid the noise of the streets, the hum of the theatre crowd, the bright lights of the ballroom – the sort of life that opens the heart and the senses like flowers in bloom. Whereas for her, life was cold as an attic facing north, and the silent spider boredom wove its web in all the shadowed corners of her heart.

She remembered prize-giving days at the convent, going up on the platform to receive the little crowns. In her white frock and open prunella shoes, with her hair in plaits, she looked a winsome child, and as she made her way back to her seat the gentlemen would lean over and say pretty things to her; the yard outside was packed with carriages, people said good-bye to her out of carriage windows, the music-master waved to her as he passed with his violin case ... How far, far away it all was!

She called Djali, took the dog between her knees, and stroked its long, delicate head.

'Come, kiss mistress! *You* haven't got any troubles!'

Then as she observed the yawn slowly forming on the graceful animal's melancholy features, she felt touched; likening it to herself, she spoke to it aloud, as though to a sufferer in need of consolation.

Sometimes a wind would blow up, a sea-breeze that came sweeping straight over the plateau of the Caux country bringing its salt freshness far inland. The rushes whistled along the ground, the beech-leaves shook with a rapid shivering, the tree-tops swayed ceaselessly to and fro with a high continuous murmur. Emma drew her shawl about her and rose to go.

The trees in the avenue shed down a dim green light on the smooth moss that crackled softly beneath her feet. The sun was setting, the sky showed red between the branches; the tree trunks, in a straight line, all alike, looked like a brown colonnade standing out on a gold ground. She felt a thrill of fear, called Djali, hurried back to Tostes along the highroad, sank into an armchair and said nothing the whole evening.

But towards the end of September something quite exceptional befell her: she received an invitation to La Vaubyessard, the home of the Marquis d'Andervilliers.

The Marquis had been Secretary of State under the Restoration, and was now making an attempt to re-enter political life. He was preparing for the parliamentary elections by de-

vious methods, with a great many distributions of firewood in
the winter and passionate demands at the General Assembly
for more and more roads in his constituency. At midsummer
he had developed an abscess in the mouth, and Charles effected
an apparently miraculous cure with a timely touch of the
lancet. The steward who was sent to Tostes to pay for the
operation reported the same evening that he had seen some
magnificent cherries in the doctor's little garden. Now the
cherry-trees were not doing well at La Vaubyessard, and so
the Marquis sent Bovary a request for some cuttings, and
afterwards made a point of coming to thank him in person. He
saw Emma, and noted that she had an attractive figure and
gave him no peasantwoman's curtsey. Accordingly it was considered at the château that it would neither overstep the
bounds of condescension nor cause any embarrassment to the
young couple to send them an invitation.

One Wednesday at three o'clock, Monsieur and Madame
Bovary set out in their dog-cart for La Vaubyessard, with a
big trunk roped on behind and a hat-box placed on the platform. Charles had a bandbox between his legs as well.

They arrived at nightfall, as the lamps were being lit to
guide the carriages through the park.

8

THE château, a modern building in the Italian style with two
projecting wings and three flights of steps in front of it,
sprawled at the bottom end of a wide stretch of parkland,
where cows grazed between ordered clumps of tall trees, and
an assortment of green shrubs, rhododendron, syringa and
guelder-rose, bulged out unevenly over the winding gravel
drive. A stream ran under a bridge, and through the mist you
could detect thatched buildings dotted about over the grassland, which was bounded on either side by a gently rising

wooded slope, while among the groves behind the house, in two parallel lines, stood the coach-houses and stables, all that remained of the old château that had been pulled down.

Charles drove up to the middle flight of steps. Servants appeared. The Marquis came forward, offered his arm to the doctor's wife, and led her inside.

The hall was lofty, paved with marble, and it echoed footsteps and voices like a church. Facing the entrance was a straight staircase; on the left, overlooking the garden, a balcony led to the billiard-room, where the click of ivory balls met you as you opened the door. As she went through to the drawing-room, Emma saw round the table a group of dignified-looking gentlemen with cravats high up round their chins, all wearing decorations, and smiling silently as they made their stroke. On the dark wood panelling hung large gilt frames with names in black lettering on their lower borders. She read: 'Jean Antoine d'Andervilliers d'Yverbonville, Comte de la Vaubyessard and Baron de la Fresnaye, killed at the Battle of Coutras, 20th October 1587.' On another: 'Jean Antoine Henry Guy d'Andervilliers de la Vaubyessard, Admiral of France and Knight of the Order of St Michael, wounded in the battle at La Hougue St Waast, 29th May 1692, died at La Vaubyessard 23rd January 1693.' The ones that followed were barely discernible, for the lamplight was directed on to the green baize of the billiard-table, and cast round the rest of the room a flickering radiance that mellowed the hanging canvases and broke into delicate streaks where it fell on the cracks in the varnish. On all those great dark gold-framed rectangles were patches of paint that stood out brighter – a pale forehead, a pair of eyes that looked straight at you, red coats with perukes flowing down over powdery shoulders, the buckle of a garter above a plump calf.

The Marquis opened the door into the drawing-room. One of the ladies rose; it was the Marchioness. She came forward to greet Emma, took her to sit beside her on an ottoman, and began talking as freely as if they were old friends. She was a woman of forty or so, with fine shoulders, a hooked nose and a drawling voice. Over her auburn hair she was wearing to-night a simple lace neckerchief that came down in a point at the back. A fair-haired young woman sat on a high-backed chair nearby, and round the fireplace gentlemen with little flowers in their button-holes stood talking to the ladies.

Dinner was at seven. The men, who were in the majority, sat down at the first table in the hall, the ladies at the second, in the dining-room, with their host and hostess.

As she went in, Emma felt herself plunged into a warm atmosphere compounded of the scent of flowers and of fine linen, of the savour of meat and the smell of truffles. The candles in the chandeliers glowed on the silver dish-covers with elongated flames. The pieces of cut glass had steamed over, and reflected a dull glimmer from one to the other. Bunches of flowers were set in a row down the whole length of the table, and on the wide-rimmed plates stood serviettes folded in the form of a bishop's mitre, each with an oval-shaped roll inside the fold. The red claws of the lobsters lay over the edge of the dishes. Luscious fruits were piled on moss in open baskets. The quails still had their feathers on them. The fumes rose. Solemn as a judge in his silk stockings and knee-breeches, his white cravat and frilled shirt, the major-domo handed the dishes, ready carved, between the guests' shoulders, and flicked the piece you chose on to your plate with his spoon. On the big porcelain stove with its copper rod, a statue of a woman draped to the chin stared fixedly at the roomful of people.

Madame Bovary noticed that several of the ladies had not put their gloves in their glasses.

At the top end of the table, alone among all these women, sat one aged man, crouched over his plate, with his serviette tied round his neck like a bib, dribbling gravy as he ate. His eyes were bloodshot, and he wore a little pigtail wound round with black ribbon. This was the Marquis' father-in-law, the old Duc de Laverdière, once favourite of the Comte d'Artois, in the days of the Marquis de Conflans' hunting-parties at La Vaudreuil; he was said to have been the lover of Marie Antoinette, between Messieurs de Coigny and de Lauzun. He had filled his life with riot and debauch, with duels, wagers and abductions; had squandered his wealth and been the terror of his family. He pointed to the dishes, mumbling, and a footman stationed behind him named them aloud in his ear. Emma's eyes kept turning in spite of themselves towards that old man with the drooping lips, as though to some august curiosity. He had lived at Court, had lain in the Queen's bed!

Iced champagne was served. Emma shivered all over at the cold taste of it in her mouth. She had never seen pomegranates before, or tasted a pineapple. Even the castor sugar looked finer and whiter than elsewhere.

After dinner the ladies went upstairs to get ready for the ball.

Emma dressed with the meticulous care of an actress making her début. She did her hair in the style her hairdresser had recommended, and put on her muslin dress, which had been laid out on the bed. Charles' trousers were too tight for him round his stomach.

'And these straps will be awkward for dancing,' he said.

'Dancing?' said Emma.

'Yes!'

'Why, you must be off your head! They'd laugh at you! You stay in your seat! It's not quite the thing for a doctor to dance, anyhow,' she added.

Charles relapsed into silence, then started pacing up and down, waiting for Emma to finish dressing.

He watched her from behind, in the mirror, between the two candles. Her black eyes looked blacker than ever. The braids of her hair, gently curving over her ears, had a rich blue lustre upon them, and in her chignon was a rose, trembling on its fragile stem, with artificial dewdrops at the tips of the leaves. Her dress was a pale saffron set off by three bunches of pompon roses and a spray of green. Charles came to kiss her on the shoulder.

'Let me alone!' she said. 'You'll rumple me.'

They heard a flourish from a violin, then the note of a horn. She descended the stairs, resisting an impulse to run.

The dancing had started. Guests were arriving, and the hall was crowded. She sat down on a little settee just inside the door.

When the quadrille was over, the floor was left to the men, who stood talking in groups, and the liveried servants bringing round large trays. Along the row of seated women went a fluttering of painted fans. Smiling faces were half hidden behind bouquets, gold-stoppered scent-bottles twirled in cupped hands whose white gloves showed the outline of finger-nails and pinched the flesh at the wrist. Lace frills, diamond brooches, medallion bracelets, trembled on their bodices, gleamed on their breasts, jingled on their bare arms. On their hair, which was stuck down firmly on their foreheads and coiled up at the nape of the neck, were forget-me-nots, jasmine, pomegranate-blossom, wheatears or cornflowers, in garlands, bunches or sprays. Red turbans crowned the wry-faced matrons who sat immovably in their seats.

Emma's heart beat a little faster when, her partner holding her by the tips of her fingers, she took her place in line and waited for the sweep of the fiddler's bow to start them off. Her nervousness soon vanished, and away she went, swaying to the rhythm of the orchestra, gently nodding her head as she glided forward. A smile rose to her lips at certain subtleties from the violin, playing solo. When the rest of the instruments were silent, you could hear the gold coins clinking on the baize tables in the next room. Then they all joined in again, the cornet blew a rousing blast, the dancers picked up the time, skirts swelled out and brushed together, hands were caught and released, eyes that lowered before you came back again to fix themselves on yours.

Scattered among the dancers, or talking in the doorways, were some dozen or more men, of twenty-five to forty, who were distinguishable from the rest of the crowd by a family likeness, which cut across all differences of age, dress or appearance. Their coats looked better cut, from finer cloth, and their hair, brought forward over the forehead in ringlets, seemed to glisten with more delicate pomades. They had the complexion of wealth, that clear white skin which is accentuated by the pallor of porcelain, the shimmer of satin, the 'finish' on handsome furniture, and is maintained at its best by a modest diet of the most exquisite foods. Their necks moved freely in low cravats, their long side-whiskers rested upon turn-down collars, the handkerchiefs with which they wiped their lips were embroidered with large monograms and emitted a delicious scent. The older among them retained a youthful air, while the young ones revealed a certain maturity. Their nonchalant glances reflected the quietude of passions daily gratified; behind their gentleness of manner one could detect that peculiar brutality inculcated by dominance in not over-exacting activities such as exercise strength and flatter vanity – the handling of thoroughbreds and the pursuit of wantons.

A few paces from Emma, a gentleman in a blue coat was talking about Italy to a pale young woman with an ornament of pearls. They extolled the size of the pillars in St Peter's; then Tivoli and Vesuvius, Castellamare and the Cascine, the roses of Genoa and the Coliseum by moonlight. With her other ear, Emma was listening to a conversation full of words she didn't understand. In the centre of a group was a youth who the week before had beaten Miss Arabella and Romulus and won two thousand pounds jumping a ditch in England. One man complained about his racers getting fat, another of the way the printers had garbled his horse's name.

It was stuffy in the ballroom. The lamps were dimming. There was a general movement into the billiard-room. A servant climbing up on a chair broke a couple of window-panes; at the sound of the glass smashing, Madame Bovary turned, and caught sight of some peasants outside, with their faces pressed to the window. It reminded her of Les Bertaux: she saw the farmhouse and the muddy pond, her father in his smock beneath the apple-trees, and herself back in the dairy again, skimming cream off the milk with her fingers. But her past life, till now so clear in her mind, had begun to slip right away from her amid the splendours of the present moment; she could not be quite sure it had ever happened. Here she was, at the ball. Outside, over everything else, hung a dark veil. She was eating a maraschino ice, holding the silver-gilt shell in her hand, half-closing her eyes as she put the spoon to her lips.

A lady sitting near her dropped her fan as a gentleman passed.

'Would you be so kind, sir,' said she, 'as to pick up my fan from behind this sofa?'

The gentleman bowed, and as he reached for the fan Emma saw the young lady's hand drop a little white triangular object into his hat. He retrieved the fan and presented it to her respectfully. She inclined her head in thanks and buried her nose in her bouquet.

After supper – at which Spanish wines and Rhine wines flowed freely, accompanied by shell-fish soup and milk-of-almond soup, Trafalgar puddings, and every variety of cold meat, in trembling aspic – the carriages began to move off in ones and twos. If you drew aside the edge of the muslin curtain you could see the lamps gliding away into the darkness. The settees emptied; but some of the card-players still sat on. The musicians moistened the tips of their fingers on their tongues. Charles leaned against a door, half-asleep.

At three in the morning the cotillion began. Emma didn't

know how to waltz. Everyone was waltzing, Mademoiselle d'Andervilliers herself, and the Marchioness. There remained now only the dozen guests who were staying the night at the château.

One of the men, who was familiarly addressed as 'Viscount' and wore a very low-cut waistcoat that looked as if it had been moulded upon him, came up and repeated his request to Madame Bovary, promising to guide her, and insisting that she would manage it successfully.

They started slowly, then got faster. They turned, and everything turned round them – the lamps and chairs, the panelling, the parquet floor – like a disc on a pivot. As they swept past a door, Emma's skirt swirled out against her partner's trousers. Their legs intertwined. He looked down at her and she looked up at him; a numb feeling came over her, she stopped still. Then they were off again, and the Viscount whirled her away still faster, till they were out of sight at the end of the gallery. She was panting for breath, she nearly fell, for an instant she leaned her head on his chest. Still turning, but more gently, he brought her back to her seat. She sank back against the wall and covered her eyes with her hands.

When she opened them again, there was a lady sitting on a footstool in the centre of the floor, with three gentlemen kneeling at her feet; she chose the Viscount, and the violin struck up again.

All eyes were upon them. Round and round they went, she holding her body quite stiff, with her head lowered, he all the while in the same pose, shoulders square, elbow rounded, chin well forward. And how that woman could waltz! They went on and on, and tired out everyone else.

After a few more minutes' conversation, the house-party said good-night, or rather good-morning, and went to bed.

Charles dragged himself upstairs clinging to the banisters; his legs were ready to drop off. He had been standing upright by the whist-tables for five hours on end, watching the play without knowing what it was all about; and it was with a deep sigh of relief that he pulled off his boots.

Emma slipped a shawl over her shoulders, opened the window and leaned out.

It was a dark night. A few drops of rain were falling. She breathed the moist wind, and felt it cool on her eyelids. The dance music was still strumming in her ears. She strained to keep awake and so prolong the spell of this luxurious life she must so soon abandon.`

Day began to break. She looked long at the windows of the château, trying to guess where abouts all the people were whom she had noticed during the evening. She would have liked to know all about them, to enter into their lives, become involved in them.

But she was shivering with cold. She undressed and huddled up against Charles, who was already asleep.

There was a large party at breakfast, which lasted only ten minutes, and at which no liqueurs were served, to the doctor's surprise. Afterwards Mademoiselle d'Andervilliers gathered up the remains of the rolls in a basket and took them to the swans in the lake, while the guests strolled round the greenhouses, where fantastic bristly plants rose up in pyramids beneath hanging vases which, with their long green intertwining tendrils falling over the edge, looked like overcrowded snakes'-nests. From the orangery at the far end a covered way led to the outhouses. To amuse the young woman, the Marquis took her to look at the stables. Above the basket-shaped racks porcelain slabs gave the names of the horses in black lettering. Each of the animals stirred in its stall as you went past and clicked your tongue. The boards of the saddle-room glittered to the eye like a parquet floor. The coach harness stood in the middle on two revolving posts, and bits and whips and stirrups and curbs were arrayed along the wall.

Meanwhile Charles went to ask one of the grooms to put

his horse to. The trap was brought round to the front, and when all the luggage had been stowed in, the Bovarys took leave of their host and hostess, and set off for home.

Emma sat silent, watching the wheels go round. Charles, perched right on the edge of the seat, drove with the reins held wide apart, and the little horse ambled gently along in the shafts, which were too wide for it. The slack reins jogging against its rump grew wet with foam, and the box roped on behind kept up a steady bumping against the body of the trap.

They had reached the high ground at Thibourville when suddenly a number of horsemen appeared in front of them and passed by, laughing, with cigars in their mouths. Emma thought she recognized the Viscount. She turned and looked back, but all she saw against the sky was a group of heads bobbing up and down in the varying tempo of trot or gallop.

A mile further on the breech-band snapped, and they had to stop and tie it together.

As he was giving the harness a final glance, Charles noticed something lying on the ground between the horse's feet. He picked up a cigar-case, with a green silk border all round it and a coat of arms in the centre, like a carriage-door.

'A couple of cigars inside, too,' he said. 'They'll do for after dinner tonight.'

'You smoke, then?' she asked.

'Sometimes. When I get the chance.'

He pocketed his find and whipped up the nag.

When they reached home, dinner was not ready. Madame flew into a rage. Nastasie answered back.

'Leave the room!' said Emma. 'The impertinence! You're dismissed!'

For dinner there was onion soup and a piece of veal cooked with sorrel. Charles, seated opposite Emma, rubbed his hands together gleefully.

'It's good to be home again!' he said.

They could hear Nastasie crying. The poor old girl had

kept him company many a long evening after his first wife died, and he was fond of her. She was his first patient and oldest acquaintance in the place.

'Have you really given her notice?' he said at last.

'Yes. Why shouldn't I?'

They warmed themselves in the kitchen while the bedroom was being got ready. Charles lit one of the cigars; he smoked with his lips rounded, spitting at each instant, recoiling at every puff.

'You'll make yourself ill,' she said scornfully.

Suddenly he put the cigar down and ran out to swallow a glass of cold water at the pump. Emma snatched up the cigar-case and hurled it to the back of the cupboard.

The next day went, oh, so slowly! She walked round the garden, up and down the same few paths, stopping in front of the flower-beds or the fruit-wall or the plaster *curé*, staring in bewilderment at all these old familiar things. How far away the ball seemed already! Why should there be such a gulf between Wednesday morning and Friday evening? The visit to La Vaubyessard had made a gap in her life, like those great chasms that a mountain-storm will sometimes scoop out in a single night. But she resigned herself to the inevitable. Reverently she put away in the chest of drawers her lovely dress and her satin slippers, the soles of which were yellowed with the wax from the dance floor. Her heart was like that. Contact with riches had left upon it a coating that would never wear off.

And so it gave Emma something to do, to think about the ball. Each time Wednesday came round she woke saying to herself, 'A week ago ... Two weeks ago ... Three weeks ago, I was there!' Gradually faces blurred in her memory, she forgot the dance tunes, no longer saw the liveried servants and the big rooms so clearly: some of the details vanished, but her yearning for it all remained.

9

OFTEN, when Charles was out, she used to go to the cupboard and take the green silk cigar-case from between the folds of the linen where she had hidden it.

She looked at it, opened it, sniffed the scent of the lining, a blend of verbena and tobacco. Whose could it be? The Viscount's! A present, perhaps, from his mistress, embroidered on some rosewood frame, a little treasure hidden from all eyes; the work of many hours, overhung by the soft curls of the pensive needlewoman. Love had breathed through the meshes of the canvas; every stitch had fastened there a yearning or a memory; and all those interwoven threads of silk were but a projection of that same silent passion. Then one morning the Viscount had taken it away with him. What words had been spoken, as it rested on the broad mantelpiece between the flower vases and the Pompadour clocks? ... She was at Tostes now; he was far away in Paris. Why 'Paris'? Such a mighty name. She said it over to herself half-aloud, just for the sound of it. It dinned in her ears like a great cathedral bell, it flamed before her eyes on the labels of her jars of cream.

She used to wake up at night when the fish-carriers passed under her window singing the *Marjolaine*, and as she listened to the sound of their metalled wheels, soon muffled by the soil as they left the village behind, she said to herself, 'Tomorrow they will be there!'

She followed them in her mind's eye, up hill and down dale, passing through villages, trundling along the highroad in the starlight. After going some distance, there was always a vague blur where her imagination failed.

She bought a guide to Paris and traced her way about the capital with the tip of her finger, walking up the boulevards, stopping at every turning along the lines of the streets and at the white squares indicating houses. Eventually she closed her tired eyes, and then in the darkness she saw gas-jets flickering in the wind, carriage-steps being let down with a great clatter at theatre entrances.

She started taking the women's papers *Work-basket* and *Sylph of the Salon*, devouring in their entirety all the accounts of first nights, race-meetings and parties, and becoming interested in a singer making her début or a shop that was being opened. She knew all the latest fashions, where to find the best tailors, the days for going to the Bois or the Opéra. She studied descriptions of furniture in Eugène Sue, and sought in Balzac and George Sand a vicarious gratification of her own desires. She even brought her book to the dinner-table, and turned over the pages while Charles ate and talked. Her memories of the Viscount always came back to her as she read. She invented relations between him and the fictional characters. But the circle of which he was the centre widened gradually about him, and the radiance of his halo was diffused upon other dreams.

So Paris swam before her eyes, like a shifting ocean glimmering through a rose-coloured haze. The teeming life that moved amid its tumult could, nevertheless, be divided and classified into separate scenes. Of these Emma saw only two or three, which shut out the rest, and represented, for her, the whole of humanity. Upon glittering parquet floors, in drawing-rooms panelled with mirrors, around oval tables covered with gold-fringed velvet cloths, stepped the ambassadorial world: here were dresses with long trains, here were high mysteries, here was anguish concealed by a smile. Next came the world of duchesses, where you looked pale and rose at four, where the women, poor angels, wore petticoats hemmed with English point, and the men – unacknowledged geniuses beneath their futile exteriors – rode horses to death for an afternoon's entertainment, spent the season at Baden, and ended up by marrying heiresses round about forty. Then there were the private rooms in restaurants where you went for supper after midnight with a motley crowd of writers and actresses, all laughing in the candlelight, who were prodigal as kings, full of idealistic ambitions and fantastical frenzies. Theirs was a higher life, 'twixt heaven and earth, amid the storm-clouds, touched with the sublime. The rest of the world came nowhere, had no proper status, no real existence. In fact, the nearer home things came, the more she shrank from all thought of them. The whole of her immediate environment — dull countryside, imbecile petty bourgeois, life in its ordinariness — seemed a freak, a particular piece of bad luck that had seized on her; while beyond, as far as eye could see, ranged the vast lands of passion and felicity. In her longing, she confounded gilded sensuality with heart's delight, elegance of manner with delicacy of feeling. Was not love like an Indian plant, requiring a prepared soil, a special temperature? Sighs in the moonlight, long embraces, hands at parting bathed with tears, all the fevers of the flesh and the languid tenderness of love — these could not be separated from the balconies of stately mansions, the life of leisure, the silk-curtained boudoir with a good thick carpet, full flower-bowls and a bed on a raised dais, nor from the sparkle of precious stones and shoulder-knots on servants' livery.

The lad from the posting-house, who came to groom the mare every morning, went clumping down the passage in his heavy wooden shoes, with his feet showing out of his list slippers, and holes in his blouse; there went the 'groom in knee-breeches' with whom she must be content! His work done, he left for the day. Charles, when he got home, used to unharness, unsaddle and tether his horse himself, while the maid brought a bundle of straw and heaved it up as best she could on to the rack.

To replace Nastasie, who eventually left Tostes in a flood of tears, Emma engaged a girl of fourteen, a sweet-faced orphan. She forbade the child to wear cotton caps, instructed her in the necessity of addressing one in the third person, serving a glass of water on a plate and knocking on doors before entering, taught her to iron, and starch, and dress her mistress, and tried to make a lady's-maid out of her. To keep the job, the new girl obeyed without a murmur ... And since Madame was in the habit of leaving the key in the sideboard, Félicité used to take a little supply of sugar up to bed with her every night, to eat all by herself after she had said her prayers.

Sometimes of an afternoon, while her mistress was upstairs, she went across and chatted with the postillions.

Emma sat in her room, her dressing-gown wrapped loosely about her, showing a frilled chemisette with three gold buttons between the trimmings of her bodice. Round her waist she had a corded girdle with big tassels, and on her little garnet-coloured slippers were two bunches of broad ribbon falling over the instep. She had bought herself a blotting-pad, writing-case, pen-holder and envelopes, though she had no one to write to. She dusted the shelves, looked at herself in the glass, picked up a book, then started dreaming between the lines and let it drop into her lap. She longed to travel – or to go back to the convent. She wanted to die, and she wanted to live in Paris.

Charles trotted across country in rain and snow. He ate omelettes at farmhouse tables, poked his arm into damp beds, let blood and caught the warm spirt of it in his face, listened to death-rattles, examined basins, tucked in a great many dirty sheets. But every evening he came home to a blazing fire and supper waiting, to a comfortable chair and a neat, attractive wife with a fresh fragrance that made you wonder where it came from, and whether it wasn't her skin that scented her petticoat.

She delighted him with a number of refinements. Now it would be a new way of making paper sconces for the candles, now the altering of a flounce on her dress, or an extraordinary name for some quite ordinary dish which the maid had spoiled but which Charles devoured happily to the last mouthful. She saw some ladies in Rouen carrying bunches of trinkets on their watches; she bought some trinkets. She wanted a pair of big blue glass vases to go on the mantelpiece, and then, some while later, an ivory workbox with a silver-gilt thimble. The less Charles understood of these pretty things, the more they appealed to him. They were a further contribution to the pleasure of his senses and the comfort of his fireside, a kind of gold-dust sprinkled all along the narrow pathway of his life.

He looked well and felt well, and his reputation was firmly established. The countryfolk were drawn to him by his unassuming manner. He patted the children on the head, kept away from the pub, and inspired confidence by his straight dealing. He was particularly successful with catarrh and chest complaints. Being scared of killing his clients, he in fact rarely prescribed anything but sedatives, with an occasional emetic, a foot-bath, or leeches. Not that he shrank from surgical treatment: he'd bleed people like horses, and had the 'devil of a grip' for pulling out teeth.

Finally, to 'keep up with things', he took out a subscription to *Medical Post*, a new paper that had sent him its prospectus. He read a bit of it after dinner. But the food inside him, and the warmth of the room, combined to send him to sleep in five minutes, and there he sprawled, with his chin on his hands, his shock of hair flopping down over the lamp-stand. Emma looked at him and shrugged her shoulders. Why hadn't she at any rate one of those silent, earnest husbands who work at their books all night – and end up, by the time that rheumatism sets in at sixty, wearing a string of decorations on their ill-fitting dress-coats! She would have liked this name of Bovary, that was hers, to be famous, on view at the bookshops, always cropping up in the papers, known all over France. But Charles had no ambition. A colleague from Yvetot with whom he had lately conferred on a case had humiliated him at the patient's very bedside, before the assembled relatives. When he told her about it that night, Emma got very angry with the man; Charles was touched, and kissed her on the forehead, a tear in his eye. She was mortified, she felt like hitting him. She ran out into the passage, opened the window and took a breath of fresh air to calm her.

'What a poor creature! what a poor creature!' she muttered, biting her lip.

She was getting generally more irritated with him. As he grew older he became grosser in his ways. He used to whittle down the corks of the empty bottles during dessert. He sucked his teeth after eating. When he drank soup he made a gulping noise at every mouthful. And now that he had begun to put on weight, his puffy cheeks seemed to be pushing his eyes, which had always been small, right up into his temples.

Emma used sometimes to tuck the red border of his undervest inside his waistcoat, or straighten his cravat, or throw away a shabby pair of gloves that he was about to put on. She did these things not, as he imagined, for his sake, but for her own, in an outburst of egoism, a nervous irritation. And sometimes she told him what she had been reading – a passage in a novel, a new play, or a bit of society gossip retailed in her paper. Charles was someone to talk to, after all – an ever-open ear, an ever-ready approbation. She confided quite enough in her greyhound! She would have confided in the logs in the fireplace, or the pendulum of the clock.

And all the time, deep within her, she was waiting for something to happen. Like a shipwrecked sailor she scanned her solitude with desperate eyes for the sight of a white sail far off on the misty horizon. She had no idea what that chance would be, what wind would waft it to her, where it would set her ashore, whether it was a launch or a three-decker, laden with anguish or filled to the portholes with happiness. But every morning when she woke she hoped to find it there. She listened to every sound, started out of bed, and was surprised when nothing came. Then at sunset, sadder every day, she longed for the morrow.

Spring came round, and with the warmer weather, while the pear-trees blossomed, she suffered from attacks of breathlessness.

As soon as it was July she began counting on her fingers how many weeks there were to October, fancying that the Marquis d'Andervilliers might be giving another ball at La Vaubyessard. September came and went without a letter or a visit.

After this dreary disappointment there was the same void in her heart again, and the succession of identical days began anew.

And so they would follow on, one after another, always the same; innumerable days that brought nothing. Other people, however drab their lives, could at least expect *something* to happen to them. One little episode would sometimes lead to endless turns of fortune and changes of scene. But for her there was nothing. Such was God's will. The future was an unlighted corridor with a stoutly locked door at the end of it.

She gave up playing the piano. What use, with no one to hear her? Since she could never play at a concert, in a short-sleeved velvet gown, lightly caressing the keys of an Erard and feeling the murmurs of ecstasy wafting all about her like a breeze – it wasn't worth the boredom of practising.

She let her drawing-folios and her needlework lie in the cupboard. What was the use? What was the use? Sewing got on her nerves.

'I've read everything,' she said to herself.

So she sat there holding the tongs in the fire or watching the rain fall.

How sad she was on Sundays when vespers rang! She listened in a trance to the cracked chimes falling one by one. On the roof opposite a cat stepped slowly, arching its back in the pale sunbeams. Along the highroad clouds of dust rose in the wind. Occasionally a dog howled in the distance. And the bell kept on tolling, a steady monotone that died away over the fields.

Then they came out of church, the women in polished clogs, the peasant-men in their new smocks, the little children skipping about bareheaded in front of them, all going home. Only the same half-dozen men would remain behind till nightfall playing 'corks' outside the front door of the inn.

The winter was a hard one. Every morning the window-panes were covered with rime, and looked liked ground-glass letting through a wan light that sometimes grew no brighter all day. The lamps had to be lit by four o'clock.

On fine days Emma went out into the garden. The dew left a silvery lace upon the cabbages, long transparent filaments hung from one to the other. No birds sang. Everything seemed asleep, the straw-covered espalier and the vine like a great sick serpent under the coping of the wall, where as one drew near one saw wood-lice crawling with innumerable feelers. Under the spruce-trees by the hedge the breviary-reading *curé* in the three-cornered hat had lost his right foot, and there were patches of white on his face where the plaster had peeled away with the frost.

She went upstairs again, locked her door, stoked up the fire, and in its overpowering warmth felt her boredom weigh yet more heavily upon her. She could have gone down to talk to the maid, but was restrained by a sense of propriety.

At the same hour every day the schoolmaster in his black silk skull-cap would fold back his shutters, the village policeman pass by with his sabre buckled over his blouse. Morning and evening the post-horses crossed the street in threes to water at the pond. Occasionally you heard the tinkle of a public-house door-bell, and when it was windy the little copper basins which formed the hairdresser's shop-sign were set creaking on their rods. The hairdresser's window display consisted of an old-fashioned plate stuck on the pane, and a

wax bust of a woman with yellow hair. The hairdresser likewise mourned a stunted career, a lost fortune, and all day long,
as he passed to and fro between the mayor's office and the
church, sombre, awaiting customers, he dreamed of a big shop
in a town – in Rouen, for instance, on the quayside, somewhere near the theatre. Whenever Madame Bovary raised her
eyes she saw him marching up and down like a guard on
sentry-go, clad in his woollen jacket, with his cap perched
over one ear.

Sometimes, of an afternoon, a swarthy black-whiskered face
would appear at the living-room window, smiling slowly with
a broad, soft grin that showed a set of white teeth. A waltz
immediately started up, and in a miniature drawing-room set
out on top of a barrel-organ, dancers the size of your finger –
women in pink turbans, Tyrolese peasants in jackets, monkeys
in frock-coats, gentlemen in knee-breeches – went circling
round and round amid armchairs, sofas and wall-tables, mirrored in fragments of looking-glass held together at the corners by strips of gold paper. As he turned the handle, the man
looked right and left and up at the windows. Occasionally he
shot a long stream of dark saliva at the kerbstone and lifted
the instrument on his knee, for its hard strap galled his
shoulder. And the music came grinding out, now long-drawn
and doleful, now quick and cheerful, through a pink taffeta
curtain held up by a copper clasp in arabesque. They were
tunes that were heard elsewhere – tunes played in the theatre,
sung in drawing-rooms, danced to at night beneath lighted
chandeliers – echoes reaching Emma from the great world outside. Sarabands unfolded endlessly in her brain. Like figures
of dancing-girls on a flowered carpet, her thoughts leapt with
the music, swinging from dream to dream, from sorrow to
sorrow. Having caught some pennies in his cap the man pulled
down an old blue cloth cover, slung his organ on his back and
stumped off. She followed him with her eyes.

It was at meal-times that her endurance was strained to the

furthest, in that little ground-floor living-room with its smoking stove, squeaking door, running walls and damp flagstones. She seemed to have all the bitterness of life served up
on her plate; the steam from the stew conjured up like fumes
of nausea from the depths of her soul. Charles was a slow
eater. She used to nibble a few nuts, or lean her elbow on the
table and beguile the time by tracing little lines on the oil-
cloth with the tip of her knife.

She let the house look after itself now, and the elder Madame Bovary, coming to spend part of Lent at Tostes, was
astonished at the change in her. She who had been once so
dainty and particular, now went all day without dressing properly, wore grey cotton stockings, and used tallow dips for
light. She kept saying that as they weren't rich they must be
thrifty, adding that she was very happy and contented and
liked Tostes very much: with other novel lines of talk that
silenced her mother-in-law. Moreover, Emma seemed no
longer inclined to follow her advice, and once when Madame
Bovary chose to maintain that masters and mistresses ought
to have an eye to their servants' religion, it brought such anger
to Emma's eyes and so cold a smile to her lips that the good
woman meddled no more.

Emma was growing capricious, hard to please. She ordered
dishes for herself and then left them untouched, drank nothing
but fresh milk one day and dozens of cups of tea the next. Often
she refused to go out, then felt stifled indoors and threw the
window open and put on a thin frock. After administering a
thorough scolding to the maid, she gave her a present or
packed her off to go and see the neighbours — just as she sometimes gave away all the silver in her purse to a beggar, though
she had little loving kindness and was not readily susceptible
to other people's emotions, any more than most people of
rustic origin, who retain for ever in their souls something of
their fathers' hornyhandedness.

Towards the end of February old Rouault came over with a

magnificent turkey, to commemorate his mended leg. He stayed three days at Tostes, and, Charles being busy with his patients, Emma kept him company. He smoked in the bedroom, spat into the grate, and chattered about farming, calves, cows, poultry, and the local council; so that when she finally shut the door on him it was with a feeling of relief that surprised herself. Not that she any longer concealed her contempt for anything or anyone. Sometimes she expressed peculiar opinions, censuring what was generally approved, and approving what was perverted or immoral: which made her husband stare at her wide-eyed.

Would this misery last for ever? Was there no escape? Was she not quite as good as all the lucky women? She had seen duchesses at La Vaubyessard with clumsier waists and commoner ways than she; she cursed the injustice of God. She propped her head against the wall and wept, for envy of those hectic lives, the shameless pleasure-seeking, the masked balls, and all the wild delights, unknown to her, that they must afford.

She grew pale, and had palpitations of the heart. Charles prescribed valerian and camphor-baths. Everything they tried seemed only to upset her.

Some days she prattled away with a feverish volubility, until suddenly her excitement would give place to a condition of torpor, in which she lay without speaking or stirring. She revived herself then by sprinkling a bottle of eau-de-Cologne over her arms.

As she was always complaining about Tostes, Charles imagined that there must be something in the locality to account for her illness. The idea grew on him, and he began seriously to think of going away and setting up elsewhere.

She then started taking vinegar to make herself slim, contracted a hard little cough and completely lost her appetite.

It was not easy for Charles to leave Tostes just as he had begun to get 'well in' after a stay of four years. Yet, if it must be ... ! He took her to Rouen to see his old master. Yes, her trouble was a nervous one, change of air was what she needed.

Charles cast about him and eventually heard of a substantial market-town in the Neufchâtel district, called Yonville-l'Abbaye, whose doctor, a Polish refugee, had decamped the previous week. He wrote to the chemist there asking him the size of the population, the distance from the nearest competitor, how much his predecessor had made in a year, and so on. The replies being satisfactory, he decided to move in the spring if Emma's health had not improved.

One day as she was tidying a drawer in preparation for her departure, she pricked her finger on something sharp. It was one of the wires of her wedding bouquet. The orange-blossom was yellow with dust, the silver-trimmed satin ribbon frayed at the edges. She tossed it into the fire. It flared up like dry straw. Then it looked like a red bush burning on the embers, slowly disintegrating. She watched it burn. The little cardboard berries popped, the wires twisted, the braid melted away and the shrivelled paper petals hovered like black butterflies at the back of the fireplace and finally vanished up the chimney.

When they left Tostes in March, Madame Bovary was pregnant.

PART TWO

YONVILLE-L'ABBAYE, so-called from an old Capucin abbey of which not a stone now stands, is a small town twenty-four miles from Rouen, between the Abbeville and the Beauvais roads, at the end of a valley watered by the Rieule, a little stream which works three water-mills before flowing into the Andelle and in which there are some trout that attract the lads with their fishing-rods on Sundays.

You leave the highroad at La Boissière and continue along the level until you reach the top of Leux Hill, where you come in full view of the valley. The river forms a dividing-line between two contrasting types of countryside, all pasture on the left, all arable on the right. The grassland stretches beneath a line of low hills to link up behind them with the grazing lands of Bray, while eastward the plain mounts gently, broadening out and flaunting its yellow cornfields as far as the eye can see. The water flowing along beside the grass makes a streak of white between the colour of the meadows and that of the ploughland, and the whole effect is of a large mantle spread out before you, its green velvet collar trimmed with silver braid.

When you reach the end of the valley, you come in sight of the oak-forest of Argueil and the escarpments of the Côte St Jean, scarred from top to bottom with irregular red lines; these are the rain-tracks, narrow streaks of a brick-red hue which stands out sharply against the grey of the mountain-side and is due to the great number of iron springs that flow through the surrounding region.

Here you are on the borders of Normandy, Picardy and the

Île de France, a bastard region whose speech is without accentuation as its scenery is without character. It is here that they make the worst Neufchâtel cheese in the whole district, while the soil is expensive to work, being crumbly, full of pebbles and sand, and needing a great deal of manure.

Until 1835 there was no proper road to Yonville, but about that date the local authorities built a by-road connecting the Abbeville and Amiens roads, which is sometimes used by wagoners from Rouen en route for Flanders. Nevertheless, despite its new outlets, Yonville-l'Abbaye has stood still. Instead of improving the soil, they cling to pasture, however depreciated its value; and the sleepy little town has turned its back on the plain and continued growing automatically in the direction of the river. You can see it a long way off, sprawled along the bank like a cowherd taking his siesta by the waterside.

At the foot of the hill, past the bridge, begins a causeway planted with young aspens which leads in a straight line to the first houses in the place. These are enclosed by hedges, and their yards are full of straggling outhouses, wine-presses, cart-sheds and distilleries dotted about beneath bushy trees amid whose branches ladders, poles and scythes are lodged. The thatched roofs, like fur caps pulled down over the eyes, hide nearly a third part of the low windows, which have thick bulging panes with a knot in the centre, like the bottom of a bottle. Against the plaster walls, diagonally crossed by black joists, leans an occasional sickly-looking pear-tree, and in the doorway is a low swing-gate to keep out the chicks that come to forage for brown bread-crumbs soaked in cider. As you go on, the yards get smaller, the houses closer together; the hedges disappear. A bundle of ferns swings on the end of a broomstick hanging down from a window. There is a blacksmith's forge, then a wheelwright's workshop, with two or three carts obstructing the roadway outside. Through an opening in the wall you see a white house with a circle of lawn in front, adorned by a Cupid with his finger on his lips, a pair of cast-iron urns standing on either side of the front steps, and a brilliant coat of arms over the door. This is the notary's house, the finest in the district.

The church is twenty yards farther along on the other side of the street, as you enter the market-place. The little grave-yard around it is enclosed by a wall elbow-high, and is so full of graves that the aged flagstones sunk into the ground form an unbroken pavement marked into regular squares by the green grass pushing its way up between. The church was re-built during the latter part of Charles X's reign. Rot has set in on top of the wooden roof, making hollow patches of black on its blue surface. Over the door, where the organ might be, is a gallery for the men, reached by a spiral staircase that re-sounds beneath their wooden shoes.

Daylight entering through the plain glass windows falls obliquely on the pews, which are set at right angles to the wall; and here and there on the wall, straw mats are nailed up with the words 'Mr —'s pew, in bold lettering underneath. Where the nave narrows farther down, the confessional box faces a little figure of the Virgin Mary, clad in a satin robe, with a tulle veil studded with silver stars on her head, and a rich crimson on her cheeks, like an idol from the Sandwich Islands. The view terminates in a picture of the Holy Family, 'presented by the Minister of the Interior', set above the high altar with four candlesticks around it. The choir stalls are of unpainted deal.

About half the big market-place at Yonville is taken up by the Market itself, which consists of a tiled roof supported by a score of pillars. The building like a Greek temple, in the corner next to the chemist's, is the Town Hall, built 'to the design of a Paris architect'. It has three Ionic pillars at ground level, a semicircular gallery on the first floor, and on top of that a pediment occupied by a Gallic cock resting one foot on the charter and holding the Scales of Justice in the other.

But what chiefly strikes the eye is Monsieur Homais the chemist's shop facing the 'Golden Lion'. At night time in particular, when his lamps shine through the big red and green glass jars that adorn his window, sending coloured rays far out over the square, you may get a glimpse, as though in Bengal lights, of the shadowy figure of the chemist bending over his desk. His house is placarded from top to bottom with advertisements in running hand, copper-plate or block capitals, for Vichy, Seltzer and Barèges waters, blood purifiers, Raspail's medicine, Arabian racahout, Darcet's pastilles, Regnault's ointment, bandages, fomentations, medicinal chocolate, and what not. His sign, taking up the whole breadth of the shop front, proclaims in gilt lettering 'Homais, Chemist'. At the back, behind the big scales screwed on to the counter, the word 'Laboratory' is inscribed above a glass door, which has another 'Homais' about half-way up in gold letters on a black ground.

And that is all there is to see at Yonville. The street – the only one – is about a gunshot in length, has a few shops on either side, and stops short at the bend of the road. If you leave it on your right and go along the bottom of St John's Hill, you come in a few minutes to the cemetery.

This was enlarged during the cholera epidemic by the removal of a section of the wall and the purchase of three acres of adjoining land. But this new section is almost entirely untenanted, the graves continuing as before to pile up towards the gate. The grave-keeper, who is also the sexton and verger – thus deriving a double benefice from deceased parishioners – has taken advantage of the empty piece of ground to plant potatoes there. His little plot narrows yearly, however, and when there is an epidemic he is not sure whether to be delighted at the deaths or pained at the burials.

'You live on the dead, Lestiboudois!' said the *curé* to him one day.

This grim remark brought him up short, set him thinking

awhile. To this day, however, he still continues to grow his tubers, coolly asserting that they come up of their own accord.

Nothing, in fact, has changed at Yonville since the events about to be recorded. The tinplate tricolour keeps turning on top of the church steeple, the draper's shop still waves its two calico streamers in the wind, the chemist's foetuses, like bundles of white tinder, rot steadily in their muddy alcohol, and above the big front door of the inn the weatherworn 'golden lion' still displays its poodle's mane to the passer-by.

On the evening when the Bovarys were due to arrive at Yonville, Widow Lefrançois, the landlady of the inn, was so busy that the sweat poured off her as she manoeuvred her saucepans. It was market-day next day, and the joints had to be carved overnight, the fowls drawn, the soup and coffee made. Then she had to get meals for her 'regulars', and for the doctor, his wife and their servant. The billiard-room rang with shouts of laughter. Three millers in the bar parlour were calling for brandy. The logs blazed, the coal crackled, and on the long kitchen-table, amid the joints of raw mutton, stood piles of plates that shook and rattled with every movement of the spinach-chopper. In the back-yard you could hear the chickens squawking as the servant-girl chased after them to wring their necks.

Warming his back at the fire was a man in green leather slippers, with a somewhat pock-marked face, and a gold-tasselled velvet cap on his head. His face expressed nothing but self-satisfaction; he had an air of being as much at peace with life as the goldfinch in the wicker cage above his head. This was the chemist.

'Artémise!' cried the landlady. 'Chop the sticks! Fill the jugs! Take 'em some brandy, look sharp! Now if only I knew what to give them for dessert, these people you've got coming ... Mercy on us, the moving-men are starting their racket in the billiard-room again! And their cart stuck right outside – why, the *Hirondelle* might come crashing into it. Shout for 'Polyte to put it up! Just fancy, Monsieur Homais, they must have played fifteen games since morning and put away eight jars of cider! ... They'll be tearing my cloth for me!' she added, watching them from a distance with her skimmer in her hand.

'No great harm if they did,' answered Monsieur Homais; 'you'd have to get a new one.'

'A new billiard-table!' exclaimed the widow.

'Yes. That one's coming to pieces, Madame Lefrançois. I've told you before, you're doing yourself no good, no good at all. Apart from anything else, they want narrow pockets and heavy cues nowadays. They don't play push-ball any more; everything's changed. You've got to keep up with the times! Look at Tellier, now ...'

The landlady flushed with resentment. The chemist went on:

'Say what you like, he's got a nicer little table than yours. Now just suppose they thought of getting up a match in aid of Poland, or the flood victims at Lyon. ... '

'We're not afraid of the likes of him!' the landlady interrupted, shrugging her fat shoulders. 'Get away with you, Monsieur Homais, as long as the Lion stands, the folks 'll come! We've got nothing to worry about! What you'll be seeing one of these fine mornings is the Café Français with the shutter up. ... New billiard-table!' she muttered, 'when it does so nicely for folding the washing, and 's slept half a dozen at shooting season! ... Oh that slow-coach Hivert!'

'Will you have to keep your gentlemen waiting for dinner?'

'Keep Monsieur Binet waiting? I ask you! On the stroke of six, in he comes, you'll see. There's not his like in this world for punctuality. He's always got to have his own place in the little room, he'd die sooner than eat his dinner anywhere else! And fussy! So particular about his cider! Not like Monsieur Léon, now: *he* comes in any time up to seven or half past, and never so much as looks at what he eats. A nice young man, he is. Never a sharp word for anyone!'

'There you have the difference between an educated man, and an old soldier turned tax-collector.'

The clock struck six. In came Binet.

He was clad in a blue frock-coat that hung straight down all round his spare frame, and a leather cap with ear-flaps fastened on top of his head, revealing beneath its turned-up peak a bald forehead flattened by years of wearing a helmet. He had on a black waistcoat, a horse-hair coat-collar, grey trousers, and – all the year round – a pair of highly polished boots with two parallel swellings where his toes turned up. Not a whisker was out of line in the fair beard that encircled his jaw like a herbaceous border, framing a long lack-lustre face with little eyes and hooked nose. He was a good shot, an expert at all card games, and he wrote a fine hand. He spent his time turning serviette-rings on a lathe which he had at his house, and these he hoarded with all the jealousy of the artist and the possessiveness of the bourgeois.

He made for the little parlour. First, however, the three millers had to be got out. Then he sat silent in his chair by the stove while they laid his place at the table. And then, as was his custom, he shut the door and took off his cap.

'Civility won't cost *him* his tongue!' said the chemist, when he and the landlady were left alone.

'You'll never get any more out of him,' she answered.'We had two cloth-travellers here last week, smart lads they were, told such a pack of yarns that night, I laughed till I cried! – What do you think – he sat there like an oyster and never said a word!'

'Quite so,' observed the chemist. 'No imagination, no sparkle, none of the social gifts!'

'Yet they say he's clever,' the landlady demurred.

'Clever?' exclaimed Homais. 'Him clever? ... Ah well, perhaps he is in his own line,' he added in a quieter tone.

He started off again:

'Now, if it were a business man in a big way, or a lawyer, a doctor, a chemist – I can understand their being so engrossed as to get eccentric, peevish even. Look at the stories in the history books! But then they've got other things to think about. Why, in my own case – the times I've searched my desk for my pen to write a label, only to find in the end that I'd put it behind my ear!'

As he spoke, Madame Lefrançois walked over to the door to see if the *Hirondelle* were in sight. She started as a man in black suddenly strode in. In the last glimmer of the fading light you could make out a ruddy face and an athletic frame.

'At your service, Monsieur le Curé!' said the landlady, reaching for one of the brass candlesticks ranged in line along the mantelpiece. 'What can I get you? A nip of cassis, a glass of wine?'

The priest very civilly declined. He had come for his umbrella, which he had left behind at the convent of Ernemont the other day. Having requested Madame Lefrançois to send it round to the vicarage during the evening, he left for the church, where the Angelus was ringing.

When the chemist could no longer hear his footsteps sounding in the square, he pronounced his behaviour to be most unmannerly. This refusal of a drink seemed to him a piece of abominable hypocrisy. All priests tippled on the sly, and were out to bring back the days of the tithe.

The landlady spoke up for her *curé*.

'He could break four of you across his knee, anyhow! He helped our people get in the straw last year, and he used to carry six bundles at a time, he's that strong!'

'Hurrah!' cried the chemist. 'There's a fine strapping lad to send your daughters to confess to! If I were the Government, I'd have all priests bled once a month: once every month, Madame Lefrançois, a generous phlebotomy, for the sake of law and order!'

'Hold your wicked tongue, Monsieur Homais! You've got no religion.'

'I have got a religion – my own religion,' the chemist answered, 'In fact I've got more than the lot of them, with all their mumbo-jumbo. – I worship God! I believe in the Supreme Being; a Creator, no matter who he be, who has placed us here below to do our duty as citizens and fathers. But I don't need to go and kiss a lot of silver-plate in a church, and support a pack of humbugs who live better than we do ourselves! You can praise God just as well in the woods and the fields, or by gazing up into the vault of heaven, like the ancients. My God is the God of Socrates, of Franklin, Voltaire and Béranger! I am for the *Savoyard Curate's Confession of Faith* and the immortal principles of '89! And I cannot worship an old fogey of a God who walks round his garden with a stick in his hand, lodges his friends in the bellies of whales, dies with a cry on his lips and comes to life again three days later: all of which is intrinsically absurd and utterly opposed, moreover, to all physical laws: which incidentally indicates that the priests have always wallowed in a shameful ignorance wherein they strive to engulf the peoples of the world along with them.'

The chemist paused and glanced round him for his audience, having for a moment imagined himself to be in possession of the floor at a council meeting. But the landlady was no longer listening to him. She was straining her ears to catch a rumbling sound in the distance: the rattle of a coach, the slip-slop of loose horseshoes striking the ground, and at long last the *Hirondelle* drove up to the door.

It was a yellow box mounted on two large wheels, which came up to the level of the tilt, spattering the passengers' shoulders and obstructing their view. Its narrow little windows rattled in their frames when the coach was closed, and showed patches of mud here and there on their ancient coating of dust, which was never washed quite clean even by a heavy rain-storm. It was drawn by three horses, two in the shafts and a leader, and when it went downhill its underside bumped on the ground.

Some of the citizens of Yonville appeared in the market-square. They all started talking at once, asking for news and explanations and game-baskets. Hivert didn't know where to begin. It was he who carried out the village's commissions in Rouen, going round the shops and bringing back rolls of leather for the shoemaker, iron for the blacksmith, a barrel of herrings for the inn, bonnets from the milliner's and tufts of hair from the hairdresser's. On the homeward journey he distributed parcels all the way along, standing up in his seat and shouting at the top of his voice as he hurled them over the garden walls, while the horses ambled along by themselves.

They had been delayed by a misadventure: Madame Bovary's greyhound had bolted across the fields. They spent a good fifteen minutes whistling for it, and Hivert even turned back a mile and a half, expecting to see it each minute. But at last they had had to come on. Emma had burst into tears and lost her temper. She said it was Charles' fault. One of her fellow passengers, Monsieur Lheureux the draper, tried to console her with various instances of long-lost dogs recognizing their masters. He had heard of one finding its way back to Paris from Constantinople. Another had gone a hundred and fifty miles in a straight line, swimming four rivers on the way. And his own father once owned a poodle which, after being away twelve years, suddenly jumped on his back in the street one evening as he was going out to dinner.

2

EMMA got out first, followed by Félicité, Monsieur Lheureux, and a wet-nurse. They had to rouse Charles out of his corner, where he had been sound asleep since darkness fell.

Homais introduced himself, presented his compliments to Madame, his respects to Monsieur, said he was delighted to have had the chance to be of service to them, and added affably that he had ventured to invite himself along, his wife being out.

Madame Bovary made for the kitchen fireplace. With the tips of her fingers she took hold of her dress at the knees, lifted it over her ankles and stretched out her black-booted foot to the fire, above the leg of mutton on the spit. The flames lit up her whole body. The texture of her dress, the smooth pores of her clear skin, even her eyelids, which she blinked from time to time, were penetrated by the glare; and when the wind blew in through the open door, a warm glow spread all over her.

On the other side of the fireplace a young man with fair hair stood watching her in silence.

Being very bored at Yonville, where he worked as a clerk at Maître Guillaumin's, Monsieur Léon Dupuis – he was the second of the 'regulars' at the Golden Lion – tended to dine late, in the hope of finding some passing visitor at the inn with whom to have an evening's conversation. But when he finished his work on time, there was nothing to do but to go there straight away and endure the company of Binet all through dinner. So it was with pleasure that he accepted the landlady's suggestion that he should join the new-comers tonight. To make an impression, Madame Lefrançois had laid a table for them in the big room, and thither the four of them now proceeded.

Homais begged leave to retain his skull-cap for fear of catching cold.

Then, turning to his neighbour:

'I expect you'll be a bit tired, Madame? That *Hirondelle* of ours bumps you about abominably.'

'That's true,' replied Emma, 'but I always enjoy a shaking-up. I like travelling.'

'It *is* so depressing,' sighed the clerk, 'to be tied to the same place.'

'If you were like me,' said Charles, 'constantly obliged to be in the saddle ... '

'Surely,' Léon broke in, addressing himself to Madame Bovary, 'nothing could be pleasanter — when one has the chance,' he added.

'As a matter of fact,' said the chemist, 'medical practice is not too arduous in these parts, for the roads are good enough for a trap, and in general you're paid pretty well, the farmers being comfortably off. Professionally speaking, apart from the usual cases of enteritis, bronchitis, bilious attacks and so on, we sometimes get intermittent fevers at harvest time, but on the whole there's not much of a serious nature, nothing especially worthy of note, unless it be a great deal of scrofula due no doubt to the peasants' deplorable living conditions. Ah, you'll find plenty of superstition to fight against, Monsieur Bovary, plenty of adherence to tradition, with which your scientific efforts will come into daily collision. They still have recourse to days of prayer, to relics, to the parish priest, rather than come along naturally to the doctor or the chemist. But, to tell the truth, the climate isn't bad. We even boast a few nonagenarians in the district. The thermometer, by my own observations, drops as low as 4° in winter, and touches 25° or at most 30° Centigrade in summer, which gives us a maximum of 24° Réaumur or 86° Fahrenheit (English scale) and no more! — though we're sheltered from the north winds by Argueil Forest on one side, and from the west winds by St John's Hill on the other. However, such a degree of heat, which on account of the water vapour given off by the river and of a considerable number of cattle in the meadows — as you know, they exhale a good deal of ammonia, that is to say nitrogen, hydrogen and oxygen (no, nitrogen and hydrogen only) — and which, sucking up the humus out of the earth, mixing together all these different emanations — doing them up in a bundle, so to speak — and combining spontaneously with the electricity, where there is any, diffused through the atmosphere, could in course of time engender noxious exhalations, such as you get in the tropics; – heat, I say, is tempered in the very quarter from which it comes – from which it *would* come, I should say – that is, in the south – by the south-easterly winds which, cooling as they cross the Seine, sometimes spring on us all of a sudden, like breezes from Russia!'

'Are there any good walks in the neighbourhood?' inquired Madame Bovary of the young man.

'Hardly any!' he replied. 'There's a place they call the Pasture, at the top of the hill, on the fringe of the woods. I go there with a book sometimes on Sundays, and lie there watching the sunset.'

'I don't think there's anything as wonderful as the sunset.' she observed. 'Especially by the seaside.'

'I adore the sea!' exclaimed Monsieur Léon.

'Don't you feel,' Madame Bovary continued, 'that your mind roves more freely over that measureless expanse? That just to gaze at it uplifts your soul, gives you glimpses of the infinite, the ideal?'

'Mountain scenery is like that, too,' said Léon. 'A cousin of mine toured Switzerland last year, and he says you can't form any idea of the magic of the lakes, the charm of the waterfalls, the gigantic spectacle of the glaciers. There are pine-trees, incredibly tall, growing across mountain torrents, huts hanging over precipices, and when there's a break in the clouds you can see whole valleys spread out a thousand feet below you. How the sight must inspire you, move you to prayer, to ecstasy! I don't wonder any more at that famous musician who used to play his piano in sight of some magnificent piece of scenery, in order to stimulate his imagination.'

'Are you a musician?' she asked.

'No, though I'm very fond of music,' he answered.

'Don't you believe him, Madame Bovary,' Homais interposed, leaning over his plate. 'That's sheer modesty! Why, my dear boy, up in your room the other day you were singing

the *Guardian Angel* beautifully. I heard you from my laboratory. You were rolling it out like a professional!'

Léon was the chemist's lodger; he had a little room on the
second floor looking on to the square. He blushed at this com-
pliment from his landlord, who had immediately turned back
to the doctor, however, and was enumerating the leading inhabitants of Yonville, furnishing him with facts and anecdotes. The solicitor's fortune wasn't known exactly. ... The
Tuvache crowd gave themselves great airs. ...

Emma resumed:

'What sort of music do you like best?'

'Oh, German ... The sort that sets you dreaming.'

'Do you know the Italian opera?'

'Not yet, but I shall go next year when I'm in Paris for my
Finals.'

'As I've had the honour of explaining to your husband,'
said the chemist, 'speaking of this poor fellow Yanoda who's
disappeared: — thanks to his extravagance you will find yourselves in possession of one of the most comfortable houses in
Yonville. Its chief convenience for a doctor is that it has a door
on to the lane, so that people can go in and out without being
seen. And it's equipped with all the amenities – wash-house,
kitchen and scullery, sitting-room, apple-loft, and so on. He
was a lad who never counted the pennies! He had an arbour
made at the bottom of the garden, by the river, just for him to
drink his beer in the summer, and if Madame is fond of gardening, she'll be able ...'

'My wife doesn't go in for that much,' said Charles. 'She's
been advised to take exercise, but she'd sooner stay in her
room all the time, reading.'

'I'm the same,' remarked Léon. 'What could be better than
a book by the fireside, with the wind beating on the window-
panes and the lamp burning ... '

'Yes! ... yes!' she said, gazing at him with her great dark
eyes wide open.

'You forget everything,' he continued. 'The hours slip by. You travel in your chair through countries you seem to see before you, your thoughts are caught up in the story, dallying with the details or following the course of the plot, you enter into the characters, so that it seems as if it were your own heart beating beneath their costumes.'

'How true! how true!' she said.

'Have you ever had the experience,' Léon pursued, 'while reading a book, of coming upon some idea you have thought of vaguely yourself, some dim picture that returns to you from afar, and seems completely to express your subtlest feeling?'

'I have felt that,' she answered.

'That is why I am fondest of poetry,' he said. 'I find it more tender than prose, and far more affecting.'

'It palls in time, though,' replied Emma. 'In fact, nowadays I'm all for stories that rush you along breathlessly and make you frightened. I hate commonplace heroes and moderate feelings such as are to be found in life.'

'Quite so,' observed the clerk, 'those books which do not touch the feelings seem to me to stray from the true end of Art. It is so sweet, amid the disappointments of life, to let the imagination dwell on noble characters, pure affections, pictures of happiness! For my part, living here far from the world, it's the one distraction I've got. Yonville has so little to offer!'

'Like Tostes, no doubt,' Emma answered. 'I always belonged to a library there.'

'If you will do me the honour of making use of it, Madame,' said the chemist, catching these last words, 'my own library is at your disposal, comprising the best authors – Voltaire, Rousseau, Delille, Walter Scott, *The Literary Echo*, and so on. In addition I take various periodicals, among them the *Rouen Beacon*, for which I have the privilege of being correspondent for the area of Buchy, Forges, Neufchâtel, Yonville and roundabouts.'

They had been sitting over the meal for two hours and a half. Artémise the serving-girl, listlessly dragging her carpet slippers over the flagstones, brought in the plates one at a time, failed to remember or understand anything she was told, and kept leaving the billiard-room door open so that the latch banged against the wall.

While he talked, Léon had unconsciously placed his foot on the bar of Madame Bovary's chair. She was wearing a little blue silk neckerchief which kept her goffered cambric collar as stiff as a ruff, and when she moved her head, the lower part of her face sank down into the linen or rose gracefully out of it. And side by side like that, while Charles chatted to the chemist, they entered upon one of those rambling conversations in which any remark may bring you back to the fixed centre of common sympathy. They discussed everything – Paris shows, names of novels, new dances, the world they had never known, Tostes where she had lived, Yonville where they now were: – so they went on till dinner was over.

When coffee had been served, Félicité went away to get the bedroom ready in the new house, and soon afterwards they all rose from the table. Madame Lefrançois had fallen asleep by the dying fire. The ostler was waiting, lantern in hand, to show Monsieur and Madame Bovary the way. Wisps of straw were stuck in his red hair, and he was lame in the left leg. He took the priest's umbrella in his free hand, and they set off.

The village was asleep. The market pillars cast long shadows over the square, and the ground looked quite grey, as on a summer night.

The doctor's house being, however, within fifty yards of the inn, they had to exchange good-nights almost at once, and the party broke up.

As she stepped inside Emma felt the chill of the plaster descend on her shoulders like a damp cloth. The walls were newly whitewashed, the wooden stairs creaked. Upstairs in the bedroom a wan light entered through curtainless windows; tree-tops were dimly discernible outside, with meadows beyond, submerged in the mist that smoked in the moonlight all along the course of the river. Scattered about the room were drawers, bottles, curtain-rods, gilt poles, mattresses over the chairs, basins on the floor. The furniture-men had just dumped everything down and left it.

It was the fourth time she had slept in a strange place. The first was at the convent, the second when she arrived at Tostes, the third at La Vaubyessard, and now this was the fourth. Each had seemed to mark the inauguration of a new phase in her life. She didn't think things could present the same aspect in different places. And since life had not been kind to her so far, the future must surely hold something better in store for her.

3

As she was getting up next morning she caught sight of the clerk crossing the market-place. She was in her dressing-gown. He looked up and raised his hat. She nodded quickly and shut the window.

Léon waited all day for six o'clock to arrive; when he got to the inn, he found no one there but Monsieur Binet, already at table.

The dinner-party the previous night had been a big event for Léon. Never before had he spent two whole hours talking to a *lady*. How on earth had he managed to expound – and with such a flow of language – a hundred things that he could never have said so well before? Normally he was timid, with the sort of reserve that is part modesty and part dissimulation. Yonville considered him 'a real gentleman'. He listened to his elders' opinions, and seemed to be no firebrand in politics, a remarkable thing in a young man. He was gifted, too. He could paint in water-colours, and read music, and when he

wasn't playing cards after dinner, he readily occupied himself
with literature. Monsieur Homais respected him for his education, Madame Homais liked him for his good nature – for he
often used to take the Homais children out to play in the garden. These were a set of grubby little urchins, badly brought
up, and somewhat lethargic, like their mother. In addition to
the maid, they had Justin to look after them. He was the
chemist's apprentice, a distant cousin of Homais' who had
been taken into the shop out of charity, and who performed
domestic duties as well.

The chemist showed himself the best of neighbours. He
gave Madame Bovary advice about tradesmen, and sent specially for his own cider merchant, tasting the brew himself and
seeing the cask well placed in the cellar. He told her how she
could get cheap butter, and fixed up an arrangement with
Lestiboudois the sexton, who in addition to his sacerdotal and
funerary functions looked after the principal gardens at
Yonville, on hourly or yearly terms as the clients preferred.

This obsequious cordiality on the part of the chemist was
not prompted by sheer altruism. There was method in
it.

He had infringed the law of 19th Ventose, Year XI, Article
1, which forbids any person not holding a diploma to practise
medicine. He had been mysteriously denounced and summoned before the King's Attorney in private, at Rouen. The
magistrate received him standing, dressed in his robes of
office, with ermine over his shoulders and his flat cap on his
head. It was in the morning, before the court sat. Policemen's
boots could be heard tramping down the corridor outside,
and there came a distant sound as of keys turning in stout
locks. There was a buzzing in the chemist's ears as though he
were going to have a stroke. He began to see himself immured
in the deepest of dungeons, his family in tears, the shop sold
and all his window-jars dispersed. He had to go straight off to
a café for a rum and Seltzer to steady his nerves.

The remembrance of this admonition gradually faded, and he continued as before giving innocuous consultations in his back room. But the mayor was against him, some of his rivals were jealous, he couldn't be too careful. His kindly attentions were meant to put Monsieur Bovary under an obligation and ensure his silence in case he ever noticed anything. And so every morning Homais brought him the daily paper, and often spared a moment in the afternoon to come round and converse with the 'Officer of Health'.

Charles was gloomy: the clients weren't coming. He sat for long hours in silence, or went into his consulting-room for a nap, or watched his wife sew. To kill time he turned odd-job man, even trying his hand at painting the attic with some spare paint left by the decorators. But money matters were weighing on him. He had spent so much on repairs at Tostes, on clothes for his wife, and then on moving house, that the whole of Emma's dowry, more than nine thousand francs, had gone in a couple of years. And then, all the things that had been lost or damaged in transit from Tostes to Yonville ...! Not least among them the plaster *curé*, who had been knocked off by a specially violent jolt of the cart and shattered into a thousand fragments on the paving-stones at Quincampoix.

A less dismal preoccupation came to distract him – his wife's pregnancy. The nearer her time drew, the fonder husband he became. It made a new bond of the flesh between them, a constant reminder of their growing union. When he watched from a distance her indolent gait, her body turning limply on her uncorseted hips, when he feasted his eyes on her as she lounged wearily in her easy chair opposite him, his happiness overflowed: he went over and kissed her, stroked her cheek, called her 'little mummy', tried to dance her round the room, and uttered between tears and laughter all manner of playful endearments that came into his head. He was overjoyed at the idea of becoming a father. Nothing was lacking to him now. He had been through the whole of human experience: serenely he settled down with both elbows firmly planted upon the table of life.

After her first feeling of astonishment Emma was eager to have the child and so find out what it felt like to be a mother. But being unable to spend money freely and buy a swing-cradle with pink silk curtains, and embroidered bonnets, she gave up her own plans in a fit of bitterness and ordered the whole outfit from a dressmaker in the village, without choosing or discussing anything. So she forfeited the pleasure of those preparations that whet the appetite of mother-love; and this perhaps enfeebled her affection from the start.

However, as Charles talked about the infant at every meal time, she soon came to take a more sustained interest in it.

She wanted a son. He should be dark and strong, and she would call him Georges. The thought of having a male child afforded her a kind of anticipatory revenge for all her past helplessness. A man, at any rate, is free. He can explore the passions and the continents, can surmount obstacles, reach out to the most distant joys. Whereas a woman is constantly thwarted. At once inert and pliant, she has to contend with both physical weakness and legal subordination. Her will is like the veil on her bonnet, fastened by a single string and quivering at every breeze that blows. Always there is a desire that impels and a convention that restrains.

The baby was born at about six o'clock one Sunday morning as the sun was rising.

'It's a girl,' said Charles.

She turned away and fainted.

Madame Homais ran round almost at once to give her a kiss, and so did old Madame Lefrançois from the Golden Lion. The chemist, a man of discretion, contented himself with a few provisional words of congratulation delivered round the edge of the door. He asked to see the baby, and thought it well formed.

During her convalescence she spent many hours wondering

what to call her daughter. First she went through all the names with Italian endings – Clara, Louisa, Amanda, Atala. She rather liked Galsuinde, and better still Yseult and Léocadie. Charles wanted the child to be named after its mother, but Emma was against this. They went through the church calendar from end to end, and sought outside opinion.

'When I mentioned it to Monsieur Léon the other day,' said the chemist, 'he wondered why you hadn't picked Madeleine, which is extremely fashionable nowadays.'

But old Madame Bovary protested strongly against giving the girl that sinner's name. Monsieur Homais, for his part, was attracted to all names which reminded you of a great man, a glorious deed or a noble conception; he had christened his four children accordingly. There was Napoléon, for glory, and Franklin for liberty. Irma was perhaps a concession to romanticism, but Athalie paid homage to the most immortal masterpiece of the French theatre. For Homais' philosophical convictions did not inhibit his artistic appreciation; the thinker never stifled the man of feeling. He could discriminate. He knew where to draw the line between imagination and fanaticism. In this tragedy of *Athalie*, for example, he censured the thought while admiring the style, denounced the conception but applauded the execution, was exasperated with the characters and spellbound by their speeches.

When he read the great passages he was carried away – until he remembered what an asset they had been to the clerical profession, and then he felt mortified: floundering in such a confusion of feelings, he longed simultaneously to crown Racine with both hands, and to give him a good piece of his mind.

At last Emma remembered hearing the Marquise at La Vaubyessard call a young woman 'Berthe', and on that name she at once decided. Monsieur Rouault being unable to come, they asked Homais to be godfather. His christening presents were all articles out of his shop, to wit: six tins of jujubes, a whole jar of racahout, three boxes of marshmallow paste, and half a dozen sticks of sugar candy which he had found in a cupboard. On the night of the ceremony they gave a big dinner party. The *curé* was present. Excitement ran high. As the liqueurs were being served, Homais struck up the *God of Good People*. Monsieur Léon sang a barcarole and the elder Madame Bovary, who was godmother, a ballad from the days of the Empire. Finally Charles' father insisted on having the baby brought down, and, tilting his glass high over its head, proceeded to baptize it in champagne. This mockery of the earliest of the sacraments roused the wrath of the Abbé Bournisien. Old Bovary countered with a quotation from the *Wars of the Gods*; the *curé* rose to go. The ladies entreated, Homais interposed, and between them they succeeded in getting the cleric back into his seat, where he picked up his saucer and quietly finished his coffee.

Monsieur Bovary senior stayed on at Yonville for a month, impressing the locals with a magnificent silver-braided forage-cap, which he wore in the mornings when he smoked his pipe in the market-place. As he habitually drank a great deal of brandy, he was constantly sending the maid to the Golden Lion for a bottle which was put down to his son's account; and to perfume his silk handkerchiefs he used up the whole of Emma's stock of eau-de-Cologne.

His daughter-in-law was by no means averse to his company. He had been about the world, and he talked of Berlin, Vienna, Strasbourg, his service as an officer, the mistresses he had had, the big lunch parties he had given. He made himself agreeable to her. Sometimes, on the stairs or in the garden, he would seize her round the waist and call out: 'Look out for yourself, Charles!'

His wife became apprehensive for her son's happiness. Fearing that her husband might exert a bad influence on the young woman if they stayed longer, she set herself to hasten their departure. Perhaps she had graver fears: Monsieur Bovary was a man to whom nothing was sacred.

One day Emma felt a sudden desire to see her baby, which had been put out to nurse with the carpenter's wife. Without consulting the almanac to see if the six weeks of the Virgin had yet elapsed, she set off for Rollet's abode at the far end of the village, at the bottom of the hill between the highroad and the meadows.

It was midday. The houses had their shutters closed, and the slate roofs, glittering in the hard glare of the blue sky, seemed to be sending up sparks from their gable-tops. A warm breeze was blowing. As she walked along, Emma began to feel weak. The pebbles on the footpath hurt her feet. She hesitated, wondering whether to turn back or to go in and sit down somewhere.

At that moment Monsieur Léon appeared out of a neighbouring doorway with a sheaf of papers under his arm. He walked up and greeted her, then stood there in the shade of the lowered grey shop-blind outside Lheureux's.

Madame Bovary told him she was on the way to see her baby, but was getting tired.

'If ... ' Léon began, but didn't dare continue.

'Have you anything to do?' she asked.

When the clerk said no, she requested him to accompany her. By nightfall news of this had spread throughout Yonville, and Madame Tuvache, the mayor's wife, declared in her maid's hearing that Madame Bovary was *compromising herself.*

To reach the nurse's house they had to turn left at the end of the street, as though making for the cemetery, and go along a narrow path bordered with privet that ran between cottages and backyards. The privet was in flower, and so were the speedwell and the dogroses, the nettles, the slender brambles that stuck out from the bushes. Through gaps in the hedge they could see inside the yards, where a pig reclined on a dunghill, or cows with poles hung across their chests rubbed their horns against the tree-trunks. Side by side they strolled along, she leaning on him, he slowing his pace to keep time with hers, while in front of them a swarm of midges hovered buzzing in the warm air.

They recognized the house by an old walnut-tree that shaded it. It was a little low house with a brown tiled roof; a string of onions was hanging down from the attic window. Some faggots propped against the thorn hedge surrounded a bed of lettuce, a few head of lavender and some sweet-peas trained on sticks. Little runnels of dirty water trickled over the grass, and all round were various nondescript rags, woollen stockings, a red calico night-dress, a large thick sheet spread out on top of the hedge. The squeak of the gate brought out the nurse, carrying in one arm a baby that she was suckling. With her other hand she dragged along a puny little boy with scabs all over his face, the son of a Rouen draper, left in the country by parents too engrossed in their business.

'Come in,' she said. 'Your baby's over there, asleep.'

The downstairs bedroom, the only one there was, had a large uncurtained bed standing against the far wall, while a kneading-trough took up the side by the window, one pane of which was stuck together with a blue paper star. In the corner behind the door, under the sink, was a row of boots with shiny hobnails and a bottle of oil with a feather in its mouth. Amid the gunflints, candle-ends and bits of tinder on the dusty mantelpiece was propped a *Mathieu Laensberg* almanac. The final unnecessary touch was added to the room by a picture of Fame blowing her trumpets, which had presumably been cut out of some advertisement for scent, and was nailed to the wall with half a dozen brads.

Emma's baby lay asleep in a wicker cradle on the floor. She picked it up in its coverlet and began crooning to it softly as she rocked it to and fro. Léon walked round the room, thinking what a strange sight it was to see that lovely woman in her nankeen dress in these squalid surroundings. Madame Bovary reddened, and he turned away, afraid he might have been looking at her somewhat impertinently. She laid the child down again. It had been sick over her collar. The nurse at once came and wiped it off, assuring her that it wouldn't show.

'She gives me worse than that, too,' she said, 'and I'm for ever cleaning her! Now if you'd be so kind as to leave word with Camus the grocer to let me have a bit of soap when I need it? That'd be easiest for you, and I needn't trouble you then.'

'Very well, very well!' said Emma. 'Good day, Madame Rollet.'

And she wiped her feet at the door as she went out.

The good woman accompanied her to the garden gate, saying what a dreadful time she had getting up during the night.

'I'm that worn out sometimes, I drop off in my chair. Now you might just let me have a pound of ground coffee, it'd last me a month, that I could take in the mornings with some milk?'

Having listened to the woman's outburst of gratitude, Emma broke away; but they had gone only a little way along the path when they heard the sound of clogs behind them. She turned round. It was the nurse again.

'Well, what is it?'

The woman drew her aside behind an elm-tree and started telling her about her husband, who with his job and the six francs a year that the Captain ...

'Make haste,' said Emma.

'Well then,' the nurse went on, heaving a sigh between each word, 'I'm afraid he won't like seeing me drink coffee all by myself. You know, men ... '

'But I'm going to give you some,' said Emma. 'You shall have some ... Don't pester me!'

'Oh dear, my poor lady, it's the terrible cramp he gets in his chest, left by his wounds. He even says cider's weakening.'

'Come to the point, Madame Rollet.'

'Well,' she went on, dropping a curtsey, 'if it wasn't too much to ask of you ... ' (she bobbed down again) 'if you'd be good enough' (her eyes begged) 'a little jar of brandy!' she got out at last, '... and I'll rub your little one's feet with it, for they're as tender as your tongue!'

Having finally shaken her off, Emma once more took Monsieur Léon's arm. She walked quickly for a while, then slowed down, and her wandering gaze alighted on the shoulder of the young man's frock-coat, with the black velvet collar over which his auburn hair fell smooth and tidy. She noticed his nails, which were longer than was customary at Yonville. Their care was one of the clerk's main occupations: he kept a special pocket-knife in his desk for the purpose.

They returned to Yonville along the river. In summer there was more of its shelving bank to be seen, and the garden walls were uncovered to their base, with several of the steps leading down to the water. The river ran noiselessly, swift, cool to the eye. Tall slender grasses leaned above it in a mass, bent by the force of the current; weeds streamed out in the limpid water like green wigs tossed away. Now and then some fine-legged insect alighted on the tip of a reed or crawled over a water-lily leaf. The sunshine darted its rays through the little blue bubbles on the wavelets that kept forming and breaking; old lopped willow-trees gazed at their own grey bark in the water. Beyond, the fields looked empty for miles around. It was dinner-time at the farms. The young woman and her companion heard nothing as they went but the sound of their own voices, their footfalls on the path, and the swish of Emma's dress as it rustled about her.

The garden walls, their copings stuck with bits of broken glass, were hot as the panes of a greenhouse. Wallflowers had pushed their way up between the bricks, and as she went by, Madame Bovary scattered some of their faded petals into a yellow dust with the point of her open sunshade; or an overhanging spray of clematis or honeysuckle would get caught in its fringe and trail for a moment on the silk.

They talked about a Spanish dancing-troupe that was due to visit Rouen very soon.

'Will you go?' she asked.

'If I can,' he answered.

Had they nothing else to say to one another? More serious communications were, to be sure, passing between their eyes. As they tried to make conversation, they felt the same languor stealing over them both, as if their whispering voices were being drowned by the deep continuous murmur of their souls. Surprised by the strange sweetness of it, they never thought to describe or to explain what they felt. Coming delights, like tropical beaches, send out their native enchantment over the vast spaces that precede them – a perfumed breeze that lulls and drugs you out of all anxiety as to what may yet await you below the horizon.

In one place the ground had been trampled by cattle, and they had to get across on big green stepping-stones set at intervals in the mud. Frequently halting to see where to tread, Emma poised precariously on the toppling stones, with her elbows in the air, glancing uncertainly forward, and laughing as she all but overbalanced into the puddles.

When they reached her garden, Madame Bovary pushed open the little gate, ran up the steps and vanished.

Léon walked back to his office. His chief was not there. He cast a glance over some papers, trimmed a quill, then finally picked up his hat and went out.

He made his way to the Pasture, at the top of Argueil Hill where the woods begin, stretched himself on the ground under the pine-trees, and looked at the sky through his fingers.

'I'm sick of it!' he said to himself. 'Sick of it!'

It was hard luck, he thought, having to live in this village, with Homais for friend and Monsieur Guillaumin for master. The latter was a man wholly absorbed in his profession, who wore gold-rimmed spectacles and red whiskers above a white cravat, and was quite without refinement, despite his affecting a stiff English manner which had impressed the clerk at first. As for the chemist's wife, she was the best wife in Normandy, placid as a sheep, cherishing her children, her father, her mother and her relatives, weeping with them that wept, leaving the house to look after itself, and hating stays; but so slow-moving, so wearisome to listen to, so common in appearance and so limited in her conversation, that although she was only thirty to his twenty, though they slept in adjacent rooms and spoke to each other every day, it had yet never crossed his mind that she could be a woman to anyone, a female in anything but dress.

Who else was there? Binet. A few shopkeepers. Two or three innkeepers. The *curé*. And lastly Monsieur Tuvache, the mayor, with his two sons: moneyed folk, surly dull-wits who farmed their own land and feasted sumptuously among themselves; regular churchgoers, and quite insufferable company.

Now, however, against this background of undistinguished humanity, Emma's face stood out, isolated from them yet still further removed from him. For he had a sense of chasms yawning between himself and her.

At first he had called on her several times in the chemist's company. Charles had shown no inordinate eagerness to have him there. And Léon didn't know how to proceed, being torn between fear of making a false move, and desire for an intimacy which he accounted well-nigh impossible.

4

WHEN the weather started to turn cold, Emma gave up her bedroom in favour of the parlour, a long low-ceilinged room with some branching coral standing in front of the mirror on the mantelpiece. Seated in her armchair by the window, she watched the villagers go by along the pavement.

Twice a day Léon went past from his office to the Golden Lion. Emma heard his step some way off and leaned forward listening; and the young man glided by behind the curtains, always dressed the same, and never turning his head. At dusk, however, as she sat there holding her chin in her left hand, with a half-finished piece of embroidery fallen on her lap, it often startled her to see his shadow suddenly move across the window. She at once got up and told the maid to lay the table.

Monsieur Homais arrived during dinner. Skull-cap in hand, he entered on tip-toe, to avoid disturbing anyone, with his invariable greeting of 'Good evening all!'

Having taken his place at the table between husband and wife, he inquired after the doctor's patients, and the doctor asked his opinion about fees. Then they discussed the contents of the paper. By this time of day Homais had it off almost by heart, and reproduced it in full, together with the journalistic comment and all the particular disasters that had occurred in France or abroad. When he had exhausted these topics he immediately proceeded to remark on the dishes before him. Sometimes, half-rising from his seat, he would delicately draw Madame's attention to a titbit, or turn round to the maid with advice on the way to deal with a stew, or on the dietetic properties of various seasonings, with much impressive talk of aromas, osmazomes, essences and gelatines. Having more recipes in his head than bottles in his shop, Homais excelled at making various kinds of preserves, vinegars and cordials, besides being an authority on the latest inventions in fuel-saving cookers, on the art of preserving cheese and that of nursing a sickly wine.

At eight o'clock Justin fetched him to shut up shop. Homais would give the boy a knowing look, particularly if Félicité were in the room; for he had noticed his apprentice's partiality to the doctor's house.

'That lad of mine,' he said, 'is beginning to get ideas into his head. Devil take me but I believe he's in love with your maid!'

A graver fault, and one for which he had taken the boy to task, was his continually listening to their conversation. On Sundays, for instance, he could not be got out of the drawing-room after Madame Homais had summoned him to fetch the children, who had been going to sleep in the easy-chairs and dragging at the oversized calico covers.

The chemist's Sunday evening gatherings were never large, his malicious tongue and his political opinions having alienated a succession of respectable citizens. But the clerk never missed. The minute he heard the door-bell, he ran down to let Madame Bovary in, to take her shawl and deposit under the shop-desk the big overshoes she wore in snowy weather.

First they had a few rounds of *trente-et-un*; then Monsieur Homais played écarté with Emma, while Léon stood behind her giving advice. His hands rested on the back of her chair; he observed how the teeth of her comb gripped into her chignon. Every time she played a card, the movement lifted her dress on the right side. From her coiled hair a dark glow ran down her back, paling gradually until it merged into shadow. As she sat back again, her dress puffed out on either side of her, in full folds that reached to the floor. When, occasionally, Léon felt the sole of his boot resting on it, he stepped aside as if he had trodden upon a living thing.

After they had finished their game, the chemist and the doctor played dominoes. Emma changed places and sat with her elbows on the table, flicking over the leaves of *Illustration*. She had brought her fashion magazine with her; Léon sat down beside her, and together they looked at the prints, waiting for each other at the bottom of the page. Often she asked him to recite some poetry. Léon delivered it in a slow, lingering voice, dying away to a studied whisper in the love passages. But he was put off by the rattle of the dominoes.

Homais was an expert and routed Charles utterly. Having reached their third hundred, they both stretched out in front of the fire and were soon asleep. The fire was dying in the grate; the teapot was empty; Léon read on. As she listened, Emma kept mechanically twirling the lampshade, looking at the clowns in carriages and tight-rope walkers with balancing-poles that were painted on the gauze. Léon stopped, indicating his sleeping audience. Then they talked quietly, and their conversation seemed the sweeter for not being overheard.

So a kind of bond was formed between them, a constant traffic in books and ballads. Monsieur Bovary was not of a jealous nature, and saw nothing odd in it.

On his birthday he received a fine phrenological head, painted blue and marked all over with figures down to the thorax. This was a kind thought of the clerk's. He was very attentive to Charles, even doing shopping errands for him in Rouen; and, a certain novel having started a craze for cactuses, he bought some for Madame and brought them back in the *Hirondelle*, holding them on his knees and pricking his fingers on their spikes.

A board with a rail was fixed at Emma's window to hold her flower-pots, and as the clerk also had his little hanging-garden, they could look across and watch each other tending their plants.

There was one window in the village that was still more frequently occupied. From morning to night on Sundays, and every afternoon when the light was good, you could see at an attic window the lean profile of Monsieur Binet bending over his lathe, whose monotonous drone could be heard as far away as the Golden Lion.

One evening Léon returned home to find a rug in his room, worked in wool and velvet, with a leaf design on a light background. He called Madame Homais, Monsieur Homais, Justin, the children and the cook. He spoke of it to his employer. Everyone was eager to see his rug. Now why should the clerk be receiving 'favours' from the doctor's wife? It looked queer. They decided that she must be his mistress.

She might well have been, from the way he was for ever harping on her charms and her wit. Once he provoked Binet to answer savagely, 'What's it to me? I don't have anything to do with her.'

He racked his brains for a way of making his declaration. Torn all the while between fear of offending and shame at his own faint-heartedness, he wept tears of dejection and desire. Then he made forceful resolutions. He wrote letters, and tore them up; gave himself a time limit, then extended it. Often he started out with a determination to dare all; but his decisiveness quickly deserted him in Emma's presence, and when Charles arrived and invited him out in his trap to see one of his patients in the neighbourhood, he accepted with alacrity, bowed to Madame, and went. Was not her husband something of hers?

Emma, for her part, never questioned herself to find out whether she was in love with him. Love, she believed, must come suddenly, with thunder and lightning, a hurricane from on high that swoops down into your life and turns it topsy-turvy, snatches away your will-power life a leaf, hurls you heart and soul into the abyss. She did not know how on the terrace of a house the rain collects in pools when the gutters are choked; and she would have continued to feel quite safe had she not suddenly discovered a crack in the wall.

5

It was a snowy Sunday afternoon in February.

They had all – Monsieur and Madame Bovary, Homais and Monsieur Léon – gone off together to see a new flax-mill that was being put up in the valley a mile and a half from Yonville. The chemist had brought Napoléon and Athalie along for exercise, and Justin escorted them, carrying umbrellas on his shoulder.

Nothing could have been less interesting than that object of interest. A large piece of waste ground, with some already rusty driving-wheels scattered about among sand and gravel heaps, surrounded a long quadrangular building riddled with little windows. It was still unfinished; the sky could be seen through the rafters. Attached to the end of the gable a bundle of straw, with a few wheat-ears in it, flapped its tricoloured streamers in the wind.

Homais was speaking. He was explaining to the company how important the mill was going to be, calculating the strength of the floor-beams and the thickness of the inner walls, and regretting that he had no yardstick such as Monsieur Binet possessed for his private use.

Emma was on his arm, leaning lightly against his shoulder, watching the sun's disc diffusing its pale brilliance through the mist. She turned round; there stood Charles, his cap pulled down over his eyes, his thick lips trembling, which lent an added stupidity to his face. Even his back, that stolid back of his, was irritating to see. His frock-coat seemed to wear upon it the whole drabness of the personality within.

As she surveyed him, tasting a kind of vicious ecstasy in her irritation, Léon moved a step forward. White with cold, his face seemed to assume a softer languor; between his neck and his cravat the collar of his shirt was loose and showed some skin; the tip of his ear stuck out beneath a lock of hair, and his big blue eyes, raised to the clouds, looked to Emma more limpid and more lovely than mountain tarns that mirror the sky.

'Little wretch!' cried the chemist suddenly, and darted over to his son, who had just jumped up on a heap of lime to get his shoes white. Severely scolded, Napoléon started howling, while Justin proceeded to wipe his shoes with a handful of straw. A knife was needed, however; Charles offered his.

'Ah, he carries a knife in his pocket, like a labourer,' she thought to herself.

Hoar-frost was settling. They turned back towards Yonville.

Madame Bovary did not accompany Charles to their neighbours' that evening. When he had gone and she felt herself alone, that contrast recurred to her, with the clarity almost of an immediate sensation but with the lengthening of perspective that things attain in memory. As she lay in bed watching the fire burn bright, the scene came back to her: Léon standing there, bending his walking-cane in one hand, and with the other holding Athalie, who had been calmly sucking a lump of ice. She found him charming; couldn't stop thinking of him; remembered how he had looked on other occasions, the things he had said, the sound of his voice, everything about him. And pouting out her lips as though for a kiss, she said over and over again:

'Charming, yes, charming! ... And in love?' she asked herself. 'In love with whom? ... With me!'

The proofs of it were there before her all in a moment. Her heart leapt. The firelight flickered merrily on the ceiling. She turned over on her back and stretched out her arms.

Then began the eternal lament: 'Oh, if only Fate had willed it ...! And why not? Why shouldn't it have been ...?'

When Charles came in at midnight she pretended to have been asleep, and as he made a noise undressing, she complained of a headache; then casually inquired what had happened during the evening.

'Monsieur Léon,' he said, 'left us early.'

She couldn't suppress a smile, and as she fell asleep her heart was filled with a new enchantment.

Next evening she had a visit from the draper, Monsieur Lheureux. A clever fellow was this shopkeeper.

Gascon by birth and Norman by choice, he had grafted upon his southern loquacity the cunning of the Cauchois. His fat, flabby, shaven face looked as if it had been tinged with a pale infusion of liquorice; his white hair enhanced the unpleasant sharpness of his little black eyes. His past was not known. Some said he had been a pedlar, others a money-agent at Routot. This much was certain, that he could do calculations in his head complex enough to frighten Binet himself. Polite to the point of obsequiousness, he always held himself bent from the middle, in the attitude of greeting or of invitation.

Hanging his crape-bound hat on the peg, he came and placed a green bandbox on the table, and started off by expressing, with a flow of courteous phrases, his regret that he had not obtained Madame's patronage before. A little shop like his wasn't one to attract a lady of *fashion* (he stressed the word); but she had only to give him the order, and he would undertake to supply her with anything she might want, be it in haberdashery or linen, hosiery or fancy goods; for he went into town four times every month, regularly. He was in touch with all the leading houses. Mention his name at the *Three Brothers*, the *Golden Beard* or the *Great Savage* – the gentlemen there all knew him like the insides of their pockets! Well, today he had just dropped in to show Madame an assortment of articles which he happened, thanks to a rare stroke of luck, to have in stock. And he took half a dozen embroidered collars out of the box.

Madame Bovary had a look at them.

'There's nothing I want,' she said.

Thereupon Monsieur Lheureux daintily exhibited three Algerian scarves, several packets of English needles, a pair of straw sandals, and finally four egg-cups carved out of coconut-shells by convicts. Resting both hands on the table, he leaned forward with neck outstretched and mouth hanging open, and followed Emma's eyes as they wandered irresolutely over his wares. Now and then, as though to flick off the dust, he ran his nail along the scarves, which were unfolded to their full extent; they rustled lightly, and the gold spangles on the material were set twinkling like little stars in the dim twilight.

'How much are they?'

'A mere trifle,' he answered. 'But there's no hurry. Any time will do. We're not Jews.'

She thought for a few moments, and again declined.

'Very well,' replied Monsieur Lheureux, quite unmoved, 'we shall come to terms another time. I've always got on well with the ladies – all but my own, at any rate.'

Emma smiled.

'What I mean is' – and he assumed an air of simple good-nature after his sally – 'the money doesn't worry me ... Why, I could give you some if need be.'

She started in surprise.

'Oh yes,' he said quickly in a lowered voice. 'I wouldn't have to look far for it, you can be sure!'

And then he switched to the subject of Tellier, the proprietor of the Café Français, whom Monsieur Bovary was then attending.

'What's he got the matter with him, old Tellier? He shakes the whole house with his coughing, and I fear that before long he'll be needing a wooden suit more than a flannel jacket. He sowed his wild oats in his young days! They were a disorderly lot, Madame! Burnt himself up with brandy! ... It's a hard thing, though, to lose an old acquaintance!'

So he went on discussing the doctor's clients as he refastened his bandbox.

'It's the weather, I suppose,' he said, glancing out of the window with a wry look on his face, 'that's the cause of all this illness. I feel out of sorts myself. I'll have to come along and see the doctor one of these days, about a pain I get in my back. ... Well, then, good evening, Madame Bovary. Always your very humble servant!'

And he shut the door quietly behind him.

Emma had her dinner on a tray in her bedroom, by the fire. She took a long time over it. She was very satisfied with everything.

'How sensible I've been!' she said to herself as she thought of the scarves.

She heard a step on the staircase: it was Léon's. She went to the chest of drawers, picked a duster off a pile that were waiting to be hemmed, and was looking very busy when he came in.

Conversation was not brisk. Madame Bovary kept breaking off, and Léon sat there looking most ill at ease. Seated on a low chair by the fire, he twirled her ivory needle-case in his fingers, while she plied her needle, occasionally holding down the cloth with her nail. She said nothing, and he remained mute, captivated by her silence as he would have been by her words.

'Poor boy!' she was thinking.

'Why is she offended?' he was wondering.

Eventually he said that he would be going into Rouen one of these days on business.

'Your music subscription is up. Should I renew it?'

'No,' she answered.

'Why?'

'Because ... ,' and pressing her lips together, she slowly drew out a long stitch of grey thread.

Her needlework irritated Léon. It seemed to be galling the tips of her fingers. A pretty speech came into his head, but he didn't risk it.

'You're giving it up?' he went on.

'What?' she said quickly. 'Music? Yes! Heavens, haven't I the house to run, my husband to look after, a hundred and one jobs, a whole host of duties that come first?'

She glanced up at the clock. Charles was late. She became the anxious wife.

'He is so kind!' she said more than once.

The clerk liked Monsieur Bovary, but Emma's tender solicitude on his account came as an unpleasant surprise. Nevertheless he continued to sound his praises, which he said he heard on all sides, particularly from the chemist.

'He's a good man!' Emma broke in.

'Yes, indeed,' the clerk replied.

He started talking about Madame Homais, whose slatternly appearance was usually a subject of mirth between them.

'What does it matter?' Emma interrupted. 'A good mother doesn't worry about what she looks like.'

And then she relapsed into silence.

It was the same on the following days. Her talk, her manner, everything about her was different. She was seen to take a new interest in her household, to attend church regularly, and to be stricter with her maid.

She fetched little Berthe home from the nurse. Félicité brought the child down whenever there were visitors, and Madame Bovary undressed her to show off her fine limbs. She declared she adored children. It was her comfort, her joy, her weakness. She accompanied her caresses with lyrical outbursts which might to any but the Yonville folk have recalled Sachette in *Notre Dame de Paris*.

When Charles came home he found his slippers warming by the fire. No longer did his waistcoats want for linings nor his shirts for buttons. It was a pleasure to see all the night-caps evenly stacked in the cupboard. She no longer grimaced at the idea of taking a stroll round the garden; Charles' suggestions were always accepted, and though she still did not anticipate his wishes, she submitted to them without a murmur. So when Léon saw him sitting at his fireside after dinner, with his hands folded over his belly, his feet on the fender, his cheeks flushed from eating, his eyes moist with contentment, while the little girl crawled about on the carpet and that slim woman leaned over the back of his chair to kiss him on the forehead –

'I must be mad!' he said to himself. 'How shall *I* ever get anywhere with her?'

She looked so virtuous and inaccessible that he relinquished every semblance of hope. In so doing, however, he endowed her with a special status, detaching her in his mind from those fleshly attributes that were not for his knowing, and raising her ever higher in his heart until she soared clear away, magnificent in flight as a soul ascending to Heaven. His was one of those pure sentiments that form no obstacle to the conduct of daily life, are cultivated for their rarity and would be more pain to lose than they are pleasure to possess.

Emma grew thinner, her cheeks paled and her face lengthened. With her black braided hair, large eyes, straight nose and bird-light step, always noiseless now, it seemed as if she went through life touching it scarcely at all, bearing on her brow the mysterious mark of some sublime destiny. She was so sad and so quiet, so sweet yet so withdrawn, that you felt in her presence a kind of icy charm, as you may shiver in church at the scent of the flowers mingling with the chill of the marble. Other people, too, came under the spell. The chemist said:

'She's a very clever woman, who wouldn't be out of place as the wife of a subprefect.'

The housewives were won by her thrift, the patients by her courtesy, the poor by her charity.

But within, she was all desire and rage and hatred. That straight-pleated dress hid a heart in turmoil, those demure lips told nothing of its suffering. She was in love with Léon; and she sought solitude that she might revel in his image undisturbed. It marred the pleasure of her daydreams to see him in the flesh. The sound of his step set her trembling. But in his presence her agitation subsided, leaving nothing but an immense astonishment that worked itself out in sadness.

Léon never knew, when he went away from her in despair, that she would immediately get up and watch him through the window. She started nervously studying his movements, covertly observing his face, and she concocted a whole rigmarole to give herself a pretext for visiting his room. She thought the chemist's wife a lucky woman indeed to be sleeping under the same roof with him, and her thoughts were for ever alighting on that house, like the pigeons from the Golden Lion who went to bathe their pink feet and white wings in the gutters there. But the more Emma became conscious of her love, the harder she strove to conceal and to suppress it. She would have been glad if he had guessed; she envisaged various happenings and catastrophes that might give him the hint. It was doubtless indolence, or fear, that held her back. Modesty, too. She wondered whether she had been too distant with him – and now the moment had gone by, and all was lost! But her pride, her joy in saying 'I am a virtuous woman', and in contemplating her own attitudes of resignation in the mirror, brought her some solace for the sacrifice she believed herself to be making.

Then the appetites of the flesh, the craving for money, the melancholy of passion, all blended together in one general misery. Instead of turning her thoughts away, she riveted them to it the more firmly; she worked up her grief, and sought out its occasions. She was irritated by a meal badly served or a door left ajar; she moped to herself about the velvet she did not possess, the happiness that was passing her by, the loftiness of her dreams and the littleness of her house.

To make it harder, Charles had apparently no notion of what she suffered. His unquestioning belief that he made her happy seemed to her a stupid insult; his complacency on the point, ingratitude. For whose sake, then, this goodness of hers? Was not he the very obstacle to all felicity, the cause of all her wretchedness, the pointed buckle, as it were, on the complicated strap that bound her?

And so on him became centred the abundant hatred which resulted from her frustrations, and which every attempt to moderate served only to augment, her vain efforts giving her an added reason for despair, and contributing further to their estrangement. She rebelled against her own meekness. Her drab surroundings drove her to dreams of luxury; marital tenderness prompted the desire for a lover. She would have liked Charles to hit her, that she might have just cause for hatred and revenge. She was surprised sometimes at the hideous ideas that occurred to her. And all the while she must go on smiling, hearing herself insist that she was very happy, pretending to be so, acting the part.

She had moods, though, when, sick of the hypocrisy of it, she was tempted to elope with Léon, and start afresh somewhere far away. But at once a vague, dark chasm yawned within her soul.

'Besides, he's not in love with me any more,' she thought. 'What will become of me? What help can I hope for? What consolation? What relief?'

She was left broken, gasping, lifeless, sobbing under her breath, her face bathed in tears.

'Why not tell the Doctor?' asked the maid when she came in during one of these attacks.

'It's just nerves,' Emma answered. 'Don't say anything, you'd only worry him.'

'Ah, yes!' returned Félicité. 'You're like old Guérin's daughter, the fisherman at Le Pollet, that I knew at Dieppe before I came to you. She was that wretched, you'd think to see her standing in the doorway there was a funeral pall hung up over the door. It seems she'd got a sort of a fog in her head, the doctors couldn't do a thing with her, and no more could the *curé*. When she got it real bad she'd go off by herself along the beach, and the coastguard often used to find her there on his rounds. Stretched flat out on the shingle she'd be, crying her eyes out. ... They say it went when she got married, though.'

'But with me,' replied Emma, 'it didn't come on till I was married.'

6

SHE had been sitting one evening by the open window, watching Lestiboudois the verger clipping the box hedge, when she heard, all at once, the chimes of the Angelus.

It was the beginning of April – when the primroses are out, and a warm breeze plays over the newly turned flower-beds, and the gardens seem to be dressing up like women for the high days of summer. Through the trellis of the arbour, and all around beyond, you saw the river tracing its winding, wandering course through the grassy meadows. The evening mist hovered between the leafless poplars, blurring their outlines with violet, paler and more transparent than a fine gauze hung over their tangling branches. Cattle moved in the distance, their tread and their lowing alike inaudible. And all the time the bell kept sounding its gentle lamentation on the air.

The reiterated chimes sent the young woman's thoughts roaming among old memories of her childhood and school-days. She remembered the altar at the convent, the tall candle-sticks that dwarfed the flower-vases and the tabernacle with the little columns. She wished she could vanish once more into that long line of white veils broken here and there by the stiff black hoods of the nuns bowed over their prie-dieus. At mass on Sundays, whenever she raised her eyes, she had seen, through the blue-grey swirls of incense rising, the gentle face of the Virgin Mary. ... Moved by the memory, she felt soft and limp as a feather tossed on the storm; and she was drawn out quite unconsciously in the direction of the church, prepared for any act of worship, if only it would absorb her soul and swallow up her entire being.

In the market-place she met Lestiboudois on his way back. Rather than cut his day short, he chose to break off from his work and resume afterwards, thus ringing the Angelus to suit his own convenience; though at the earlier hour it also served to summon the youngsters to their catechism class.

Some of the children were there already, playing marbles on the flagstones in the churchyard or swinging their legs astride the low wall, mowing down with their wooden shoes the tall nettles that grew between the wall and the nearest of the graves. The nettles made the only patch of green in the place; all beside was stone, constantly covered with dust despite the verger's broom. The children ran about in their sandals as though on a floor specially laid for them; their voices rang above the reverberations of the bell, which were dying away now with the oscillations of the great rope that hung down from the belfry and trailed on the ground. Swallows darted by with little cries, cutting through the air, making for their brown nests under the eaves. At the far end of the church a lamp – a nightlight wick inside a hanging glass – was burning: it looked from a distance like a little white cloud quivering above the oil. A long ray of sunlight shone down the nave, making the aisles and the recesses still darker.

'Where is the *curé*?' Madame Bovary asked a small boy who was amusing himself by waggling the turnstile, which was loose in its socket.

'He's coming,' the boy answered.

And just then the vicarage door grated on its hinges and the Abbé Bournisien appeared. The children scampered off helter-skelter into the church.

'Young rascals! Always the same!' muttered the priest. 'Nothing sacred!' he added as his foot encountered a battered catechism, which he stooped to pick up.

He caught sight of Madame Bovary.

'Excuse me,' he said; 'I didn't recognize who it was.'

He stuffed the catechism into his pocket and stood swinging the heavy vestry-key in his fingers.

The glow of the setting sun struck full on his face, and paled his woollen cassock, which was shiny at the elbows and

He stood swinging the heavy vestry-key in his fingers.

frayed in the skirt. Grease spots and tobacco stains followed the line of little buttons down his broad chest, showing most plentifully beside his bands, upon which rested the ample folds of his ruddy neck. This was flecked with yellow spots that vanished into the stubble of his greying beard. He had just had dinner, and was breathing heavily.

'How are you?' he asked.

'Not well,' Emma answered; 'I feel dreadful.'

'So do I!' the cleric exclaimed. 'Must be the warmer weather, don't you think? Surprising how it takes it out of you! But then, there you are — we are born to suffer, as St Paul says. ... What does Monsieur Bovary think about it, though?'

'He!' said she with a scornful gesture.

'What!' cried the good man in surprise. 'Hasn't he given you something for it?'

'Ah, it's no earthly remedy I need!' said Emma.

However, the *curé* was constantly peering into the church, where the youngsters were on their knees, shoving into one another and tumbling over like a row of ninepins.

'I want to ask you ...' she began again.

'Stop that, Riboudet!' shouted the priest. 'Just you wait, I'll come and warm your ears for you, you young scamp!'

He turned to Emma.

'That's Boudet the carpenter's son. His parents are well off, and they spoil him. He'd learn fast enough if he wanted to, though; he's got some brains. I sometimes call him Riboudet for a joke, you know, like the hill on the way to Maromme, and sometimes I say 'Mon Riboudet' – 'Mont Riboudet', you know, ha, ha! I told that to the Bishop the other day, and he laughed – he deigned to laugh at it. ... Well, and how's Monsieur Bovary?'

She seemed not to hear. He continued:

'Busy as ever, I expect? He and I are certainly the two hardest-worked people in the parish. But he tends the body,' he added with a heavy laugh, 'while I tend the soul.'

She fixed a gaze of entreaty upon him.

'Yes,' she said, 'you heal all ills.'

'Well may you say so, Madame Bovary. Why, this very morning I had to go over to Bas-Diauville to see a cow that was blowing; they thought there was a spell on it. I don't know how it is, but every single cow they've got ... Excuse me. ... Longuemarre and Boudet, for goodness' sake, will you stop it?' And he darted into the church.

The youngsters were crowding round the big lectern, clambering up on the cantor's stool and looking inside the missal. Others were stealing towards the confessional box, and in another moment would have ventured into its sanctity. All at once the *curé* was among them, handing out a volley of cuffs. He picked them up by the scruff of the neck and dumped them down on their knees on the floor of the choir, with some force, as if he would have liked to plant them in the flag-stones.

'There!' said he as he walked back to Emma, opening out his large calico handkerchief, with one corner of it stuck between his teeth. '... Yes, the farmers have a hard time of it.'

'They're not the only ones,' she replied.

'No, certainly! Workers in the towns, for instance.'

'No, not them ...'

'I beg your pardon, but I've known poor mothers with families, in the towns – good women, I assure you, real saints – who wanted for their daily bread!'

'But what of those,' rejoined Emma – and her mouth twisted at the corners as she spoke – 'those, Monsieur, who may have bread, but haven't ...'

'A fire in the winter?' said the priest.

'Oh – what does it matter!'

'What does it matter? Well! I should say myself that good food and good fire ... after all ...'

'O God, O God!' she breathed.

'Is something wrong?' he asked, stepping forward anxiously. 'Something you've eaten, no doubt ... You go home and have a cup of tea, Madame Bovary. That'll set you right. Or a glass of cold water with some brown sugar in it.'

'What for?' She looked like one waking from a dream.

'Well, you put your hand to your forehead – I thought you must be feeling dizzy.'

It suddenly struck him:

'There was something you were asking me. What was it, now? I can't recall.'

'Was there; Oh no, nothing – nothing,' Emma repeated.

Her wandering gaze slowly alighted on the old man in the cassock, and they looked at one another face to face, without speaking.

'Well, Madame Bovary,' he said at last,' you'll excuse me, but – Duty First, you know. I must polish off these brats of mine. First Communion will be on us soon, I'm afraid we'll be caught out again! That's why I'm going to keep them at it an hour extra every Wednesday after Ascension. Poor little mites, we can't begin too soon to set them in the way of the Lord – as indeed He bade us do through the mouth of His Divine Son. ... I wish you well, Madame. My respects to your husband!'

And with a genuflexion at the door he passed into the church.

Emma watched him go, stumping out of sight between the rows of pews, bending his head a little to one side, his hands hanging down with the palms turned outwards.

Then she wheeled round like a statue on a pivot, and started homewards. The gruff voice of the priest and the shrill treble of the children followed her as she went:

'Are you a Christian?'

'Yes, I am a Christian.'

'What is a Christian?'

'A Christian is one who, being baptized ... baptized ... baptized ...'

She climbed upstairs, clinging to the bannisters, and once inside her room dropped straight into an easy chair.

The grey light rippled gently down through the windows. The chairs seemed more firmly embedded in their places, enveloped in a fathomless ocean of shadow. The fire was out, the clock ticked, and Emma felt vaguely astonished that there should be such calm about her and such turmoil within. But little Berthe was there, toddling about in her knitted boots, between the work-table and the window. She came up to her mother and tried to take hold of her apron-strings.

'Leave me alone!' said Emma, holding her off.

The little girl was soon back again; she clung to her mother's knees, leaned her arms on them and gazed up at her with big blue eyes, while a stream of fresh saliva dribbled out of her mouth on to the silk of the apron.

'Leave me alone!' the young woman repeated in annoyance. Frightened by the look on her face, the child started whimpering.

'Oh, leave me alone, will you!' And she pushed her away with her elbow.

Berthe fell against the chest of drawers, and cut her cheek on the brass curtain-holder. The blood began to flow. Madame Bovary swooped down upon her and gathered her up, pulled the bell-cord right off, shouted for the maid at the top of her voice, and was beginning to scold herself severely when Charles appeared. He had just come in for dinner.

'Look, dear!' said Emma quietly. 'She's just fallen over and hurt herself playing.'

Charles assured her it was nothing serious, and went to fetch some plaster.

She refused to go down to dinner, and stayed upstairs alone to look after her child. Any remaining anxiety she had was gradually dispelled as she watched the child sleeping: and then she thought herself a very good, silly mother to have been worried over such a trifle. Berthe had ceased to sob. Her breathing now scarcely lifted the cotton coverlet. Big tears stood at the corners of her half-closed eyelids, and between her lashes you could see a pair of pale, sunken eye-balls. The skin on her cheek was drawn awry by the plaster.

'Strange,' thought Emma, 'what an ugly child she is!'

When Charles came home from the chemist's at eleven o'clock – he had gone there after dinner to return the plaster – he found his wife standing beside the cradle.

'It's really nothing to worry about,' he said, kissing her on the forehead. 'Don't fret, poor darling, you'll make yourself ill.'

He had stayed at the chemist's a long time. Though he hadn't appeared greatly upset, Homais had gone out of his way to 'buck him up'. They had talked about the various dangers with which childhood is beset, and about the carelessness of servants. Madame Homais knew something of that, for she bore on her chest the scars of a bowlful of hot gravy which a cook had spilt down her pinafore once long ago. These good parents accordingly took every kind of precaution. They never had an edge on the knives, or polish on the floor. Iron bars were over the windows and a strong guard at the fireplace. The Homais children, for all their independent spirit, never moved without someone to keep an eye on them. Their father swathed them in chest-protectors at the slightest sign of a cold, and till they had turned four they were all strapped, relentlessly, into padded caps. This, it is true, was a fad of Madame Homais', and a source of inward anxiety to her husband, who was apprehensive of the effect such compression might have on the mental organs; he even went so far as to ask her, 'Do you want to turn them into Caribs or Botocudos?'

Charles had been making several attempts to interrupt the conversation.

'I'd like a word with you,' he whispered in the ear of the lawyer's clerk. The latter rose to lead the way upstairs.

'Does he suspect something?' Léon wondered, his heart in his mouth.

At last Charles, having shut the door behind them, asked him to find out the price of a good daguerreotype in Rouen. It was to be a little surprise for his wife, a token of affection – namely, a portrait of himself in his dress-coat. But he wanted to know what he was letting himself in for, first. It shouldn't be any trouble to Monsieur Léon, who went into town practically every week for …

For what? Homais suspected a flirtation. But he was wrong. Léon had no light of love. He was gloomier than ever, a fact that was brought home to Madame Lefrançois by the amount of food he left on his plate nowadays. Anxious to know more, she questioned the tax-collector. Binet answered haughtily that he wasn't a paid detective.

At the same time, he did think his companion was behaving oddly. Léon would frequently fling himself back in his chair, stretch out his arms and complain about life in general.

'You need more amusement,' said the tax-collector.

'Such as?'

'If I were you I'd get a lathe!'

'I wouldn't know what to do with it,' answered the clerk.

'Ah no, that's true,' observed the other, stroking his jaw with an air of scorn tinged with complacency.

Léon was tired of loving without results. And he was beginning to feel that discouragement which is engendered by a life of repetition, when no interest guides nor expectation sustains it. He was so bored with Yonville and the Yonvillites that the very sight of certain people and certain buildings could irritate him beyond endurance; the chemist, for all his good nature, was becoming intolerable. Nevertheless, the prospect of a change alarmed as much as it attracted him.

His nervousness soon turned to impatience, and he began to hear an echo of Paris in his ears – the fanfare of its masked balls, the laughter of its *grisettes*. Since he was to finish his studies there, why not go at once? Why not? He started making inward preparations, arranging in advance how he should spend his time. He furnished a room for himself, in his imagination. He would lead the artist's life, learn to play the guitar, and wear a dressing-gown, a beret and blue velvet slippers. Already he was gazing with admiration at the crossed foils over his mantelpiece, with a skull and the guitar above them.

The difficulty lay in getting his mother's consent. Yet it sounded a perfectly reasonable scheme; his employer had actually been advising him to widen his experience in some other office. Léon compromised by looking for a place as second clerk in Rouen. Failing to find anything, he at last wrote a long, detailed letter to his mother, setting out the advantages of going to Paris at once. She gave her consent.

He didn't hurry. Every day for a whole month Hivert conveyed boxes, cases and parcels for him from Yonville to Rouen and from Rouen back to Yonville. And after he had restocked his wardrobe, had his three armchairs restuffed, bought a new supply of handkerchiefs, made, in short, enough preparations for a voyage round the world, he still delayed from week to week, until a second letter arrived from his mother, urging him to go at once, since he wished to take his exams before the vacation.

When the moment came to say good-bye, Madame Homais burst into tears; Justin sobbed; Homais concealed his emotion like a man, and insisted on carrying his friend's overcoat up to the lawyer's gate. The lawyer was taking Léon to Rouen in his carriage. There was just time for the young man to run over and say good-bye to Monsieur Bovary.

At the top of the stairs he halted, quite out of breath. Madame Bovary rose quickly as he entered.

'Once more!' said Léon.

'I knew you'd come!'

She bit her lip, and a rush of blood beneath the skin sent the colour flooding over her face, from the roots of her hair to the line of her collar. She remained standing, leaning against the panelling.

'The Doctor's not here?' he went on.

'He's out.'

She repeated, 'He's out.'

And then there was silence. They gazed at one another, and their thoughts, clinging close together like two throbbing bosoms, met in a single anguish.

'I'd like to kiss Berthe good-bye,' said Léon.

Emma went out to the stairs and called Félicité.

Quickly his glance ranged round the room, over the walls, the shelves and the fireplace, as if he would probe into everything and stamp it on his memory.

She came back, and the maid brought in Berthe, who was carrying a toy windmill upside-down and twirling it on a string.

Léon gave her several kisses under the chin.

'Good-bye, little one! Good-bye, dear little Berthe!'

And he handed her back to her mother.

'Take her,' said she to the maid.

They were alone again.

Madame Bovary rested her face against the window, her back turned to him. Léon held his cap in his hand, tapped it gently against his thigh.

'It's going to rain,' said Emma.

'I've got my coat,' he answered.

'Ah!'

She turned, lowering her chin, and her forehead was like marble where the light slid over it down to the curve of her brows — without revealing what it was she gazed at in the distance, nor what she was thinking in the depths of her.

'Good-bye, then!' he breathed.

She raised her head abruptly.

'Yes, good-bye ... Go!'

They both stepped forward. He held out his hand. She hesitated.

'English fashion, then!' she said, forcing a little laugh as she gave him hers.

Léon felt it in his own, and the very substance of his being seemed to flow down into that moist palm.

Then he released it: their eyes met once more, and he was gone.

When he reached the market-hall, he stopped and hid behind one of the pillars, to take one last look at the white house with four green blinds. He thought he saw a shadow at her bedroom window; but just at that moment the curtain must somehow have escaped from its holder, for it slowly stirred and all at once shook out its long slanting folds, then fell into place as straight and still as a plaster wall. Léon set off at a run.

He saw his chief's carriage standing on the highroad, with a man in a workman's apron beside it, holding the horse. Homais was chatting to Monsieur Guillaumin while they waited for him.

'Come and shake hands,' said the chemist with tears in his eyes. 'Here's your overcoat, my boy. Mind you don't get cold! Take great care of yourself! And don't overdo things!'

'Come on, Léon. Jump up!' said the solicitor.

Homais leaned over the splashboard, and in a voice broken with sobs let fall the one sad word, 'Farewell!'

'Farewell to you!' answered Monsieur Guillaumin. 'Right! Let go!'

They were off; Homais turned back home.

Madame Bovary had opened the window looking on to the garden, and was watching the clouds.

They were massing in the west over Rouen, rapidly rolling their black convolutions nearer, while long shafts of sunlight struck round their edges like golden arrows on a hanging trophy: the rest of the sky was clear and white as porcelain. A gust of wind bowed the poplars, and all at once the rain came, pattering down on the green leaves. Afterwards the sun shone out again, the hens clucked, sparrows shook their wings in the wet shrubs, and puddles of water running over the gravel carried off a scattering of pink acacia blossoms.

'How far away he'll be already!' thought Emma.

Homais came round as usual at half past six, during dinner.

'Well, so we've launched our young friend!' he said as he sat down.

'That's right,' the doctor answered. He turned in his chair. 'And what's the news with you?'

'Nothing much. My wife was a bit upset this afternoon. You know what women are – put out by the least thing. Mine in particular! But we mustn't be impatient with them: their nervous system is so much more sensitive than ours.'

'Poor Léon!' said Charles. 'How will he get on in Paris? Do you think he'll get used to it?'

Madame Bovary sighed.

'Never fear!' said the chemist, clicking his tongue. 'Little dinner parties at the restaurants, masked balls, champagne! He'll be well away, I can tell you!'

'I don't think he'll go wrong, though,' Charles demurred.

'No more do I,' answered Homais quickly, 'though he'll have to fall in with the rest, if he doesn't want to be taken for a Jesuit. Oh, you've no idea what a gay life they lead in the Latin Quarter, with their actresses! And students are very well thought of in Paris, too. If they've any sort of social gifts at all, they can get into the best circles. Ladies of the Faubourg St Germain have been known to fall in love with them, even, and that gives them a chance to make an excellent match eventually.'

'Yes, but I'm a bit afraid for him – *there* ...' said the doctor.

'Quite right,' the chemist interrupted, 'there are two sides to the picture. You've always got to keep one hand on your pocket in Paris, you know. ... Say you're in the Park: a stranger comes up to you, well dressed, a decoration perhaps, you'd take him for a diplomat: gets into conversation, makes himself agreeable, offers you snuff, picks up your hat for you. You get on famously: he takes you to a café, invites you down to his place in the country, introduces you over the drinks to all manner of acquaintance – and more often than not it's for nothing but to filch your purse or to lead you into evil ways.'

'That's true,' replied Charles, 'but I was thinking about dangers to health, mainly. Typhoid, for instance, which often attacks students from the country.'

Emma shuddered.

'Because of the change of diet,' the chemist agreed, 'and the way it upsets the general physical economy. And then the Paris water! And restaurant cooking: all that spiced food of theirs overheats your blood in the long run, and still doesn't beat a good stew, when all's said. I've always liked home-cooking best myself; it's far more wholesome. When I was studying in Rouen, you know, I boarded at a boarding-school. I used to have my meals along with the staff. ...'

So he went on expounding his general opinions and personal preferences, until Justin came to fetch him away to make a mulled egg that had been ordered.

'Never a moment's rest!' he exclaimed. 'Always tied! Can't leave the place an instant! For ever sweating blood like a farm-horse. What a yoke of drudgery!'

'By the by,' he added as he reached the door, 'have you heard the news?'

'What's that?'

'It is very likely,' answered Homais, raising his eyebrows and putting on his weightiest expression, 'that the Seine-Inférieure Agricultural Show will this year be held at Yonville-l'Abbaye. At any rate, that's the rumour. There was some mention of it in the paper this morning. It would be of the highest importance for the district. ... However, we'll talk of it another time. No, I can see my way, thank you; Justin has the lamp.'

7

NEXT day was a day of mourning to Emma. Everything seemed wrapped in a drifting, clinging darkness, and sorrow sank deep in her soul with a muffled wailing, like the winter wind in a derelict château. It was the spell cast by the departed, the lassitude that follows the event, the pain caused by any accustomed motion breaking off or prolonged vibration abruptly ceasing.

Sombrely melancholy, numbly despairing as when she had returned from La Vaubyessard with the dance-tunes whirling in her head, she now saw a taller, handsomer, a more delightful, and a vaguer Léon. He was far away, and yet he had not left her, he was here still, his shadow seemed to linger on the walls. She could not take her eyes from the carpet on which he had walked, the chairs in which he had sat. The river still flowed by, pushing its little waves along the slippery bank. Many a time they had strolled beside it, listening to that same murmuring of the water over the mossy pebbles. The fine sunny days they had had! The lovely afternoons, alone together in the shade at the bottom of the garden! He used to read aloud to her, perched on a footstool of dry sticks, bareheaded, while the cool breeze off the meadows fluttered the pages of his book and the nasturtiums round the arbour. ... He was gone – her only joy in life, her only hope of happiness! Why had she not seized that happiness when it offered? Why had she not held it, knelt to it, when it threatened to fly away? She cursed herself for not having given Léon her love. She thirsted for his lips. An impulse seized her to run after him, to throw herself into his arms and say 'It is I! I am yours!' But at once Emma felt dismayed at the difficulties of such an undertaking; and the vanity of the hope served but to intensify the desire.

From that moment her remembrance of Léon became the

centre of her discontent; it crackled there more fiercely than a fire left burning in the snow by travellers in the Russian steppes. She ran to it, huddled herself against it, carefully stirred it when it flagged, and cast about for fresh fuel to revive it; and all that the distant past or the immediate present could offer, all she felt and all she fancied, her sensual longings that now melted into air, her plans for happiness that creaked like dead branches in the wind, her sterile virtue, her fallen hopes and her domestic martyrdom – anything and everything she gathered up and used to feed her grief.

Still the flames subsided, whether from an insufficiency or an overload of fuel. Little by little love was dimmed by absence, yearning smothered by habit, and that red glow that had lit up her pale sky became shrouded deeper in shade and by degrees obliterated. To her drowsed consciousness an aversion from the husband seemed like an aspiration towards the lover; the sear of hatred like the warmth of tenderness. But since the storm still blew, and passion burned to ashes, and no help came nor sun shone out, it was on all sides darkest night, and she remained lost in a ghastly cold that cut right through her.

The black days she had known at Tostes began again. She accounted herself far more wretched this time, for she had learnt what sorrow was, and knew that it was endless.

A woman who had imposed such sacrifice on herself might be permitted a certain licence. She bought a Gothic prie-dieu, spent fourteen francs in a month on lemons for cleaning her nails, wrote to Rouen for a blue cashmere dress, and picked out the loveliest sash at Lheureux's, to wear round her waist over her dressing-gown. So arrayed she reclined on the sofa, with the blinds drawn and a book in her hand.

She often changed her hair-style, doing it in Chinese fashion, in soft curls or in plaits, or parting it at the side and rolling it under like a man.

She decided to learn Italian: she bought dictionaries, a

grammar, and a stock of paper. She attempted serious reading, history and philosophy. Sometimes Charles used to jump up out of his sleep at night, mumbling 'All right', under the impression that someone had come to fetch him to a patient; but it was only Emma striking a match to re-light her lamp. However, it was with her reading as with her needlework, which cluttered up the cupboard all unfinished: she picked it up, put it down, passed on to something else.

In certain moods she needed little encouragement to go quite wild. One day she maintained against her husband that she could drink a tumbler of brandy, and as Charles was foolish enough to dare her to it, she drained it to the last drop.

Despite her 'giddy' airs – as the housewives of Yonville termed them – Emma still didn't look cheerful. Almost always she had a fixed little line at the corners of her mouth, such as puckers the faces of old maids and thwarted success-seekers. Her skin was pale, white as a sheet all over, and pinched at the nostrils; her eyes stared out at you vacantly. Having discovered three grey hairs at her temples, she talked of ageing.

She had frequent attacks of faintness, and one day spat blood. Charles fussed about her anxiously.

'Pah, that's nothing!' she exclaimed.

Charles took refuge in his surgery and wept, slumped over the table in his office chair beneath the phrenological head.

He then wrote and asked his mother to come, and they had long talks together about Emma.

What should they do? What *could* they do, when she refused all treatment?

'I'll tell you what your wife needs,' said his mother, 'and that's hard work – manual work! If she were obliged to earn her bread, like a lot of other people, she'd never get these hysterical moods of hers. It all comes of the pack of ideas she's stuffed her head with, and the idle life she leads.'

'But she's always doing something,' said Charles.

'Doing something! Yes, reading novels – wicked books –

works against religion, that ridicule the priests with quotations out of Voltaire! It's playing with fire, that is, my boy! Anyone without religion will always go wrong in the end!'

So they decided to prevent Emma reading novels. It seemed no light undertaking. The good lady said she would do it, by stopping at the lending-library on her way through Rouen and telling them that Emma was giving up her subscription. If the shopkeeper still persisted in his poisoner's trade, would they not have the right to inform the police?

Mother and daughter-in-law bade one another a chilly farewell. In three weeks together in the house they hadn't exchanged half a dozen words apart from the customary greetings and inquiries at meals or at bedtime.

Madame Bovary senior left on a Wednesday. This was market-day at Yonville; and all morning the square had been cluttered up with carts, which stretched in a line along the houses from the church to the inn, all of them tipped up with their shafts in the air. On the opposite side were canvas booths selling cotton goods, counterpanes and woollen stockings, halters for horses and packets of blue ribbon with their ends streaming out in the breeze. Heavy ironmongery was laid out on the ground between pyramids of eggs and little hampers of cheese with bits of gluey straw sticking out. Alongside the corn-cutters were fowls clucking inside their low coops, thrusting their heads out between the bars. The crowds, jammed in one spot and unwilling to budge from it, threatened at times to smash in the front of the chemist's shop. On Wednesdays that establishment never emptied; people shoved their way in, less for medicine than for medical advice, so tremendous was M. Homais' reputation in the surrounding villages. His robust assurance had fascinated the rustics: they regarded him as a greater doctor than all doctors.

Emma was leaning out of her window — where she was often to be found, for in the country the window takes the place of theatres and park parades — and was amusing herself surveying the herd of yokels down below, when she saw a gentleman in a green velvet frock-coat. He wore yellow gloves, though his legs were clad in sturdy gaiters; and he was steering his way towards the doctor's house, followed by a peasant walking pensively with his eyes on the ground.

'Can I see the doctor?' he inquired of Justin, who was talking to Félicité on the doorstep. Taking him for the doctor's servant he added, 'Tell him it's Monsieur Rodolphe Boulanger, of La Huchette.'

It was no pride in his demesne that prompted the new-comer to add 'of La Huchette', but simply the desire to make himself known. La Huchette was in point of fact a large estate near Yonville, of which he had just acquired the house, along with a couple of farms that he was working himself in a semi-serious manner.

He was a bachelor and said to be worth 'at least six hundred a year'.

Charles came into the dining-room. Monsieur Boulanger presented his man, who wanted to be bled because he'd got 'pins and needles all over'.

'It'll clear me,' was his answer to all arguments.

So Bovary sent for a bandage and a basin, which he asked Justin to hold.

'Don't be afraid, my man,' he said to the already white-faced villager.

'No, no, go ahead!' the man answered. And he held out his brawny arm with a touch of bravado. At the prick of the lancet the blood spurted out and splashed against the mirror.

'Nearer with the basin!' Charles exclaimed.

'Lookee!' said the peasant. 'It's like a young fountain flow-ing! What red blood I've got. Should be a good sign, eh?'

'Sometimes,' the Officer of Health remarked, 'they don't feel anything at first: the syncope occurs afterwards, especially with strong chaps like this.'

Instantly the yokel let go of the lancet-case which he had

been twirling in his fingers: a jerk of his shoulders snapped the back of his chair: his cap fell to the floor.

'I thought as much,' said Bovary, putting his fingers over the vein.

The basin began to wobble in Justin's hands. He quaked at the knees. His face went white.

'Emma!' Charles called out, 'Emma!'

She was down the stairs in a flash.

'Vinegar!' he cried. 'Good Lord, two at once!'

He was so agitated, he had difficulty in applying the compress.

'It's nothing,' said Monsieur Boulanger quite calmly, as he lifted Justin in his arms and set him down on the table with his back to the wall.

Madame Bovary began to untie his cravat. There was a knot in his shirt-strings, and she was some minutes plying her dainty fingers at the lad's neck. Then she poured vinegar on to his cambric handkerchief, dabbed it over his forehead and blew on it delicately.

The man had come to. Justin remained unconscious, his pupils vanishing into the white of his eyes like blue flowers in milk.

'Don't let him see that,' said Charles.

Madame Bovary picked up the basin. As she bent down to put it under the table, her dress, a yellow summer dress with four flounces, long in the waist and full in the skirt, spread out around her on the floor. Emma put out her arms to steady herself as she crouched down, and the material clung to her here and there following the curve of her bosom. Then she went to fetch a jug of water, and was dissolving some lumps of sugar in it when the chemist arrived; the maid had been round to fetch him in the midst of the fray. When he saw that his apprentice had his eyes open, he breathed again. He walked all round him, eyeing him up and down.

'Ass!' he said. 'Proper little ass! Ass in three letters! A fine thing to make a fuss about, a paltry bit of blood-letting! A young fellow that's not afraid of anything, too! A regular squirrel, as you can see, who goes up to the dizziest heights nut-gathering! Oh, ah, you can talk, you can brag! A promising look-out for a future chemist! Who knows, you may find yourself called on in grave circumstances one day to enlighten the magistrates in the law-courts; and then it's essential to keep cool, to argue your case and show what you're made of, if you don't want to be taken for an idiot!'

Justin said nothing.

'Who asked you to come, anyway?' continued the chemist. 'You're always worrying Monsieur and Madame. Besides, I need you more than ever on Wednesdays. There's a score of people in the shop now. I've left everything on your account. Now, then – look sharp and get back – and keep an eye on the jars till I come!'

Having re-tied his cravat, Justin made off, and they started talking about fainting fits. Madame Bovary had never had one.

'That's remarkable for a lady!' said Monsieur Boulanger. 'You do find some very delicate people about, though. Do you know I've seen one of the seconds at a duel lose consciousness merely through hearing the pistols being loaded!'

'I'm not affected at all,' said the chemist, 'by the sight of other people's blood, but the mere idea of seeing my own flowing would be enough to make me faint, if I thought about it too much.'

Monsieur Boulanger now sent his man off, telling him not to worry, since his whim had been gratified.

'It's given me the pleasure of your acquaintance,' he added; and his eyes were on Emma as he spoke.

Then he deposited three francs on the edge of the table, bowed carelessly, and went.

He was soon over the river, on his way back to La Huchette, and Emma watched him striding across the meadow, under the poplars, every now and then slowing up like one in thought.

'Very nice!' he was saying to himself. 'Very nice, this doctor's wife! Pretty teeth, dark eyes, trim little foot, turned out like a Parisian! Where the deuce can she have come from? Where can that clumsy oaf have found her?'

Monsieur Rodolphe was thirty-four years old, hard of heart and shrewd of head, with much experience and understanding of women. This one had attracted him; so his mind was occupied with her, and with her husband.

'A stupid creature, he looks. Of course she's sick of him. Dirty nails and three days' growth of beard!... While he trots off on his rounds, she sits and darns the socks. And is bored! Longs to live in town and dance the polka every night! Poor little thing! Gasping for love, as a carp on a kitchen table for water. Three pretty words, and she'd adore you, I'll be bound. Tender, charming it'd be ... Yes, but how to shake it off afterwards?'

The drawbacks to pleasure, glimpsed in advance, set him thinking by contrast of his mistress. This was an actress at Rouen, whom he kept. Seeing her in his mind's eye – sated at the very thought of her – he said to himself:

'Madame Bovary is far prettier – fresher, above all! Virginie has been getting decidedly too fat. She's so tiresome, with her wants. And her mania for prawns ...'

The countryside was deserted, and Rodolphe could hear nothing as he went but the rhythmical swish of his boots in the long grass and the distant cry of the grasshoppers under the oats. He saw Emma standing there in the dining-room, in that dress ... ; he proceeded to undress her.

'Oh, I'll have her!' he shouted, scattering a clod of earth in front of him with a swing of his stick.

He immediately turned his attention to the tactical aspect of the enterprise.

'How and where to meet?' he mused. 'There'll be the brat for ever at her apron-strings: there'll be the maid, the neighbours, the husband, all sorts of nuisances to reckon with. Oh damn it!' he said, 'it'd take too long.'

He started off again:

'It's her eyes, they pierce your heart. And that pale complexion ... I adore pale women!'

By the time he reached the top of Argueil Hill, his mind was made up.

'So it only remains to watch out for opportunities. Right: I'll pay them a call or two, send them some game and poultry, have myself bled if necessary. We'll get friendly. I'll ask them over. ... By Jove, yes!' he thought, 'there's this Agricultural Show coming! She'll be there, I shall see her. Off we go, then, and boldly too – it's the best policy!'

8

THE famous Show did indeed arrive. From early morning on the great day the village folk had been standing at their doors discussing the preparations. The façade of the Town Hall was festooned with ivy, a marquee had been erected in one of the meadows, and in the middle of the market-place, opposite the church, stood a kind of cannon that was to announce the arrival of the Prefect and salute the successful competitors. The militia from Buchy – there was none at Yonville – had come to augment the fire-brigade, captained by Binet. He wore an even higher collar than usual today; and, buttoned tight into his uniform, the upper part of his body was so stiff and motionless that it seemed as if all the life in him had descended to his legs, which rose and fell with wooden exactitude as he marked time. A certain rivalry existed between the tax-collector and the colonel of the militia, and to display their talents they drilled their men separately. Red epaulettes and black breastplates crossed and recrossed alternately, starting off again and again, never ending. Never had there been such a parade! A number of citizens had washed their houses overnight; tricolours hung from open windows; all the inns were full. In the fine weather, starched bonnets, gold crosses and coloured neckerchiefs stood out dazzling as snow, glittering in the bright sunshine, relieving with their scattered motley the sombre monotony of the frock-coats and blue smocks. The farmers' wives from the surrounding district had tucked their dresses up, to avoid getting them splashed, with thick pins which they removed on dismounting. Their menfolk were concerned rather with their hats, covering them with their pocket-handkerchiefs, one corner of which they held between their teeth.

The crowds were flocking into the main street from both ends of the village, pouring out of lanes and byways and houses. Now and then a door-knocker banged back behind a lady in cotton gloves who was stepping out to see the sights. The principal attraction was a pair of long stands covered with fairy lights, flanking the platform on which the authorities were to sit. And against each of the four pillars of the Town Hall stood a pole bearing a little dark-green pennant emblazoned with an inscription in gold lettering. One said 'Trade', another 'Agriculture', the third 'Industry' and the fourth 'The Arts'.

However, the jubilation that beamed on every face seemed to cast a cloud upon Madame Lefrançois at the 'Lion'. She stood on her kitchen steps muttering under her breath.

'Tomfoolery! A lot of tomfoolery, with their tent thing! I suppose they imagine the Prefect'll enjoy having his dinner down there under canvas, like a circus clown? And all that nonsense is – "for the good of the district". ... Then why go and get that bottle-washer of theirs all the way from Neufchâtel? And who's it for, anyway – a lot of cowherds and ragamuffins. ...'

The chemist came in sight. He was wearing a dress-coat and nankeen trousers, beaver shoes and, unusually for him, a hat – a hat with a low crown.

'How d'ye do!' he called. 'You'll excuse me, I'm in a hurry.'

The stout widow asked where he was going.

'Aha, surprised to see me out? A man who's for ever poked away in his laboratory, like the rat in the old chap's cheese!'

'What cheese?' said the landlady.

'Oh, nothing, nothing,' answered Homais, 'I was merely trying to convey to you, Madame Lefrançois, that in the ordinary course of things I am quite a recluse. Today being a special occasion, however, I have to ...'

'Ah, that's where you're going!' she said with an air of scorn.

'Why, yes!' replied the chemist in astonishment. 'Am I not a member of the committee?'

Widow Lefrançois stared at him a moment and then replied with a smile:

'Oh, I see! But how do you come to be mixed up with farming? Do you know anything about it?'

'Certainly I do. I am a chemist. And chemistry being, Madame Lefrançois, the study of the reciprocal molecular action of all natural bodies, it follows that agriculture falls within its sphere! After all – composition of manures, fermentation of liquids, analysis of gases, effect of miasmas – what is all that, I ask you, but chemistry pure and simple?'

The landlady made no answer.

'Do you think,' Homais continued, 'that you need actually till the soil or fatten fowls yourself to be an agriculturist? No: it's the chemical composition of the relevant substances that you must know about, the geological deposits, atmospheric effects, soil properties, properties of minerals and rain-water, the varying densities of bodies, their capillary attraction and so on and so forth. Then you must have your principles of hygiene off thoroughly, in order to supervise and criticize the construction of buildings, the feeding of your livestock, the provisioning of your men! Furthermore, Madame Lefrançois, you must master botany! Be able to tell one plant from another, you follow me? Know which ones are beneficial and which deleterious, which unproductive and which nutritive, whether you'd do well to pull them up here and reset them there, to propagate some and destroy others. In short, you've got to keep abreast of science in the pamphlets and published papers, and always be on the alert, to point out improvements. ...'

The landlady was gazing steadfastly at the door of the Café Français.

'Would to heaven our farmers were trained chemists,' Homais proceeded, 'or at least paid more attention to scientific teaching! You know, I myself recently wrote a striking little work, a treatise of over seventy-two pages, entitled "Cider: its Manufacture and Operation; with some original observations thereon", and I sent it up to the Agricultural Society of Rouen. It earned me the distinction of being admitted to membership of that body, in the Agricultural Section, Pomology Sub-section. Well, now, if my work had only been given to the general public ...'

The chemist paused, noting the landlady's air of preoccupation.

'Look at 'em!' she said. 'It's beyond everything! A cookshop like that!'

And with a shrugging of her shoulders, that pulled her jumper up over her bosom, she pointed with both hands to her rival's establishment, whence issued the sound of singing.

'Well, it won't be for long now,' she added. 'Another week'll see the end of it!'

Homais stepped back in amazement. She came down the three steps and spoke in his ear:

'D'you mean to say you've not heard? The bailiffs are going in this week. Lheureux's selling him up. He's been the death of 'em with his bills.'

'What a shocking tragedy!' exclaimed the chemist, who always had the right form of words for every conceivable occasion.

The landlady proceeded to tell him what had happened.

She had heard it from Théodore, the man at Monsieur Guillaumin's. Much as she abominated Tellier, she censured Lheureux; he was a wheedling, grovelling creature.

'Hullo, there he is!' she said. 'Going through the market! He's bowing to Madame Bovary. She's got a green hat on: and look, she's on Monsieur Boulanger's arm!'

'Madame Bovary!' exclaimed Homais. 'I must run and pay her my respects. She might like to have a seat in the enclosure, under the peristyle.'

And turning a deaf ear to the rest of the Widow Lefrançois' story, the chemist hurried off, with a smile on his lips, a jaunty stride, and any number of bowings in all directions, taking up a great deal of space with the long tails of his dress-coat flapping in the breeze behind him.

Rodolphe had noticed him from a distance and quickened his pace, but as Madame Bovary got out of breath, he slowed up again, smiling at her as he explained brusquely:

'That was to escape from the heavy fellow – you know, the chemist.'

She gave him a nudge.

'What's the meaning of that?' he asked himself, and as he walked along he surveyed her out of the corner of his eye.

Her calm profile gave no hint. It showed clear in the light, framed in the oval of her bonnet, which was tied with pale reed-like ribbons. She was looking straight in front of her, beneath her long curving lashes, and though her eyes were fully open they appeared slightly narrowed because of the blood that pulsated gently beneath the fine skin that covered her cheek-bones. Where her nostrils met was a pale pink glow. Her head leaned a little to one side, and between her parted lips you saw the pearly tips of her white teeth.

'Is she laughing at me?' Rodolphe wondered.

Emma's nudge had been simply a warning, however. Monsieur Lheureux was walking along beside them. Every now and then he made some conversational remark, such as 'What a glorious day!' 'Everybody's out of doors!' 'The wind's in the east!'

Madame Bovary took as little notice of his advances as did Rodolphe, though the draper came sidling up to them at their least movement, touching his hat and saying, 'Beg pardon?'

Outside the blacksmith's, instead of keeping on up to the gate along the roadway, Rodolphe turned abruptly down a side-path, drawing Madame Bovary with him.

'Farewell, Monsieur Lheureux!' he called out. 'Till we meet again!'

'How you got rid of him!' she said with a laugh.

'Why let people hang on to one?' he answered. 'And to-day, when I'm fortunate enough to be with you ...'

Emma blushed. He left the sentence unfinished, and started talking about the lovely weather, and the delight of walking on the grass.

Some daises were growing there.

'What pretty daisies!' he said. 'Oracles in plenty for all the local girls in love! ... Suppose I pick one,' he added. 'What do you say?'

'Are *you* in love?' she asked, with a little cough.

'Eh! eh! who knows?' answered Rodolphe.

The show-ground was beginning to fill up, and the women helpers kept bumping into you with their big umbrellas, their baskets and their babies. You had frequently to be getting out of the way of a long row of peasant-girls, maidservants in blue stockings and flat shoes, with silver rings on their fingers, who smelt of milk when you came close to them. They spread out hand in hand all across the field, from the row of aspens up to the marquee. By now the judging was due to start, and one after another the farmers were filing into a kind of arena marked off by a long rope hung on stakes.

Inside were the animals, their muzzles towards the rope, their rumps jostling together in a rough line. Somnolent pigs sank their snouts in the ground, calves lowed, sheep bleated, cows sprawled their bellies out on the grass, with one leg bent beneath them, and chewed with deliberation, blinking their heavy eyelids as the midges buzzed round them. Shirt-sleeved wagoners were holding the restive stallions, which kept neighing vociferously in the direction of the mares. These stood quite quiet, stretching out their necks, their manes drooping, while their foals rested in their shadows, or came up from time to time to suck. Above the undulating line of massed beasts, you saw a white mane ruffling up like a wave in the breeze, a pair of sharp horns jutting out, or the heads of some men running. Outside the arena, a hundred yards farther on, a big black bull stood apart, muzzled, with an iron ring through its nostrils, moving no more than an animal of bronze. A ragged child held it by a rope.

Sundry gentlemen were now advancing with heavy tread between the two rows of animals, examining each in turn and then conferring together in low tones. One, who looked more important than the rest, made jottings in a notebook as he went. This was the chairman of the judges, Monsieur Derozerays de la Panville. The minute he recognized Rodolphe he stepped briskly towards him.

'What's this, Monsieur Boulanger?' he said, with a pleasant smile. 'Are you deserting us?'

Rodolphe assured him he was coming directly. But when the chairman was once more out of earshot he said, 'I think not! When I can be with you!'

While ridiculing the Show, Rodolphe nevertheless produced his blue ticket, so that they could move about wherever they pleased, and he even halted occasionally in front of one of the fine 'exhibits'. Noticing, however, that Madame Bovary was unimpressed by these, he started making fun of the Yonville ladies and the way they were turned out. He apologized for being so carelessly dressed himself. His clothes were an incongruous mixture of the workaday and the elegant, such as is taken by the vulgar to denote an eccentric way of life, an emotional disturbance, or a subservience to aesthetics, combined always with a certain contempt for convention, by which they are either fascinated or exasperated. Frilly at the cuffs, his cambric shirt fluttered out in front between the revers of his grey drill waistcoat wherever the breeze took it. His broad-striped trousers terminated at the ankle above a pair of nankeen boots vamped with patent leather. These were so highly polished that you could see the grass in them; and in them he went trampling over the horse-dung, with one hand in his jacket pocket, his straw hat tilted to the side of his head.

'But then, when you live in the country ...' he added.

'... There's no point in bothering,' said Emma.

'Exactly!' Rodolphe replied. 'Just fancy, there's not one of all these good people who's capable of understanding so much as the cut of a coat.'

They spoke of the dullness of the country, the lives that were smothered by it, the illusions that perished there.

'That's why,' said Rodolphe, 'I'm sinking into such a state of gloom. ...'

'You!' she exclaimed in surprise. 'Why, I thought you were a very cheerful person.'

'Oh, on the surface, yes. I wear my jester's mask in public. But how often I've looked at a graveyard in the moonlight and wondered whether I wouldn't be better off lying there asleep with the rest of them!'

'Oh! But what about your friends?' she said. 'Don't you think of them?'

'My friends? What friends? Have I got any? Is there anyone who cares about me?' – and he accompanied these last words with a little hissing sound.

However, they had to step aside for a man coming up behind them with an immense scaffolding of chairs. He was so loaded that you could see nothing of him but the toes of his sabots and the tips of his outstretched arms. It was Lestiboudois the sexton, carting round the church chairs among the crowd. Full of ideas where his own interests were concerned, he had hit upon this method of turning the Show to account; and his enterprise was rewarded, for he had more customers than he could cope with. The villagers, feeling the warmth, had actually started squabbling over those straw seats that reeked of incense; and against their stout backs, covered with blobs of candle-grease, they were leaning with a certain awe.

Madame Bovary took Rodolphe's arm again.

'Yes,' he went on as though to himself, 'I've missed a lot, always being alone. If only I'd had some aim in life. If I'd met with affection. If I'd found someone ... Oh, I'd have used all the energy I possessed – conquered everything, smashed down every obstacle.'

'It doesn't seem to me you've got much to grumble about,' said Emma.

'You think not?'

'After all, you're free' – she hesitated – 'and rich.'

'You're laughing at me!' he exclaimed.

She assured him she was not. As she spoke, they heard the boom of a cannon. Everybody at once started rushing back to the village.

It was a false alarm; there was no sign of the Prefect. The judges were in a quandary: should they wait, or open the proceedings?

At last, from the far end of the square, appeared a large hired landau drawn by a pair of skinny horses, which were being roundly lashed by a coachman in a white hat. Binet just had time to shout 'Fall in!' and the Colonel to follow suit. There was a dive for the piled rifles. In the commotion, some of the men forgot to fasten their collars. The official equipage seemed to divine their discomfiture, however, for the pair of hacks slowed up, tugging at their chain, and ambled to a halt outside the Town Hall, just as the militia and the fire-brigade were deploying to the beat of the drums.

'Mark time!' shouted Binet.

'Halt!' shouted the Colonel. 'Into line – left – turn!'

After a 'Present arms', in which the smacking of the bands came rattling out like a copper kettle rolling downstairs, all the rifles were lowered again.

Thereupon a gentleman in a short silver-trimmed jacket was seen to step out of the carriage. He was bald in front and tufted behind, sallow-complexioned, and with an appearance of the utmost benignity. He narrowed his large heavy-lidded eyes to scan the crowd, lifted his pointed nose in the air and set a smile on his sunken mouth. Recognizing the mayor by his sash, he explained that the Prefect had been prevented from coming. He himself was an official on the Prefect's staff. He added a few words of apology. Tuvache responded in complimentary terms. The visitor declared himself over-whelmed. So they stood there face to face, their foreheads almost touching, surrounded by the judges, the councillors, the important personages, the militia, and the crowd at large. Holding his little black three-cornered hat against his chest, the great man reiterated his greetings, while Tuvache, bent like a bow, smiled back at him, stuttering and stammering and making protestation of his loyalty to the throne and his appreciation of the honour that was being done to Yonville.

Hippolyte, the groom from the inn, came limping up on his club-foot to take the reins from the coachman, and led the horses off beneath the archway of the Golden Lion, where a crowd of peasants gathered round to inspect the carriage. There was a tattoo on the drums, the howitzer thundered, and the gentlemen filed up and took their places on the platform, in the easy-chairs of red Utrecht velvet lent by Madame Tuvache.

A homogeneous group they were, with their soft, fair, slightly tanned faces, the colour of new cider, and their bushy whiskers sticking out above tall stiff collars supported by white cravats tied in a floppy bow. Every one of the waistcoats had velvet revers, every watch carried an oval cornelian seal at the end of a long band. Hands all rested on thighs, carefully lifting the creases of their trousers, which were of unsponged cloth and shone more brilliantly than their stout leather boots.

The ladies of the party kept at the back, between the pillars in the vestibule, while the body of the crowd faced them, standing up, or seated on Lestiboudois' chairs. For he had brought a load along with him from the meadow, and was all the while running off to get more from the church, causing such congestion with his trade that one had great difficulty in reaching the platform steps.

'I think myself,' said Monsieur Lheureux to the chemist, as the latter passed along to take his seat, 'that they ought to have put up a couple of Venetian masts, with something rich and a bit severe in the way of draping. It would have made a fine sight.'

'Certainly it would,' answered Homais. 'But there, what can you expect? The mayor *would* do the whole thing on his own. Poor old Tuvache, he hasn't got much taste; in fact, he's completely lacking in any sort of artistic sense.'

Meanwhile Rodolphe and Madame Bovary had gone up to the Council Chamber on the first floor of the Town Hall. It was empty, and so he declared that they would be able to enjoy the spectacle in comfort up there. Fetching three stools from the oval table under the bust of the King, he placed them by one of the windows, and they sat down side by side.

There was a great commotion on the platform, much whispering and parleying, and at last the Prefect's deputy rose. His name, now known to be Lieuvain, was being passed round among the crowd. After collecting his papers together and holding them close up to his eyes to see them better, he began:

'Gentlemen,

'Let me first be permitted, before addressing you on the object of our gathering here today – and this sentiment will,

I am sure, be shared by all of you – let me be permitted, I say, to pay a fitting tribute to the Authorities, to the Government and, gentlemen, to our beloved Monarch and Sovereign Lord the King, to whom no branch of public or private prosperity is indifferent, and who steers the chariot of state with a hand at once so firm and so wise, amid the ceaseless perils of a stormy sea – who knows, moreover, how to gain respect for peace no less than for war – for Trade and for Industry, for Agriculture and for the Arts.'

'I ought to get a bit farther back,' said Rodolphe.

'Why?' said Emma.

But at that moment the official's voice rose to a remarkable pitch as he declaimed:

'Those days are past, gentlemen, when civil discord stained our public places with blood, when landowner, merchant, and working-man alike, as they courted peaceful slumbers, would tremble lest they be awakened by the clang of the tocsin; when the most subversive slogans were aimed in all audacity at the very foundations – '

'They might see me from down there,' Rodolphe explained, 'and then I'd have to spend a fortnight apologizing. And with my bad reputation ...'

'What a thing to say about yourself!'

'No, no, it's abominable, I assure you.'

'However, gentlemen,' the speaker proceeded, 'if, driving those sombre pictures from my mind, I turn my gaze now to the present state of our fair land, what do I see? Everywhere, trade and the arts flourish. Everywhere new paths of communication, new arteries within the body politic, are opening up new contacts. Our great manufacturing centres thrive once more. Religion finds new strength and smiles in every heart. Our ports are full. Confidence returns. At last France breathes again!'

'Though I dare say I deserve it by ordinary standards,' Rodolphe added.

'How is that?' she asked.

'Why, do you not know that there are souls for ever in turmoil? Souls that must have dream and action turn and turn about – a passion of utter purity, and an orgy of self-indulgence? It leads one into all kinds of adventures and escapades.'

She gazed at him then as one might gaze at a traveller who has journeyed through strange lands.

'We poor women haven't even that diversion,' she remarked.

'Sorry diversion, for it never brings happiness.'

'Does anything?'

'Yes,' he answered, 'it comes along one day.'

'And this,' the distinguished visitor was saying, 'this you have realized, you who cultivate the land and labour in the fields, peaceable pioneers in a true task of civilization! Progressive and high-minded men! You have realized, I say, that the storms of political strife are, in very truth, more devastating than the riot of the elements!'

'It comes along one day,' Rodolphe repeated, 'all of a sudden, just when you are despairing of it. Then, new vistas open. It's as if a voice cried out "Behold!" You feel you must reveal yourself, give everything, sacrifice everything, to that person. Nothing need be said. You know! You have seen each other in your dreams' – and his eyes rested on hers. 'There before you, shining, sparkling, is the treasure you have sought so long. Still you doubt. You dare not believe. You stand dazed as if you had stepped out of darkness into light.'

Here Rodolphe helped out his words with motions, passing his hand over his face like a man in a trance. Then he let it fall on Emma's. She withdrew hers. The official read on:

'And who can wonder at it, gentlemen? Only he who remains so blind, so immersed, so deeply immersed, I do not fear to say, in the prejudices of a past age, as still to misconceive the spirit of our agricultural communities. Where, indeed, can one find more patriotism than in the country, more devotion to the common weal, in a word, more intelligence? I do not mean, gentlemen, a superficial intelligence – that vain embellishment of idle minds – but a profound and balanced intelligence that applies itself first and foremost to the pursuit of useful ends, contributing thus to the good of each, to the general advancement, and to the upholding of the State – the fruit of respect for law and fulfilment of duty!'

'Duty again!' said Rodolphe. 'Always on about duty. I'm sick to death of the word. What a lot of flannel-waistcoated old fogeys they are, pious old women with beads and bed-socks, for ever twittering in our ears about "Duty, duty!" To feel nobly and to love what is beautiful – that's our duty. Not to accept all the conventions of society and the humilia-tions society imposes on us.'

'Still ... all the same ...' Madame Bovary demurred.

'No! Why inveigh against the passions? Are they not the one beautiful thing there is on earth; the source of all heroism and enthusiasm, poetry, music, art, everything?'

'All the same,' said Emma, 'we must take some notice of what the world thinks, and conform to its morality.'

'But you see, there are two moralities,' he replied. 'One is the petty, conventional morality of men, clamorous, ever-changing, that flounders about on the ground, of the earth earthy, like that mob of nincompoops down there. The other, the eternal morality, is all about and above us, like the country-side that surrounds us and the blue heavens that give us light.'

Monsieur Lieuvain had just wiped his mouth with his hand-kerchief. He resumed:

'Now what should I be doing here, gentlemen, demonstrat-ing the usefulness of farming to *you*? Who supplies our wants, who provides us with the means of life, but the farmer? The farmer, gentlemen, who, sowing with laborious hand the fer-tile furrows of our countryside, brings forth the corn which, crushed and ground by ingenious machinery, issues thence in the guise of flour, to be conveyed to our cities and speedily delivered to the baker, who makes it into a food for rich and poor alike. Is it not the farmer, again, who fattens his rich flocks to give us clothes? How should we clothe, or feed, ourselves were it not for the farmer? Nay, gentlemen, need we go even so far afield for our examples? Who has not frequently pondered on the great importance to us of that homely animal, the adornment of our poultry-yards, that provides us with soft pillows to sleep on, succulent flesh for our tables, and eggs? – But I could go on for ever enumerating, one by one, the various products that the well-tended earth lavishes like a bountiful mother upon her children. Here the vine, there the cider apple, elsewhere colza, cheese, or flax – gentlemen, let us not forget flax! – which has made such strides in recent years, and to which I would more especially draw your attention.'

He had no need to draw it, for the multitude sat open-mouthed to drink in his words. Tuvache, next to him, listened with staring eyes. Monsieur Derozerays gently closed his now and then. Farther along, the chemist, with his son Napoléon between his knees, had his hand cupped behind his ear so as not to lose a single syllable. The rest of the judges nodded their chins slowly up and down in their waistcoats to signify assent. The fire-brigade leaned on their bayonet-scabbards at the foot of the platform, and Binet stood motionless, his elbow stuck out, the point of his sabre in the air. He may have heard, but he could not have seen anything for the visor of his helmet, which came right down over his nose. His lieutenant, Monsieur Tuvache's youngest son, had his visor at a still more exaggerated angle. He was wearing an enormous helmet that wobbled on top of his head and allowed one end of his calico handkerchief to slip down behind. He smiled beneath it with a perfectly child-like sweetness, and his little white face, running with sweat, wore an expression of enjoyment, exhaustion and somnolence.

The crowd stretched right across to the houses on the far side of the square. There were people leaning out of every window, standing in every doorway. Justin, outside the chemist's shop, seemed quite transfixed by the sight that met his eyes. In spite of the silence, Monsieur Lieuvain's voice failed to carry in the air, and reached you only in fragmentary phrases, drowned here and there by the scraping of chairs among the crowd. Then all of a sudden you heard the long lowing of a bullock behind you, or lambs bleating to each other at the corners of the streets. They had been driven down by the shepherds and cowherds, and gave voice from time to time as their tongues snatched at a morsel of foliage hanging above their muzzles.

Rodolphe had drawn closer to Emma and was talking rapidly in a low voice.

'Doesn't this conspiracy of society revolt you? Is there a single feeling it does not condemn? The noblest instincts, the purest sympathies, are reviled and persecuted, and if ever two poor souls do meet, then everything is organized to prevent their union. They'll attempt it all the same, they'll flap their wings and call to one another. And no matter what happens, sooner or later, in six months or ten years, they'll meet again and love – because Fate ordains it, because they were born for one another.'

He sat with his arms folded on his knees. Raising his eyes to Emma's, he gazed at her closely, fixedly. She saw little gleams of gold playing about his dark pupils. She was near enough to him to smell the cream on his glossy hair. She felt limp, she remembered the Viscount who had waltzed with her at La Vaubyessard: his beard had exhaled that same perfume of lemon and vanilla. Mechanically her eyelids narrowed as she breathed in the scent. She straightened up in her chair, and as she did so she caught a glimpse, right away on the farthest horizon, of the ancient *Hirondelle* slowly descending Leux Hill, trailing a long plume of dust behind it. It was in that yellow coach that Léon had so often come back to her; and along that road that he had gone from her for ever. She had a vision of him at his window across the way. Then everything blurred, the sky clouded over, and it seemed to her that she was still circling in the waltz, in the glare of the chandeliers, on the Viscount's arm, and Léon was not far away, he was just coming. ... But all the while she was conscious of Rodolphe's face beside her. Her old desires became imbued with the sweetness of the present sensation, and, on this subtle breath of perfume that was being shed upon her soul, they were tossed about like grains of sand in a gust of wind. Her nostrils dilated rapidly, vigorously, breathing in the freshness of the ivy round the tops of the columns. She took off her gloves, wiped her hands, fanned her face with her handkerchief, while through the throbbing at her temples she could hear the hum of the crowd below and the speaker still droning out his singsong.

'Keep steadily ahead!' he was saying. 'Listen neither to the voice of hidebound habit nor to the impulsive counsels of rash experiment! Work above all at the improvement of the soil, at producing rich fertilizers, at breeding fine horses and cattle, fine sheep and pigs! Let this Agricultural Show be a peaceful arena where victor extends the hand of brotherhood to vanquished and wishes him success next time! ... And now, to all those venerable retainers, lowly servants whose laborious toils have never before been recognized by any Government, I say: Come forward and receive the meed of your silent virtues! Rest assured that from this day forth the State will never lose sight of you, that it will encourage and protect you, will satisfy your just demands, and lighten, so far as in it lies, the painful burden of your sacrifice!'

And Monsieur Lieuvain sat down.

Monsieur Derozerays rose and began his speech. This was far less ornate than the official's, and recommended itself by a more positive flavour – a matter of more specialized knowledge and more exalted reflections. Eulogistic reference to the Government had less place in it, farming and religion had more. The bond that existed between the two was made clear

– they had always worked together for civilization ... While Rodolphe was talking to Madame Bovary about dreams, presentiments and magnetic attraction, the speaker went back to the infancy of society, to those savage times when men lived on acorns in the heart of great forests; from which he passed on to the period at which they had given up animals' skins for a covering of cloth, had ploughed the land and planted the vine. Now was this an improvement? Were there not perhaps more disadvantages than advantages in these discoveries? Monsieur Derozerays asked himself the question. Rodolphe had led on gradually from magnetism to affinities; and while the Chairman alluded to Cincinnatus at his plough, to Diocletian among his cabbages, to the Chinese emperors ushering in the new year with the sowing of seed, the young man was explaining to the young woman that the cause of these irresistible attractions lay in some previous existence.

'We, now, why did we meet? What turn of fate decreed it? Was it not that, like two rivers gradually converging across the intervening distance, our own natures propelled us towards one another?'

He took her hand, and she did not withdraw it.

'General Prize!' cried the Chairman.

'Just now, for instance, when I came to call on you ...'

'Monsieur Bizet of Quincampoix.'

'... how could I know that I should escort you here?'

'Seventy francs!'

'And I've stayed with you, because I couldn't tear myself away, though I've tried a hundred times.'

'Manure!'

'And so I'd stay tonight and tomorrow and every day for all the rest of my life.'

'To Monsieur Caron of Argueil, a Gold Medal!'

'For I have never been so utterly charmed with anyone before.'

'To Monsieur Bain of Givry St Martin.'

'And so I shall cherish the memory of you.'

'For a merino ram ...'

'But you'll forget me. I shall have passed like a shadow ...'

'To Monsieur Belot of Notre-Dame ...'

'No, say I shan't! Tell me I shall count for something in your thoughts, in your life?'

'Pigs: Prize divided! Monsieur Lehérissé and Monsieur Cullembourg, sixty francs each!'

Rodolphe squeezed her hand. He felt it warm and vibrant in his, like a captive turtle-dove trying to take wing. Whether she was trying to withdraw it, or responding to his pressure, her fingers made a movement.

'Oh, thank you, you do not repulse me!' he said. 'How sweet you are! You know that I am yours! Only let me look at you, let me gaze upon you!'

A breeze from the window ruffled the cloth on the table, and down in the square the peasant women's big bonnets lifted up, fluttering like white butterflies' wings.

'Oil-cake,' the Chairman continued. He began to go faster: 'Flemish fertilizer – Flax – Drainage – Long Leases – Domestic Service.'

Rodolphe had stopped speaking. They looked at one another, and their dry lips quivered in a supreme desire. Gently, effortlessly, their fingers interwined.

'Catherine Nicaise Elisabeth Leroux of Sassetot la Guerrière: For fifty-four years' service at the same farm: Silver Medal, value twenty-five francs!'

'Where is she? Catherine Leroux!' the official repeated.

There was no sign of her. Voices could be heard whispering:

'Go on!'

'No.'

'Over there on the left!'

'Don't be afraid!'

'Stupid creature!'

'Well, is she there or not?' cried Tuvache.

'Yes, here she is!'

'Then let her come up!'

Thereupon a timorous-looking little old woman was seen to step up on to the platform, wizened and shrunken in her tattered garments. She wore heavy clogs on her feet and a big blue apron round her waist. Her thin face, framed in a borderless cap, was wrinkled as a withered russet, and from the sleeves of her red bodice appeared two drooping hands, gnarled at the joints, and so caked and chapped and hardened by barn-dust, wool-grease and washing-soda that they looked dirty though they had been rinsed in fresh water. Years of service had left them hanging open as if to bear their own humble witness to the many hardships they had endured. A touch of cloistral austerity lent some expression to her face, but her pale stare was softened by no shade of sadness or of feeling. Living among animals, she had grown placid and mute as they. This was the first time she had ever found herself the centre of such a crowd of people. Inwardly terrified by the flags and drums, the frock-coated gentlemen and the official's Legion of Honour, she stood stock still, not knowing whether to advance or to run, or why they kept pushing her forward or why the judges smiled at her. There she stood, before those beaming bourgeois, an embodied half-century of servitude.

'Come, venerable Catherine Nicaise Elisabeth Leroux!' said the official, who had taken the list of prizewinners from the Chairman. 'Come along, come along!' he coaxed her in fatherly fashion, looking alternately at the sheet of paper in his hand and at the aged crone in front of him.

'Is she deaf?' said Tuvache, bouncing up in his armchair. He started shouting in her ear:

'Fifty-four years' service! Silver Medal! Twenty-five francs! For you!'

Having got her medal, she gazed at it, and a blissful smile

overspread her features. As she trotted off, she could be heard muttering: 'I'll give it to our *curé*, to say mass for me.'

'Fanatical!' exclaimed the chemist, leaning across to the lawyer.

The proceedings were over. The crowds dispersed. The speeches had been delivered, and now everybody resumed his station and things reverted to normal. Masters bullied servants. Servants belaboured the animals – those indolent conquerors returning to their sheds, their horns garlanded with green.

Meanwhile the militia had gone up to the first floor of the Town Hall, with cakes spitted on their bayonets, and the regimental drummer carrying a basketful of bottles. Madame Bovary took Rodolphe's arm and he saw her home. They parted at her door, and then he went off for a stroll in the meadow until it was time for the feast to begin.

The feast was long and noisy and badly served. The guests were wedged in so tight they could hardly move, and the narrow planks that were doing duty as benches very nearly gave way beneath the weight of the assembled company. They ate hugely. Everyone set to and did his share. Sweat poured down every forehead, and a pallid stream hovered between the lamps above the table, like a river mist on an autumn morning. Rodolphe leant back against the side of the marquee, too deep in his thoughts of Emma to hear a thing. On the grass behind him, servants were piling up the dirty plates. His neighbours spoke to him and received no answer. They refilled his glass, but though the hubbub grew around him, all was quiet within his mind. He was thinking of the things she had said, and of the shape of her lips. Her face appeared to him in the cap badges of the militia, shining as in a magic mirror. The pleats of her dress hung down the walls; and days of love unfolded endlessly before him in the long vistas of the future.

In the evening he saw her again, at the fireworks, but she was with her husband and Monsieur and Madame Homais.

The chemist, much perturbed about the danger of stray squibs, kept breaking away from the party every other minute to go and offer Binet his advice.

The fireworks had been delivered to Monsieur Tuvache, who, with excessive caution had stored them in his cellar. The powder was consequently damp and wouldn't light, and the principal feature, which was to have been a dragon biting its tail, completely miscarried. Occasionally a paltry little Roman candle went off and drew from the gaping crowd a great roar of applause, with which there mingled the shrieks of women who were being tickled under cover of the darkness. Emma nestled silently against Charles, then raised her chin as she followed the flash of the rockets across the black sky. Rodolphe watched her in the glimmer of the lanterns.

The lanterns burned down one by one. The stars shone out.

A few drops of rain began to fall, and Emma tied her scarf over her hair.

At that moment the official's cab drove out of the inn yard. The coachman was drunk and immediately dropped into a doze, and from some way off you could see, above the hood, between the two lamps, his unwieldy body swinging to and fro with the rocking of the vehicle.

'Drunkenness really ought to be dealt with severely!' said the chemist. 'I'd like to see a special list put up every seven days on the door of the Town Hall, with the names of all those who have been under the influence of alcohol during the week. From the statistical point of view, you'd have a kind of public record, which might come in ... Excuse me!' – and once more he ran off to speak to the Captain.

That gentleman was just going home – home to his lathe.

'It wouldn't be a bad idea,' said Homais to him, 'if you sent one of your men, or went round yourself ...'

'Don't come bothering me. There's nothing to make a fuss about,' answered the tax-collector.

'Nothing to worry about!' said the chemist as he rejoined

his friends. 'Monsieur Binet assures me that everything has been attended to. There won't be any sparks, and the pumps are full. We can go home to bed.'

'My word, I can do with it, too!' observed Madame Homais, who was yawning tremendously. 'But who cares? We've had a lovely day for our Show.'

'A very lovely day!' agreed Rodolphe under his breath, his eyes tender.

They said good-night and went their ways.

Two days later, a big report of the Show appeared in the *Rouen Beacon.* Homais had composed it in style the following morning.

'Whence these festoons, these flowers, these garlands? Whither bound these throngs like the billows of a raging ocean, beneath a tropical sun that pours upon our leas its warmth torrential?'

He went on to speak of the condition of the peasants: the Government was doing a great deal, certainly, but not enough.

'Be bold!' he cried to it. 'A thousand reforms must be achieved. Let us achieve them!'

Coming to the scene of the great man's arrival, he omitted neither the 'martial bearing of our militia', nor 'our sprightly village lasses', nor the bald-headed ancients who contributed their patriarchal presence – some of them the 'survivors of our immortal legions', who 'felt their hearts beat once more in time to the manly roll of the drums'. He mentioned himself among the foremost of the judges, and even reminded his readers in a footnote that M. Homais, pharmacist, had sent a treatise on cider to the Agricultural Society. When he got to the prize-giving, he painted the delight of the winners in dithyrambic strokes. Brother embraced brother, the father his son, the husband his wife. Many a one displayed his modest medal with pride, and doubtless, when he returned home to his good wife, hung it up, with tears in his eyes, on the wall of his humble cottage.

'At six o'clock a banquet, held in Monsieur Liégeard's meadow, assembled the leading personages of the Show. The utmost cordiality reigned throughout. Divers toasts were drunk, Monsieur Lieuvain proposing "The King", Monsieur Tuvache "The Prefect", Monsieur Homais "Industry and The Arts, those twin sisters", and Monsieur Leplichey "Progress". At night the sky was suddenly illumined by a brilliant fire-work display. 'Twas a veritable kaleidoscope, an operatic scena. For an instant our little town imagined itself trans-planted into the midst of an Arabian Night's dream.

'Be it said that no untoward event came to upset our happy family gathering.'

And he added:

'Only the absence of the clergy was remarked. No doubt the churches have their own idea of progress. ... As you will, reverend apostles of Loyola!'

9

Six weeks went by, with no sign of Rodolphe. At last, one evening, he appeared.

'Wouldn't do to go back too soon,' he had said to himself the day after the Show, and at the end of the week he went off for some shooting. After that he wondered if he had left it too long. But then he reasoned like this:

'If she fell in love with me the first day, she must have been dying to see me again, and she'll be more in love with me than ever now. Very well, proceed!'

And when he saw Emma turn pale at his entrance, he knew he had not miscalculated.

She was alone, in the fading light. The little muslin curtains over the windows deepened the dusk; the gilt on the baro-meter, touched by a last ray of sunshine, threw a blaze of fire on to the looking-glass, between the indentations of the coral.

Rodolphe remained standing, Emma hardly answered his words of greeting.

'I've been busy,' he said. 'I haven't been well.'

'Nothing serious?' she asked quickly.

'Well, no,' he admitted, sitting on a stool at her side. 'The truth is, I decided not to come.'

'Why?'

'Can't you guess?' He turned and looked at her so passionately that she lowered her eyes with a blush.

'Emma!'

'Sir!' – and she moved away a little.

'You see! I was right,' he observed in a gloomy voice, 'I was right, not wanting to come back. For that name that fell from my lips – the name that fills my heart – is forbidden me. Madame Bovary: everybody calls you that! And it isn't your name, anyway, it's someone else's. Someone else's,' he repeated; and he hid his face in his hands.

'Oh, I think of you constantly. It drives me to despair. ... Forgive me! I'll leave you. ... Good-bye! I'll go away, far away, and you'll hear no more of me. But today, some mysterious force has impelled me to you. One cannot fight with fate! Or resist when the angels smile! One is simply carried away by what is charming and lovely and adorable!'

Emma had never been told such things before, and her pride stretched out luxuriously in the warmth of his words, as though she were relaxing in a hot bath.

'Though I didn't call on you,' he continued, 'though I couldn't see you, at any rate I kept a watchful eye on all about you. I used to get up at night, every night, and come here. I used to gaze at your house, at the moonlight shining on the roof, the trees in the garden swaying to and fro outside your window and the little lamp gleaming out on to the darkness. ... Ah, little did you guess that down there, so near and yet so far, was a poor wretch ...'

'Oh, you are good!' she said, turning to him with a sob.

'No, I love you, that is all. Can you doubt it? Tell me – one word, one little word!'

And imperceptibly Rodolphe slipped from the stool to the floor. The next minute they heard a clatter of clogs in the kitchen. He noticed that the door wasn't fastened.

'It would be very kind of you,' he remarked, hoisting himself up again, 'if you would gratify a whim of mine!'

This was, to be shown over her house, which he was most eager to see. Madame Bovary had no objection, and they were both rising to their feet when Charles came in.

'Good evening, Doctor,' said Rodolphe.

Flattered by the unexpected use of the title, the Officer of Health started being profusely obsequious: of which the other took advantage to pull himself together a little.

'Your wife has been telling me about her health ...'

Charles broke in: yes, it was indeed a great anxiety to him: her attacks of breathlessness were coming on again.

Rodolphe asked whether riding would do her any good.

'Why, of course, excellent! Just the thing! There's an idea, now. What do you say, dear?'

She said she didn't possess a horse. Monsieur Rodolphe offered her one of his. She declined; he did not press her. Then, by way of accounting for his visit, he told them that his carter, the man whom the doctor had bled, was still having bouts of giddiness.

'I'll call in,' said Bovary.

'Oh, no, no, I'll send him to you. I'll bring him along. That'll be more convenient for you.'

'Very well! I'm much obliged to you!'

When Rodolphe had gone –

'Why don't you accept Monsieur Boulanger's offer?' said Charles. 'It's extremely kind of him.'

She pouted and hedged and finally declared that 'it might look a bit queer'.

'Who cares what it looks like?' said Charles, pivoting on his heel. 'No sense in that! Health comes first!'

'But how can I go riding without a riding-habit?'

'You'll have to have one,' he answered.

The riding-habit decided her.

When it was ready, Charles wrote to Monsieur Boulanger to say that his wife awaited his convenience, and that they would be most grateful.

Next day at noon, Rodolphe arrived at Charles' door with two saddle-horses, one of which had pink rosettes at its ears and a buckskin side-saddle. He had put on some riding-boots of soft leather, reflecting that she would probably never have seen their like before. And Emma was indeed charmed when he made his appearance on the landing, in his long velvet coat and white worsted breeches. She was ready and waiting for him.

Justin slipped out of the chemist's shop to have a look at her, and the chemist himself interrupted his labours to come and deliver a word of warning to Monsieur Boulanger.

'Accidents happen so quickly. Take every care! Are they lively horses?'

Emma heard a noise up above: Félicité was drumming on the window to amuse little Berthe. The child blew her mother a kiss, and Emma gave an answering signal with the knob of her whip.

'Good riding!' called Monsieur Homais. 'And safety first, remember, safety first!' He waved his newspaper as he watched them out of sight.

As soon as it felt the turf beneath it, Emma's horse broke into a canter. Rodolphe bounded along beside her. Occasionally they exchanged a word. With her face slightly lowered, her hand well up and her right arm stretched out, she abandoned herself to the rhythmic motion, jogging up and down in the saddle.

At the foot of the hill Rodolphe let go the reins and they

shot away together – to halt suddenly at the top so that her big blue veil dropped down over her face.

It was the beginning of October. A mist lay over the land, swirling away to the horizon between the folds of the hills, or tearing asunder and drifting up into nothingness. Sometimes a ray of sunshine striking through a rift in the clouds gave them a glimpse of Yonville away behind them, with the gardens by the riverside, the yards, the walls, the church steeple. Emma half-closed her eyes to pick out her own house; and that little village in which she lived had never looked so tiny. From where they were, high up, the whole valley was like a vast white lake melting into the air. Clumps of trees stood out here and there like black rock, and the tall rows of poplars topping the haze reminded one of a wind-swept beach.

Over the smooth green turf between the pines a dim brown light played in the warm air. Red-brown, like tobacco dust, the earth deadened the sound of their footfalls, and as the horses went along their hooves kicked the fallen fir cones in front of them.

So they rode round the edge of the wood. From time to time Emma turned away to avoid his eyes, and then she saw nothing but the long line of pine-trunks stretching away in an unbroken succession that made her feel a little dizzy. The horses panted, the saddle-leather creaked.

As they entered the forest the sun came out.

'The gods are with us,' said Rodolphe.

'You think so!' said she.

'On we go, on we go!' was all his answer.

He clicked his tongue and the horses broke into a trot. Tall ferns at the side of the pathway were getting caught in Emma's stirrup, and Rodolphe kept leaning over and pulling them out as they went. At other times he came abreast of her to hold back the branches, and then Emma felt his knee brush against her leg. The sky was blue now, the leaves quite still. They passed long stretches of heather in full bloom. Patches of violet alternated with the tangled undergrowth of the trees, which were a medley of grey and fawn and gold. Often they heard a furtive flutter of wings beneath the bushes or a soft cawing of rooks among the oak-trees.

They dismounted. Rodolphe tethered the horses. She walked ahead over the moss between the cart-tracks.

Her long riding-habit hampered her though she held up the skirt behind. Rodolphe, following her, had his eyes on the dainty white stocking that showed like a morsel of her naked flesh between the black cloth and the black boot.

She stopped.

'I'm tired,' she said.

'A bit farther!' he answered. 'Don't give in yet!'

A hundred yards farther on she stopped again. Through her veil, which hung down to her waist slantwise from the man's hat she was wearing, her features were discernible in a haze of blue, as though she were floating beneath azure waves.

'Where are we going, then?'

He didn't answer. Her breath was coming in little jerks. Rodolphe cast his eyes about him, biting his moustache.

They reached a clearing where young trees had been cut. They sat down on a log, and Rodolphe proceeded to declare his love.

He avoided frightening her with gallant speeches at the outset. He was calm, serious, melancholy.

Emma listened with bowed head, raking among some chips of wood with the toe of her boot. But when he said 'Are not our destinies now one?' —

'No, no!' she answered. 'You know that. It cannot be.'

She rose to her feet. He took hold of her wrist. She stopped still. After gazing at him for a minute with moist, loving eyes, she jerked out:

'Oh, don't, don't say any more. Where are the horses? Let's go back.'

He made a weary, angry gesture.

'Where are the horses? Where are the horses?' she repeated.

Smiling a strange smile, his eyes set and his teeth clenched, he advanced upon her with outstretched arms. She shrank back trembling.

'You frighten me!' she stammered. 'You make me feel ill! Let's go back!'

'If it must be –' he replied with a changed expression on his face. And at once he became respectful, attentive, timid again. She gave him her arm and they turned to go.

'What is the matter?' he said. 'What is it? I don't understand. You've a wrong idea of me, you must have. You are in my heart as a Madonna on a pedestal, lifted high, secure and immaculate. ... Only, I can't live without you. I need you, your eyes, your voice, your thoughts! Oh, be my friend, my sister, my angel!'

And he stretched his arm about her. She tried feebly to disengage herself. He was half-supporting her as they went along.

They heard their horses cropping.

'Stay, stay awhile!' said Rodolphe.

He drew her farther on, round the edge of a pond where duckweed grew green on the ripples and faded water-lilies lay motionless among the reeds. At the sound of their steps in the grass, frogs leapt up and darted away into hiding.

'It's wrong, wrong,' she said, 'it's madness to listen to you.'

'Why? Emma! Emma!'

'Oh, Rodolphe!' the young woman slowly sighed, and she leaned her head on his shoulder.

The stuff of her habit clung to the velvet of his coat. She tilted back her white neck, her throat swelled with a sigh, and, swooning, weeping, with a long shudder, hiding her face, she surrendered.

The evening shadows were falling. The sun, low on the skyline, shone through the branches dazzling her. Here and there around her the leaves and the earth were dappled with a flickering brightness, as though humming-birds had shed their wings in flight. Silence was everywhere. Sweetness seemed to breathe from the trees. She felt her heart beginning to beat again, and the blood flowing inside her flesh like a river of milk. Then, far away beyond the forest, on the other side of the valley, she heard a strange, long-drawn cry that hung on the air, and she listened to it in silence as it mingled like music with the last vibrations of her jangled nerves. Rodolphe, cigar in mouth, was mending one of the bridles with his pocket-knife.

They went the same way back to Yonville. There before them lay their own tracks side by side in the mud, the same bushes, the same stones in the grass. Nothing around them had changed, and yet for her something more tremendous had happened than if the mountains had moved from their places. Now and then Rodolphe leaned over, took her hand and kissed it.

She was charming on horseback, a straight, slim figure, with her knee flexed upon the animal's mane, her colour heightened by the fresh air, in the glow of the evening.

Going into Yonville she pranced her horse on the cobbles. Eyes watched her from windows.

At dinner her husband said she looked well, but she seemed not to hear when he asked about her ride. She sat with her elbow beside her plate, between the two lighted candles.

'Emma!' he said.

'What?'

'Ah! ... I called on Monsieur Alexandre this afternoon, and he's got an old mare, that's still very good-looking, only a bit broken at the knees, that I'm pretty certain we could have for three hundred francs. ... So, as I thought you'd like the idea, I said we'd have it – I bought it! Have I done right? Tell me!'

She nodded her head in assent. A quarter of an hour later she asked,

He stretched his arm about her.

'Are you going out tonight?'

'Yes. Why?'

'Oh, nothing, dear, nothing.'

As soon as she was rid of Charles, she went upstairs and shut herself in her room.

At first she felt in a kind of daze. She could see the trees, the paths, the ditches, Rodolphe; could feel his arms about her still, among the shivering leaves and the whistling grasses.

Noticing her reflection in the mirror, she started in surprise. Never had her eyes looked so big, so dark, so deep; her whole person had undergone some subtle transfiguration.

'I've a lover, a lover,' she said to herself again and again, revelling in the thought as if she had attained a second puberty. At last she would know the delights of love, the feverish joys of which she had despaired. She was entering a marvellous world where all was passion, ecstasy, delirium. A misty-blue immensity lay about her; she saw the sparkling peaks of sentiment beneath her, and ordinary life was only a distant phenomenon down below in the shadowy places between those heights.

She remembered the heroines of the books she had read, and that lyrical legion of adulteresses began to sing in her memory with sisterly voices that enchanted her. She was becoming a part of her own imaginings, finding the long dream of her youth come true as she surveyed herself in that amorous role she had so coveted. Gratified revenge too was hers. Had she not suffered enough? Now was her hour of triumph. Love, so long pent up within her, surged forth at last with a wild and joyous flow, and she savoured it without remorse, disquiet or distress.

The next day passed in a new delight. They exchanged vows. She told him her sorrows, Rodolphe interrupted her with kisses. Gazing at him with eyes half-closed, she bade him call her by her name once more and tell her again that he loved her. They were in the forest, as on the previous day, in a sabot-maker's hut. The walls were of thatch, and the roof was so low they had to stoop. They sat close together on a bed of dry leaves.

Starting from that day, they wrote to each other regularly every evening. Emma used to place her letter in a crevice in the wall at the bottom of the garden, and Rodolphe came to fetch it and left his own, which was always too short for her liking.

One morning when Charles had set off before daybreak, she was taken with a fancy to see Rodolphe on the instant. She could quickly reach La Huchette, stay there an hour, and be back in Yonville before anyone was awake. The thought of it set her panting with desire, and soon she was half-way across the meadow, hurrying along with never a glance behind her.

Day was beginning to break. From a distance Emma recognized her lover's house, with its two swallow-tailed weathervanes standing out dark in the pale light of dawn.

Beyond the farmyard was a large building that must be the château itself. She glided in as though the walls had parted magically at her approach. A big straight staircase led up to a corridor. Emma lifted a door-latch and at once picked out a man's form asleep on the far side of the room. It was Rodolphe. She gave a cry.

'It's you! You!' he said. 'How did you get here? Ah, your dress is damp!'

'I love you!' she answered, sliding her arms round his neck.

This first venture having succeeded, from now on whenever Charles went out early Emma hastily dressed and tiptoed down the steps to the edge of the water.

When the cow-plank was not in place, she had to make her way along by the garden-walls beside the river. The bank was slippery and she clung to the tufts of withered wallflowers to prevent herself from falling. Then she struck across ploughed fields, sinking in, floundering, getting her thin shoes clogged with mud. A breeze blew across the meadows fluttering the silk scarf over her hair. The oxen scared her, and she started running, to arrive all out of breath, with roses in her cheeks, her whole body exhaling a fragrance of sap and verdure and fresh air. Rodolphe, at that hour, would still be asleep. It was like a spring morning coming into his room.

The yellow curtains over the windows let in a heavy golden light. Emma blinked and groped her way, the dewdrops on her hair framing her face in an aureole of topazes. Rodolphe drew her to him with a laugh and pressed her to his heart.

Afterwards she would explore the room, open all his drawers, use his comb, look at herself in his shaving-mirror. Often she put into her mouth a big pipe that lay on the bedside-table along with the lemons and lumps of sugar and the jug of water.

It took them a good quarter of an hour to say good-bye. Emma cried, then. She wished she could stay with him for ever. Something stronger than herself was driving her to him; until one day when she arrived unexpectedly, Rodolphe knit his brows in apparent annoyance.

'What's the matter?' she said. 'Aren't you well? Speak to me!'

At length he declared with an air of seriousness that her visits were becoming foolhardy – she was compromising herself.

10

LITTLE by little these fears of Rodolphe's took possession of her. At first she had been intoxicated with love, had had no thought beyond. But now that it was indispensable to her, she dreaded losing anything of that love, dreaded the least difficulty that might befall it. On her way back from his house she cast nervous glances to right and left, watched every figure moving along the skyline, every attic window in the village from which she might be visible. She listened for footsteps, voices, ploughs at work, and sometimes stopped dead in her tracks, paler and more tremulous than the leaves of the poplars swaying overhead.

One morning as she was making her way back like this, she suddenly thought she saw a rifle pointing at her. Its long muzzle projected obliquely over the side of a tub half-buried in the grass at the edge of a ditch. Emma walked straight on, though she was ready to faint with terror, and a man popped up out of the tub like a jack-in-the-box. He had leggings buckled at the knee, a cap pulled down over his eyes, chattering teeth and a red nose. It was Captain Binet, on the lookout for wild duck.

'Why didn't you shout out?' he cried. 'When you see a gun you should always give warning.'

This he said to prevent her seeing what a fright she had given him. There had been an official order forbidding duck-shooting except from a boat, and Monsieur Binet, despite his respect for the law, was at present on the wrong side of it. He had been expecting to hear the village policeman arrive at any minute. The risk lent a certain piquancy to the enjoyment, however, and in the solitude of his tub he had been congratulating himself on his luck and his wickedness.

The sight of Emma seemed to relieve him of a great weight. He at once broke into conversation.

'Cold morning,' he said. 'There's a nip in it!'

Emma said nothing.

'You're out early?' he pursued.

'Yes,' she faltered, 'I've been to the nurse's, to see my baby.'

'Ah, splendid! Splendid! I've been out here like this since the crack of dawn. But it's such dirty weather, that unless you get the bird right on the tip ...'

'Good day, Monsieur Binet,' she cut in, turning on her heel.

'Pleasure, ma'am,' he answered drily, and climbed back into his tub.

Emma knew she oughtn't to have left him so abruptly. His

suspicions would certainly be aroused. The story about the nurse was the lamest invention. Everyone in Yonville knew that the Bovary child had been back at home for the past year. Besides, no one lived in that direction; the path led only to La Huchette. So Binet would have guessed where she'd been! And he wouldn't keep it to himself. He'd chatter, for sure.

All day long she racked her brains, trying over every conceivable lie. That idiot with the game-bag came constantly before her eyes.

After dinner, Charles, seeing a worried look on her face, proposed a visit to the Homais' to cheer her up. The first person she saw in the chemist's shop was Binet. Standing at the counter, in the glow cast by the big red jar, the tax-collector was saying:

'Give me half an ounce of vitriol, will you?'

'Justin!' the chemist shouted. 'Bring the sulphuric acid!' — Then to Emma, who was about to go up to Madame Homais' room:

'No, don't bother, she'll be down directly. Warm yourself at the stove while you wait. Excuse me. ... Good evening, Doctor.' (The chemist was very fond of bringing out the word 'Doctor', as though in addressing it to someone else he procured a certain reflected glory for himself.) 'Don't upset those mortars, boy! Go and get the chairs from the little room — you know we never move the armchairs out of the drawing-room.'

As Homais darted out from behind the counter to return his easy-chair to its place, Monsieur Binet asked for half an ounce of sugar acid.

'Sugar acid?' The chemist was contemptuous. 'What's that? Never heard of it. You want oxalic acid, I dare say? Oxalic, isn't that it?'

Binet explained that he wanted an abrasive to make metal-polish to get rust off his shooting-gear. Emma gave a start.

'Unfavourable weather, to be sure, with this humidity in the air!' the chemist observed.

'Some people don't seem to mind it, though,' replied the tax-collector with a sly look.

Her heart was pounding.

'Next, I want ...'

'He'll never go,' she thought.

'Half an ounce of resin and turpentine, four ounces of beeswax, and an ounce and a half of bone-black for my patent leather, if you please.'

The chemist began to cut the wax, and Madame Homais appeared, with Irma in her arms, Napoléon at her side and Athalie trailing on behind. She went and sat down on the plush window-seat, while the little boy squatted on a stool and his elder sister hovered round the jujube-box beside her daddy, who was funnelling and corking and labelling and tying parcels. All was silent around him. You heard only the occasional clatter of weights in the scales, and a few muttered words from the chemist as he gave instructions to his apprentice.

'And how is your little lady?' inquired Madame Homais suddenly.

'Quiet!' exclaimed her husband, entering figures in his daybook.

'Why didn't you bring her with you?' she went on in a loud whisper.

'Sssh!' Emma indicated the chemist.

However, Binet seemed too intent on checking his bill to have heard anything. At last he went. Emma heaved a deep sigh of relief.

'How hard you're breathing!' said Madame Homais.

'Ah, it's a bit warm,' she answered.

Next day, accordingly, they discussed how they could organize their meetings. Emma was for bribing her maid with a present. It would be better, however, if they could find a house where they would be safe in Yonville. Rodolphe promised to look for one.

All through the winter, three or four times every week, he used to arrive in the garden at dead of night. Emma purposely removed the key from the gate; Charles thought it had been lost.

Rodolphe announced himself by tossing a handful of gravel against the shutters. She would start to her feet. But sometimes she had to wait, for Charles had a way of chattering on interminably by the fireside; she grew frantic with impatience then, and if looks could have done it, he would have been hurled out of the window. At last she began to undress, then picked up a book and sat there reading very quietly, simulating interest. Eventually Charles would call out to her from the bedroom: 'Come on, Emma, it's time!'

'All right, I'm coming,' she answered.

But as the candles shone in his eyes, he soon turned over to the wall and fell asleep. Immediately she slipped out, holding her breath, smiling, quivering, all undressed.

Rodolphe had a large cloak in which he enveloped her; putting his arm round her waist, he led her in silence to the end of the garden – into the arbour, to that same garden seat on which Léon had gazed at her so lovingly on bygone summer evenings. She had little thought for Léon now.

The stars shone through the leafless jasmine branches. Behind them they heard the river flowing by, and an occasional rustling of dry reeds on the bank. Clumps of shadow loomed up here and there in the darkness, rising at times in a concerted shudder and leaning over like immense black waves advancing to engulf them. The chill of the night made them cling the closer, the sighs they breathed seemed louder, their eyes, only just visible in the gloom, looked larger, and in the midst of the silence their whispered words fell clear as crystal on their hearts and lingered there in prolonged vibrations.

On rainy nights they took shelter in the consulting-room,

between the shed and the stable. Emma lit one of the kitchen lamps, which she had hidden behind the bookcase. Rodolphe used to make himself quite at home there; the sight of the bookshelves, the desk, the whole room, provoked his mirth, and he couldn't resist making a great many jokes at Charles' expense, which disconcerted Emma. She would have liked to see him more serious – more dramatic, on occasion. Once she thought she heard footsteps in the lane.

'There's someone coming!' she said.

He blew out the light.

'Have you got your pistols?'

'What for?'

'Why, to defend yourself,' Emma replied.

'From your husband? Ha! Poor little man!' – and Rodolphe helped out his words with an eloquent flip of his fingers.

She was impressed by his bravery, though she felt in it a kind of coarseness, a straightforward vulgarity, that shocked her.

Rodolphe gave much thought to this matter of the pistols. If she was in earnest, she was being highly ridiculous, not to say odious, for *he* hadn't any quarrel with the worthy Charles, not being exactly what you would call consumed with jealousy. In the same connexion Emma had sworn him a solemn vow which he likewise considered to be hardly in the best of taste.

She was getting very sentimental, too. It had been necessary to exchange miniatures, and cut off handfuls of hair, and now she was asking for a ring, a virtual wedding-ring, in token of a lifelong union. She made frequent mention of the 'bells of evening' and the 'voices of nature'. She talked of her mother, and asked about his. It was twenty years since Rodolphe had lost his, but Emma comforted him with the kind of arch prattle one might use to an orphan child, and sometimes, as she looked at the moon, she said:

'I am sure that, together up there, they both give their blessing to our love.'

But – she was so pretty! So artless a creature he had seldom possessed. This 'love affair' was a new experience for him. It had drawn him out of his easy ways; it tickled both his senses and his vanity at once. Emma's emotionality, which his bourgeois common sense disdained, yet delighted him in his heart of hearts because he was the object of it. And now, certain of her love, he began to be careless; imperceptibly his manner changed.

Gone were those tender words that had moved her to tears, those tempestuous embraces that had sent her frantic. The grand passion into which she had plunged seemed to be dwindling around her like a river sinking into its bed; she saw the slime at the bottom. She refused to believe it. She redoubled her tenderness. And Rodolphe took less and less care to hide his indifference.

She didn't know if she regretted yielding to him, or whether she didn't rather aspire to love him still more. The humiliation of feeling her weakness turned to a bitterness tempered only by sensual pleasure. It was not an attachment but a continual enticement. He was subjugating her; she went almost in fear of him.

Yet on the surface things were smoother than ever, Rodolphe having succeeded in managing the affair his way; and at the end of six months, when spring came round, they were to one another as husband and wife tranquilly nourishing the domestic flame.

That was the time of year when Monsieur Rouault sent his turkey to commemorate the setting of his leg. A letter always accompanied the present. Emma cut the string that fastened it to the hamper, and read the following lines:

My dear children,

I trust this finds you in good health and that the bird will be up to standard. He looks to me a bit tenderer, if I may say so, and weightier. Next time I'll give you a cockerel for a change, unless you'd rather keep to gobblers, and send me back the hamper, if you will, with the other two. I've been having trouble with the shed, one night as it was blowing hard, the roof flew off into the trees. The harvest wasn't up to much either, and I don't know when I shall get over to see you. I can't very well leave the place now I'm all on my own, my poor Emma!

Here there was a gap between the lines, as if the old fellow had dropped his pen to dream.

I'm all right myself but for a cold I caught the other day going over to Yvetot fair to hire a shepherd, having given mine the sack he being so particular about his food. They do lead us a dance, the rogues! He was a saucy rascal into the bargain.

I heard from a pedlar that'd had a tooth out when he was in your parts in the winter, that Bovary was working hard as ever, it doesn't surprise me either, and he showed me the tooth. We had a cup of coffee together. I asked him if he'd seen you and he said no but he'd seen a couple of horses in the stable, so it sounds as though business is good. I'm glad to hear it, my dear ones, and may God in His goodness send you all the happiness you can wish for.

It goes hard with me that I've not yet made the acquaintance of my beloved granddaughter Berthe Bovary. I've planted an Orleans plum tree for her in the garden, underneath your window, and I'll not have it touched unless it's to bottle some fruit by and by that I'll keep in the cupboard for when she comes.

Good-bye, my dear children. My love to you, my girl, and you too, son-in-law, and a kiss for the little one on both cheeks.
I am, with every good wish,
Your loving father,
Théodore Rouault.

She stood a few minutes with the rough paper in her hands, following the kindly thoughts which went cackling through its tangle of spelling mistakes like a hen half-hidden in a thorn hedge. The ink had been dried with ashes from the grate, for a handful of grey dust slid off the letter on to her dress: she could almost see her father bending down over the hearth to pick up the tongs. How long it was since she had sat at his side, on the settee by the fire, holding a stick in the great crackling furze flames. She remembered summer evenings filled with sunshine; foals that whinnied as you passed, and went galloping, galloping away; and under her window was a beehive and sometimes the bees, circling in the sunlight, would bounce against the panes like golden balls. Happy days, days full of hope and freedom, days rich in illusions! She had no illusions now. She had laid them out in all the varied ventures of her soul, the successive phases of maidenhood, marriage and love, strewing them along her path like a traveller who leaves behind a portion of his gold at every wayside inn.

But if that were so, why was she unhappy? Where was the rare catastrophe that had cast her down? She raised her head and glanced about her as though to detect the cause of her suffering.

An April sunbeam glistened on the china in the cabinet. The fire blazed. She felt the carpet soft beneath her slippers. It was a bright warm day. She could hear her little girl shouting with laughter.

The child was rolling about on the grass, which was being cut for hay. She lay face downwards on top of a haycock, with her nurse holding on to her by her skirt. Lestiboudois raked close by, and every time he came up she leaned forward, flapping her arms in the air.

'Bring her to me!' said her mother, rushing out and gathering her up in her arms. 'Oh how I love you, my little pet, how I love you!'

Noticing some dirt on the tips of her ears, she at once rang for hot water and gave her a wash, changed her underclothes, shoes and stockings, asked a hundred and one questions about her, as though she had been away on a journey, and finally, with more kisses and some tears, handed her back to the maid, who stood in astonishment at such a display of tenderness.

Rodolphe found her graver than usual that night.

'Only a mood,' he decided. 'She'll get over it.' And he stayed away three evenings in succession.

When he did come again she treated him coldly, almost disdainfully.

'You're wasting your time, my beauty!' he thought to himself, and he took no notice of her doleful sighs or of the handkerchief she kept producing.

Then it was that Emma repented.

She went so far as to ask herself why she detested Charles so much, and whether it wouldn't be better to love him, if she could. But there was little in him that could invite to such a requital of affection; and her desire to make a gesture was proving a considerable embarrassment to her, when the chemist happened to come along and provide her with an opportunity.

II

HE had lately read of a marvellous new treatment for club-feet, and being an apostle of progress and a local patriot, had conceived the idea of bringing Yonville to the fore with operations for strephopodia.

'What risk is there?' he asked Emma. 'Look!' – and he counted the 'pros' on his fingers. 'Success, practically certain. An end of suffering and disfigurement for the patient. Immediate fame for the operator. Now, why shouldn't your husband operate on poor old Hippolyte over at the Lion? He'd be sure to tell all the visitors, don't forget; and then,' Homais lowered his voice and looked over his shoulder, 'what's to prevent me sending a little paragraph to the paper about it? An article gets discussed, you know. Lord, yes, the thing spreads like wildfire. And who knows, who knows ...?'

Bovary might, indeed, be successful; might be an able surgeon, for all Emma knew. And how satisfying for her to have urged him to a step that would bring him fame and fortune! Her one wish was for something more solid than love to lean upon.

She and the chemist joined forces, and Charles let himself be persuaded. He sent to Rouen for Dr Duval's treatise and buried himself in it every evening, clasping his head in his hands.

And while he studied equinus, varus and valgus, which is to say strephocatopodia, strephenopodia and strephexopodia, or to put it more clearly, the varying deviations of the foot downwards, inwards or outwards, as well as strephypopodia and strephanopodia – otherwise downward or upward torsion – Monsieur Homais was using all manner of arguments to induce the stableman to submit to the operation.

'I dare say you'll feel practically nothing. It's only a little prick like a mild blood-letting. Not as bad as corns can be sometimes.'

Hippolyte rolled his eyes stupidly, pondering.

'Mind you,' the chemist went on, 'it's no concern of mine. I'm only thinking of you! Sheer humanity! I'd be glad to see you rid of your hideous deformity, my boy, and that swinging of the lumbar region which must, whatever you say, be a great handicap to you in the exercise of your calling.'

Homais next pointed out how much brighter and brisker he'd feel afterwards, and went so far as to hint that he'd be more likely to succeed with the women; at which the groom grinned sheepishly. Then he attacked his vanity.

'Gracious me, you're a man, aren't you? Just suppose you'd had to join up, and go and serve with the colours? Ah, Hippolyte ...!' And he left him, vowing that it beat him how anyone could be so obstinate, so blindly hostile to the benefits of science.

The poor fellow gave in, for it was as if there were a conspiracy against him. Binet (who never meddled in other people's business), Madame Lefrançois, Artémise, the neighbours, everyone from the mayor down, urged and shamed and lectured him. But the decisive factor was that it *wouldn't cost him anything*. Bovary had undertaken to provide the necessary apparatus – a generous suggestion of Emma's which Charles had readily accepted, remarking inwardly that he had an angel of a wife.

With the chemist's advice and two false starts, he had a kind of box, weighing about eight pounds, constructed by the carpenter and the locksmith, with a prodigal amount of iron, wood, sheet-iron, leather, nails and screws.

Meanwhile he had to find out to which class of clubfoot Hippolyte's belonged, so as to know which tendon to cut.

The foot formed almost a straight line with the leg, yet at the same time had an inward deviation. Hence it was an equinus with a touch of varus about it, or, if you prefer, a slight varus with pronounced equine characteristics. But on that equine foot, which was indeed as broad as a horse's hoof, with horny skin, hard tendons, great thick toes and black toe-nails like the nails of a horseshoe – on that foot the strephopod galloped about like a stag from morn till night. He was constantly to be seen in the market-place, hopping round the carts, putting his odd foot foremost, for he seemed actually stronger on that leg than on the other. With long service it had developed as it were moral qualities of energy and endurance, and on it he preferred to shore his weight when he had heavy work to do.

Now, since it was an equinus, Charles would have to cut the Achilles tendon, and then if necessary he could deal with the anterior tibial muscle afterwards, to clear up the varus. For the doctor was afraid to risk a double operation; was, in fact, already quaking at the possibility of injuring some important region unknown to him.

Not Ambroise Paré, applying an immediate ligature to an artery for the first time since Celsus, at an interval of fifteen hundred years: not Dupuytren, piercing through a thick layer of brain to open up an abscess: not Gensoul, when he performed the first removal of an upper maxillary, can have felt such a strain upon hand and heart and intellect, as Monsieur

Bovary when he took his tenotome to Hippolyte. On a side-table, just as in a hospital, lay a pile of lint, some waxed thread, a heap of bandages – a pyramid of bandages – all the bandages there were in the chemist's shop. Monsieur Homais it was who had been organizing the event all morning, alike to impress the multitude and to flatter his own conceit. Charles made an incision. They heard a sharp snap. The tendon was cut, the operation was over. Hippolyte, speechless with astonishment, bent over Bovary's hands to cover them with kisses.

'Now, calm down,' said the chemist, 'you shall show your gratitude to your benefactor another time.' And he went out to announce the result to a half-dozen curious souls who had collected in the yard, and who were expecting to see Hippolyte emerge walking properly. Having fastened the patient into his apparatus, Charles returned home, where Emma was anxiously awaiting him on the doorstep. She flung her arms round his neck. They sat down to dinner. He ate heartily, and even asked for a cup of coffee with the dessert – an orgy he normally permitted himself only when they had company on Sundays.

The evening passed pleasantly in chatter and daydreams. They talked of their coming fortune and the improvements they could have in the house, and he saw himself growing in esteem and prosperity, his wife for ever loving him. She too enjoyed the freshness of a new sentiment, the finer, wholesomer delight of feeling some sort of affection for this poor lad who loved her. A fleeting thought of Rodolphe came to her, but her eyes returned to Charles; and she noted with surprise that his teeth weren't bad at all.

They were in bed when Monsieur Homais arrived. He brushed past the cook and burst into their room holding up a freshly written sheet of paper in his hand. It was his notice for the *Beacon*. He had brought it over to show them.

'Read it to us,' said Bovary.

He read:

' "Despite the web of superstition that still covers part of the face of Europe, light nevertheless begins to filter through into our country places. So it was that our tiny city of Yonville found itself on Tuesday last the scene of a surgical experiment that was also an act of high philanthropy, when Monsieur Bovary, one of our most distinguished practitioners ..." '

'Ah, that's too much, too much!' said Charles, a lump rising in his throat.

'Oh no, it isn't, not a bit of it! "... operated on a clubfoot." I haven't used the scientific term. In a newspaper, you know ... everybody might not understand; and the masses must ...'

'That's right,' said Bovary. 'Go on!'

'I proceed. "Monsieur Bovary, one of our most distinguished practitioners, operated on a clubfoot. The patient was one Hippolyte Tautain, for twenty-five years ostler at the Golden Lion Hotel (proprietress the Widow Lefrançois) in the Place d'Armes. The novelty of the enterprise, and public interest in the patient, had attracted such a concourse of people, that the entrance to the establishment was positively blocked. The operation went like magic, only a few drops of blood appearing on the skin, as though to announce that the refractory tendon had at last yielded to the surgeon's art. Strange to relate – we affirm it *de visu* – the patient seemed to feel no pain. His condition so far leaves nothing to be desired. Everything points to a speedy convalescence. Who knows but what, at our next village fête, we may see our stalwart Hippolyte joining in the Bacchic dance, in a ring of jolly fellows, cutting such capers as will prove to every eye that he is completely mended! Honour to the nobly wise! Honour to those tireless souls who sacrifice their sleep to the advancement or the healing of their fellow-men! Honour, thrice honour! Can we not now cry aloud that the blind shall see and the lame walk? But what fanaticism once promised its elect, science now achieves for all mankind! We shall keep our readers informed of the successive stages of this remarkable cure." '

All of which did not prevent old Madame Lefrançois running round five days later in a rare fright, screaming: 'Help! Help! He's dying! I don't know what to do with him!'

Charles dashed over to the Golden Lion. Seeing him run across the square, hatless, the chemist deserted his shop, and arrived out of breath, flushed and apprehensive, inquiring of everyone on the way up: 'What can have happened to our famous strephopod?'

The strephopod was writhing in frightful convulsions; the machine in which his leg was encased was banging against the wall hard enough to stave it in.

Taking every precaution to avoid moving the limb, they withdrew the box, and laid bare a hideous sight. The foot was swollen to an unrecognizable shape, the whole of the skin looked about to burst, and it was covered with patches of ecchymosis caused by the wonderful machine. Hippolyte had complained of pain before, but they hadn't taken any notice. Now they were forced to admit that he had not been entirely in the wrong, and he was freed for a few hours. No sooner had the oedema subsided a little, however, than the two experts saw fit to replace the limb in the apparatus, clamping it in still tighter to hurry things along. After another three days, Hippolyte being at the end of his tether, they again removed the contraption, and were astonished at the sight that met their eyes. A livid tumour had spread right up the leg, with pustules here and there discharging a dark liquid. Things had taken a serious turn. Hippolyte was beginning to lose heart, and Madame Lefrançois put him in the little parlour, near the kitchen, so that at any rate he should have something to take his mind off it. But the tax-collector, who dined there every day, raised strong objections to such companionship, and they had to move Hippolyte across into the billiard-room.

There he lay, groaning under his thick blankets, white-faced, unshaven, hollow-eyed, now and then turning his sweaty head on the dirty pillow where the flies crawled.

Madame Bovary came to see him, brought cloths for his poultices, gave him comfort and encouragement. Not that he
lacked for company, which on market-days especially was
plentiful, with the yokels all round him playing or fencing
with their cues, smoking, drinking, singing and shouting.

'How goes it?' they asked, clapping him on the shoulder.
'Not up to much, are you?' It was his own fault, though. He
ought to do such-and-such, or so-and-so ...

They told him of people who had all been cured by other
forms of treatment than his, adding by way of consolation:
'Fact is, you coddle yourself too much. You ought to get up.
Lounging about like a prince of the realm! All the same, you
old humbug, you don't smell nice.'

The gangrene had, indeed, spread higher and higher. It
made Bovary feel ill himself. He called in every hour, every
minute. Hippolyte looked up at him with terror-stricken eyes.

'When am I going to get better?' he sobbed. 'Make me
well! It's awful! It's awful!'

The doctor always advised light meals.

'Don't you listen to him, lad,' said Madame Lefrançois after
he had gone. 'They've put you through the mill quite enough
as it is. You'll only get weaker and weaker. Here, swallow
this!' And she gave him a good rich broth or a slice of mutton
or a rasher of bacon, with now and again a nip of brandy,
which he was too nervous to raise to his lips.

Hearing that he was getting worse, the Abbé Bournisien
asked to see him. He started off by commiserating, but declared in the same breath that he ought to rejoice in his sufferings, since they were the will of Heaven, and take this opportunity of putting himself right with God.

'You've been rather neglectful of your duty,' said the cleric
paternally. 'We haven't seen much of you at Divine Service.
How many years is it since you approached the communion-
table? I realize that your daily toils, amid the hurly-burly of
life, may have turned you aside from the pursuit of salvation:

but now is the time to think of it! You need not despair. I have known great sinners who cast themselves upon the mercy of the Lord when about to be summoned before His presence – oh, I know you have not yet come to that! – and most certainly they died in a state of grace. Let us hope you too will be another shining example. Now, why not, by way of precaution, say a "Hail Mary" and an "Our Father" every night and morning? Yes, do that for my sake. It costs nothing. Will you promise?'

The wretched creature promised. The *curé* called again on the following days. He gossiped with the landlady, told anecdotes and interlarded them with jests and puns that were lost on Hippolyte. Then as soon as an opportunity arose he reverted to religious matters, modifying his features to suit.

It seemed that his zeal was rewarded, for before long the cripple expressed a desire to make a pilgrimage to Bon-Secours if he were cured. Bournisien said he saw nothing against it, it was an extra safeguard, it 'couldn't do any harm'.

The chemist was annoyed at what he called the machinations of the priest, alleging that they prejudiced Hippolyte's recovery.

'Let him be, let him be,' he told Madame Lefrançois repeatedly. 'You're sapping his morale with all this mysticism.'

But the good woman had had enough of Homais. It was he who'd 'started it all'. In sheer contrariness she set a full font of holy water, with a sprig of box in it, at the head of the patient's bed.

However, religion seemed no more efficacious than surgery, and the inexorable mortification kept mounting from his extremities towards his stomach. Vary the potions, change the poultices though they might, the muscles got looser every day, and at last Charles nodded his assent when Madame Lefrançois asked if as a last resort she could send for the celebrated Canivet of Neufchâtel.

A Doctor of Medicine, fifty years old, of some standing and

great self-confidence, this personage jeered unceremoniously when he uncovered the leg with the gangrene risen to the knee. Flatly declaring that he would have to amputate, he went off to the chemist's to rail at the asses who could have reduced a poor fellow to such a plight. Gripping Homais by the button of his frock-coat, he bawled all over the shop:

'Tricks from Paris, eh! Bright ideas from the gentlemen in the metropolis! It goes with strabismus and chloroform and lithotrity, a lot of monstrous rubbish that ought to be stopped by the Government. They want to be smart, and so they ram their remedies down you regardless. Oh, *we*'re not as clever as *they* are. We're not specialists – dandies – elegants! We're practitioners, healers: and we'd never dream of operating on a man who was perfectly fit! Straighten a clubfoot – how can you straighten a clubfoot? Might as well try levelling up a hunchback!'

All of which was gall to Homais. However, he dissembled his discomfiture beneath a courtier's smile, for he needed to humour Monsieur Canivet, whose prescriptions occasionally reached Yonville. Instead of standing up for Bovary, therefore, he kept his mouth tight shut, abandoning principle and sacrificing dignity to the more important interests of his business.

It was a big event in the village, a thigh-amputation by Dr Canivet. Everybody rose early that day. The main street, crowded as it was, wore an air of mourning, as though it were an execution that was to take place. A debate on Hippolyte was in progress at the grocer's. The shops were doing no trade at all. Madame Tuvache never budged from her window, in her eagerness to see the surgeon arrive.

He came in his gig, driving himself. In course of time his corpulent figure had weighed down the right-side springs, and inside the tilting vehicle could be seen a huge box with a red sheepskin cover and three brass clasps, resplendent with authority.

Bowling in beneath the archway of the Lion, the doctor shouted for someone to unharness his nag, then went to the stable himself to see if the animal was being properly fed. Whenever he called to see a patient, he first looked after his mare and his trap, which provoked the comment, 'He's a character, is Dr Canivet'. And for that unshakeable equanimity he was but the more esteemed. The universe might perish to a man, without causing him to abandon the least of his habits.

Homais appeared.

'I shall need you,' the doctor told him. 'Are we ready? Forward, march!'

The chemist went red in the face and confessed that he was too sensitive to witness an operation of that sort.

'When you're only an onlooker, you know, it works on the imagination, and my nervous system is so very ...'

'Rubbish, man!' Canivet interrupted him. 'Matter of fact, you look more like an apoplectic to me. Wouldn't surprise me either. You chemist chaps are for ever cooped up in your little kitchens, it can't but damage the constitution in the long run. Now look at me. Up at four every morning. Shave in cold water – never feel the cold. Never wear flannel, never catch a chill, sound in wind and limb! I eat anything that comes, and make the best of what I've got. And that's why I'm not squeamish like you. I'd just as soon carve up a Christian as a chicken on the table. ... Of course, you'll say it's habit, just habit. ...'

And with not a scrap of consideration for Hippolyte, who was sweating with agony under the bed-clothes, these gentlemen launched into a long discussion, wherein the chemist likened the imperturbability of the surgeon to that of a general, and Canivet, gratified by this comparison, proceeded to expatiate on the requirements of his art. He looked upon it as a sacred calling – degraded, however, by these 'Officers of Health'. Finally, reverting to the case before him, he examined the bandages Homais had brought – the same ones that had made their appearance at the original operation – and asked for somebody to hold the limb for him. They sent out for Lestiboudois. Monsieur Canivet rolled up his sleeves and passed through into the billiard-room, while the chemist stayed behind with Artémise and the landlady, who had both gone whiter than their aprons and glued their ears to the door.

During this time, Bovary didn't dare stir from his house. He sat by the empty grate in the dining-room, chin sunk on his chest, hands clasped, eyes staring. 'What a calamity!' he thought, 'what a failure!' And yet he had taken every conceivable precaution. Fate had a hand in it. But what of that? If Hippolyte should die, it would be his doing. What could he say for himself when they asked about it on his rounds? *Had* he made a slip somewhere? He couldn't think of anything. And after all, the most eminent surgeons made mistakes. Ah, no one would believe that. He'd be laughed at, talked about! It would spread to Forges, to Neufchâtel, Rouen, everywhere. Some of his professional colleagues might attack him. That would mean a controversy, he'd have to reply in the papers. Hippolyte might even sue him. He saw himself disgraced, ruined, done for! Assailed by so many possibilities, his imagination tossed and tumbled about among them like an empty barrel rolling on the waves of the sea.

Emma sat opposite, watching him. She did not share his humiliation, she had her own to bear: that of ever having expected ability from such a man. As if she hadn't perceived his mediocrity quite clearly a score of times already!

Charles started moving about the room. His boots creaked on the parquet.

'Sit down. You get on my nerves,' she said.

He sat down.

How could she have deceived herself again, she who was so intelligent? What lamentable idiocy had led her to abase her being in such constant sacrifice? She remembered all her luxurious instincts, all the privations of her soul, the squalors of married life and housekeeping, her dreams dropping in the mud like wounded swallows, the things she had wanted and denied herself, the things she might have had! And all ...

In the midst of the silence that hung over the village, a heart-rending shriek pierced the air. Bovary turned a deathly white. She knit her brow with a nervous twitch, and went on: all for what? for him! for that creature, that man without feeling or understanding, who sat there in perfect placidity, never dreaming for a moment that the ridicule attaching to his name would now sully her as well. She had tried to love him; had repented in tears her surrender to another man.

'Perhaps it was a valgus, then?' exclaimed Bovary suddenly out of his meditations.

The words dropped upon her thoughts with the sudden shock of a leaden bullet tossed into a silver dish. Emma started, raised her head to see what he was saying, and they gazed at one another in silence, as though astonished at the sight of one another, so widely sundered were their trains of thought. Charles surveyed her with a fuddled look as he listened, motionless, to the last cries of the victim following one upon another in long-drawn modulations, broken by sudden sharp screams, like the howling of some animal being slaughtered in the distance. Emma bit her pale lip. Her fingers twisted a piece of coral she had broken off. The blazing points of her pupils were fixed on Charles like two flaming arrows about to be released. Everything about him grated on her now, his face, his clothes, the things he didn't say, his whole person, his very existence. She repented her past virtue as though it were a crime; what still remained of it collapsed beneath the savage onslaught of her pride. She revelled in all the malicious ironies of adultery triumphant. The thought of her lover returned to her with a dizzy seductiveness, she gave herself up to it utterly, drawn to him with a new enthusiasm. Charles seemed as completely alien to her, as irrevocably estranged from her, as impossible and finished with, as if he were suffering the last agony of death before her eyes.

Footsteps sounded on the pavement. Charles looked up. Through the lowered blinds he could see Dr Canivet going along by the market, in the broad sunshine, mopping his brow with a silk handkerchief. Homais followed carrying a big red box, and together they made their way towards the chemist's shop.

With a sudden despondent tenderness Charles turned to his wife. 'Kiss me, my dear!'

'Let me alone!' she flung out, crimson with rage.

'Why? Why?' he stammered in astonishment. 'Come, you're not yourself! You know I love you! Come to me!'

'Stop!' she cried in a terrible voice. And bursting from the room, Emma slammed the door behind her so hard that the barometer crashed to the floor.

Charles fell back in his chair. He was beaten. What could be the matter with her? Was it some nervous disorder? He burst into tears, feeling vaguely as though some baneful, incomprehensible influence were hovering about him.

When Rodolphe arrived in the garden that night he found his mistress waiting for him at the foot of the steps. They put their arms about each other, and all their bitterness melted away like snowflakes in the warmth of that embrace.

12

THEIR love began again. Often Emma used to write to him during the day, on the spur of the moment, beckoning through the window to Justin who would untie his apron and run off at once to La Huchette. Rodolphe came: to be told that she felt bored, that her husband was odious and life intolerable.

'Well, what can I do about it?' he burst out impatiently one day.

'Ah, if you wanted to ...'

She was sitting on the floor between his knees, her hair unbraided, a vacant look in her eyes.

'Well, what?' Rodolphe demanded.

She sighed. 'We could go away and live ... somewhere else ...'

'You must be mad!' he said with a laugh. 'How could we?'

She kept coming back to the subject. He pretended not to understand, and turned the conversation.

What baffled him was that there should be all this fuss about something so simple as love.

She must have a motive, a reason, a driving-force behind her affection.

Her feeling for him was, indeed, augmented daily by her aversion to her husband. The more she gave herself to the one, the more she loathed the other. Never had Charles seemed so unpleasant, his fingers so stubby, his wits so dull or his manners so common, as when she sat with him after a rendezvous with Rodolphe. Then, even as she played the virtuous wife, she was afire at the image of that sunburned brow with its curl of black hair, that figure at once so strong and so elegant, that man so mature in judgement and so passionate in desire! For him it was that she filed her nails with all a sculptor's care. For him, she could never have enough cold cream on her skin or patchouli on her handkerchief. She loaded herself with bracelets, rings, necklaces. When he was coming, she filled her big blue vases with roses, and prepared her room and her person like a courtesan awaiting a prince. The maid had to be for ever washing linen. All day long Félicité never went outside the kitchen, where she was frequently watched at her work by Justin.

Resting his elbows on the ironing-board, the boy would gaze with greedy eyes at all those feminine things spread out around him: dimity petticoats, neckerchiefs, collars, drawers with running strings, wide at the hip and gathered at the knee.

'What's this for?' said the young lad, running his hand over a crinoline or some hooks and eyes.

'Haven't you ever seen anything?' Félicité answered with a laugh. 'As if your Madame Homais didn't wear them!'

'Oh, ah, Madame Homais.' Meditatively he added, 'But is she a *lady*, like Madame?'

It annoyed Félicité, however, to have him hanging round her all the time. She was six years older than he, and Monsieur Guillaumin's man Théodore had started courting her.

'Let me be!' she said, moving her starch pot. 'Run away and pound the almonds! You're for ever dangling round the women. Wait till you've got some fluff on your chin before you start meddling with such things, you bad boy!'

'All right, don't be cross. I'll go and do her shoes for you.'

At once he took down Emma's shoes from the shelf. They were caked with mud, acquired at her rendezvous; it crumbled beneath his fingers, and he watched the dust rise slowly in a ray of sunlight.

'What a fuss you make of 'em!' said the maid, who wasn't so particular when she cleaned them herself, for her mistress used to pass them on to her as soon as the stuff had lost its freshness.

Emma had a great number of pairs in her wardrobe, and got through them at a reckless rate, without Charles' venturing the least remonstrance.

In the same docile spirit he paid up twelve pounds for a wooden leg which she thought they ought to present to Hippolyte. Cork-topped and spring-jointed, it was an elaborate contrivance, with a black trouser leg to cover it and a patent-leather boot to finish it off. But Hippolyte didn't care to use such a handsome leg for everyday, and begged Madame Bovary to get him another, more serviceable, one. Needless to say, the doctor defrayed the cost of that purchase also.

The ostler gradually resumed his duties. He was once more to be seen getting about the village; and if ever Charles heard him stumping along in front of him, he hastily turned a corner.

The order for the leg had been placed with Lheureux. It gave him an excuse for several visits to Emma. He told her of the new deliveries from Paris, talked about various objects of feminine interest, was most obliging and never asked for money, so that Emma found it only too easy to gratify her every wish. For instance, she wanted to give Rodolphe a handsome riding-whip that was to be had at an umbrella-shop in Rouen: Monsieur Lheureux deposited it on her table the following week.

The day after that, however, he called with a bill for over ten pounds. Emma was taken aback: the drawers were all empty, they owed Lestiboudois for over a fortnight and the maid for six months, there were a host of other debts besides, and Bovary was waiting impatiently for Monsieur Derozerays to settle his account, which he was in the habit of doing round about midsummer.

She succeeded in putting him off for a time; but eventually Lheureux lost patience: he was being pressed for money, his own was laid out, and unless he called some of it in he would be obliged to take back all the goods she'd had off him.

'Take them!' said Emma.

'Ah, no, that was just my joke,' he replied. 'Though I could have done with the riding-whip. ... I know, I'll ask the Doctor to let me have it back!'

'No, don't do that!' she cried.

'Aha, I've got you!' thought Lheureux to himself, and feeling sure he had hit upon something, he went away saying under his breath, with his habitual little hissing noise: 'Right! We shall see, we shall see!'

She was wondering how to get out of this predicament, when the maid came in and laid on the mantelpiece a little fold of blue paper – 'from Monsieur Derozerays'. Emma pounced upon it. Inside were fifteen napoleons – the payment of the account! She heard Charles coming upstairs, threw the money to the back of the drawer and locked it.

Three days later Lheureux appeared again.

'Let me make you a proposition,' he said. 'If, instead of paying the said sum, you would like to take ...'

'Here you are,' said she, placing fourteen gold pieces in his hand.

The shopkeeper was dumbfounded. To cover up his disappointment he started apologizing profusely and making her various offers of service, all of which Emma refused. Then she stood a moment with the change in her apron pocket, fingering the two five-franc pieces. She made a resolution to economize, so as to be able to pay back in time ...

'Heavens, no, he'll forget!' she decided.

Besides the riding-whip with the silver knob, Rodolphe had also been given a signet-ring engraved with the words *Amor nel cor*, a scarf to use as a muffler and a cigar-case exactly like the Viscount's, the one which Charles had picked up in the road and which Emma still kept. These presents humiliated him, however. Several he refused to take. She became insistent; and in the end Rodolphe would yield, thinking her tyrannical and interfering.

She had some odd notions, too.

'When midnight chimes,' she said, 'you are to think of me!'

And if he confessed that he had not thought of her, there was a torrent of reproaches, ending always with the eternal question: 'Do you love me?'

'Of course I do!'

'A lot?'

'Certainly!'

'You've never loved anyone else?'

'Did you think I was a virgin?' he exclaimed with a laugh.

Emma cried. He did his best to comfort her, enlivening protestation with pleasantry.

'I love you so much!' she burst out. 'So much, I can't live without you! I long for you sometimes till my heart almost breaks with jealousy! I say to myself, Where is he now? Talking to other women, perhaps. They smile at him, he comes ... Ah no! No! Tell me there's none you care for! There are women more beautiful than I, but none that can love as I can. I am your slave, your concubine. You are my king, my idol – you are good, handsome, intelligent, strong!'

He had listened to so many speeches of this kind that they no longer made any impression on him. Emma was like any other mistress; and the charm of novelty, gradually slipping away like a garment, laid bare the eternal monotony of passion, whose forms and phrases are for ever the same. Any difference of feeling underlying a similarity in the words escaped the notice of that man of much experience. Because wanton or mercenary lips had murmured like phrases in his ear, he had but scant belief in the sincerity of these. High-flown language concealing tepid affection must be discounted, thought he: as though the full heart may not sometimes overflow in the emptiest metaphors, since no one can ever give the exact measure of his needs, his thoughts or his sorrows, and human speech is like a cracked kettle on which we strum out tunes to make a bear dance, when we would move the stars to pity.

Nevertheless, with that advantage in clarity that belongs to the one who lags behind in any relationship, Rodolphe perceived further pleasures to be exploited in this affair. Refusing to be inconvenienced by a sense of shame, he treated her as he pleased, and turned her into something pliant and corrupt. Her attachment to him was a thing of idiocy, full of wonderment for him, full of voluptuous pleasure for her, a drugged blessedness; and her soul sank deep in its intoxication, drowned and shrivelled up in it like the Duke of Clarence in his butt of malmsey.

Solely as a consequence of these amorous habits, a change was apparent in Madame Bovary. Her eyes grew bolder, her talk freer. She even committed the impropriety of going out with Monsieur Rodolphe with a cigarette in her mouth, as though to snap her fingers at the world; and those who still doubted, doubted no longer when they saw her step out of the *Hirondelle* with her figure squeezed into a waistcoat, like a man; the elder Madame Bovary, who had come to take refuge in her son's house after a shocking scene with her husband, was not the least scandalized of matrons. There was much besides of which that lady disapproved. In the first place, Charles had disregarded her advice as to the prohibition of novels. Further, she didn't like the 'tone of the house'. She passed a few remarks on this subject. Once in particular, feeling ran high over Félicité.

Going down the passage the previous night, Mother Bovary had caught the girl with a man – a man of about forty, with a brown beard, who, when he heard her footstep, quickly slipped out into the garden. Emma burst out laughing at all this. The good lady flew into a rage, and declared that you ought to keep an eye on your servants' morals – unless morals were to be treated as a laughing-matter.

'Where have you lived all your life?' said her daughter-in-law, with so impertinent a look on her face that Madame Bovary asked her if it were not her own case that she was defending.

'Get out!' the young woman shouted, springing to her feet.

'Emma! Mamma!' cried Charles, trying to restore peace.

But both had fled in their exasperation. He found Emma stamping on the floor, muttering: 'What manners! What a peasant-woman!'

He ran to his mother. She was beside herself, stammering with rage: 'She's an insolent girl, a giddy hussy! Worse, maybe!' And she was for leaving on the instant unless Emma came and apologized. Charles went back to his wife and implored her, on his knees, to give in.

'Very well. I'll go,' she replied at last. And she did indeed hold out her hand to her mother-in-law, and say, with the dignity of a duchess: 'I apologize, Madame.' Then she went back upstairs, flung herself on her bed, buried her face in the pillow and cried like a child.

They had arranged, she and Rodolphe, that in case of emergency she was to fasten a sheet of paper to the blind, and if he happened to be in the village he would go at once to the lane behind the house. Emma put up the signal. She had been waiting for three-quarters of an hour when suddenly she saw Rodolphe at the corner of the market. She was tempted to open the window and call out; but he vanished again immediately. She fell back in despair.

Soon, however, she thought she heard someone coming along the pavement. It must be he. She ran downstairs and across the yard. He was there, waiting outside. She threw herself into his arms.

'Take care!' he said.

'Ah, if you only knew ...' she answered, and then she told him everything, hurriedly, disjointedly, overstating the facts, inventing several, with such a wealth of parentheses that he couldn't make head or tail of it.

'Come, my poor darling, be brave! Take heart! Be patient!'

'I've been patient and suffered for the last four years! Love like ours should be proclaimed from the roof-tops! They're tormenting me! I can't stand any more of it! Save me!'

She clung close to Rodolphe. Her tear-filled eyes were sparkling like flames under water, her breast heaved rapidly. Never had he loved her so much. He lost his head.

'What do you want me to do?' he said.

'Take me away!' she cried. 'Take me away, I entreat you!' And she fastened upon his lips, as though to extract from them the unexpected consent that was breathed forth in a kiss ...

'But ...'

'What?'

'Your little girl.'

She reflected a moment, then answered: 'We'll have to take her, that's all!'

'What a woman!' he thought as he watched her go. For she had slipped back into the garden. Someone was calling her.

The elder Madame Bovary was astonished at the transformation in her daughter-in-law on the following days. Emma was indeed more submissive, carrying deference to the point of asking for a recipe for pickling gherkins.

Was this a trick to fool them both? Was it an orgy of stoicism, a desire to drain her cup of bitterness to the dregs before she set it down? No, for she was blind to everything around her, absorbed in the foretaste of her promised happiness. With Rodolphe this was the one, the endless, topic. 'Ah, when we're in the coach!' she would murmur, nestling into his shoulder. 'Do you think about it? Can it be? I believe, when the carriage drives off, I shall feel as if we were going up in a balloon, bound for the clouds. How I count the days! Do you?'

Madame Bovary had never looked so lovely as now. There was about her that indefinable beauty which comes of joy, of enthusiasm, of success, and which is simply the harmony of temperament with circumstance. Her yearnings and her griefs, her experience of pleasure, her still youthful illusions, had brought her on by easy stages, as manure and rain and sun and wind bring on the flowers, and now at last she blossomed forth in all the fullness of her nature. Her eyelids seemed fashioned expressly for those long looks of love in which her pupils lost themselves; every eager breath she took set her slender nostrils dilating and curled up the fleshy corners of her lips, with that shadow of dark down upon them. One skilled in the arts of corruption, you would say, must have arranged those tresses round her neck, that thick mass rolling carelessly

down wherever the daily dishevelments of love might take it.
There were softer inflexions in her voice and in her figure.
Some subtle, pervasive essence flowed from the very folds of
her dress, from the arch of her foot. Charles thought her as
delicious, as utterly irresistible, as when they were first
married.

When he came home at dead of night he never dared to
wake her. The globe of the nightlight cast a flickering ring on
the ceiling; the cradle with its curtains drawn looked like a
little white hut jutting out in the darkness beside the bed.
Charles gazed at them. He thought he could hear the child's
light breathing. Soon, now, she would start to grow. Every
year, every month would see her shooting up. He saw her in
his mind's eye, coming home from school at the end of the day,
laughing merrily, with ink-stains on her tunic and her satchel
over her arm. Then they'd have to send her away to school.
That would cost money. Where was it to come from? He
started thinking. He wondered whether he should hire a little
farm in the neighbourhood, which he could visit every morning on his rounds. He would save up what it brought him and
put it in the bank. Then he could buy shares in something or
other. His practice would grow, too. He was counting on that,
for he wanted Berthe to have a good schooling, to be accom-
plished, to learn the piano. Ah, how pretty she'd be at fifteen!
Just like her mother, wearing one of those same broad-
brimmed straw hats in the summer. Why, at a distance they'd
be taken for sisters! He pictured her sitting by their side of an
evening, sewing in the lamplight. She would embroider some
slippers for him, she would busy herself about the house, filling it with her grace and gaiety. And then they'd have to find
her a good young fellow to settle down with – somebody
pretty soundly placed, who'd make her happy, happy ever
after. ...

Emma was not asleep, only pretending to be. While he
dozed off beside her, she was awake in a very different dream-

land. ... A coach-and-four had been whirling them along for a week, towards a new world from which she would never return. On and on they drove, their arms entwined, in silence. Often from a mountain height they would suddenly catch sight of a splendid city below them, with domes, ships, bridges, forests of orange-trees, cathedrals of white marble with storks' nests on their spiky steeples. They slowed down to a foot-pace over the big flagstones, and by the wayside were bunches of flowers, proffered you by women in red bodices. You heard bells chime and mules bray. You heard guitars murmuring and fountains splashing, their spray flying up to freshen the fruits standing in pyramids at the feet of white statues that smiled beneath the spirting jets of water. And then one night they came to a fishing village with brown nets drying in the wind all along the huts and under the cliff. Here they would stay, in a little low house with a flat roof and a palmtree shading it, at the head of a gulf by the sea. They would swing in a hammock or drift in a gondola. Life would be large and easy as their silken garments, all warm and starry as the soft nights they would gaze out upon. ... And yet, in the vast spaces of that imagined future, no particular phenomenon appeared. The days, all magnificent, were all alike as waves. The vision hovered on the horizon, infinite and harmonious, in a haze of blue, in a wash of sunshine ... Then the baby started coughing in its cradle, or Bovary snored more loudly, and Emma didn't get to sleep till morning, as dawn was whitening the window-panes and young Justin already taking down the chemist's shutters across the square.

She had sent for Lheureux and said to him: 'I shall be wanting a cloak, a large one with a deep collar and a lining ...'

'You're going on a journey?' he asked.

'No, but – never mind, I can rely on you? And quickly?' He bowed.

'Then I shall need a case – not too heavy, a handy size ...'

'Yes, yes, I know, about three feet by one and a half, as they're making them nowadays.'

'And a travelling-bag.'

'Must be a row on, all right!' thought Lheureux.

'And here!' said Madame Bovary, pulling her watch from her waist-pocket, 'you can take it out of the price of this.'

The shopkeeper threw up his hands in protest. Why, they weren't strangers. Could he have any doubts of her? Ridiculous! She insisted that at any rate he should take the chain; and Lheureux had put it in his pocket and was on his way out, when she recalled him.

'Leave it all at your place. The coat' – she appeared to ponder – 'don't bring that either, just give me the workman's address and tell him to keep it till I call.'

They were to run away the following month. She would leave Yonville ostensibly to go shopping in Rouen; Rodolphe would have booked seats, obtained passports, even written to Paris to ensure their having the mail-coach to themselves as far as Marseilles, where they would buy an open carriage and go straight on to Genoa. She was to deal with her luggage, sending it to Lheureux's to be put straight on to the *Hirondelle*, so that no suspicions would be aroused. And in all this, nothing was said of the child. Rodolphe avoided the subject; Emma had perhaps forgotten. He wished to have a clear fortnight in front of him to wind up some business affairs. At the end of the week he asked for two more. Then he said he wasn't feeling well. Then he went off on a journey. August ran by, and after all these delays, they decided that it should be, irrevocably, the fourth of September, which was a Monday.

The final week-end arrived.

Rodolphe came on Saturday evening, earlier than usual.

'Is everything ready?' she asked.

'Yes.'

They strolled round the flower-beds and sat down by the terrace, on the edge of the wall.

'You're sad,' said Emma.

'No. Why?' But as he spoke he looked at her strangely, with tenderness.

'Is it because you're going away,' she said, 'away from all that's dear to you, all that makes up your life? Yes, I understand, though *I've* got nothing in the world – you're all in all to me! And I shall be everything to you, family, country, everything! I will care for you, I will love you!'

'How sweet you are!' he said, folding her in his arms.

'Am I?' she said, with a voluptuous laugh. 'Do you love me? Swear it, then!'

'Do I love you? Love you? I adore you, my love!'

Full and flushed, the moon came up over the skyline behind the meadow, climbed rapidly between the branches of the poplars, which covered it here and there like a torn black curtain, rose dazzling white in the clear sky, and then, sailing more slowly, cast down upon the river a great splash of light that broke into a million stars, a silver sheen that seemed to twist its way to the bottom, like a headless snake with luminous scales; or like some monstrous candelabra dripping molten diamonds. The soft night was all about them. Curtains of shadow hung amid the leaves. Emma, her eyes half-closed, breathed in with deep sighs the cool wind that was blowing. They did not speak, caught as they were in the rush of their reverie. Their early tenderness returned to their hearts, full and silent as the river flowing by, soothing-sweet as the perfume the syringas wafted, casting huger and more melancholy shadows on their memory than those the unmoving willows laid upon the grass.

Often some night-animal, hedgehog or weasel, would scuffle through the undergrowth as it started after its quarry; now and again a ripe peach could be heard softly dropping from the tree.

'What a lovely night!' said Rodolphe.

'We shall have many!' answered Emma. She went on as

though speaking to herself: 'Yes, it will be good to travel. ... Then why am I sad at heart? Is it dread of the unknown, the wrench of parting? Or is it ...? No, it's just that I'm too happy! What a weak creature I am! Forgive me!'

'There is still time!' he cried. 'Think! You may repent!'

'Never!' she declared impetuously. And, moving closer to him – 'What harm could come to me? There is no desert or precipice or ocean where I would not follow you. Our life together will be every day a closer, completer embrace. We shall have no worries or cares, nothing will stand in our way. We shall be all alone, all to ourselves, for always. ... Speak to me, answer me!'

He put in a 'Yes ... yes,' at regular intervals. Her fingers played with his hair, and through the big tears that rolled down her cheeks she kept saying in a baby-voice: 'Rodolphe! Rodolphe! Ah, Rodolphe, my dear little Rodolphe!'

Midnight struck.

'Midnight!' she said. 'Tomorrow we go! Only one more day!'

He rose to leave; and as though that movement were somehow the signal for their flight, Emma suddenly assumed an air of gaiety.

'You've got the passports?' she said.

'Yes.'

'You haven't forgotten anything?'

'No.'

'Are you sure?'

'Quite sure.'

'And you'll be waiting for me at the Hôtel de Provence at twelve o'clock?'

He nodded.

'Till tomorrow!' said Emma in a final kiss. And she watched him go.

He did not look round. She ran after him, and leaning over the water's edge, amid the bulrushes, called out 'Till tomorrow!'

He was already on the opposite bank, striding rapidly across the meadow.

After a minute or two Rodolphe halted, and when he saw her white-clad form gradually vanishing into the darkness like a phantom, his heart began to beat so fast that he leaned against a tree to prevent himself falling.

'What an idiot I am!' he said, with a terrible oath. 'All the same, she was a pretty mistress!'

At once Emma's beauty, all the pleasure of their love, came back to him. For a while he softened. Then he hardened his heart against her.

'After all,' he exclaimed, flinging up his arms, 'I can't flee the country! And saddle myself with a child!'

This he said to strengthen his resolution.

'Besides, look at all the difficulties, the expense. ... No, no, by Heaven, no! It would have been too stupid!'

13

As soon as he got home, Rodolphe hurriedly ensconced himself in his desk-chair, underneath the stag's head that hung trophy-wise on the wall. But with the pen in his hand, he could find nothing to say; so he leaned his elbows on the desk and thought. It was as though Emma had already receded into a distant past, as though the decision he had taken had suddenly placed an immense gulf between them.

To conjure her back, he went to the cupboard by his bedside and got out an old Rheims biscuit-tin, in which he was in the habit of storing his letters from women. It exuded an odour of damp dust and withered roses. First he found a handkerchief covered with pale stains. It was hers. She had had an attack of nose-bleeding once when they were out together. He had forgotten all about it. Beside it, stubbed at the corners, was a miniature of her that she had given him; he thought her dress showy and her ogling look quite deplorable. As he concentrated on the portrait, trying to visualize the original, Emma's features blurred in his memory, as though the living and the painted face were rubbing together and obliterating each other. Then he read some of her letters. They were largely concerned with arrangements for their journey: brief, practical, businesslike. He wanted to have a look at the longer ones that she had written in the early days; he turned the whole tin upside down to find them, and started mechanically rummaging amid the jumble of papers and other objects, coming upon bouquets, a garter, a black mask, pins, locks of hair – fair hair, dark hair – some of which had caught in the hinge of the little box and broke when he opened it.

As he dallied among these souvenirs, he examined the handwriting of the letters and their style, both as varied as their spelling. They were tender or gay, facetious or melancholy. Some asked for love, others for money. A word would bring back a face, a gesture, a tone of voice; but sometimes he could recall nothing.

All flocking into his mind at once, these women cramped, diminished one another to a single level of love where all were equal. Taking a handful of letters from the disarray, he played with them for a few minutes, cascading them from his right hand into his left. Finally, growing bored and drowsy, Rodolphe put the tin back in the cupboard, saying to himself: 'What a lot of humbug!'

Which summed up his opinion. For his pleasures had so trampled over his heart, like schoolboys in a playground, that no green thing grew there, and whatever passed that way, being more frivolous than children, left not so much as its name carved on the wall.

'Well, here goes!' he said to himself.

He wrote: 'Be brave, Emma, be brave! I do not want to ruin your life. ...'

'That's true, damn it all,' thought Rodolphe. 'It's for her own good, I'm playing fair.'

'Have you thoroughly pondered your resolution? Do you know to what an abyss I was dragging you, poor darling? No, I think you do not! You were coming in blind trust, believing in happiness, in the future. ... Ah, what poor senseless creatures we are!'

Here Rodolphe paused to think of a good excuse. 'Suppose I say I've lost all my money? No. That wouldn't clinch the thing, anyway; I'd have it starting all over again. How can you make such women listen to reason?'

After some thought he proceeded: 'Be sure I shall never forget you. I shall always be deeply devoted to you. But one day, sooner or later, these ardent feelings of ours would doubtless have cooled. Such is the human lot. We should have grown tired of one another. Who knows but what I might have suffered the agony of witnessing your remorse – of sharing it myself, since I should have been the cause of it! The very thought of your suffering is torture to me, Emma. Forget me. Why did we have to meet? Why were you so beautiful? Am I to blame? No, by Heaven; blame only Fate!'

'Always an effective word,' he said to himself.

'Ah, had you been one of those frivolous-hearted women one sees, then indeed I might selfishly have embarked upon an adventure which would in that case have had no danger for you. But that delicious exaltation which is at once your charm and your torment, has prevented you from understanding – adorable woman that you are! – the false position in which we should have been placed. Neither had I thought of it at first. I was at ease in the shade of that ideal happiness, lying under the mango-tree, as it were, regardless of consequences.'

'She may think it's the money I grudge. Can't help it if she does; it's got to be finished.'

'Society is cruel, Emma. It would have pursued us everywhere we went. There would have been awkward questions,

ugly words. They might have snubbed you – insulted you!
You, that I would set upon a throne! You, whose memory
will go with me as a talisman. For I am leaving the country, as
a penance for all the harm I have done you. I shall go at once.
Where, I do not know. I am past thinking! Good-bye. Be always good and kind. Keep a place in your memory for this
unhappy man who has lost you. Teach your child my name,
and let her say it over in her prayers.'

The two candles flickered. Rodolphe got up to close the
window, then sat down again.

'There, I think that's all. Oh, just in case she comes to
ferret me out. ...'

'I shall be far away when you read these sad lines. I have
decided to leave immediately, so that I shan't be tempted to see
you again. No wavering! I shall come back, and some day,
perhaps, we may talk to one another quite calmly of our past
love. *Adieu!*'

And there was a final *adieu* – separated into two words, *A
Dieu!* – which he thought in excellent taste.

'Now, how shall I sign it?' he wondered. 'Your devoted?
No. Your friend? Yes that's it.'

'Your friend.'

He read the letter through, and felt satisfied.

'Poor little woman!' he thought with a movement of pity.
'She'll think I've a heart of stone. It could have done with a
few tears over it. Well, it's not my fault if I can't cry ...'

He poured out a glass of water, dipped his finger in, and let
one big drop fall on the paper. The ink smudged. As he was
looking for a seal, he came across the '*Amor nel cor*' signet-
ring.

'Not quite the thing in the circumstances! ... Oh well, what's
the difference?'

After which he smoked three pipes and went to bed.

When he got up next day – it was about two o'clock, he had
slept late – Rodolphe had a basket of apricots picked. Placing

his letter at the bottom, under some vine-leaves, he sent his ploughman Girard off with it at once, with instructions to carry it carefully to Madame Bovary's. This was a method of communication he employed, sending her fruit or game according to the season.

'If she asks after me,' he said, 'tell her I've gone away on a journey. And give the basket to *her*, into her own hands. Off, now, and mind your step!'

Girard put on his best blouse, covered over the apricots with his handkerchief, and, lumbering along in his heavy, studded boots, set off tranquilly in the direction of Yonville.

Madame Bovary was in the kitchen when he arrived, help-ing Félicité lay out a bundle of washing on the table.

'Master sent this, ma'am,' said the ploughman.

Her fears were roused. As she felt in her pocket for a tip, she gazed at the man wild-eyed; and he stared back in amaze-ment, unable to comprehend how anyone could be so affected by a present like that. At last he went. Félicité was still there. She couldn't wait any longer. She pretended to be taking the apricots into the dining-room, turned the basket upside-down, snatched away the leaves, found the letter, opened it, and, as though a fire were raging at her back, Emma fled upstairs in a panic.

She saw Charles in the bedroom; he said something, she didn't hear, but rushed on up the stairs, breathless, aghast, out of her wits, all the while clutching that horrible sheet of paper, which crackled in her fingers like a piece of sheet-iron. On the second landing she halted outside the attic door, which was shut.

Then she tried to collect herself. The letter – she must read it through. She didn't dare. How – where – without being seen?

'Oh, in here,' she thought, 'I'll be safe.'

Emma pushed open the door and entered.

The roof-slates cast down a stuffy heat that gripped her

216

temples and stifled her. She dragged herself across to the shuttered window and drew the bolt; the dazzling sunlight flooded in.

Opposite, away over the roof-tops, the open country stretched as far as eye could see. Down below, the village square was deserted. The pebbles glittered on the pavement, weathercocks stood motionless on the houses. From a lower floor at the corner of the street came a kind of droning sound with strident modulations: Binet was at his lathe.

She leaned against the window-frame and read the letter through, hysterical with rage. But the more she tried to fix her thoughts on it, the more confused they became. She seemed to see him, to hear his voice, to be clasping him in her arms; her heart pounded against her ribs like a battering-ram, thudding faster and faster, leaping wildly. She cast her eyes all round her, wishing she could sink into the earth. Why not have done with it? What was to stop her? She was free. She stepped forward and looked down at the pavement.

'Go on! Go on!' she said to herself.

The ray of light coming up from directly below was dragging the weight of her body towards the abyss. The ground seemed to start swaying up the walls, the floor dipped beneath her like a vessel heeling over. She stood at the very edge, swinging out into space. The blue of the sky pressed down upon her, the air was circling in her hollow head, she had only to give way, to let herself go ... And all the time the lathe went on whirring, whirring, like a voice furiously calling her.

'Emma! Emma!' shouted Charles.

She stopped still.

'Where are you? Come on down!'

The thought that she had just been saved from death made her almost faint with terror. She shut her eyes. A touch on her sleeve made her shudder. It was Félicité.

'The doctor's waiting, Madame. The soup is served.'

And down she must go, and sit with him!

She tried to eat. The food choked her. She opened out her serviette as though to examine the darns in it, and actually set herself to the task of counting the stitches. Suddenly she remembered the letter. Where had she put it? Had she dropped it somewhere? She felt too exhausted to think of an excuse for getting up from the table. She was losing her nerve, too. She was afraid of Charles. She knew he knew! Oddly enough, he broke into her thoughts with the words: 'It seems we shan't be seeing Monsieur Rodolphe for a while.'

She started. 'Who told you?'

'Who told me?' he echoed in surprise at the sharpness of her tone. 'Why, I met Girard just now outside the Café Français. He's gone away on a journey, or is about to go.'

A sob broke from her.

'Does it surprise you? He goes off like that now and then for a holiday and, my word, I don't blame him either! With money – and a bachelor! A fine time he has too, does our friend. He's a gay dog! Monsieur Langlois was telling me ...'

He broke off tactfully as the maid came in. Félicité picked up the apricots that were scattered over the dresser and put them back in the basket. Not noticing how red his wife had gone, Charles told the girl to bring them to him, picked out an apricot and took a bite at it.

'Ah! Perfect!' he said. 'Try one!' And he handed her the basket, which she gently pushed away.

'Just smell! What a delicious odour!' he exclaimed, passing the basket to and fro under her nose.

'I'm choking!' she cried, springing to her feet. But with an effort she conquered the spasm. 'It's nothing, nothing,' she said. 'Just nerves. ... Sit down and get on!'

For she dreaded being questioned and nursed and never left alone.

To humour her, Charles sat down again and went on eating. He spat out the apricot-stones into his hand, then deposited them on his plate.

All at once a blue tilbury trotted briskly across the market-place. Emma gave a shriek and fell flat on the floor.

After much thought, Rodolphe had decided to go away to Rouen. And as you cannot get from La Huchette to Buchy without coming through Yonville, through Yonville he had had to come. Emma had recognized him in the gleam of the lamps which came flashing through the dusk like lightning.

Hearing an uproar, the chemist dashed in. The table had been overturned, the meat and gravy, the cutlery, the salt-cellar, the cruet-stand, were strewn about the room, Charles was shouting for help, Berthe howling with fright, Félicité, with hands that shook, unlacing her mistress, whose whole body was writhing convulsively.

'I'll run and get my aromatic vinegar,' said the chemist.

When she sniffed the bottle, her eyes opened.

'There!' said he. 'That stuff would waken the dead.'

'Say something!' Charles implored her. 'Speak to us! Emma! It's me – your Charles who loves you – don't you know me? Look, here's your little girl. Give her a kiss!'

The child held out her arms, to put them round her mother's neck. Emma turned away.

'No ... nobody!' she jerked out. And then she fainted again. They carried her up to bed.

She lay with mouth hanging open, eyes closed, hands straight down at her sides, motionless, white as a waxen image. Two streams of tears welled out of her eyes and trickled slowly on to the pillow.

Charles stood at the back of the alcove. The chemist, beside him, preserved that meditative silence which befits the graver occasions of life.

'Set your mind at rest,' he said eventually, laying a hand on Charles' elbow. 'I think the paroxysm is over.'

'Yes, she's a bit easier now,' answered Charles, watching her as she slept. 'Poor girl, poor girl, the old trouble again!'

Homais asked how it had happened. Charles told him the

attack had come on quite suddenly, while she was eating apricots.

'Extraordinary!' the chemist remarked. 'Though it's possible the apricots caused the syncope. Some people are so sensitive to certain odours. That would be an excellent subject to study, you know, both in its pathological and in its physiological aspects. Its importance is acknowledged by the priests, who have always introduced aromatic perfumes into their ceremonies; they lull the intellect and induce a condition of ecstasy – no difficult matter with members of the other sex, who are more finely adjusted than we are. Cases are cited of women fainting at the smell of burnt hartshorn, or of newly baked bread. ...'

'Careful, you'll wake her!' whispered Bovary.

'And it isn't only human beings who are subject to such vagaries,' continued the chemist; 'animals are as well. You must know, for instance, of the powerfully aphrodisiac effect that is produced on the feline tribe by *Nepeta cataria*, commonly called catmint; while on the other hand, to mention an example the authenticity of which I can vouch for myself, an old colleague of mine named Bridoux – now in business in the Rue Malpalu – owns a dog that has fits if you hold a snuff-box in front of it. He often gives a demonstration to his friends at his villa in the Bois-Guillaume. Would you believe that a common-or-garden sternutatory could work such mischief on a quadrupedal organism? Fascinating, don't you think?'

'Yes,' said Charles, not listening.

'It goes to show,' the other went on, smiling with an air of benign complacency, 'how innumerable are the irregularities of the nervous system. Now, your wife, I confess, has always looked to me the true sensitive type. Hence I should by no means recommend to you, my friend, any of those so-called remedies which claim to attack the symptoms but in reality undermine the constitution. No, none of that idle quackery! Diet – there's the whole secret. With sedatives, emollients and syrups. And then, don't you think we ought perhaps to strike at the imagination?'

'How? In what way?' said Bovary.

'Ah, that is the question. Such is indeed the question. "C'est là la question", as the paper was saying the other day.'

Emma woke, shouting: 'The letter! The letter!'

They thought she must be delirious. By midnight she was. Brain-fever had set in.

For forty-three days Charles never left her side. He forsook his patients, sat up all night with her, and was continually feeling her pulse or applying mustard plasters or cold-water compresses. He sent Justin to Neufchâtel for ice; it melted on the way back; he sent him off again. He called in Monsieur Canivet, and had Dr Larivière, his old master, come from Rouen to see her. He was desperate. What alarmed him most was Emma's condition of prostration. She didn't speak, and she didn't hear anything. She appeared even to be without pain, as though body and soul were resting together from all the shocks that they had suffered.

By the middle of October she was able to sit up in bed with pillows at her back. Charles shed tears when he saw her eating her first slice of bread and jam. Her strength began to return. She got up for a few hours in the afternoon, and then one day when she was feeling much better, he tried taking her on his arm for a walk round the garden. The gravel paths were almost obliterated with dead leaves. She shuffled along in her slippers, one step at a time, leaning on Charles and smiling continuously.

In this fashion they walked as far as the terrace at the bottom. She drew herself up slowly and, shading her eyes with her hand, gazed into the distance; but she could see only a few bonfires smoking on the hills.

'You'll tire yourself, darling,' said Bovary, and he pushed her gently towards the entrance to the arbour. 'Sit down on the bench, you'll be all right there.'

'Oh! No, not there, not there!' said she in a lifeless voice.

An attack of dizziness came on; and that evening her illness began again, though this time it was of a more uncertain nature, with more complex symptoms. Sometimes she had pains in her heart, sometimes in her chest, then in the head or limbs. She started vomiting – and in that Charles thought he saw the first signs of cancer.

On top of everything, the poor fellow was worried about money.

14

In the first place, he had no idea how he was going to settle with Homais for all the medical supplies they had been having from him, and though as a doctor he needn't have paid for them at all, he would have felt ashamed to incur such an obligation. Then there were the household expenses, which had risen alarmingly now that the maid was in charge. Bills rained in, tradesmen were getting restive; Monsieur Lheureux was particularly importunate. At the critical stage of Emma's illness, that gentleman, taking advantage of the situation to present an inflated bill, had hurried round with the cloak and travelling-bag, two trunks instead of one and a host of other things besides. No use for Charles to say he didn't want them – the shopkeeper retorted high-handedly that they'd all been ordered and he wasn't going to take them back: besides, it might upset Madame during her convalescence: Monsieur had better think it over: not to waste words, he was determined to take him to court sooner than give up his rights and cart the goods back. Eventually Charles gave orders for them to be sent back, but Félicité forgot; he had other things to think about, and so they were left. Lheureux returned to the attack, and by alternately blustering and whining, manoeuvred Bovary into signing a note of hand to fall due in six months. As soon as he had put his name to it, Charles had a bold idea –

that of borrowing forty pounds from Lheureux. Awkwardly he asked if such a loan were possible – for a year, he added, on any terms desired. Lheureux hurried off to fetch the money and made out another bill whereby Bovary undertook to pay to his order, on the 1st September next, the sum of forty-three pounds: which with the seven already stipulated made a round fifty. So, with interest at six per cent plus a quarter commission and a good thirty-three-and-a-third on the articles supplied, Lheureux should clear five pounds in twelve months. He hoped that matters would not stop there, that Bovary would be unable to pay and have to renew the bills; so that his little capital, nourished at the doctor's like a patient in hospital, would return to him one day considerably plumper, heavy enough to burst the bag.

Lheureux was prospering generally. He had won a contract for supplying cider to the workhouse at Neufchâtel; Monsieur Guillaumin had promised him some shares in the peatworks at Grumesnil; and it was his ambition to set up a new Argueil-Rouen coach service, which would presumably drive the Lion's old bone-shaker off the road in no time, and, by being faster and cheaper and carrying a bigger load, bring the whole of the Yonville trade into his hands.

Charles often wondered how he was going to meet so large a debt next year. He turned over various expedients in his mind. Should he apply to his father? His father would turn a deaf ear. Should he sell something? He had nothing to sell. He began to see such difficulties ahead that he promptly banished from his mind so unpleasant a subject of speculation. He reproached himself for having let it distract him from Emma – as though his every thought belonged to that woman, as though to think of anything else, even for a moment, were to steal something from her.

The winter was a hard one. Madame's recovery was slow. On fine days they wheeled her armchair to the window overlooking the market-place – for the garden was repugnant to her now, and the blinds were always drawn on that side. She wanted to sell their horse; everything she had formerly been fond of she now disliked. Her whole outlook seemed contracted to self-solicitude. She used to lie in bed and have little meals brought up to her, or ring for the maid to ask about her invalid drinks, or just to have a chat. And every day the snow on the market-roof cast its still white glitter into the room. When the snow went, the rain came. Emma would wait, in a kind of suspense, for each small daily event to come inexorably round, little though it might concern her. The biggest moment was when the *Hirondelle* drew up in the evening, and she heard the landlady shouting and other voices answering, and saw Hippolyte's stable-lamp twinkling like a star in the darkness as he hunted among the boxes on the tilt. At noon, Charles came in. After he had gone again, she drank her broth. And when dusk began to fall at about five o'clock, the children went by on their way home from school, scraping their sabots on the pavements and all in turn rapping on the shutter-hooks with their rulers.

Bournisien called about this time of day. He asked how she felt, told her the news and exhorted her to religion in a little wheedling prattle that was not without its charm. The very sight of his cassock was a comfort to her.

One day, at the crisis of her illness, believing herself at death's door, she had asked for the sacrament. While they got her room ready, setting out the chest of drawers, with its array of medicine bottles, as an altar, and while Félicité strewed dahlia petals over the floor, Emma felt a powerful influence sweep over her, relieving her of all pain, all perception, all feeling. Her flesh found rest from thought; a new life had begun; it was as if her soul, ascending to God, were about to be swallowed up in His love like burning incense vanishing in smoke. The sheets were sprinkled with holy water, the priest took the white wafer from the sacred pyx, and as she parted her lips to receive the Body of the Saviour, she swooned with a celestial bliss. The curtains swelled softly around the bed like clouds, the beams of the two tapers on the chest of drawers appeared as dazzling aureoles of light. Then she let her head drop back on to the pillow, seeming to hear through space the harps of the seraphs playing, and to see, seated upon a throne of gold in an azure Heaven with His Saints around Him bearing branches of green palm, God the Father, resplendent in majesty, at whose command angels with wings of flame descended to Earth to carry her up in their arms.

This glorious vision remained in her memory as the most beautiful dream that could be dreamed. She strove to recapture the sensation of it, which lingered, if with a less exclusive purity, yet with as profound an enchantment. Her soul, deformed by pride, found rest at last in Christian humility. Relishing the pleasures of weakness, Emma contemplated the destruction of her will within her, which was to leave the way wide open to the flowing tide of grace. So then, in place of happiness there existed greater felicities, above all loves a higher love, without end or intermission, a love that would grow to all eternity. Amid the illusions that her wishes prompted, she glimpsed a realm of purity, floating above the earth, melting into the sky, where she aspired to be. She wanted to become a saint. She bought rosaries, wore amulets, and asked for a little reliquary set in emeralds to be placed at the head of her bed, that she might kiss it every night.

The *curé* marvelled at this frame of mind in her, though he feared the very fervour of her faith might lead her to the borders of the heretical, even the extravagant. However, not being highly conversant with these matters once they went beyond a certain range, he wrote to Monsieur Boulard, bookseller to the Bishop, asking for 'some work of note, for a female with brains'. As indifferently as if he were shipping hardware to Negroes, the bookseller packed up all the works then current in the religious book trade and bundled them off. They included little manuals of question and answer, haughty-toned pamphlets in the manner of Monsieur de Maistre, and some novels of a sort, in pink bindings and sugary style, turned out by academic hacks or penitent blue-stockings. There were *Think on These Things*; *The Man of the World at the Feet of Mary*, by the distinguished Monsieur de — ; some *Errors of Voltaire, for the Use of Young People*, and so on.

Madame Bovary was in point of fact not yet sufficiently clear-headed to apply herself seriously to anything at all. Moreover, she went at her reading too precipitately. The ritual ordinances annoyed her; she disliked the arrogance of the controversial writings and the furious zeal with which they attacked people she had never heard of; while the secular stories flavoured with religion seemed to her written in such ignorance of life that they insensibly diverted her from the truths she was seeking to have proved. Still she persevered, until when the volume at last fell from her hands she saw herself as possessed by the finest Catholic melancholy that ever ethereal soul could conceive.

All memory of Rodolphe she had sunk deep in her heart, and there it remained, more still and solemn than a king's mummy in a catacomb. This embalmed passion gave off an all-pervasive effluence, imbuing with tenderness the atmosphere of immaculate purity in which she wished to dwell. When she knelt on her Gothic prie-dieu, she addressed to her Lord the same sweet words she had once murmured to her lover in the heart-easings of illicit passion. She was trying to make faith come. But no bliss descended from the heavens, and she rose with weary limbs and the vague feeling that it was all a vast deception. Her quest seemed only an added merit; and in the pride of her piety, Emma likened herself to those great ladies of old, whose glory she had dreamed of over a portrait of La Vallière, who, trailing so majestically long robes with gorgeous trains, would retreat into solitude to shed at the feet of Christ all the tears of a heart that life had wounded.

She now devoted herself to an extravagant charity, sewed clothes for the poor and sent firewood to women in confinement; Charles returned one day to find three ragamuffins being fed with soup at the kitchen table. The little girl, whom he had sent to the nurse's during her illness, she now fetched home again. She decided she would teach her to read; and however much Berthe cried, she never got angry with her now. She had chosen the path of resignation; a universal indulgence was declared. She used exalted phrases on all occasions: '*My angel,* has your tummy-ache gone?' she would say to the child. ...

Her mother-in-law could find no fault with her, unless it was her mania for knitting vests for orphans instead of mending her own dusters. But, worn out as she was by wrangling in her own home, the good woman liked this quiet household and even stayed till after Easter, to escape the taunts of her husband, who invariably ordered pork sausages for Good Friday.

Besides her mother-in-law, whose right judgement and staid manner were a great source of strength to her, Emma had other visitors nearly every day: Madame Langlois, Madame Caron, Madame Dubreuil, Madame Tuvache, and regularly from two to five the excellent Madame Homais, who for her part had never been one to listen to all the tittle-tattle that went on about her neighbour. The Homais children came to see her too, accompanied by Justin, who took them up to her room and then stood stiffly silent by the door. Madame Bovary would often forget he was there and sit down at her dressing-table, take out her comb and shake her head in an abrupt movement. And the first time he saw that mass of hair tumble down to her knees, the dark ringlets uncurling, it was as if the poor boy had suddenly been thrust into an extraordinary new world whose splendour scared him.

His silent eagerness, his blenchings and tremblings, were no doubt lost on Emma. She never dreamt that love (which had gone out of her life) pulsated so close at hand beneath that coarse shirt, in that youthful heart that had opened to the influence of her beauty.

For she enfolded everything now in so complete an indifference, she spoke so affectionately and looked so haughtily, had such diverse moods, that one could no longer distinguish in her the charitable from the self-regarding impulse, depravity from virtue. One evening she lost her temper with the maid, who had asked permission to go out and was fumbling for an excuse; then suddenly asked her, 'Do you love him?' And without waiting for an answer from the blushing Félicité, she said gloomily: 'All right! Run along and enjoy yourself!'

At the beginning of spring she had the whole of the garden turned upside-down, despite some remonstrance from Bovary. Not that he was sorry to see her showing signs of interest in something. She asserted herself the more as her health improved. First she contrived to evict Madame Rollet the wet-nurse, who, during Emma's convalescence, had acquired the habit of coming to the kitchen rather too often, bringing with her her pair of nurslings and her lodger, who had an appetite like a cannibal. Then she shook off the Homais tribe and successively dismissed the rest of the callers. Even her church-going dropped off, to the high contentment of the chemist, who thereupon informed her amicably: 'You were getting somewhat involved with the cloth!'

Bournisien continued, however, to pay his daily visit on the way back from his catechism class. He liked to sit out of doors, taking the air in the 'grove', as he called the arbour. Charles usually came home about the same time, and they sent for a bottle of sweet cider to cool them, and drank together to Madame's complete recovery.

Binet would be there, too – a little lower down, by the terrace wall, catching crayfish. Bovary invited him in for a drink. He was an expert at uncorking stone bottles. 'Like this!' he used to say, casting a complacent glance all round him and away to the very limit of the view. 'Hold the bottle upright on the table, so, and after cutting the strings, give the cork a few little pushes, gently, gently – as they do with Seltzer water in the restaurants.'

During the demonstration the cider frequently squirted up into their faces, at which the priest invariably laughed his thick laugh and made the same joke: 'Its goodness leaps to the eye!'

A 'good chap', was Bournisien – who showed no signs of being shocked when one day the chemist was advising Charles to take Madame, by way of a change, to hear the celebrated tenor Lagardy at Rouen. Surprised at his silence, Homais asked the priest what he thought; he replied that he saw less danger to morals in music than in literature.

The chemist rallied to the defence of letters, contending that drama served to tilt at prejudice and taught virtue beneath the mask of entertainment.

'*Castigat ridendo mores*, Monsieur Bournisien! Look at the greater part of Voltaire's tragedies – how cleverly they're interspersed with philosophical reflections, which make them a real popular education in morals and diplomacy.'

'*I* once saw a play,' said Binet, 'called the *Street-boy of Paris*, where there's an old General who's hit off to a T! He takes down a young blood who had seduced a working girl, who in the end ...'

'Certainly,' Homais went on, 'there are bad writers as there are bad chemists. But to condemn wholesale the greatest of the arts, strikes me as a gross piece of philistinism, worthy of those dark ages when they threw Galileo into prison!'

'I'm well aware,' countered the *curé*, 'that there *is* good writing, good authors do exist. But where you have these couples brought together in luxurious surroundings, with all the adornment of worldly display, the barbarous dressing-up, the grease-paint and the lights, the effeminate voices – surely, in time, all that must breed a certain laxity, and give rise to unclean thoughts, impure temptations! Such is, at any rate, the unanimous opinion of the Fathers. After all,' he added, suddenly assuming a mystical tone of voice, while he twirled a pinch of snuff between his finger and thumb, 'if the Church has condemned the playhouse, the Church has her reasons for so doing. We must accept her decrees.'

'What reason *is* there,' asked the chemist, 'for excommunicating actors? Time was when they participated openly in religious ceremonies. They used to act in the chancel itself; they did a farcical sort of a play called a "mystery", which frequently offended against the laws of decency.'

The priest contented himself with a groan, and the chemist went on: 'The same as in the Bible! You know what I mean, there's a lot of lively stuff! Oh yes, some really spicy bits!'

Monsieur Bournisien made a movement of annoyance.

'Ah, now you'll own it's not a book to be put into the hands of young people, and I should be sorry to find Athalie ...'

'But it's the Protestants, not us, that recommend the Bible!' cried the other, losing patience.

'No matter!' said Homais, 'I'm surprised that in these days, in this age of enlightenment, you should still persist in condemning an intellectual recreation which is quite harmless and moral, and sometimes even good for the health, isn't that so, Doctor?'

'I dare say,' the doctor answered half-heartedly, either because he shared the opinion expressed but wished to avoid giving offence, or because he had no opinion.

The conversation seemed at an end, when the chemist saw fit to fire off a parting shot.

'I've known priests dress up in ordinary clothes to go and watch show-girls kicking their legs!'

'Come!' ejected the *curé*.

'Oh yes, I've known them.' And pronouncing each syllable distinctly, Homais repeated: 'I – have – known – them.'

'Well, it was wrong of them,' said Bournisien, resigned to hearing the worst.

'And, my goodness, they don't stop there!' said the chemist.

'Sir!' the priest broke out, with such a wild glare in his eyes that the chemist was intimidated.

'I only mean,' he resumed in a less offensive tone, 'that tolerance is the surest way to win people to religion.'

'Yes, that's true, that's true,' the good man conceded, sitting down again. But he stayed only a couple of minutes more.

'Well, that was a set-to if you like!' said Homais when he had gone. 'You saw how I licked him! Good and proper! Anyhow, if I were you, I'd take your wife to see the show if only to annoy one of those old crows once in your life, by George! I'd come with you if there were anyone to do my work here. Be quick about it, too, for Lagardy's only giving one performance. He's had a magnificent offer from England. I'm told he's a fly one, rolling in money, takes three mistresses and his own chef about with him. These great artists are all night-birds. They need to lead rackety lives, to stimulate their imagination. They die in the workhouse, though, not having the sense to put a bit by when young. Well, enjoy your dinner! See you tomorrow!'

This theatre project quickly took root in Bovary's mind. He broached it to his wife at once. She as promptly refused: it would be too tiring, too much trouble, too expensive. But for once in a way Charles persisted, so certain was he that the excursion would do her good. He could see nothing against it. His mother had lately forwarded twelve pounds, of which he had given up hope; there was nothing out of the way in the debts immediately owing; and it was still so long before he had to pay Lheureux, that there was no point in worrying about that. Fancying, moreover, that she was refusing out of tact, Charles became the more pressing, until in the end he wore down her resistance. At eight o'clock next morning they stowed themselves into the *Hirondelle*.

The chemist, who although there was nothing to keep him

at Yonville, felt that he couldn't possibly stir from the place, sighed as he saw them off.

'Enjoy yourselves! Lucky mortals that you are!' And to Emma, who was wearing a blue silk dress with four flounces: 'You're as pretty as a picture! What a hit you'll make in Rouen!'

The coach stopped at the Red Cross Hotel in the Place Beauvoisine. It was one of those inns you find on the outskirts of any country town, with big stables and little bedrooms, and hens scratching for oats in the yard, underneath the commercial travellers' muddy gigs: good old-fashioned hostelries with worm-eaten balconies that creak in the wind on winter nights: always full of people, noise and victuals, with sticky marks of coffee-and-brandy on the black tables, thick windows yellowed by flies, stains of cheap wine on the damp serviettes; still retaining a countrified air, like farm-hands dressed up in their Sunday suits – having a street café in front and a kitchen-garden at the back.

Charles went straight off to buy tickets. He got the stalls mixed up with the gallery, the pit with the boxes; he asked for explanations but failed to understand them, was sent from the box-office to the manager, returned to the inn, set out for the theatre once more, and so measured the length of the town, between the theatre and the boulevard, several times.

Madame bought herself a hat, gloves, and a bouquet. Monsieur was in dread of missing the start, and, without stopping even to gulp down a plate of broth, they arrived at the theatre to find the doors still shut.

15

THE crowds were lining up along the wall, penned symmetrically inside the railings. Gigantic posters at the corners of the neighbouring streets announced in gaudy lettering: 'Bride of

Lammermoor – Lagardy – Opera', and so on. It was a fine day, everyone felt hot, curls ran with perspiration, handkerchiefs were being fetched out to mop red foreheads. Now and then a warm breeze from the river set the fringe of the drill awnings fluttering over the tavern doors. A little farther down, however, came a refreshing draught of ice-cold air, bringing a smell of tallow, oil and leather with it. This was the emanation from the Rue des Charrettes, a street of great dark warehouses and trundling barrels.

So as not to stand there looking foolish, Emma suggested a stroll by the harbour before going in. Bovary kept the tickets cautiously clutched in his hand inside his trousers pocket, which he held tight against his belly.

Her heart beat as she entered the foyer. She smiled involuntarily, out of vanity, as she saw people jostling down the passage on the right while she went up to the boxes. She took a child's delight in pushing open the large upholstered doors with one finger, she breathed deep into her lungs the dusty smell of the corridors, and when she was ensconced in her box she drew herself up in her seat as to the manner born.

The theatre was beginning to fill up. Opera-glasses emerged from their cases; seat-holders, catching sight of their friends, waved greetings. They had come to find relaxation in the arts from the cares of business. Nevertheless they were still talking shop – cotton, proof spirit, indigo, they couldn't forget it. There were old men with peaceful, expressionless faces, bleached hair and bleached complexions, heads like silver medals tarnished by a leaden vapour. There were young bloods strutting about in the stalls, showing off their rose-pink or apple-green cravats in the opening of their waistcoats, and being admired from up above by Madame Bovary as they leaned on their gold-knobbed walking-canes, with the palms of their yellow gloves stretched taut.

Then the orchestra candles were lit and the chandelier was let down from the ceiling, its glittering facets shedding a sudden gaiety upon the house. The musicians filed in; and after a confused din of rumbling double-basses, scraping fiddles, braying cornets, chirruping flutes and flageolets, there came three taps from the stage: a roll of drums: sustained chords from the brasses, and the curtain rose upon a country scene.

It was a crossways in a wood, with a fountain on the left shaded by an oak-tree. Peasants and chieftains with plaids over their shoulders were singing a hunting-chorus. A captain came on and, raising both arms to Heaven, invoked the Spirit of Evil. A second character appeared. Then both departed, and the huntsmen struck up again.

Emma found herself back in the books of her youth, in the land of Sir Walter Scott. She seemed to hear the skirl of the bagpipes echoing through the mist across the heather. Remembering the novel, she could understand the libretto without difficulty, and as she followed the plot, sentence by sentence, elusive thoughts came back to her, to be dispersed immediately by the thunder of the music. She let herself be lulled by the melodies: she felt a vibration pass through her whole being, as if the bows of the violins were being drawn across her own nerves. She hadn't eyes enough to take in all the costumes and the scenery, the characters, the painted trees that shook when anyone took a step, the velvet caps, the cloaks and swords, the whole creation moving to the music as in the atmosphere of another world. A young woman came forward and threw a purse to a squire in green. She was left alone, and a flute started playing, like the murmur of a fountain or the warbling of birds. Gravely Lucy entered upon her cavatina in G major. She plained of love, she longed for wings. So too Emma would have liked to escape from life and fly away in an embrace. ... Suddenly Edgar Lagardy made his entrance.

He had a splendid pallor of the sort that lends a marmoreal majesty to the ardent races of the South. His vigorous frame was tightly clad in a brown-coloured jerkin. A small carved dagger swung at his left thigh. He rolled his eyes languorously and showed his white teeth. It was said that a Polish princess had fallen in love with him hearing him sing one night on the beach at Biarritz, where he had been a boat-mender. She had thrown everything to the winds for him. He had left her for other women; and his fame as a lover served but to enhance his reputation as an artist. This canny player was always careful to slip into the advertisements some lyric phrase about the fascination of his person and the sensitivity of his soul. A fine voice, imperturbable self-possession, more personality than intelligence and more power than poetry, went to complete the armoury of this admirable mountebank-type, with its ingredients of the hairdresser and the toreador.

He cast an immediate spell. He clasped Lucy in his arms, he left her, returned to her, seemed in despair. He burst out in anger, then agonized with an infinite elegiac tenderness, and the notes rolled forth from his bare throat laden with sobs and kisses. Emma leaned forward to watch him, her fingernails clutching at the plush on the box, and took her heart's fill of those melodious lamentations that poured out to the accompaniment of the double-basses like cries of the drowning amid the tumult of the tempest. She recognized the ecstasy and the anguish of which she had all but died. The heroine's voice seemed simply the echo of her own consciousness, and all this fascinating make-believe a part of her own life. Yet none on earth had ever loved with a love like that. *He* had not wept like Edgar, that last evening in the moonlight when they had said, 'Till tomorrow! Till tomorrow!' ... The theatre was ringing with applause. The whole of the finale was begun over again. The lovers spoke of the flowers on their tomb, of vows, exile, fate, hope. When they sang their last *adieu* Emma uttered a sharp cry which was drowned in the reverberations of the final chords.

'Why is that lord being cruel to her?' asked Bovary.

'No, no, no, he's her lover,' she answered.

'Well, he's swearing vengeance on her family, whereas the other one, the one that came on just now, said "I love Lucy and believe that she loves me", and then he went off arm-in-arm with her father. That *is* her father, isn't it, the ugly little chap with the cock's feather in his hat?'

Emma explained. But when they got to the duet in which Gilbert unfolds his nefarious schemes to his master Ashton, Charles, seeing the supposed wedding-ring that was to deceive Lucy, imagined it to be a love-token from Edgar. Not that he claimed to understand the story: the music did so interfere with the words.

'What does it matter?' said Emma. 'Be quiet!'

'You know I always like to get things straight,' he answered, leaning over her shoulder.

'Quiet, quiet!' she said impatiently.

Lucy came forward, half-supported by her women, with a wreath of orange-blossom in her hair, her face paler than her white satin dress. Emma thought of her own wedding-day; she saw herself back in the cornfields again, walking along the little path on the way to church. Oh, why, why hadn't she resisted, entreated, like that girl there? Instead she had plunged blindly, blithely, over the precipice. ... If only in the freshness of her beauty, before the soilure of marriage and the disillusionment of adultery, she could have grounded her life upon some great, strong heart – then everything would have gone together, virtue and love, the pleasures and the duties, never would she have descended from that height of felicity. But, of course, such happiness must be a fiction, invented to be the despair of all desire. She knew now the littleness of those passions that art exaggerates. Accordingly, Emma strove to deflect her thoughts, to see no more in this reproduction of her sorrows than an embodied fantasy, an ornament for the eye. And she was actually smiling to herself, a smile of contemptuous pity, when from the velvet hangings at the back of the stage a man in a black cloak appeared.

He made a gesture and his broad-brimmed Spanish hat fell to the floor. Immediately orchestra and singers attacked the sextet. Edgar, flashing fury, dominated them all with his clear tenor. Ashton hurled his murderous challenge in deeper notes, Lucy moaned her shrill plaint; Arthur modulated aside in the middle register, the Minister's baritone pealed forth like an organ, while the women's chorus echoed his words deliciously. All the characters were now gesticulating in a line across the stage; and anger and vengeance, jealousy, pity, terror and astonishment all breathed forth together from their parted lips. The outraged lover brandished his naked sword. His lace ruffle jerked up and down with the heaving of his chest as he crossed from left to right with great strides, in buckskin boots that folded back over the ankles, clanking his spurs on the boards. There must, thought Emma, be an endless fund of love within him, that he should lavish it upon the audience in such plenteous draughts. She lost all wish to cavil as the romance of the role took hold of her. Drawn to the man by his creation of the character, she tried to picture to herself the life he led, that extraordinary, hectic, splendid life, that might have been hers if only chance had so ordained it. For they might have met, and loved. With him she would have visited all the kingdoms of Europe, travelling from capital to capital, sharing the fatigue and the glory, gathering up the flowers they flung at his feet, embroidering his costumes with her own hand; in the evening sitting at the back of a box, behind the gilt trellis-work, listening with parted lips to the profusion of that man who would be singing for none but her. He would look up at her as he sang his part on the stage. ... A wild idea seized her: he was looking at her now, yes, she was certain he was! She longed to run to his arms, to shelter in his strength as in the very incarnation of love, and to say to him, to cry out to him, 'Take me! Carry me away! Away! Yours, yours be all my ardour, all my dreams!'

The curtain fell.

The smell of gas mingled with the smell of breath, the waving of fans made the air still stuffier. Emma wanted to go out, but the corridors were jammed with people; she sank back into her seat with palpitations that took her breath away. Afraid that she was going to faint, Charles went off to the refreshment-room to fetch her a glass of barley-water.

He had the greatest difficulty in getting back to the box. Carrying the glass in both hands, he got his elbows jogged at every step and spilt three-quarters of it over the shoulders of a Rouen lady in a short-sleeved dress, who screamed like a peacock, as though she were being murdered, when she felt the cold liquid running down her back. Her husband, a mill-owner, got furious with the clumsy fellow, and while she took her handkerchief and dabbed at the stains on her beautiful cherry taffeta, he muttered surlily the words compensation, expense, repayment. ...

At last Charles reached his wife.

'Heavens,' he gasped, 'I thought I'd never get here! It's packed! Packed! ... And you'll never guess,' he added, 'whom I ran into up there! Monsieur Léon!'

'Léon?'

'Himself! He's coming along to pay you his respects.'

The words were hardly out of his mouth when the ex-clerk of Yonville entered their box.

He held out his hand with an aristocratic nonchalance, and Madame Bovary mechanically extended hers, yielding no doubt to the attraction of a stronger will. She had not touched that hand since that spring evening when the rain pattered on the green leaves and they stood at the window saying goodbye. ... In an instant, however, she recalled herself to the requirements of the situation, shook herself out of her trance with an effort and began to stammer a few hurried phrases.

'Oh! Good evening! Well! fancy you here!'

'Ssh!' came a voice from the pit, for the third act was beginning.

'So you're at Rouen now.'

'Yes.'

"How long have you been here?'

'Ssh!' 'Quiet there!' 'Go outside!' People were looking round at them. They stopped talking.

But from that moment she listened no more. The wedding chorus, the scene between Ashton and his manservant, the great duet in D major, for her it all happened at a distance, as though the instruments had been muted and the stage set farther back. She was thinking of those card-games at the chemist's, their walk to the nurse's house, the times when he had read to her in the arbour, or when they had sat together by the fireside: all that sorry little love, so quiet and so patient, so tactful and so tender – which she had none the less forgotten. Why had they met again? What chain of circumstance had brought him back into her life? He sat behind her, leaning against the partition, and every now and then a little shiver ran down her spine as she felt the warm breath of his nostrils on her hair.

'Does this stuff amuse you?' he said, leaning over so close that the point of his moustache brushed her cheek.

'Oh, heavens, no, not much,' she answered indifferently.

He suggested that they should go off and have ices somewhere.

'Oh, not yet! Stay a bit!' said Bovary. 'She's got her hair down – looks like being tragic, this does.'

But the mad scene was little to Emma's taste, and Lucy seemed to her to be overacting.

'She shouts,' said Emma, turning to Charles, who was drinking it in.

'Yes – maybe – a bit,' he answered, torn between the genuineness of his pleasure and the respect he felt for his wife's opinion.

'The heat – !' said Léon with a sigh.

'You're right, it's unbearable.'

'Is it too much for you?' Bovary asked.

'Suffocating! Let's go.'

Monsieur Léon arranged her long lace shawl daintily over her shoulders, and they all three went down to the quayside and sat outside a café in the open air.

Emma's illness was their first topic; now and again she interrupted Charles, for fear, she said, of boring Monsieur Léon. The latter told them he had come to spend two years in a big office in Rouen, to learn the business, which was very different in Normandy from the sort you handled in Paris. Then he inquired after Berthe, the Homais family, the Widow Lefrançois; and then, as there was nothing more to say in the presence of the husband, the conversation petered out.

Some people who had just left the theatre came by along the pavement, humming or bawling at the top of their voices, 'Lucy, my beautiful angel!' Léon aired his musical knowledge. He had heard Tamburini, Rubini, Persiani, Grisi, Beside them, Lagardy, for all his sound and fury, came nowhere.

'All the same,' Charles, who had been sipping his rum and sherbet, broke in, 'he's supposed to be really fine in the last act. I wish we'd stayed. I was beginning to enjoy it.'

'Never mind,' said the clerk, 'he's giving another performance soon.'

Charles said they were going home in the morning. 'Unless you'd like to stay on by yourself, my pet?' he added, turning to his wife.

Switching his tactics to meet this unexpected opportunity, the young man struck up the praises of Lagardy in the last act. Yes, that was something superb, sublime. Charles became more pressing.

'You can come home on Sunday. Now, make up your mind. If you feel it'll do you the least bit of good, you ought not to say no.'

Meanwhile the tables were being cleared all round them, and a waiter came and posted himself tactfully behind them.

Charles took the hint and pulled out his purse, but the clerk laid a hand on his arm to stop him – and even remembered to leave a couple of silver coins for the waiter, dropping them with a clink on the marble-topped table.

'Really, I don't like you spending ...' mumbled Bovary.

The other waved this aside with lofty cordiality and reached for his hat.

'It's fixed, then?' he said. 'Six o'clock tomorrow?'

Charles insisted that *he* simply couldn't stay any longer, but that was no reason why Emma shouldn't. ...

'It's just,' she faltered with an odd smile, 'that I'm not sure...'

'Ah well, sleep on it, and we'll see how you feel in the morning.' Then to Léon, who was coming along with them: 'Now you're back in these parts, I hope you'll come and take some dinner off us now and then?'

The clerk said he certainly would: as a matter of fact he would be visiting Yonville soon on business. They separated by St Herbland's Passage as the cathedral clock was striking half past eleven.

PART THREE

_____

I

WHILE studying for his law degree, Monsieur Léon had been a not infrequent visitor at the *Thatched Cottage,* where he made quite a hit with the *grisettes,* who thought he looked 'distinguished'. He was the most presentable of the students, he wore his hair neither too short nor too long, he did not squander his term's allowance on the first of the month, and he kept on good terms with his tutors. And he had always abstained from excesses, as much from pusillanimity as from fastidiousness.

Many a time when he stayed indoors reading, or when he sat under the lime-trees in the Luxembourg of an evening, his law-book would drop from his hands, and thoughts of Emma would return to him. But little by little his feeling for her lost its force and was overlaid by a mass of other appetites, though never quite extinguished by them, for Léon had not entirely abandoned hope, and the future dangled a vague promise before him, like a golden fruit hanging from some fantastic tree.

Now, seeing her again after a gap of three years, his passion reawakened. This time, he thought, he must be bold, and try to win her. His shyness had, in fact, been rubbed off by contact with his gay companions, and he came back to the provinces full of contempt for whosoever had not trodden the asphalt of the boulevards in patent-leather shoes. In the presence of a Parisian lady in lace, or in the salon of some scholastic celebrity, some honoured personage with a carriage-and-four, the humble clerk would doubtless have trembled like a child. But here on the quayside at Rouen, talking to this country practitioner's wife, he felt at his ease, secure in the foreknowledge that he would shine. Assurance depends on one's surroundings. Words that go well enough in the top attic are useless in the drawing-room; the wealthy woman seems to have all her bank-notes about her to defend her virtue, like so much armour-plate inside the lining of her bodice.

After taking leave of Monsieur and Madame Bovary the night before, Léon had followed them at a distance along the street. When he saw them go in at the Red Cross, he had about-turned and spent the rest of the night thinking out a plan.

Consequently, at about five o'clock next day, he walked into the lobby of the hotel, with a tight feeling in his throat, a white face, and that coward's courage that nothing can stop.

'The gentleman isn't in,' a servant told him.

That augured well. He went up.

Far from being disconcerted by his arrival, Emma apologized for having forgotten to tell him where they were staying.

'Oh, I guessed!' said Léon.

'How?'

He pretended he had been guided to her by instinct. She started smiling, and he hastened to retrieve that asininity by saying that he had spent the morning calling at every hotel in the place in search of her.

'So you decided to stay.'

'Yes, though I ought not to,' she said, 'for there's no sense in acquiring tastes you can't indulge, when there are a hundred and one things that have a claim on you. ...'

'Oh yes, I can imagine.'

'I doubt if you can. You're not a woman.'

Ah, but men had their trials too. ... The conversation got under way with sundry philosophical reflections. Emma dwelt on the poverty of all earthly affection and the perpetual isolation that enshrouds the human heart.

Whether he wished to sound impressive, or whether his mood were naïvely following the lead of her melancholy, the young man declared that he had been prodigiously bored all the time he was a student. Legal procedure got on his nerves, other professions had attracted him, his mother never stopped nagging at him in every letter she wrote. ... So they went into ever greater detail on the subject of their sorrows, each growing somewhat excited as they went further in confidence. At times they stopped short of expressing all they had in mind — yet felt for phrases to convey their meaning none the less. She did not confess her love for another man; he did not say he had forgotten her.

Perhaps he could no longer recall those suppers after the dance with the girls in fancy dress. Presumably she had no recollection of those assignations of old, those mornings when she used to run through the long grass to her lover's mansion. The noises of the town scarcely reached them here; the room seemed small, as though to emphasize their intimacy. Emma, wearing a dimity dressing-gown, leant back against the aged armchair. The yellow wallpaper behind her gave her a sort of gold background, and her bare head was reflected in the mirror, with the white line of the parting in the middle and the tips of her ears peeping out from under the plaits of her hair.

'But forgive me, I must be boring you with all my troubles,' she said.

'No, never, never!'

'If you only knew,' she said, and she lifted her beautiful eyes to the ceiling as a tear formed, 'if you only knew the dreams I've dreamed.'

'I, too! I've suffered! I often used to go out and wander along by the river, trying to deaden my thoughts in the noise of the crowd, yet still unable to banish the obsession that pursued me. There's a picture-shop along the Boulevard with an Italian print in the window, of one of the Muses. She's draped in a tunic, looking at the moon, and she's got forget-me-nots in her flowing hair. Something was for ever drawing me towards that shop. I've stood there for hours on end.' In a trembling voice he added: 'She was something like you.'

Madame Bovary turned away to hide the smile she felt rising irresistibly to her lips.

'Many a time I wrote to you, and then tore up the letter,' he went on.

She made no answer.

'I fancied sometimes that chance would bring you to me. I thought I saw you at street-corners, I went chasing after a cab whenever I caught sight of a shawl or a veil like yours fluttering at the window.'

She seemed determined to let him talk on without interruption. Folding her arms and lowering her head, she gazed down at the rosettes on her slippers, and now and then gently moved her toes inside the satin.

At last she sighed. 'What can be more distressing than to drag out a futile existence like mine? If only our sorrows could be of use to someone, we might find some consolation in the thought of our sacrifice.'

He proceeded to pay tribute to virtue, duty, and silent immolation. *He* had an unbelievable, unsatisfied longing to dedicate himself.

'I should very much like to be a Sister of Mercy,' she said.

'Alas,' he replied, 'there are no such sacred missions for men, nor any vocation at all, as far as I can see, unless perhaps that of a doctor. ...'

With a little shrug of her shoulders, Emma broke in to tell him how dreadfully ill she had been, how near she had come to dying. A pity she hadn't died: she would now be suffering no more. ... Immediately Léon yearned for the 'peace of the tomb'. One night he had actually made his will, asking that he should be buried in the beautiful rug with the velvet stripes which she had given him. ... For this was how they would have liked it all to be: they were both constructing an ideal of themselves and adapting their past lives to it. Speech acts invariably as an enlarger of sentiments.

However, this tale about the rug made her ask, 'Why?'

'Why?' He hesitated. 'Because – I loved you!'

And while he congratulated himself on having taken the leap, he watched her face out of the corner of his eye.

It was like the sky when the wind blows the clouds away. The dark mass of sombre thoughts seemed to lift from her blue eyes, her whole face was radiant.

He waited, and at last she said, 'I always suspected it.'

And then they recounted all the little events of those far-off days whose joys and sorrows they had just summed up in a single word. He spoke of the bower of clematis, the dresses she used to wear, the furniture in her room, everything in the house.

'And our poor cactuses, what of them?'

'The frost killed them this winter.'

'Ah, you don't know how I used to think about them. I saw them in my mind's eye, with the sun beating down on the blinds of a summer morning, and your bare arms moving among the plants.'

'Poor Léon!' said she, holding out her hand to him.

Léon promptly pressed it to his lips. Then, when he had taken a deep breath –

'You had a sort of mysterious, captivating power over me in those days. There was one time, for instance, when I came to call – but I don't suppose you remember?'

'Yes, I do. Go on.'

'You were downstairs in the hall, at the foot of the stairs, just going out – yes, you were wearing a hat with little blue flowers on it! Without waiting to be asked, I went with you, I couldn't help it. Yet every moment I grew more and more conscious of my silliness. I went along at your heels, not quite daring to walk beside you, yet unable to leave you. When you turned into a shop, I stood fast in the street and watched through the window as you took off your gloves and counted out the money. Then you went and rang at Madame Tuvache's. Someone let you in, and I stood there like an idiot staring at the big door closing behind you.'

Listening to him, Madame Bovary was surprised to discover how old she was. All those glimpses of the past returning made her life seem larger; gave her, as it were, vast tracts of feeling over which she might rove. From time to time, with eyes half-closed, she murmured, 'Yes, that's right. That's right.'

They heard eight o'clock strike from the various clocks in the Beauvoisine quarter, which is full of boarding-schools, churches, and big derelict mansions. They had stopped talking, but as they looked at one another they felt a humming in their heads, as though some vibrant message had passed between their gazing eyes. They had joined hands; and past and future, memory and dream, all mingled together in the sweetness of their ecstasy. The shadows deepened along the walls; only the four crudely coloured prints that hung there, showing scenes from *La Tour de Nesle*, with inscriptions underneath in French and Spanish, still gleamed faintly in the twilight. Through the sash-window a patch of dark sky was visible between gabled roofs.

She rose to light a pair of candles on the chest of drawers, then came and sat down again.

'Well?' said Léon.

'Well?' she replied.

He was wondering how to resume after this interruption, when she said, 'How is it no one has ever expressed such sentiments to me before?'

The clerk declared that idealistic natures were not easily understood. *He* had fallen in love with her at first sight. It made him frantic to think of the happiness they might have had, if it had only been granted them to meet earlier in life and be joined together in an indissoluble union.

'I have thought of that sometimes,' she said.

'What a dream!' murmured Léon. And delicately toying with the blue border of her long white girdle, he added, 'Why shouldn't we begin again now?'

'No, my friend,' she replied. 'I am too old, you're too young. Forget me. Other women will love you ... you will love them.'

'Not as I love you!' he cried.

'What a child you are! Come, we must be sensible. I ask it of you.'

She pointed out all the reasons why love was impossible between them. They should remain just good friends, as they had been before.

Was she in earnest when she said that? Emma could hardly have known herself – preoccupied as she was with the temptation to which she was exposed and the necessity of withstanding it. Gazing at the young man with pity in her eyes, she gently repelled the shy caresses that his trembling hands essayed.

'I'm sorry!' he said, drawing back.

And Emma felt vaguely alarmed at this timidity, more dangerous for her than Rodolphe boldly advancing upon her with open arms. No man had ever seemed to her so handsome; there was an exquisite candour in his bearing. He lowered his long, fine, curving lashes. His smooth cheek flushed – with desire for her, she thought. Emma felt an almost ungovernable yearning to lay her lips upon it.

She bent forward and pretended to look at the clock. 'Goodness, how late it is! How we chatter!'

He took the hint and reached for his hat.

'I've forgotten all about the opera, too. And poor Charles left me here especially for it! I was going with Monsieur and Madame Lormeaux from the Rue Grand-Pont.'

And it had been her last chance. She was leaving next day.

'Leaving?' exclaimed Léon.

'Yes.'

'But I must see you again,' he said. 'There's something I want to tell you. ...'

'What is it?'

'Something – important. Something very serious. No, no, you can't, you mustn't go. If you only knew. ... Listen. ... You haven't understood me, then? You haven't guessed?'

'But you've talked very well!'

'You're laughing at me. Please! For pity's sake let me see you once more – just once!'

'Well ...,' she said and paused; then, as a thought struck her, 'No, not here!'

'Anywhere you like.'

'Will you ...' She seemed to ponder. Then, tersely: 'Eleven tomorrow, in the Cathedral.'

'I shall be there,' he cried, and seized her hands; she pulled them away.

And as they were both standing up now, he behind her, Emma with lowered head, he bent over and kissed her, very deliberately, on the nape of the neck.

'Oh, you're crazy, you're crazy!' she cried, giving vibrant little laughs as the kisses rained down.

Leaning his head over her shoulder, he seemed to be seeking her eyes' consent. They fell upon him full of a frigid majesty.

Léon stepped back, to go. He halted at the door and whispered in a trembling voice, 'Till tomorrow!'

She nodded in reply and vanished into the next room.

That night Emma wrote the clerk a long rambling letter withdrawing from the appointment: it was all a thing of the past, for their own good they ought not to meet again. But when the letter was sealed, Emma realized that she didn't know Léon's address. She was in a quandary.

'I'll give it him myself,' she said. 'He'll come.'

Next day, with his window flung open and a song on his

lips, Léon sat on his balcony polishing away at his pumps. He put on white trousers, smart socks and a green coat, drenched his handkerchief in every kind of scent he possessed, and after having his hair curled, uncurled it again to give it a greater natural elegance.

'Too soon yet!' he thought as he glanced at the hairdresser's cuckoo-clock, which pointed to nine.

He flicked through an old fashion-magazine, went out, smoked a cigar, wandered along three streets, then decided it was time to set off in the direction of Notre Dame.

It was a fine summer morning. Silverware glittered in the jewellers' shops; the light sloping down on the Cathedral set little points of brilliance dancing on the grey stones. A flock of birds wheeled in the blue sky, round the trefoiled bell-turrets. The square resounded with cries. It was fragrant with the flowers that bordered its pavement – roses, jasmine, pinks, narcissi, tuberoses, alternating irregularly with moist green plants, catmint and chickweed. The fountain gurgled in the centre, and under broad umbrellas, among pyramids of melons, bare-headed flower-women were wrapping bunches of violets in twists of paper.

The young man asked for a bunch. It was the first time he had ever bought flowers for a woman, and as he sniffed their scent his bosom swelled with pride, as though the homage intended for her came home again to him.

However, he was afraid of being observed. He walked resolutely into the Cathedral.

On the threshold, in the centre of the left-hand porch, under the *Marianne Dancing*, stood the beadle, his plumed hat on his head, rapier at his calf and cane in hand, more majestic than a cardinal and as highly polished as a sacred pyx.

He came forward to greet Léon, with that smile of wheedling benignity that churchmen use when they address children.

'A stranger hereabouts, I expect, sir. You wish to see over the Cathedral?'

'No,' said Léon. And first he walked round the aisles. Then he went out and looked across the square. No sign of Emma. He turned back and walked up into the choir. The nave was mirrored in the brimming fonts, with the beginnings of the arches and part of the windows. The reflection of the stained glass broke at the edge of the marble and continued on the flagstones beyond like a chequered carpet. Broad daylight shone in through the three open doors and stretched down the whole length of the Cathedral in three enormous rays. Now and again a sacristan crossed at the far end, making the oblique genuflexion of piety in a hurry. The crystal chandeliers hung motionless. In the choir a silver lamp was burning. From the side-chapels and darker corners of the church came occasionally a sound like the exhaling of a sigh, and a clanking noise, as a grating was shut, that echoed on and on beneath the vaulted roof.

Léon walked gravely round the walls. Never had life seemed so good to him. Presently she would come, charming and animated, glancing round at the eyes that followed her; in flounced dress and dainty shoes, with her gold eye-glass and all manner of adornments new to his experience; and in all, the ineffable charm of virtue surrendering. The Cathedral was like a gigantic boudoir prepared for her. The arches leaned down into the shadows to catch her confession of love, the windows shone resplendent to light her face, and the censers would burn that she might appear as an angel in an aromatic cloud.

But still she did not come. He sat down on a chair, his eyes lighted on a blue window depicting fishermen with baskets. He looked at it long and attentively, counting the fishes' scales and the button-holes in the jerkins, while his thoughts strayed in quest of Emma.

The beadle kept his distance, inwardly furious with this individual who presumed to admire the Cathedral by himself. It seemed to him a monstrous way to behave – a kind of stealing what was his – sacrilege, almost.

There was a rustle of silk over the stone slabs, the brim of a hat, a black cape – she had come! Léon rose and hastened to meet her.

Emma was white-faced, walking quickly.

'Read this!' she said, holding out a sheet of paper – 'No, don't!' – and she snatched her hand back again. Then she went into the Lady Chapel, where she knelt down against a chair and began to pray.

The young man felt annoyed at this sudden piety. But then he found a certain charm in seeing her, at their place of tryst, thus wrapped in her devotions, like an Andalusian marquesa. Then he grew impatient, for she seemed to be going on for ever.

Emma was praying, or trying to pray, in the hope that Heaven would suddenly fill her with resolution. To elicit the divine aid she feasted her eyes on the splendours of the tabernacle, breathed in the scent of the white rocket-flowers blooming in the big vases, and listened to the stillness of the Cathedral – which only emphasized the tumult in her heart.

She rose, and they were about to leave, when the beadle came hurrying up to them.

'A stranger hereabouts, I expect, ma'am! You wish to see over the Cathedral?'

'No!' said the clerk.

'Why not;' said she – her tottering virtue clinging for support to the Virgin, the sculptures, the tombs, whatever offered.

To do the thing properly, the beadle took them right back to the entrance on the square, where he pointed with his cane to a large circle of black paving-stones with no inscription or carving.

'Here,' he proclaimed majestically, 'you see the outer casing of the lovely bell of Amboise. It weighed eighteen tons. There was not its like in all Europe. The workman who cast it died of joy. ...'

'Come on,' said Léon.

The old fellow started off again. Returned to the Lady Chapel, he spread out his arms in a comprehensive gesture of demonstration, prouder than a country smallholder showing off his wall-fruit.

'Beneath this plain stone lies Pierre de Brézé, Lord of Varenne and Brissac, Grand Marshal of Poitou and Governor of Normandy, killed at the Battle of Montlhéry on the 16th July, 1465.'

Léon bit his lip, fuming.

'While on the right, this nobleman encased in iron, on a prancing steed, is his grandson Louis de Brézé, Lord of Breval and Montchauvet, Count of Maulevrier and Baron of Mauny, King's Chamberlain, Knight of the Order, and likewise Governor of Normandy, who died on the 23rd July, 1531, a Sunday, as the inscription tells. This figure underneath, about to descend into the tomb, shows you once more the self-same man. It would surely be impossible to find a more perfect representation of death!'

Madame Bovary held up her eye-glass. Léon stood still and watched her, no longer attempting the least word or gesture, utterly discouraged by this double defence of volubility and indifference. The interminable guide ran on: 'This woman on her knees beside him, weeping, is his wife Diane de Poitiers, Countess of Brézé and Duchess of Valentinois, born 1499, died 1566. And on the left, with the child in her arms, is the Blessed Virgin. Now turn this way. Here we have the Amboise tombs. Both were Cardinals and Archbishops of Rouen. That one was a Minister under King Louis XII. He did much for the Cathedral. In his will he left thirty thousand gold crowns to the poor.'

Talking all the time, he pushed them straight on into a chapel which was cluttered up with hand-rails, one or two of which he moved aside to reveal a sort of block that might once have been a crudely carved statue.

'Once upon a time,' he said with a long groan, 'it adorned

253

the tomb of Richard Cœur-de-Lion, King of England and Duke of Normandy. It was reduced to its present state, sir, by the Calvinists. They buried it, for spite, in the ground beneath the episcopal throne. Look, here is the doorway leading to the Bishop's residence! We pass on now to the Dragon Windows. ...'

Léon quickly pulled a silver coin from his pocket, and took Emma by the arm. The beadle was left standing in amazement, unable to comprehend such premature munificence, when there were still so many things for the strangers to see. He shouted after him, 'The spire, sir, the spire!'

'No, thanks,' said Léon.

'You shouldn't miss it, sir. It is four hundred and forty feet high, only nine less than the Great Pyramid of Egypt. It is all of cast iron, it ...'

Léon fled, for it seemed to him that his love, which for close on two hours had been immobilized like the stones around him in the church, was now about to vanish like smoke through that kind of truncated funnel, oblong cage or fretwork chimney, that perches so grotesquely on top of the Cathedral like an essay in the extravagant by some whimsical tinker.

'Where are we going?' said Emma.

He strode on without answering; and Madame Bovary was actually dipping her finger in the holy-water font at the door, when they heard a heavy, panting breath behind them, punctuated by the tap-tap of a stick. Léon turned round.

'Sir!'

'What is it?'

There stood the beadle, a score or so of stout paper-bound volumes stuffed under his arm or balanced against his belly. They were works 'treating of the Cathedral'.

'Idiot!' growled Léon, and he darted outside.

A street urchin was playing on the pavement.

'Go and get me a cab!'

The youngster shot off down the Rue des Quatre Vents, and they were left for a minute face to face, in some embarrassment.

'Oh, Léon! Really – I don't know – whether I ought ...', she simpered affectedly. Then she looked serious. 'You know it's not the thing!'

'Why not?' retorted the clerk. 'It's done in Paris!'

And that word, with its unassailable logic, decided her.

The cab hadn't arrived yet, though; Léon was afraid she might retreat inside the Cathedral again. At last it came in sight.

'At any rate you ought to go out through the North Door!' cried the beadle, who had halted in the porch, 'and see the *Resurrection,* the *Last Judgement,* the *Paradise, King David,* and the *Damned in the Flames of Hell*!'

'Where to, sir?' said the cabby.

'Where you like!' said Léon, pushing Emma into the carriage; and the lumbering machine set off.

It went down the Rue Grand-Pont, across the Place des Arts, along the Quai Napoléon, over the Pont Neuf, and pulled up sharply before the statue of Pierre Corneille.

'Keep on!' came a voice from inside.

The cab started off again, and gathering speed down the hill beyond the Carrefour La Fayette, drove into the station yard at full gallop.

'No! Straight on!' cried the voice again.

It passed out through the iron gates, and presently striking the Drive, trotted gently along between the tall elms. The cabby mopped his brow, stuck his leather hat between his legs and turned off beyond the side-avenues towards the green by the waterside.

All along the river, on the pebble-paved towing-path, went the fiacre, past the islands and a good way towards Oyssel.

Then suddenly it switched off through Quatre Mares, Sotteville, the Grande Chaussée, the Rue d'Elbeuf, and halted for the third time outside the Botanical Gardens.

'Go on, will you!' cried the voice yet more furiously.

Immediately it moved off again, past St Sever, the Quai des Curandiers, the Quai aux Meules, back over the bridge, across the Drill Square and behind the workhouse gardens, where old men in black jackets are to be seen strolling in the sunshine along the ivy-mantled terrace. It drove along the Boulevard Bouvreuil, down the Boulevard Cauchoise, and all the way up Mont Riboudet as far as the Côte de Deville.

There it turned and came back again, then went roaming at random, without aim or course. It was seen at St Pol and Lescure, at Mont Gargan, at the Rouge Mare and in the Place du Gaillardbois; in the Rue Maladrerie, the Rue Dinanderie, outside St Romain, St Vivien, St Maclou and St Nicaise; at the Customs House, at the Old Tower, the 'Three Pipes', the Monumental Cemetery. Every now and then the driver, perched up on his box, would cast despairing glances at the public houses. He couldn't conceive what mania for locomotion possessed these individuals that they should want to drive on for ever. Once or twice he did slow up, and angry exclamations immediately broke out behind him; whereupon he whipped up his sweating hacks still harder, jolting the cab recklessly, banging into things right and left and not caring, demoralized, almost weeping with thirst, fatigue and despondency.

And by the harbour, in the midst of the wagons and barrels, in the streets, at every corner, the citizens opened their eyes wide in amazement at the spectacle, so extraordinary in a provincial town, of a carriage with drawn blinds, continually reappearing, sealed tighter than a tomb and being buffeted about like a ship at sea.

Once, in the middle of the day, when they were right out in the country and the sun was beating down at its fiercest on the old silver-plated carriage-lamps, an ungloved hand stole out beneath the little yellow canvas blinds and tossed away some scraps of paper, which were carried off on the wind and landed like white butterflies in a field of red clover in full bloom.

At about six o'clock the cab drew up in a side-street in the Beauvoisine quarter, and a woman got out; she walked away with her veil lowered, and without a backward glance.

2

REACHING the inn, Madame Bovary was surprised to see no sign of the coach. After waiting fifty-three minutes for her, Hivert had finally set off.

Not that she was obliged to go home. But she had promised Charles she would return that evening. He was expecting her. She already felt in her heart that inert submissiveness that is to many a woman both the penalty and the atonement for her adultery.

Hastily packing her trunk, she paid the bill, hired a trap in the yard and, urging on the driver, asking him again and again what time it was and how far they had come, succeeded in overtaking the *Hirondelle* as it drove into Quincampoix.

She sank down in her corner and shut her eyes. When she opened them again, the coach was at the foot of the hill and she could see Félicité in the distance, posted on the watch outside the smithy. Hivert reined in, and the maid, stretching up to the window, said mysteriously: 'You've got to go to Monsieur Homais at once, Madame. It's something urgent.'

The village was quiet as ever. At the corners of the streets little pink heaps were steaming in the air: it was the jam-making season, and at Yonville they all made their supply on the same day. Outside the chemist's shop a far larger mound was attracting general attention, towering above the rest with that superiority which the kitchen stove must concede to the factory and individual caprice to public demand.

She went in. The big armchair was overturned, the *Rouen Beacon* itself lay spread out on the floor, held by two pestles. She opened the passage door, and in the middle of the kitchen, amid brown jars full of loose red currants, grated sugar, lump sugar, scales on the table and pans on the fire, she saw the whole of the Homais family, great and small, with aprons up to their chins and forks in their hands. Justin was standing with bowed head while the chemist bellowed at him:

'Who told you to go up to the Capharnaum for it?'

'What is it? What is the matter?' asked Emma.

'The matter?' said the chemist. 'We're making jam. We put it on the fire. It's going to boil over, because it's not thick enough, so I call for another pan. And he, the feeble good-for-nothing, goes and takes — takes off its nail in my laboratory — the key of the Capharnaum!'

This was the chemist's name for his store-room at the top of the house, where he kept all his professional utensils and supplies. He used to spend long hours alone up there, labelling, decanting, re-tying; and he regarded it not as a mere store-room, but as a veritable sanctuary, whence issued, the work of his hands, all manner of pills and pellets, infusions, lotions and potions, that went to spread his fame abroad. No one else ever set foot in it. His reverence for it was such that he swept it out himself. In fact, if the shop was the arena wherein he revealed his glory to the public gaze, the Capharnaum was the retreat in which he shut himself off from the world to indulge his private interests. Consequently, Justin's thoughtlessness struck him as a piece of monstrous irreverence. Redder than the currants, he repeated:

'The key of the Capharnaum! The key that locks up the acids and the caustic alkalis! To go and take a pan from store! A pan with a lid! One I may never use! Everything has its importance in the delicate operations of our art, but damn it all, we must preserve certain distinctions, and not employ for purposes little more than domestic, instruments intended for pharmaceutical use! It's like carving a chicken with a scalpel. It's as if a magistrate ...'

'There now, calm down, dear,' Madame Homais kept saying, and Athalie, tugging at his coat, piped up, 'Papa! Papa!'

'No! Let me alone!' he ranted. 'Let me alone, damn it. Why, I might as well set up as a grocer and have done with it. All right, go ahead! break! smash! do your worst! Let loose the leeches! Burn the marshmallow! Pickle gherkins in the window-jars! Slash up the bandages!'

'You had something ...' began Emma.

'One moment! Do you know what peril you were in? Did you see nothing in the corner on the left, on the third shelf? Speak! Answer me! Say something!'

'I d-don't know,' stammered the lad.

'Oh, you don't know. Well, I *do* know! You saw a blue glass bottle, sealed with yellow wax, which contains a white powder, and on which I had written the word *Dangerous*. Do you know what it is? Arsenic! And you go and touch it, you take a pan that stands next to it!'

'Next to it!' cried Madame Homais, wringing her hands. 'Arsenic! You might have poisoned the lot of us!'

The children started howling, as though they could feel horrible pains in their vitals already.

'Yes, or a patient,' the chemist went on. 'I suppose you'd like to have me in the dock at next assizes? To see me dragged to the scaffold? Haven't you noticed how carefully I handle everything—I with *my* wealth of experience? Why, it frightens me myself sometimes when I think of my responsibility. For the Government's persecuting us, and the absurd regulations that rule our lives are a veritable sword of Damocles suspended over our heads!'

Emma had given up hope of finding out why she was wanted. Breathlessly the chemist swept on: 'And that's your return for all we do for you. That's how you repay my fatherly care. Where would you be without me, eh? What would you do? Who is it feeds you, teaches you, clothes you? Who's giving you your chance to take an honourable place in the world one of these days? But you've got to pull up your sleeves and sweat for it, my boy! *Fabricando fit faber, age quod agis.*'

In his wrath he had broken into Latin. He would have broken into Chinese or Icelandic if he had been acquainted with either language, for he was now at one of those crises in which the soul, like a storm-cleft ocean, gives a glimpse of all it contains, from the seaweed round its shores to the sand dredged up from its depths.

'I'm beginning to feel confoundedly sorry I ever took you on,' he continued. 'I'd have done a sight better to leave you to wallow in the filth and squalor you were born in. You'll never be fit for anything but cowherding. You've no gift for science. You hardly know how to stick on a label! And you live here in my house, lording it on the fat of the land, like a pig in clover!'

Emma turned to Madame Homais. 'They told me to come ...'

'Oh, my goodness, yes!' that lady broke in dolefully. 'I don't know how to tell you. It's bad news. ...'

She couldn't go on. The chemist was thundering: 'Empty it! Scour it! Take it back! Look lively!' And seizing Justin by the scruff of the neck, he shook him so hard that a book flew out of his pocket.

The boy stooped down. Homais forestalled him, picked up the volume, and stared at it, his eyes popping out of his head and his jaw dropping.

'*Married ... Love!*' he said, pronouncing the words deliberately and distinctly. 'Capital, capital! Very pretty. Illustrations too! ... Oh, it's beyond everything!'

Madame Homais took a step forward.

'No, don't touch it!'

The children wanted to see the pictures.

'Leave the room!' he exclaimed imperiously.

They left the room.

First he strode up and down, keeping the volume open between his fingers, rolling his eyes, choking, swollen, apoplectic. Then he advanced straight upon his pupil and planted himself in front of him with folded arms.

'So you've got all the vices, have you, you little wretch? Take care! You're on a slippery slope. It never occurred to you that this wicked book might fall into the hands of my sons and daughters, might sow the seeds in their minds — tarnish the purity of Athalie — corrupt Napoléon? He is no longer a child! Can I even be sure that they haven't already seen it? Can you swear ...?'

'Monsieur Homais!' said Emma. 'Had you something to tell me?'

'I had, Madame. Your father-in-law is dead!'

Monsieur Bovary senior had indeed met his end, quite suddenly, two days ago. He had been seized with a stroke after dinner. Out of an over-scrupulous regard for Emma's feelings, Charles had asked Homais if he would employ his tact to break the dreadful news to her.

Homais had thought out his speech with care, had rounded it, polished it, given it rhythm; it was a masterpiece of gradual revelation and stylistic subtlety. But anger had routed rhetoric.

Emma stayed no longer. Nothing more was to be gleaned, for the chemist had resumed the course of his vituperations. His temper had somewhat abated, however, and now he was grumbling in a fatherly way while he fanned himself with his skull-cap.

'Not that I entirely disapprove of the work! The author was a doctor. There are certain scientific aspects of the thing that it does a man no harm to know — I'd even say that he ought to know. But not yet, not yet. Wait at least till you're a man yourself, till your temperament matures.'

Charles, who had been waiting for Emma's knock, advanced to meet her with open arms.

'Ah, my dear,' he said, with tears in his voice; and gently he bent down to kiss her. The touch of his lips reminded her of Léon and she passed her hand over her face with a shudder.

'Yes ... I know ... I know,' she managed to say.

He showed her the letter, in which his mother had related the facts without any hypocritical sentimentality. Her only regret was that her husband had not received the succour of religion, having died at Doudeville, in the street, at the door of a café after an ex-officers' reunion dinner.

Emma handed back the letter. At dinner she thought it well-bred to affect a disinclination to eat, but when Charles pressed her, she fell-to with determination, while he sat opposite, unmoving, a picture of dejection.

From time to time he raised his head and directed at her a look of utter distress.

'I wish I could have seen him again!' he sighed once.

She was silent.

Eventually, however, she thought she ought to say something. 'How old was he?'

'Fifty-eight.'

'Ah!'

And that was all.

A quarter of an hour afterwards he added: 'Poor mother! What will she do now?'

She gave a shrug.

Attributing her taciturnity to grief, Charles forced himself to say no more about it, to avoid stirring her feelings. Instead, giving a wrench to his own, he asked, 'Did you enjoy yourself yesterday?'

'Yes.'

When the table had been cleared, Bovary still sat on, and so did Emma. And little by little, as she eyed him, the monotony of that spectacle drove all pity from her heart. He seemed so weak, so puny, a cipher, a poor creature in every way. How could she get rid of him? Would the evening never end? She felt a drowsiness as of opium fumes stealing over her senses.

They heard a rap of timber on the boards in the hall. It was Hippolyte bringing Madame's luggage. To set it down he had to describe a painful arc on the floor with his artificial leg.

'He's forgotten all about it!' she said to herself as she watched the poor fellow, whose mop of red hair dripped with sweat.

Bovary fumbled in his purse for a copper, apparently unconscious of all the humiliation there was for him in the mere presence of that man standing there, the living rebuke to his incurable ineptitude.

'What a pretty bunch of flowers!' he said, noticing Léon's violets on the mantelpiece.

'Yes,' she answered casually, 'I bought them just now from a beggar-woman.'

Charles picked up the violets, cooled his tear-stained eyes on them, sniffed at them gingerly. She grabbed them from his hand and went to put them in a glass of water.

Next day his mother arrived. She and her son wept many tears, and Emma disappeared pleading household duties.

The day after that, the question of mourning had to be gone into. They took their work-boxes and sat out in the arbour by the waterside.

Charles thought of his father, and was surprised to feel so much affection for a man of whom he had never imagined himself to be more than moderately fond. ... His mother thought of her husband: the worst days of the past seemed enviable now: everything was glossed over in her instinctive clinging to long-established habit, and from time to time as she plied her needle a big tear would trickle down her nose and hang for a moment at the tip. ... Emma was thinking that barely forty-eight hours ago they had been together, away from everyone, ecstatic, wishing for a thousand eyes to gaze upon each other. She tried to recapture the least detail of that vanished day; but she was irked by the presence of her mother-in-law and her husband. She wished she could hear nothing and see nothing, so as to garner undisturbed those memories of love which, do what she might, were being swamped by external impressions.

She was unstitching the lining of a dress; bits of stuff lay scattered all around her. Her mother-in-law never once raised her eyes from her squeaking scissors. Charles, in felt slippers and the old brown overcoat he used as a dressing-gown, sat with both hands in his pockets, silent as they. Nearby, Berthe, in a little white pinafore, was raking the gravel path with her spade.

All at once they saw Monsieur Lheureux coming in at the gate.

He had called to offer his services 'in their sad bereavement'. Emma didn't think she needed anything. The draper was not so easily beaten.

'Very sorry!' he said. 'But I should like a few words in private.' To Charles he murmured, 'About that matter – you know!'

Charles crimsoned to the roots of his hair.

'Ah, yes, yes, of course. Darling, would you ...?'

He turned to his wife in his embarrassment.

She seemed to understand, for she got to her feet.

'It's nothing,' Charles told his mother; 'some little household matter, no doubt.' For he dreaded what she would say if she found out about the note he had signed.

As soon as they were alone, Lheureux began to congratulate Emma in pretty plain terms on the money she would inherit. Then he turned to neutral topics, the wall-fruit, the harvest, his own health, which was always 'so-so, fair to middling' – for he worked like a million niggers, and still didn't make enough to put butter on his bread, whatever people might say.

Emma let him talk. She had been so prodigiously bored these last two days!

'And so you're quite set up again?' he inquired. 'My word, what a state your husband was in! He's a good fellow, though we haven't always seen eye to eye.'

She asked what he meant; for Charles had not told her of the quarrel over the bill.

'You know!' said Lheureux. 'Those little wants of yours — the travelling-cases.'

He had pulled his hat down over his eyes, and with his hands clasped behind his back, he smiled, pursed his lips in a whistle, and stared her full in the face, in an insufferable manner. Did he suspect something? She waited, a prey to all kinds of apprehension, until at last he went on: 'We made it up, however, and I was just coming to put a further proposition to him.'

This was a renewal of the note that Bovary had signed. Of course, the Doctor would act as he thought best, and he mustn't be worried, especially now that he was going to have such a host of things to attend to.

'Come to that, it'd be a good idea if he handed it all over to someone else — yourself, for example. It'd be quite simple with a Power of Attorney. You and I could see to these little matters together.'

She didn't understand. He broke off; then, reverting to business, declared that Madame would hardly be able to manage without having something from him: he'd send her a dozen yards of black barège for a dress.

'The one you're wearing is all right for the house, but you'll want another for visiting. I could see that the minute I came in. I don't miss much!'

Instead of sending the material, he brought it. Then he came back for the measurements, and again on other pretexts, always trying to make himself agreeable and obliging — enfeoffing himself, as Homais would have said — and invariably slipping in a few words about the Power of Attorney. He didn't mention the note again, and she wasn't curious about it. Charles must have told her when she was beginning to get better, but her head had been in such a whirl since then that it had slipped her memory. Moreover, she purposely refrained from starting any discussion of money matters: a reserve which surprised the elder Madame Bovary, who ascribed her changed disposition to the religious sentiments she had contracted when ill.

As soon as her mother-in-law had departed, however, Emma set to work, and astonished Bovary by her practical common sense. Various inquiries would have to be made and mortgages verified. They must see if it were a case for auction or clearance. The technical terms rolled out, together with imposing words like 'order', 'foresight', 'the future'; and she always magnified the difficulties of the probate: until at last, one day, she showed him the copy of a general authorization to 'manage and administer his affairs, effect all loans, sign and endorse all notes, pay all debts ...' and so on. She had profited by Lheureux's instruction.

Charles asked innocently where the document had come from.

'From Monsieur Guillaumin.' And with all the coolness in the world she added, 'I don't trust him too far, though. Lawyers have such a bad reputation! Perhaps we ought to consult ... but there's ... no, there's nobody!'

'Unless Léon ...' said Charles, pondering.

Yes, but it was difficult to settle things by post. Emma offered to go to Rouen herself. Charles wouldn't hear of it. She insisted. It was a contest in obligingness. Finally, affecting a mock-rebellious tone of voice:

'Please! No more! I'll go.'

'How sweet you are!' he said, kissing her on the forehead.

The very next morning she took her seat in the *Hirondelle*, to go and consult Monsieur Léon at Rouen. She stayed there three days.

THREE full, exquisite, splendid days they were: a real honeymoon.

They stayed at the Hôtel de Boulogne, on the quayside; there they lived, behind drawn blinds and locked doors, with flowers strewn over the floor and iced drinks brought up every morning.

When evening came they took a covered boat and went to have dinner on one of the islands.

It was the hour of day when you hear the caulkers' mallets ringing against the ships' hulls along the dockside. Smoke from the tar rose up among the trees, and on the surface of the water, undulating unevenly in the crimson glow of the sun, floated great oily patches like medallions of Florentine bronze.

They threaded their way between the moored vessels, whose long slanting cables skimmed the top of their boat.

The noises of the town receded gradually – the rattle of carts, the hubbub of voices, the yelping of dogs on the decks of the boats. Emma untied her hat, and they landed on their island.

They went to a tavern with dark fishing-nets hung up at the door, and sat down in its low-ceilinged dining-room; they ate fried smelts, cream, and cherries. Then they went to lie down on the grass, and kissed beneath the poplars out of sight. They wished they could dwell for ever, Crusoe-fashion, in that little spot which seemed to them in their happiness the most magnificent on earth. It wasn't the first time they had seen trees and blue sky and green grass, or heard the sound of water flowing and the wind rustling in the leaves; but they had never, surely, appreciated it all till now. It was as though Nature had not existed before, or had only begun to be beautiful since the gratification of their desires.

They returned at nightfall. The boat kept close in to the

islands, and they lay in the stern, both hidden in the shadow, without speaking. The square oars grated in the iron row-locks, striking on the silence like the beat of a metronome, while the rope trailing behind never ceased its soft little ripple in the water.

Once the moon came out, and then of course they rhap-sodized about that melancholy, romantic orb; and she began to sing:

'*One night, do you remember, we were drifting ...*'

Her weak, melodious voice was lost on the water; the wind carried away the trills that brushed like a fluttering of wings about Léon's listening ears.

She sat facing him, leaning against the side of the boat, where the moonlight entered through the openings in the canvas. Her black dress, with the skirt fanning out around her, made her look taller and more slender. Her head was raised, her hands were clasped, her eyes looked up to the heavens. Sometimes she would be wholly hidden by the shadow of the willows – to reappear of a sudden like a vision in the light of the moon.

On the floor beside her Léon's hand encountered a flame-coloured silk ribbon.

The boatman examined it.

'Ah, yes,' he said at last, 'that'll likely belong to a party I took out the other day. A lively lot of ladies and gentlemen they were. Cakes, champagne, hunting-horns and I don't know what all! One of 'em there was in particular, a tall hand-some fellow with a little moustache, who was a real joker. "Come on", they kept saying, "tell us another one... Adolphe... Dodolphe", I think it was.'

Emma shivered.

'What's the matter, dear?' said Léon, drawing closer to her.

'Nothing! It must be the night air. ...'

'... Regular lady-killer he'd be, too!' added the old sailor softly by way of complimenting the stranger. Then he spat on his hands and grasped his oars again.

At last the time came to say good-bye. It was a sad parting. Léon was to send his letters to Madame Rollet's. She gave him such precise instructions about using a double envelope that he thought her a wonderfully astute intriguer.

'And I can say it's all right?' she said as she kissed him for the last time.

'Absolutely!' – But why, he wondered afterwards as he walked back through the streets alone, should she be so keen on this Power of Attorney?

4

LÉON soon began to adopt superior airs in front of his friends, avoided their company, and completely neglected his work.

He waited eagerly for her letters, and read and re-read them. He wrote to her. He conjured up her image with all the force of desire and memory. Far from fading with absence, his longing for her grew, until, one Saturday morning, he managed to escape from his office.

When he reached the top of the hill and saw the church steeple down below him in the valley, with its tinplate tricolour turning in the wind, he felt that pleasurable blend of triumph and sentimentality that must come to a millionaire revisiting his native village.

He went and prowled round her house. There was a light on in the kitchen. He watched for her shadow to appear behind the curtains. Nothing came.

Old Mother Lefrançois exclaimed with surprise at the sight of him, and thought he was 'taller and thinner'; whereas Artémise thought he was 'broader and browner'.

He had dinner in the little parlour, as in the old days, though without the tax-collector; for Binet, 'fed-up' with waiting for the *Hirondelle*, had decided to put his meal-time an hour earlier, and now dined sharp at five, still remarking as often as not that 'that perishing clock was slow'.

Léon summoned up his courage and went to knock at the doctor's door. Madame was upstairs; and she didn't come down for a quarter of an hour. The doctor seemed delighted to see him; but stayed in all the evening and all next day.

He saw her alone, late at night, in the lane at the end of the garden – the lane where she had once met the other! A storm was raging. They talked under an umbrella, while the light-ning flashed.

It was becoming intolerable to be apart.

'Better death!' said Emma.

She writhed on his arm, weeping.

'Good-bye! Good-bye! ... When shall I see you?'

They turned back for one last embrace, and it was then that she promised to devise some arrangement which would allow them to see each other in complete freedom, at least once a week, regularly. Yes, she would find a way. Emma was full of hope. Some money would soon be coming to her.

In expectation of this, she bought a pair of broad-striped yellow curtains for her bedroom, which Lheureux had de-clared a bargain. She hankered after a carpet, and Lheureux politely undertook to procure her one, assuring her that it would be no great labour. He had become indispensable to her. She sent for him a score of times a day, and he would promptly leave what he was doing and come along without a murmur. Equally incomprehensible was Mother Rollet's go-ing there every day for her lunch and even calling to see her in private.

It was about this time, towards the beginning of winter, that she appeared to be smitten with a sudden passion for music.

One night when Charles was listening to her, she began the same piece over again four times running, vexed with herself each time, while he, never noticing anything odd, cried out, 'Bravo! Well done! Don't stop, though, keep on!'

'No, it's frightful, I'm all thumbs!'

Next day he asked her to play to him again.

'Well, if you want me to.'

And Charles had to admit she was a bit out of practice. She mixed up the staves, fumbled for the notes and finally came to a sudden stop.

'No, it's no good, I need some lessons, but ...' She bit her lip and added, 'They're too expensive, at twenty francs a time.'

'Yes, they are ... they are rather,' said Charles, sniggering foolishly. 'But I believe you might do it for less. You often find teachers who haven't got much of a name, who are better than those that have!'

'Find one!' said Emma.

When he came home next day he gave her a sly look; but he couldn't keep it to himself for long.

'You do get ideas into your head sometimes! Do you know I've been to Barfeuchères today, and Madame Liégeard tells me her three girls at the Miséricorde are getting lessons at two and a half francs a time – and from a well-known teacher too!'

She shrugged her shoulders and didn't open the piano again.

But whenever she went near it she would sigh (if Bovary were in the room): 'Oh, my poor piano!' And when she had visitors she made a point of telling them how she had given up music, and couldn't start again, in their present circumstances. They sympathized with her and said, what a pity it was, when she had such a gift. They even spoke to Bovary about it. The chemist in particular shamed him.

'You're making a great mistake! We should never let our natural faculties lie fallow. Besides, my friend, remember that if you encourage your wife to study now, you'll be saving on your little girl's musical instruction later on. It's my opinion that children *ought* to be taught by their own mothers. It's an idea of Rousseau's, still a bit new perhaps, but one that's bound to prevail in the end, I'm sure, like mother's milk and vaccination.'

So Charles returned to the subject once again. Emma answered sourly that they'd do better to sell the thing. Though to see that old piano go, that had given so much gratification to her vanity, would have been for Madame Bovary rather like destroying a part of herself.

'If you'd like to have a lesson or two now and again,' he said, 'that wouldn't be too ruinous, after all.'

'But it's no use unless you keep it up regularly,' she replied.

And that was how she managed to obtain her husband's permission to go into Rouen once a week to see her lover. At the end of the first month she was thought to have made considerable progress.

5

THURSDAY came round. She got up and dressed very quietly to avoid waking Charles, who would have asked why she was getting ready so early. Then she paced up and down, or stationed herself at the window to look out over the square. The dawn light was winding its way between the market pillars, and in the pale glow of the sunrise you could read the chemist's name in block capitals above the closed shutters of his shop.

When the clock said quarter past seven she went across to the Golden Lion. Artémise came down yawning to let her in, and raked out a few embers for Madame. Then Emma was left alone in the kitchen. From time to time she strolled outside, where Hivert was harnessing the horses in leisurely fashion, listening the while to Madame Lefrançois, who was thrusting her night-capped head out of a little window to give him his orders, in a long rigmarole that would have bewildered a lesser man. Emma tapped the soles of her shoes on the paving-stones. At last, when he had gulped down his soup, shrugged himself into his driving-coat, lit his pipe and grabbed hold of his whip, he clambered up and settled himself serenely on his box.

The *Hirondelle* moved off at a gentle trot, stopping several times in the first two miles to pick up passengers, who stood looking out for it at their garden gates by the side of the road. Those who had booked seats overnight kept the coach waiting; some were still in bed. Hivert called and shouted and cursed, then got down from his seat to go and hammer on their doors, while the wind whistled in through the cracked blinds of the carriage.

Gradually the four rows of seats filled up, the coach went bowling along, orchards of apple-trees sped by, and ahead the road ran on between two long ditches of stagnant water that seemed to meet in the far distance.

Emma knew every inch of the way. After a stretch of meadowland came a signpost, an elm-tree, then a barn or a navvy's hut. Sometimes she shut her eyes for a while to give herself a surprise. But she always retained an exact awareness of the distance still to go.

At last the brick houses followed faster, the road rattled under the wheels, and the *Hirondelle* glided between gardens in which you caught a glimpse, through an opening in the wall, of statues, a rockery, clipped yews, or a swing. All at once you looked and saw the town ahead of you.

Sweeping down in great tiers, plunged in the mist, it spread out far and wide beyond the bridges, confusedly. Behind it the open country rose in a monotonous movement, to touch the pale sky at the blurred horizon. Seen from above like this, the whole landscape looked still as a picture. In one corner ships crowded at anchor. The river curved round the green hills, the oblong islands looked like great dark fishes resting on its surface. Immense brown billows of smoke poured from the factory chimneys, to drift away in the wind. The roar of the foundries clashed with the clear chimes pealing from the churches that rose up above the mist. Bare trees on the boulevards showed as clumps of purple amid the houses; the rain-wet roofs made a glistening patchwork all across the slopes of the town. Occasionally a gust of wind would carry the clouds towards St Catherine's Hill, like aerial breakers tumbling soundlessly against a cliff.

That mass of life down there gave her a dizzy feeling. Her heart swelled, as though those hundred and twenty thousand throbbing hearts had sent up to her all at once the fumes of the passions she imagined to be theirs. Her love expanded in that vast space before her. It was filled with tumult at the vague hubbub that arose. Then she poured it out again upon the squares and promenades and streets; and that ancient Norman city lay outspread beneath her eyes like an enormous metropolis, a Babylon awaiting her. She leaned out of the window, holding on with both hands, and sniffed the breeze. The three horses were galloping along, the pebbles grinding in the mud, the coach rocking, Hivert hailing the traffic from afar, while the good citizens who had been spending the night at the Bois-Guillaume peacefully descended the hill in their little family carriages.

They stopped at the city gates. Emma unbuckled her overshoes, put on a fresh pair of gloves, rearranged her shawl, and twenty yards farther on stepped out of the *Hirondelle*.

The town was waking. Shop fronts were being polished by assistants in caps, and at the street corners women with baskets at their hips uttered occasional resonant cries. She slipped along by the wall, her eyes on the ground, smiling for joy beneath her lowered black veil.

To avoid the main streets, where she might be seen, Emma plunged into dark alley-ways, and emerged, wet with perspiration, at the lower end of the Rue Nationale, close by the fountain. This is the district of the theatres, bars and brothels. Often a cart would pass by loaded with rickety stage scenery. Aproned waiters scattered sand over the pavement, between the tubs of evergreen. She walked amid a smell of absinthe, cigars and oysters.

She turned a corner, and recognized his crimped hair curling out beneath his hat.

Léon continued along the pavement. She followed him to the hotel. He climbed the stairs. He opened the door. He went in. ... What an embrace! And after kisses, such a flood of words, as they recounted the troubles of the week, their misgivings, their anxiety about the letters. But it was all over now, and they gazed at one another with voluptuous laughter and tender endearments on their lips.

The bed was a large mahogany bed in the form of a cradle, with red damask curtains sweeping down from the ceiling in a wide curve. And there was nothing in the world so beautiful as her brown head and white skin against that crimson background, when she folded her naked arms in a gesture of modesty and hid her face in her hands.

The warm room with its noiseless carpet, its gaudy decorations and soft light, seemed made for the intimacies of passion. The arrow-headed curtain-rods, the brass-work, the big knobs on the fender, all lit up at once when the sun shone in. Between the candlesticks on the mantelpiece lay two of those large pink shells in which you hear the sound of the sea when you hold them to your ear.

How they loved that friendly room, full of gaiety despite its somewhat faded splendour! They always found the furniture set out the same, and sometimes under the clockstand were hairpins that she had left behind the previous Thursday. They lunched by the fire at a little round table inlaid with rosewood. Emma carved and served, babbling the while all manner of coquettish badinage. She laughed a rich wanton laugh when the champagne frothed over the brim of her delicate glass and on to the rings on her fingers. They were so utterly engrossed in the possession of one another, they fancied they were in their own home, there to dwell for the rest of their lives, an eternal young-married-couple. They used to say 'our room', 'our carpet', 'our armchairs'. There were even 'my slippers' — a pair to which she had taken a fancy and which Léon had given her. They were of pink satin trimmed with swansdown. When she sat on his knees, her legs would dangle in the air, while the pretty heelless slippers swung on the toes of her bare feet.

He was savouring for the first time the inexpressible delight of feminine elegance. Never had he known such grace of language, such quiet taste in dress, such languid drowsy-dove postures. He marvelled at the elevation of her soul and the lace on her petticoat. Besides, was not she a lady of style, and a married woman! A real mistress, in fact?

In the variety of her moods, by turns gay and other-worldly, garrulous and taciturn, fiery and indifferent, she provoked a thousand desires in him, appealed both to his instincts and to his memories. She was the 'woman in love' of all the novels, the heroine of all drama, the shadowy 'she' of all the poetry-books. On her shoulders he saw reproduced the amber colours of the *Odalisque Bathing*. She had the deep bosom of a feudal châtelaine. She bore a resemblance to the *Pale Woman of Barcelona* ... but she was above all Angels!

Often as she gazed, it was as if his soul went out from him and were shed like a wave about the curving contour of her head, then drawn down into the whiteness of her bosom.

He used to sit on the floor at her feet, resting his elbows on his knees and twisting round to smile up at her.

She leant over him, murmuring, breathless with ecstasy: 'Don't move! Don't speak! Only look at me! There's something so tender in your eyes, it does me so much good.'

She used to call him 'child'.

'Child, do you love me?'

And she scarcely heard his answer for the haste with which his lips rose to her mouth.

On the clock was a little bronze Cupid, who smirked, curving his arms beneath a gilded garland. They often laughed at him. But when they had to part, everything seemed very serious.

Standing quite still, face to face, they said over and over: 'Till Thursday! Till Thursday!'

Suddenly she took his head in her hands, kissed him quickly on the forehead, cried out 'Good-bye!' and rushed from the room.

She went to a hairdresser in the Rue de la Comédie to have her hair braided. Night was falling; the gas was lit in the shop.

She heard the theatre-bell summoning the players to the performance, and saw men with white faces and women in faded dresses go by across the way and vanish through the stage door.

It was hot in that little room with the too-low ceiling, where the stove hummed in the midst of wigs and hair-creams. The smell of the curling-tongs and those fat hands at work on her head soon made her sleepy, and she dozed off gently in her dressing-gown. The assistant who did her hair would frequently offer her tickets for the masked ball.

At last she escaped. She threaded her way back through the streets, reached the Red Cross, retrieved her over-shoes, which she had hidden under one of the benches in the morning, and squeezed into her seat beside her impatient fellow-passengers. Some of these got out at the foot of the hill, and she was left alone inside the carriage.

At every turn in the road you obtained a fuller view of the lights in the town behind you, forming a broad luminous vapour above the labyrinth of houses. Emma knelt on the cushioned seat till her eyes were dazzled by the glare. She sobbed, called out 'Léon', breathed forth tender messages, and kisses that were lost in the wind.

Up the hill, in the midst of the carriages, trudged an old tramp with his stick. A mass of rags covered his shoulders, his face was hidden by a battered beaver hat stuck on like an inverted bowl. When he removed this, he revealed where his eyelids should have been a pair of gaping holes all stained with blood. The flesh was shredded into red ribbons, discharging matter which had congealed in green scabs down to his nose. His black nostrils twitched convulsively. To address you, he threw back his head with an idiot laugh; and then his glaucous eye-balls, rolling in perpetual motion, shot up towards his temples and knocked against the open sore.

As he followed the carriages he sang a little song:

'*When the sun shines warm above,*
It turns a maiden's thoughts to love.'

And the rest of it was all birds and summertime and green leaves.

Sometimes he would bob up suddenly behind Emma, with his head uncovered. She would spring back with a cry. Hivert started twitting him, telling him he ought to take a booth at the Fair of St Romain, or asking him with a laugh how his sweetheart was keeping.

Often he thrust his hat in at the window as the coach was moving off, clinging to the footboard with his other arm and getting splashed by the wheels. His voice, at first a feeble whine, rose shrilly, rending the darkness like a plaintive utterance of some obscure distress. Heard through the jingle of the horse-bells, the murmur of the trees and the rumbling of the empty carriage, it had a suggestion of remoteness that upset Emma. It penetrated to the very depths of her being like a whirlwind in an abyss. It swept her away into the vast spaces of a limitless melancholy. However, Hivert, noticing a weight dragging on one side, lashed out at the blind man with his whip. It cut across his sores, and he dropped in the mud with a howl of pain.

Eventually the passengers fell asleep, some with their mouths open, others with chin sunk on chest, toppling over on to their neighbour's shoulders, or with one arm through the strap, rocking rhythmically to the motion of the carriage. The lamp swinging outside above the rumps of the shaft-horses shone in through the curtains of chocolate-coloured calico, casting blood-red shadows over all those motionless forms. Besotted with sadness, Emma shivered in her clothes; an ever-sharper cold crept into her feet, and death into her soul.

Charles was waiting for her at home; the *Hirondelle* was always late on Thursdays. At last Madame arrived. She hardly kissed her daughter. Dinner was not ready: no matter! She forgave the maid. It seemed nowadays as if the girl could do no wrong.

Often, noticing her pallor, her husband asked if she were feeling quite well.

'Yes,' said Emma.

'But you're very strange tonight?'

'Oh, it's nothing, nothing!'

There were some days when she went straight to her room, and Justin, who was there, would move about on padded feet, more resourceful in her service than a first-class chambermaid. He set out matches and candlestick and a book, laid out her night-dress, turned down the sheet.

'All right, that'll do,' she said, 'run along!'

For he still stood there, hands hanging, eyes wide open, as though caught in a sudden trance, entwined in innumerable threads.

The next day was terrible, and those that followed still harder for Emma to bear, in her impatience to resume her happiness; a stark longing it was, fired with trite images, that on the seventh day burst freely forth in Léon's arms. His own passion remained hidden behind his outpourings of wonderment and gratitude. Emma savoured that love of his with a quiet absorption, fed it by all the devices her affection prompted, and quaked a little lest time should take it from her.

'You'll leave me,' she used to tell him in a voice tender with melancholy. 'Ah, yes, you'll marry; you'll be like the rest.'

'The rest?' he asked.

'Men!' she answered. And pushing him away with a languorous gesture, she added, 'You're all villains!'

One day when they were talking philosophically of earthly disillusionment, she chanced to say — testing his jealousy, or yielding perhaps to an imperative need to unburden herself — that she had loved someone before him. 'Not like you!' she put in quickly; and she swore on her daughter's life that 'nothing had happened'.

The young man believed her. Nevertheless he questioned her as to that 'someone's' occupation.

'He was a ship's captain, my dear.' — For would not that preclude investigation, and at the same time raise her high above him — that claim to have exercised her fascination on a man who must of necessity be combative by nature and accustomed to deference?

And the clerk felt the lowliness of his position. He longed for epaulettes, rank, medals. She must like that sort of thing; it was to be inferred from her expensive habits.

In point of fact, Emma harboured a host of extravagant wishes that she never mentioned, such as the desire to have a blue tilbury to take her to Rouen, drawn by an English horse and driven by a groom in top-boots. Justin it was who had put this idea into her head, by begging her to take him into her service as a footman. And if the want of it detracted nothing from the pleasure of arrival at each rendezvous, it certainly aggravated the bitterness of homecoming.

When they talked about Paris, she often ended by murmuring, 'How happy we could be there!'

'Aren't we happy?' the young man asked gently, stroking her hair.

'Yes, of course,' she said, 'I'm being silly. Kiss me!'

To her husband she was more charming than ever, making him pistachio-creams and playing him waltzes after dinner.

He thought himself, in consequence, the luckiest of mortals; and Emma had been feeling free of all anxiety, when, one evening, quite suddenly —

'Isn't it Mademoiselle Lempereur you go to for lessons?'

'Yes.'

'Well, I've just met her,' Charles went on, 'at Madame Liégeard's. I mentioned you to her. She's never heard of you.'

It was a thunderbolt.

'Oh, I expect she's forgotten my name,' she answered quite naturally.

'Maybe there are several Mademoiselles Lempereur who teach the piano at Rouen?' said the doctor.

'It's possible.' Then quickly: 'But I've got her receipts. Look, I'll show you!'

She went to the writing-desk, rummaged in all the drawers, mixed up all the papers, and ended in such a state of confusion that Charles implored her not to go to all that trouble for the sake of a few paltry receipts.

'Oh, I'll find them!' she said. And sure enough, on the following Friday, as Charles was putting on his boots in the dark little closet in which his clothes were kept, he felt a sheet of paper between the leather and his sock. He picked it up and read:

'Received, for three months' lessons with articles provided, the sum of sixty-five francs. — Félicie Lempereur, Teacher of Music.'

'What on earth's it doing in my boots?'

'Oh, it must have fallen out of the old bill-box up on the edge of the shelf,' she answered.

From that moment her existence became nothing but a tissue of lies, in which she hid her love from view.

It became a need, a craving, an indulgence: to the point that if she said she had gone along the right side of a street yesterday, it was to be inferred that she had in fact taken the left.

One morning, soon after she had set off, as usual pretty

lightly clad, it suddenly came on to snow. Charles was watching it out of the window, when he caught sight of Monsieur Bournisien ensconced in the Tuvache dog-cart, about to be driven into Rouen. He went out and entrusted the cleric with a thick shawl to give to Madame on his arrival at the Red Cross. On reaching that establishment, Bournisien inquired for the doctor's wife from Yonville, and was told that that lady was seldom to be found there. In the evening, recognizing Madame Bovary in the *Hirondelle*, the priest told her of his fruitless errand – without appearing to attach any importance to the matter, however, for he at once began singing the praises of a preacher who was just now working wonders at the Cathedral, and whom all the ladies were flocking to hear.

But if the *curé* had asked no questions, another time it might be someone less discreet. She thought it would be as well to get off at the Red Cross every time, and then the good folk from the village, seeing her go up the stairs, would never suspect a thing.

One day, however, Monsieur Lheureux met her coming out of the Hôtel de Boulogne on Léon's arm. She took fright, fancying that he would gossip. He was not so stupid.

Three days later he walked into her room and closed the door behind him.

'I need some money,' he said.

She declared she had none to give him. Lheureux launched forth upon a stream of complaints, reminding her what forbearance he had already shown her.

It was true that Emma had so far paid off only one of the notes that Charles had signed. For the second she had requested the dealer to substitute two fresh ones, and these had also been renewed for a very long term. He now fetched from his pocket a list of goods not paid for, to wit curtains, carpet, material for the easy-chairs, several dresses and various toilet requisites, the total value of which amounted to approximately eighty pounds.

She lowered her eyes.

'And if you haven't got any cash,' he added, 'you've got some property.'

He named a tumbledown cottage situated at Barneville, near Aumale, which brought in very little. It had once belonged to a small farm which old Monsieur Bovary had sold. Lheureux knew all about it, even to its acreage and the names of the neighbours.

'Now, if I were you,' he said, 'I'd sell off, settle up, and pocket the difference!'

But where would they find a purchaser? He held out hopes of finding one. She asked how she could effect the sale.

'Haven't you got that Power of Attorney?' he answered.

The words came like a breath of fresh air.

'Leave me the bill,' said Emma.

'Oh, we won't bother about that,' replied Lheureux.

He called again the following week, and belauded himself for having succeeded, after a deal of effort, in discovering one Langlois, who had had an eye on the property for long past but hadn't yet named his price.

'The price doesn't matter!' she cried.

On the contrary: they must go slowly, and sound the fellow. The thing was worth the trouble of a journey. He offered to go himself – since she couldn't – and confer with Langlois on the spot. On his return he announced that the buyer's figure was a hundred and sixty pounds.

Emma brightened at the news.

'Frankly,' he added, 'it's a good price.'

Half the sum was made over to her immediately. When she asked to settle her account, the dealer said: 'It hurts me, on my honour it does, to see you part with so – so significant a sum all at once.'

She looked at the bank-notes, seeing the unlimited number of rendezvous with Léon that those eighty pounds represented.

'What, what do you say?' she stammered.

'Oh!' he laughed guilelessly. 'Anything can be put on a bill. Don't I know the little tricks they play?' And he stared at her fixedly while he ran his finger-tips down the two lengthy documents he held in his hand.

Finally, opening his pocket-book, he laid on the table four notes payable to order, each for forty pounds.

'Give me your name to those and keep the lot!' said he.

She made a shocked protest.

'But if I give you the balance,' Lheureux answered brazenly, 'I'm doing *you* a service, am I not?' And picking up a pen, he wrote across the account: 'Received from Madame Bovary, one hundred and sixty pounds.'

'Why should you worry, seeing that you'll be getting the balance due on your little shack in six months' time, and I'm making the last of the notes payable *after* that?'

Emma felt a bit lost in her calculations; there was a ringing in her ears as though pieces of gold were bursting from their bags and clinking all around her on the floor. Lastly Lheureux explained that a friend of his, Vinçart, a banker at Rouen, would discount the four notes, and then he himself would make over to her the balance from the actual debt.

Instead of eighty pounds, however, he brought only seventy-two, his friend Vinçart—'as was fair'—having deducted eight for commission and discount.

Then he casually demanded a receipt. 'You understand, in business, there are times ... And with the date, please, the date.'

A vista of wishes coming true now opened in front of Emma. She had sense enough to keep a hundred and twenty pounds in reserve, with which she paid off the first three notes as they fell due. The fourth happened to drop into the letter-box on a Thursday. Charles, in great consternation, waited patiently for his wife to return and explain.

If she had told him nothing of this note, it was simply to spare him household worries. She sat on his knee, caressed him, cooed at him, and went through a long list of all the indispensable things she had had on credit.

'In fact, you'll agree that for all that amount, it's not too much to charge.'

Charles, at his wits' end, presently had recourse to the inevitable Lheureux, who gave his word to put matters right if the Doctor would sign two notes, one of them for twenty-eight pounds and payable in three months. To put himself into a position to meet this, Charles wrote a pathetic letter to his mother.

Instead of sending a reply she came herself. When Emma asked him if he had got anything out of her —

'Yes,' he answered. 'But she wants to see the account.'

The first thing in the morning Emma ran across to Lheureux's and asked him to make out a fresh bill for not more than forty pounds. She couldn't have shown the one for a hundred and sixty without revealing that she had paid off three-quarters of it and consequently confessing to the sale of the property, a transaction which had been skilfully handled by the dealer and which in fact only came to be known some time afterwards.

Despite the very low price charged for each article the elder Madame Bovary could not be turned from the conclusion that it represented an excessive expenditure.

'Couldn't you have done without a carpet? Why d'you need new covers for the easy-chairs? In my day there was only one easy-chair in the house – for elderly people. At least, that was the way in my mother's house, and she was a respectable woman, I assure you! Everybody can't be rich! Squander, and you'll get through any fortune! I'd be ashamed to pamper myself as you do – and I'm an old woman who needs attention! ... There you are, frills and fal-lals! What, silk for linings at one-and-eight when you can pick up jaconet at fivepence, or even fourpence, that does perfectly well!'

Emma, leaning back on the sofa, replied as calmly as might be: 'Oh, stop, stop, Madame!'

The other continued to lecture her, predicting that they'd end in the poor-house. Yes, and it was Bovary's fault. Just as well he'd promised to cancel that Power of Attorney. ...

'What!'

'Ah, he's given me his word,' the good woman told her.

Emma opened the window and called Charles. The poor fellow had to confess to the promise his mother had dragged out of him.

Emma disappeared and came quickly back, majestically holding out to her a thick sheet of paper.

'I thank you,' said the old woman. And she threw the document in the fire.

Emma burst out laughing, a long, loud, strident laugh; she was hysterical.

'Oh, Lord!' cried Charles. 'You're to blame too! You come and stir up trouble ...'

His mother shrugged her shoulders and said it was just 'tantrums'.

Charles, in revolt for the first time in his life, took his wife's part. Old Madame Bovary said she had better go. And next day she went. On the doorstep, in answer to all his efforts to prevent her, she said: 'No, no, you love her more than me, and I can't blame you, it's only natural. Anyhow, it's your own lookout. You'll see! ... Look after yourself. ... For I shan't be coming to "stir up trouble", as you call it.'

Despite this, Charles was left extremely abashed in front of Emma, who made no secret of the grudge she bore him for his lack of trust in her. A great many entreaties were required before she would agree to renew her Power of Attorney; he even accompanied her to Monsieur Guillaumin to have a second, identical, one drawn up for her.

'I quite understand,' said the lawyer; 'a man of science cannot be burdened with the practical details of life.' And Charles felt solaced by this piece of blandishment, which clothed his weakness in a flattering semblance of loftier preoccupations.

What an outpouring there was next Thursday with Léon in their room at the hotel! She laughed, cried, sang, danced, sent down for sherbet, asked for cigarettes, and seemed to him wild, but adorable, magnificent.

Some reaction of her whole being, he knew not what, was driving her to hurl herself more eagerly upon the good things of life. She was growing irritable, greedy, voluptuous. She walked through the streets with him, her head held high, unafraid, she said, of compromising herself. Sometimes, however, Emma thought with a sudden shudder of the possibility of meeting Rodolphe. Though they had parted for ever, it seemed to her she was not yet entirely freed from her dependence on him.

One night she failed to return to Yonville. Charles was distraught. Little Berthe wouldn't go to bed without her mummy and was sobbing as though her heart would break. Justin had set off down the road at a venture, Homais had been fetched from his shop.

Finally, at eleven o'clock, Charles could bear it no longer; he harnessed the trap, jumped in, whipped up his nag, and at two in the morning reached the Red Cross. No one there. He wondered if the clerk might have seen her. Where did he live? Luckily Charles remembered his office address; he made for it.

Day was beginning to break. He saw a scutcheon over a door and knocked. No one came, but someone called out an answer to his question, accompanying it with much abuse of people who came and caused a disturbance in the middle of the night.

The house in which the clerk lived had neither bell nor knocker nor porter. Charles banged on the shutters with his fist. A policeman came in sight. He felt scared and turned tail.

'Of course! What a fool I am!' he thought. 'She'll have stayed to dinner with Monsieur Lormeaux.' But the Lormeaux family had left Rouen. 'Then she'll have stopped to look after

Madame Dubreuil. Eh? ... Madame Dubreuil has been dead these ten months. Where *can* she be?'

He had an idea. He went to a café, asked for a Directory and hastily looked up the name of Mlle Lempereur. She lived at No. 74, Rue de la Renelle-des-Maroquiniers.

As he turned into that street, Emma appeared at the other end of it. He not so much embraced as threw himself upon her.

'Why didn't you come back?' he cried.

'I wasn't well.'

'How? Where? What was it?'

She passed her hand across her forehead and answered, 'At Mademoiselle Lempereur's.'

'I was right then! I was on my way there.'

'Oh, it's not worth going back now,' said Emma, 'she's just gone out. But don't ever worry in future. I feel tied, you see, if I know you're so upset by the least delay.'

She was granting herself a sort of general dispensation from inconvenience in her escapades. And she made free and generous use of it. Whenever she had an impulse to see Léon, off she would go, on no matter what pretext; and as he wouldn't be expecting her, she went to call for him at the office.

These were very happy times at first. But he did not long conceal from her his employer's severe disapproval of these distractions.

'Nonsense! Come on!' said she. And he came.

She wanted him to dress all in black and grow a little pointed beard, to look like the portraits of Louis XIII. She was anxious to see where he lived, and then said it wasn't much of a place. He blushed for it. She took no notice of that, and told him he ought to buy some curtains like hers. He said they were expensive.

'Ha! How you count your little pennies!' she laughed.

On each occasion, Léon had to give her a report of everything he had done since their last meeting. She asked him for a poem, a poem written to her, a love poem in her honour. He never could manage to make the second line rhyme, and in the end he copied out a sonnet from a keepsake-album.

He was prompted less by vanity than by the sole desire of pleasing her. He never questioned her ideas, he concurred in all her tastes. He had become her mistress rather than she his. Murmuring tender words, she kissed his soul away. Where could she have learnt that gift of corruption – so profound and so well-dissembled as to be scarcely a physical thing?

6

ON the trips he made to see her at Yonville Léon had often dined with the chemist, and felt in courtesy obliged to invite him in turn.

'With pleasure!' had been Homais' answer. 'Matter of fact I need a pick-me-up, for I'm getting into a rut here. We'll go to the theatre and the restaurants, we'll have high jinks!'

'Ah, my dear!' murmured Madame Homais tenderly, terrified of the unknown risks he was proposing to run.

'Well, what is it? Don't you think I ruin my health enough, living amid the constant emanations of the pharmacy? Now, there's a woman for you! Jealous of Science – and then she objects to your enjoying the most harmless diversions! No matter, you can count on me. One of these days I'll skip off to Rouen, and then we'll make the money fly!'

Such an expression as this would once have been studiously avoided by the chemist; but nowadays he was becoming addicted to a gay Parisian style which he considered to be in the best of taste; like his neighbour Madame Bovary he questioned the clerk with great curiosity about life in the capital, and talked slang to impress ... the bourgeois; saying 'digs', 'outfit', 'swell', 'slick', 'Breda Street', and 'I'll cut along' for 'I'm going'.

And so one Thursday, entering the kitchen of the Golden

Lion, Emma was surprised to find Monsieur Homais there, dressed in travelling-clothes – that is to say, wrapped up in an old cloak that had never been seen on him before – carrying a case in one hand and in the other the foot-warmer out of his shop. He had confided his plan to nobody, in case the public should be alarmed at his absence.

He must have been excited at the prospect of revisiting the scenes of his youth, for he never stopped talking all the way; and almost before the coach had come to a standstill he leapt out to hurry off in search of Léon. Struggle as he might, the clerk was dragged off to the big Café de Normandie, which Homais entered majestically without removing his hat, for he regarded it as most 'provincial' to uncover in a public place.

Emma waited for Léon three-quarters of an hour, then hurried round to his office. A prey to every kind of conjecture, accusing him of indifference, reproaching herself for her weakness, she spent the afternoon with her forehead glued to the window-panes.

At two o'clock the two men were still seated opposite one another at table. The spacious dining-room was emptying. The flue of the stove, shaped like a palm, rounded its gilt sheaf on the white ceiling. Through the window beside them they could see in the broad sunlight a little fountain gurgling into a marble basin, where among watercress and asparagus three torpid lobsters were stretched out with some quails lying on their side all in a heap.

Homais was enjoying himself. Although he was drunk on luxury more than on good fare, the Pomard was somewhat quickening his faculties, and when the rum omelette appeared he expounded immoral theories on women. The thing that chiefly fascinated him was *chic*. He adored an elegant dress in tasteful surroundings, and in the matter of physical qualities was not averse from a slim morsel.

Léon eyed the clock in despair. The chemist drank and ate and talked.

'You must feel quite bereft at Rouen,' he said suddenly. 'But then your love's not far away!'

The other reddened.

'Come on, own up! Can you deny that at Yonville ...'

The young man mouthed.

'... At Madame Bovary's, were you not courting ...?'

'Whom?'

'The maid?'

He meant no more than he said. Nevertheless Léon protested in spite of himself, vanity routing all discretion; the fact was, he only liked dark women.

'I agree,' said the chemist, 'they've got more *temperament.*'

And leaning over to whisper in his friend's ear, he outlined the symptoms whereby one could tell that a woman had temperament. He even launched into an ethnographical excursus: the German woman was vapourish, the French wanton, the Italian passionate.

'And the Negress?' asked the clerk.

'An artistic taste,' said Homais. 'Waiter! Two coffees!'

'Shall we go?' said Léon at last, his patience ebbing.

'Yes.'

But first he must see the manager and offer him his congratulations. After that the young man tried to get away by pleading business.

'Ah, I'll escort you!' said Homais.

As they walked down the street he chatted about his wife and his children, their future, his shop, the state of decay in which this had been formerly, and the pitch of perfection to which he had brought it.

When they reached the Hôtel de Boulogne Léon broke away from him and dashed up the stairs to find his mistress in a ferment.

The mention of Homais set her in a rage. He heaped one good excuse upon another: it wasn't his fault, surely she knew Monsieur Homais? Could she imagine that he preferred the chemist's company to hers? She turned away. He stopped her, sank down on his knees, put both arms round her waist in a languorous posture full of desire and entreaty.

She stood with her big flaming eyes fixed on him, with a serious, an almost terrible, look. Then they were dimmed with tears; her red eyelids lowered; she gave him her hands, and Léon was pressing them to his lips when a servant arrived to tell Monsieur that someone wanted him.

'You'll come back?' she said.

'Yes.'

'Soon?'

'Straight away.'

'That was a dodge,' said the chemist when he saw Léon. 'I thought I'd come and rescue you, for you didn't seem to be relishing your visit. Come to Bridoux's and take a glass of *garus* with me!'

Léon swore that he must return to the office. The chemist started being facetious about documents and red tape. 'Why not leave Cujas and Barthole alone a bit, damn it? Be a good fellow and come to Bridoux's! You'll see his dog; it's most interesting.'

And as the clerk still stood out –

'I'll come with you. I can read the paper while I wait, or take a look through the statute-book.'

Léon, dazed by Emma's anger and Homais' chatter, perhaps also by the weight of lunch inside him, stood wavering, seemingly under the spell of the chemist, who kept repeating: 'Come to Bridoux's! Only a couple of minutes away! Rue Malpalu!'

And out of cowardice or stupidity, on that mysterious impulse that drives us to the most antipathetic actions, he let himself be taken to Bridoux's. They found that gentleman in his little backyard, supervising three of his men who were breathlessly turning the big wheel of the Seltzer-water machine. Homais gave them a few tips, shook Bridoux by the hand and ordered *garus*. A score of times Léon tried to go, but the other caught him by the arm and said, 'Just a minute and I'll be coming. We'll go to the *Beacon* and see that crowd. I'll introduce you to Thomassin.'

Léon got rid of him, however, and ran to the hotel. Emma was not there.

She had just left, fuming. She hated him now. To fail her like that on their day together – it was outrageous. She cast about for further reasons for breaking with him: he was incapable of heroism, weak, commonplace, effeminate, as well as parsimonious and chicken-hearted.

Then she grew calmer, and eventually decided she had most likely been slandering him. But the denigration of those we love always severs us from them a little. Idols must not be touched; the gilt comes off on our hands.

They began to talk more of things indifferent to their love. Emma's letters were all about flowers, poetry, the moon and the stars – ingenuous shifts of an enfeebled passion endeavouring to recoup its powers from any and every external source. She would look forward to a profound happiness at next meeting, then have to admit that she felt nothing remarkable. Disappointment was quickly overlaid by fresh hope, and Emma returned to him still more ardent and more avid. She snatched off her dress and tore at the thin laces of her corsets, which whistled down over her hips like a slithering adder. She tiptoed to the door on bare feet to make quite sure it was locked; then made a single movement and all her clothes fell to the floor. Pale, silent, serious, she sank into his arms with a long shudder.

And yet, on that cold-beaded brow, on those stammering lips, in those wandering pupils, in the clasp of those arms, there was something extreme, mysterious, mournful, which seemed to Léon to come subtly stealing between them, to set them apart.

He dared not question her; but seeing how experienced she

was, he thought to himself that she must have passed through every ordeal of suffering and of pleasure. What had charmed him once, now frightened him a little. Moreover he resented her progressive absorption of his personality. He could not forgive Emma that continual conquest. He strove to stop loving her; but he had only to hear the creak of her boots and he felt unmanned as a drunkard at the sight of strong liquor.

She went out of her way, it is true, to lavish all sorts of attention upon him — exquisite dishes at table, coquetry in her dress, languor in her glances. She came from Yonville with roses in her bosom, and strewed them over his face; she showed concern for his health, advised him on questions of behaviour, and in order to bind him more closely to her — hoping she might enlist the aid of Heaven — hung a medallion of the Virgin round his neck. She inquired about his companions, like a virtuous mother. 'Don't see them,' she would say, 'don't go out, don't think of anyone else. Love me!'

She wished she could have him continually under her eye, she thought of getting him shadowed in the street; there was a tramp-like individual always to be found outside the hotel, accosting the visitors, who would certainly be willing. ... No: her pride revolted.

'Ah well, that's that. Let him deceive me if he wants to, what do I care?'

One day when they had parted early and she was going back alone along the boulevard, she came in sight of the walls of her convent. She sat down on a bench under the elms. Ah, those peaceful days! How she had yearned for — how she had tried to imagine — those ineffable love-sentiments she read about in books!

The first months of her marriage, her rides to the forest, the Viscount waltzing, Lagardy singing, everything passed before her eyes once more; and Léon seemed suddenly as remote as the rest.

'And yet,' she told herself, 'I love him!'

She snatched off her dress and tore at the thin laces of her corsets, which whistled down over her hips like a slithering adder. (This illustration was originally suppressed in the American edition.)

No matter, she still wasn't happy, she never had been. What caused this inadequacy in her life? Why did everything she leaned on instantaneously decay? ... Oh, if somewhere there were a being strong and handsome, a valiant heart, passionate and sensitive at once, a poet's spirit in an angel's form, a lyre with strings of steel, sounding sweet-sad epithalamiums to the heavens, then why should she not find that being? Vain dream! There was nothing that was worth going far to get: all was lies! Every smile concealed a yawn of boredom, every joy a misery. Every pleasure brought its surfeit; and the loveliest kisses only left upon your lips a baffled longing for a more intense delight.

A metallic rattle smote the air and four strokes chimed from the convent bell. Four o'clock. She felt she had been there an eternity. An infinitude of passions can be got into a minute, like a crowd in a small space. And in her passions, Emma's whole life was taken up. She had no more concern for money than an archduchess.

However, one day an undersized individual with a bald head and a red face called on her and introduced himself as coming from Monsieur Vinçart of Rouen. He took out the pins which fastened the side-pocket of his long green topcoat, stuck them into his sleeve, and politely handed her a document.

It was a bill for twenty pounds bearing her signature, which Lheureux – after all his assurances to the contrary – had passed to Vinçart.

She sent the maid to fetch Lheureux. He was busy and couldn't come.

The stranger, who had remained standing, casting inquisitive glances to right and left under cover of his fair bushy eyebrows, asked dispassionately: 'What answer am I to give Monsieur Vinçart?'

'Well,' said Emma, 'tell him – I haven't got it now. I'll have it next week. He must wait till – yes, next week.'

The visitor left without another word.

But at noon the following day she received a demand note. When she saw the stamped paper, with *Maître Hareng, Bailiff of Buchy* scrawled all over it in large letters, she was so frightened she ran across to the draper's as fast as she could go. She found him in his shop tying a parcel.

'At your service, Madame!' he said – continuing none the less with his task, at which he was helped by a young girl of about thirteen, slightly hump-backed, who worked for him as both shop-assistant and housemaid.

Then, clattering across the floor-boards in his wooden shoes, he led the way upstairs and showed Madame into a tiny office where a number of ledgers lay on a heavy deal desk behind a padlocked grating. Against the wall under some remnants of calico stood a safe, of such dimensions that it must surely contain other things besides bills and money. In fact, Monsieur Lheureux did some business as a pawnbroker. Here it was that he had deposited Madame Bovary's gold chain and old Tellier's ear-rings. That unfortunate had eventually been forced to sell out, and had bought a struggling grocery business at Quincampoix, where he was dying of his catarrh, his face yellower than the candles around him.

'What is it today?' said Lheureux, sitting down in his big wicker armchair.

'Look!' She showed him the paper.

'Well, what can I do about it?'

She flew into a rage, reminding him of his promise not to pass on her I.O.U.s. He admitted it. 'But I was forced. I had the knife at my throat.'

'What'll happen now?' she demanded.

'Oh, quite simple. Court order. Bailiffs. ... *Finis!*'

Emma had to restrain herself from hitting him. In a level voice she asked if there were no way of keeping Vinçart quiet.

'Keep Vinçart quiet! H'm. You don't know him. He's a Tartar!'

But Monsieur Lheureux must help.

'Now look here, it seems to me I've been pretty decent with you up to now. Here,' and he opened one of his ledgers, 'look at this ... and this' (running his finger up the page) 'August 3rd, eight pounds ... June 17th, six pounds odd. March 23rd, two pounds. In April ...'

He stopped, as though afraid of making a slip.

'And that's quite apart from the notes signed by Monsieur, one for twenty-eight pounds, one for twelve. As for your little bills and payments, they go on and on; they're a hopeless tangle. No, I wash my hands of the matter.'

She cried. She even called him her 'dear Monsieur Lheureux'. He persisted in laying the blame on 'that scoundrel Vinçart'. In any case, he hadn't a farthing. No one had been paying him. They were taking the clothes off his back. A poor shopkeeper like him couldn't advance money.

Emma said no more, and Lheureux, biting the feathers of a quill, doubtless grew alarmed at her silence, for he added: 'Of course, if I did get anything coming in one of these days ... I might ...'

'After all,' she said, 'as soon as the Barneville payments ...'

'What?' And he appeared much surprised to learn that Langlois had not yet paid her. At once, in a honeyed voice: 'What terms did you say ...?'

'Oh, anything you like!'

Thereupon he shut his eyes to think, jotted down a few figures, and, declaring that it would be anything but easy, it was a ticklish business, he was 'bleeding himself white' – he made out four bills for ten pounds each to fall due at monthly intervals.

'Provided that Vinçart will agree! Otherwise, it's settled. I don't shilly-shally. I'm straight as a die!'

After that he casually showed her a number of new articles he had in the shop, though there was nothing, in his opinion, that was good enough for Madame.

'Look at this. Dress material at threepence a yard, and

guaranteed fast colours! They swallow it, though. They don't get told any better, you can imagine,' said he, hoping to convince her of his honesty by confessing how he swindled other people.

He called her back again to see three ells of lace he had lately picked up at a sale. 'Beautiful, isn't it? Very popular nowadays for chair-backs. Quite the fashion?' And with the deftness of a conjuror he wrapped the lace in blue paper and slipped it into Emma's hand.

'Tell me, at any rate, how ...'

'Oh, another time!' he answered, and turned on his heel.

That evening she persuaded Bovary to write to his mother and ask her to send them the remainder of the inheritance as soon as she could. Her mother-in-law replied that there was nothing more to send: the estate had been wound up and, apart from Barneville, they had just twenty-five pounds a year remaining to them, which she would forward punctually.

Madame then sent out bills to two or three clients, and as this expedient proved a success she started making considerable use of it. She was always careful to add in a postscript: 'Don't say anything to my husband, you know how proud he is. I greatly regret ... Your obedient servant ...' There were some protests, which she intercepted.

She took to raising money on her old gloves and hats, and on the old junk in the house. She drove a hard bargain, the lust for profit running in her peasant blood. On her vists to Rouen she picked up various knick-knacks that Lheureux would certainly take off her if no one else did. She bought ostrich feathers, Chinese porcelain, wooden chests. She borrowed from Félicité and Madame Lefrançois, from the landlady of the Red Cross, from anyone and everyone. With the money that finally came in from Barneville she paid off two of the notes; the remaining sixty pounds melted away. She signed fresh undertakings, and so it went on.

True, she sometimes tried to reckon things up – only to

arrive at figures too exorbitant to be credible; she started off again, soon got into a muddle, then packed it all away and forgot about it.

It was a gloomy house now. Tradesmen were seen leaving with angry faces. Handkerchiefs were left lying about on the stove, and little Berthe, to Madame Homais' horror, had holes in her stockings. If ever Charles ventured some timid remonstrance, she answered savagely that *she* couldn't help it.

Why these outbursts? He put it all down to her old nervous trouble. Feeling ashamed of having taken her infirmities for faults, he cursed his own selfishness and longed to run to her and take her in his arms. ... 'No, it'd vex her,' he thought, and he sat tight.

After dinner he used to stroll round the garden by himself. Then he took Berthe on his knee, opened his medical journal and tried to teach her to read. The little girl, who was not in the habit of learning, would soon gaze up at him with big, sad eyes and start to cry. He comforted her, fetched her some water in the garden-can to make rivers in the gravel, or broke off sprays to plant trees in the flower-beds: which could do little harm to the garden, choked as it was with weeds – so many days' wages were owing to Lestiboudois! After a while the child felt cold and wanted her mother.

'Call your nanny, dear,' said Charles. 'You know mummy doesn't like to be disturbed.'

Autumn was coming on, the leaves already falling, just like the year before last when she had been ill! Oh, when would it all be finished with? ... He started pacing up and down again, hands clasped behind him.

Madame was in her room. No one went up to her. She stayed there all day long, half-awake, half-dressed, occasionally burning some aromatic pellets that she had bought at an Algerian shop in Rouen. To avoid having her husband lying asleep beside her at night, she managed with a great deal of fuss to relegate him to the floor above; and she would lie awake till morning reading fantastic fiction, all blood and orgies.

Often she screamed out in terror and Charles came running in.

'Oh, go away!' she said.

And when she felt herself burned more fiercely by that secret flame her guilty love had kindled – then, panting, shaking, throbbing with desire, she flung the window wide, breathed in the cold air, let the weight of her tresses stream out on the wind, and yearned, as she gazed at the stars, for a princely lover. She thought of *him* – of Léon; and she would then have given anything for a single one of those rendezvous of which she had grown so weary.

Those days of meeting were her gala days; they must be glorious! When he couldn't pay for everything himself, she contributed freely; which happened nearly every time. He tried to make her see that they would be just as comfortable somewhere else, in a cheaper hotel. She raised objections.

One day she took from her bag six little silver spoons (they were old Rouault's wedding-present to his daughter) and asked Léon to go and pawn them at once. He obeyed, though he disliked doing it. He was afraid of compromising himself.

Thinking it over afterwards, he decided that his mistress was getting into strange ways and that perhaps, after all, people had been right in trying to part him from her.

His mother had received an anonymous letter informing her at some length that he was 'ruining himself with a married woman'. The good lady, having visions of that eternal bugbear to family life, the vague pernicious creature, the siren, the monster that dwells fantastically in the deep places of love, at once wrote to Maître Dubocage, Léon's employer. That gentleman rose to the occasion splendidly and kept Léon for three-quarters of an hour trying to open his eyes, to warn him of his peril. Such an intrigue would damage him when it came to setting up on his own. He implored him to break it off, and if he would not make the sacrifice in his own interest, then to do it for him, Dubocage!

Léon had finally promised not to see Emma again. Now he was sorry he hadn't kept his word – seeing all the trouble and the gossip that that woman might still draw down upon him; not to mention the banter he had to endure from his colleagues round the stove every morning. Furthermore, he was about to become chief clerk. It was time to be serious. Accordingly he was renouncing the flute, elevated sentiments, and the imagination. Every bourgeois in the ferment of his youth, if only for a day or a minute, has believed himself capable of a grand passion, a high endeavour. Every run-of-the-mill seducer has dreamed of Eastern queens. Not a lawyer but carries within him the débris of a poet.

It bored him nowadays when Emma suddenly started sobbing on his chest. Like those people who cannot endure more than a certain dose of music, his heart grew drowsily indifferent to the clamour of a love whose niceties he could no longer appreciate.

They knew each other too well to feel that astonishment in possession which multiplies its joy a hundredfold. She was as sated with him as he was tired of her. Emma had rediscovered in adultery all the banality of marriage.

But how to break free? Humiliated though she might feel by that low-level happiness, she clung to it from habit or depravity, worrying it the harder every day, exhausting all felicity by demanding too much of it. She blamed Léon for her disappointment, as though he had deceived her; she even wished for some catastrophe that would bring about their separation, since she couldn't make up her mind to it herself.

She continued none the less to write him love-letters, in accordance with the view that a woman should always write to her lover.

But as she wrote she saw another man, a phantom made of

her most ardent memories, of the finest things she had read, of her most violent longings; who became in the end so real and so accessible that he set her thrilling with wonder, though she had no clear picture of him, for he receded like a god behind the abundance of his attributes. He dwelt in an azure region where silken ladders swing from balconies, in the breath of flowers, by moonlight. She felt him near her; he would come and would carry her away, body and soul, in his embrace. ... Then she fell back prostrate, shattered; for these transports of imaginary loving fatigued her more than a grand debauch.

She was living now in a state of chronic general collapse. Emma frequently received writs – so many sheets of stamped paper that she scarcely looked at. She would have liked to stop living, or else to remain continuously asleep.

On the day of mid-Lent she did not return to Yonville. Instead she went in the evening to a masked ball. She wore velvet breeches and red stockings, a knotted wig, a cocked hat tilted over one ear. She pranced all night to the blare of the trombones; people thronged round her; and at daybreak she found herself on the steps of the theatre, with five or six of the dancers, all in fancy dress, friends of Léon's, who were proposing to go and have supper.

The neighbouring cafés were full. They found an inferior sort of eating-house down on the quayside, and the proprietor showed them into a little room on the top floor.

The men whispered together in a corner, no doubt conferring on the cost. There were a clerk, two medical students, a shop-assistant: what company for her! The women, Emma quickly perceived from their twangy voices, were nearly all of the lowest class. She felt frightened, pushed back her chair and dropped her eyes.

The rest began to eat. She ate nothing. Her forehead was on fire, her eyelids tingling, her flesh icy. She could feel the ballroom floor still reverberating in her head with the rhythmic pulsation of a thousand dancing feet. Then the smell of the punch and the cigar-smoke made her feel dizzy. She fainted; they carried her over to the window.

Day was beginning to break, a big patch of crimson widening in the pale sky over St Catherine's. The livid river shuddered in the wind; the bridges were deserted, the street-lamps were going out.

She came to herself and thought of Berthe, sleeping away yonder, in the maid's room. But just then a cart loaded with long iron rods went by, hurling a deafening metallic vibration against the walls of the houses.

She made an abrupt escape, changed out of her costume, told Léon he must go home, and was at last left alone at the Hôtel de Boulogne. Everything, herself included, was intolerable to her. She wished she could fly away like a bird and grow young again somewhere far out in the stainless purity of space.

She went out and along the boulevard, across the Place Cauchoise, towards the outskirts of the town, till she came to an open street overlooking some gardens. She walked quickly; the fresh air soothed her and little by little the faces of the crowd, the masks, the quadrilles, the chandeliers, the supper and those women, all vanished like mists being blown away. Reaching the Red Cross, she threw herself on her bed in the little second-floor room with the scenes from *La Tour de Nesle*. Hivert woke her at four o'clock in the afternoon.

When she got home, Félicité pointed to a grey sheet of paper behind the clock. She read: 'In formal execution of the order, whereof this is a true ...' Order? What order? Another document had, in fact, been delivered the night before, but knowing nothing of that, she was thunderstruck by the words: 'By Order of His Majesty, in the Name of the Law, to Madame Bovary ...'

Skipping several lines she saw: 'Within twenty-four hours'. — What? — 'To pay the sum total of three hundred and twenty pounds.' And further down: 'Which is to be enforced by the utmost rigour of the law, and notably by execution of distraint upon all her furniture and effects.'

What was to be done? Twenty-four hours. Tomorrow! Lheureux must be trying to frighten her again, she thought. Immediately she saw through all his machinations, guessed the purpose behind all his complaisance. The very size of the sum served to reassure her.

However, as a result of buying on credit, borrowing, signing notes and then renewing those notes, which swelled at each expiry, she had eventually accumulated a capital sum for Lheureux, which he was impatient to get hold of to use in his speculations.

She strolled nonchalantly into his shop. 'You know what's happened? It's a joke, I suppose!'

'No.'

'What do you mean?'

He slowly turned and folded his arms.

'Did you think, my little lady, that I was going to go on supplying you with goods and money till the end of time, out of the sheer kindness of my heart? I must get back my outlay – that's fair, isn't it?'

She protested at the amount he was claiming.

'Well, that's what it is. The court upheld it, judgement has been given, you've had notice! And anyway, it's not my doing, it's Vinçart!'

'Couldn't you ...?'

'Not a thing!'

'But ... all the same ... let's talk it over.' And she started rambling; she had known nothing about it: it came as a surprise ...

'Whose fault's that?' said Lheureux with an ironic bow. 'While I slave like a nigger here, you go off enjoying yourself.'

'Don't preach!'

'It never does any harm,' he replied.

She went weak; she begged and prayed; she even laid her pretty, long white hand on the draper's knee.

'Let me alone! Anyone'd think you were trying to tempt me!'

'You cur!' she cried.

'Oho, how you go on!' he answered, laughing.

'I'll tell people what you are. I'll tell my husband ...'

'Well, well. I've got something to show your husband, too.' And Lheureux took from his safe the receipt for seventy-two pounds which she had given him at the time of the Vinçart transaction.

'Do you imagine,' he added, 'that the poor dear man won't understand your little theft?'

She sank back, stunned as by a knock-out blow.

'Yes, I'll show it to him ... I'll show it to him,' he repeated, pacing to and fro between the window and the desk.

Then he came up to her and said softly: 'I know it's no joke; but after all it never killed anyone, and since it's the only way left you of paying me back my money ...'

'Where can I get it?' said Emma, wringing her hands.

'Pah! When people have friends, as you have!' And he gave her so penetrating and terrible a look that she froze to the very marrow.

'I promise you,' said she, 'I'll sign ...'

'I've had quite enough of your signatures!'

'I'll sell something ...'

'Come!' he exclaimed with a shrug of the shoulders. 'You've nothing left to sell!'

He called through the peep-hole into the shop: 'Annette! Don't forget those three remnants of No. 14!'

The servant appeared; Emma understood. She asked, how much money would be required to stop all proceedings?

'It's too late!'

'But if I brought you fifty pounds – a quarter of the sum – a third – nearly all of it?'

'No, it's no use.' He pushed her gently towards the staircase.

'I beg you, Monsieur Lheureux, just two or three more days!' She started sobbing.

'Hallo! Tears!'

'You drive me to desperation!'

'That's too bad!' he said as he closed the door behind her.

7

SHE bore it bravely next day when Maître Hareng the bailiff arrived, with two witnesses, to draw up a list of goods to be distrained.

They started with Bovary's consulting-room. His phrenological head they ruled out as being 'professional equipment'. But in the kitchen they counted the plates and the pots, the chairs and the candlesticks, and in the bedroom all the knick-knacks in the cabinet. They examined her linen, her clothes, her dressing-room; her whole existence was spread out like a corpse at a post-mortem, for the three men to pry into its inmost secrets.

Maître Hareng was buttoned up in a thin black coat, and wore a white cravat and tightly fastened boot-straps. 'If you'll allow me, Madame, if you'll allow me,' he would say from time to time – with frequent exclamations of 'Charming!' or 'Very pretty!' – after which he would resume his writing, dipping his pen into the ink-horn which he carried in his left hand.

When they had been over the rest of the house, they went up to the attic.

There was a desk up there in which she kept Rodolphe's letters. It had to be opened.

'Ah! Your correspondence,' Maître Hareng smiled discreetly. 'I must make sure the box contains nothing else, however. Allow me.'

He tilted the papers gently as though he would shake out the gold pieces. That made her furious, to see that thick hand, the fingers red and soft like slugs, resting on the pages she had held to her beating heart.

At last they went. Félicité came back indoors – she had been put on guard to keep Bovary away – and they hurriedly installed the bailiff's man at the top of the house, where he promised to remain.

During the evening Charles seemed preoccupied. Emma watched him in an agony, reading accusation in every line of his face. Then, as her eyes travelled over the fireplace with its ornamental Chinese screens, over the big curtains, the armchairs, all the things that had softened the bitterness of her life, she was smitten with remorse, or rather with an immense regret which, far from extinguishing her passion, served only to awaken it. Charles sat with his feet on the fender, placidly poking the fire.

Once the bailiff's man, bored no doubt in his hiding-place, made a slight noise.

'Is that someone upstairs?' said Charles.

'No,' she answered, 'it's only an open window rattling in the wind.'

The following day, a Sunday, she set off for Rouen, to call on all the bankers whose names she knew. They were out of town, or away on a journey. She refused to give in. Those she did manage to see she asked for money, declaring that she *must* have it and would pay it back. Some of them laughed in her face; all of them refused.

At two o'clock she hurried to Léon's and knocked at his door. No answer. Eventually he appeared.

'What brings you here?'

'Do you mind?'

'No, but ...' and he admitted that the landlord didn't like them to have 'women' there.

'I've got to talk to you,' she said.

He reached for his key, but she stopped him. 'No, let's go to our place.'

They went to their room at the Hotel de Boulogne. As soon as they got inside, she drained a large glass of water. She was very pale.

She said to him:

'Léon, you've got to do something for me.'

She gripped his hands tight and gave him a shake.

'Listen. I need three hundred pounds.'

'You're crazy.'

'Not yet ....'

She told him about the bailiffs and the predicament she was in. Charles knew nothing of it. Her mother-in-law hated her. Her father couldn't help. But he, Léon, he must set about finding this sum that she must have.

'And how do you expect ...?'

'Oh, don't be so helpless!' she cried.

Stupidly he said: 'It can't be as bad as you make out. A hundred or so would probably keep the fellow quiet.'

All the more reason for trying to do something! Surely it wasn't impossible to find a hundred pounds? And Léon could stand surety instead of her.

'Go on, go and try! You must! Oh, hurry, hurry! I will love you so!'

He went away. At the end of an hour he returned looking solemn. 'I've been to three people,' he said. 'Nothing doing.'

They sat facing one another on either side of the fireplace, motionless, silent. Emma shrugged her shoulders, tapped her foot on the floor.

'I'd soon get it if I were in your place,' he heard her murmur.

'Where from?'

'Your office!' And she gave him a look.

In her blazing eyes was a diabolical recklessness; their lids narrowed with sensual invitation. The young man felt himself succumbing to the mute will-power of this woman who was

urging him to a crime. He took fright, and to forestall anything more explicit, clapped his hand to his forehead with an
exclamation:

'Morel is coming back tonight! I shouldn't think he'd refuse
me.' (Morel was a friend of his, the son of a wealthy business
man.) 'I can bring it you tomorrow.'

Emma didn't appear to welcome this idea as cordially as he
had hoped. Did she guess he was lying? He reddened and
went on: 'Don't wait, though, darling, if I'm not there by
three o'clock. Now, I'm afraid I must be off. Good-bye!'

He grasped her hand, but it was quite lifeless in his. Emma
had no energy left to feel anything.

The clock struck four. Yielding mechanically to force of
habit, she rose to return to Yonville.

The weather was fine. It was one of those sharp, bright
March days when the sun shines in a perfectly clear sky. The
folk of Rouen were strolling contentedly in their Sunday
clothes. She reached the Cathedral. Vespers were just over,
and the people were pouring out through the three doors like
a river beneath the arches of a bridge; in the middle, firmer
than a rock, stood the beadle.

She remembered the day when she had gone in there, tense
and expectant, with that great vault rising high above her, yet
overtopped by her love. ... She walked on, weeping beneath
her veil, dazed, unsteady, almost fainting.

'Look out!' came a cry as a carriage gate swung open.

She stopped to let a tilbury emerge, with a black horse
prancing in the shafts and a gentleman in sable furs driving.
Who was it? Where had she seen ... The carriage sprang forward and was gone.

Why, it was he! The Viscount! She turned round. The
street was empty. She felt so overwhelmed with misery that
she leaned against a wall to prevent herself falling.

Then she thought she must have been mistaken. She could
be sure of nothing now. She felt lost, forsaken by everything

within and around her, whirling through a bottomless chaos; and it was almost with joy that she arrived at the Red Cross to find the good Homais watching a crate of chemist's supplies being loaded on to the *Hirondelle*, and with a silk handkerchief in his hand in which he was carrying six *cheminots* for his wife.

Madame Homais was very fond of these small, heavy loaves, shaped like a turban, which are eaten with salt butter during Lent: a last survival of Gothic fare, perhaps going back to the time of the Crusades, with which the sturdy Normans used once to gorge themselves, fancying that they saw in the yellow torchlight on the table, between the jugs of mead and the huge joints of pork, Saracens' heads to devour. The chemist's wife crunched them up in the same heroic manner despite her dreadful teeth, and Homais never failed to bring some back from his trips into Rouen, always buying them at the big shop in the Rue Massacre.

'Delighted to see you!' he greeted Emma, and offered his hand to help her up into the coach.

He hung the *cheminots* on the netting of the rack and sat with bare head and folded arms, in a pensive Napoleonic attitude. But when the blind man came in sight as usual at the foot of the hill, he broke out:

'I can't understand the authorities tolerating such scandals nowadays. The poor wretches ought to be shut up and forced to work. Upon my word, progress goes at a snail's pace! We wallow in utter barbarism.'

The blind man proffered his hat. It swung to and fro outside the carriage window, like a piece of upholstery hanging loose.

'That,' said the chemist, 'is a scrofulous complaint.' And though he knew the poor devil well enough, he pretended he had never seen him before, muttered the words 'cornea', 'corneal opacity', 'sclerotic', 'facies', then asked him paternally: 'Have you had that terrible affliction long, my friend?

Instead of getting drunk at the pub, you'd do better to go on a diet.'

He advised him to take good wine, good beer, and good roast meat.

The blind man went on singing his song; he seemed half-witted. At last Monsieur Homais opened his purse.

'Here you are, here's a penny: give me back a halfpenny. And don't forget my advice; it'll do you good.'

Hivert ventured openly to doubt its efficacy, but the chemist guaranteed to cure the man himself, with an antiphlogiston ointment of his own preparation, and he gave him his address. 'Monsieur Homais, Market-place. Anyone'll tell you.'

'Now then,' said Hivert, 'after all that, you can do your act.'

The blind man crouched down on his haunches, threw back his head, rolled his dark green eyes and stuck out his tongue, rubbed his stomach with both hands and uttered a sort of dull howl, like a famished dog. Disgusted, Emma tossed him a half-crown piece over her shoulder. It was the sum of her wealth; it seemed glorious to fling it away like that.

The carriage was moving off again when Homais suddenly leaned out of the window and called after him: 'No starch, no milk food! Wear wool next the skin and expose the diseased parts to the smoke of juniper berries!'

The familiar sights rolling by gradually distracted Emma from her present miseries. An intolerable weariness overcame her, and she arrived home in a dispirited stupor, almost asleep.

'What will be, will be,' she said to herself.

And you never knew, something quite unexpected might happen at any moment. Lheureux might even die.

At nine o'clock the next morning she was awakened by voices in the square. A mob of people was gathered round the market to read a large notice pasted up on one of the pillars. She saw Justin climb up and tear at it; as he did so, the hand of the village policeman descended on his shoulder.

Homais came out of his shop; old Mother Lefrançois could be seen in the middle of the crowd, apparently delivering a harangue.

'Madame! Madame!' cried Félicité, running in. 'It's a scandal!' And in great agitation the poor girl handed her a sheet of yellow paper she had just torn off the door. Emma read at a glance that all her furniture was for sale.

They gazed at one another in silence. Servant and mistress had no secrets from one another now.

'If I were you, Madame,' Félicité sighed at last, 'I'd go to Monsieur Guillaumin.'

'You would?' said she. Which meant: 'Has your Théodore's master ever spoken of me, then?'

'Yes, you go. It's the best thing you can do.'

She dressed, put on her black frock and her bonnet with the jet beads, and to avoid being seen (for there were still a number of people in the market-place) she turned away from the village and went along the path by the water.

She reached the lawyer's gate quite out of breath. The sky was heavy, with a little snow falling.

In answer to her ring Théodore appeared at the top of the steps in his red waistcoat; he came and let her in almost familiarly, as he might have let in an acquaintance, and showed her into the dining-room.

A large porcelain stove was humming in a recess, the remainder of which was filled up with a cactus. In black wooden frames against oak-grained wallpaper hung Steuben's *Esmeralda* and Schopin's *Potiphar*. The table ready laid, the two silver dish-warmers, the crystal door-knobs, the parquet floor and the furniture, all shone with a meticulous, English cleanness. The windows were decorated at each corner with little square panes of coloured glass.

'This is the sort of dining-room,' thought Emma, 'that I ought to have.'

The notary entered, clasping his palm-leaf dressing-gown

against his body with his left arm, while with his other hand he quickly raised and replaced the maroon velvet cap that he wore tilted pretentiously to the right side of his head, over the ends of three strands of fair hair which were gathered up at the back and twisted round his bald skull.

Having offered her a chair, he sat down to breakfast with much apology for his incivility.

'Monsieur,' said she, 'I want to ask you ...'

'What, Madame? I am listening.'

She proceeded to explain her position.

Maître Guillaumin was aware of it, for he had a secret connexion with the draper, from whom he used to obtain capital for mortgages.

He knew even better than she the long story of the notes – trifling at first, endorsed by various signatures, made payable at long intervals and continually renewed, until the day when the dealer had gathered up all his claims and deputed his friend Vinçart to institute the necessary proceedings in his own name – for Lheureux did not wish to be considered a shark among his fellow-townsmen.

She punctuated her account with recriminations against Lheureux, and from time to time the lawyer grunted noncommitally in response.

Eating his cutlet and drinking his tea, he kept his chin thrust down into his sky-blue cravat, which was fastened by a pair of diamond tie-pins linked with a little gold chain; and he smiled a peculiar, sugary, ambiguous smile.

He noticed that her feet were damp.

'Come and dry them by the stove. ... Higher up ... against the porcelain.'

She was afraid of dirtying it.

'Pretty things never do any harm,' the lawyer remarked with gallantry.

She set to work upon his feelings, became moved herself, started telling him of her household troubles, her difficulties, her needs. Yes, he could understand – a smart woman like her! Without ceasing to eat, he turned right round to face her, so that his knee brushed against her boot, the sole of which curled up as it steamed against the stove.

But when she asked him for a hundred and twenty pounds, he pursed his lips and declared that he was extremely sorry not to have had the management of her property earlier; for there were any number of ways, even for a lady, of turning one's money to account. She could have invested in the Grumesnil peat-bogs or the building sites at Le Havre and got big returns with practically no risk at all. He worked her into a devouring rage at the thought of the fabulous profits she would have been certain to make.

'Why didn't you come to me?' he asked.

'I don't really know,' she said.

'I wonder. Were you frightened of me? Well, it's my loss, for we hardly know each other! Though I'm most interested in you: I hope you don't doubt that?'

He put out his hand and took hers, covered it with a greedy kiss, then held it on his knee, daintily toying with her fingers while he whispered softly in her ear.

His toneless voice babbled on like a running brook. Through his shiny spectacles she saw a glint in his eye. His hands slid up Emma's sleeve and stroked her arm. She felt a panting breath on her cheek. The man revolted her.

She sprang to her feet.

'I am waiting, sir!' she said.

'What, what ...' stammered the lawyer, turning suddenly white.

'The money ...'

'But ...' Then, yielding to the uprush of an overpowering desire: 'All right – yes!'

He dragged himself on his knees towards her, careless of his dressing-gown. 'For pity's sake stay! I love you!'

He seized her round the waist.

A wave of crimson flooded Madame Bovary's face. She drew back, terrible to see.

'You take a despicable advantage of my distress, Monsieur! I am to be pitied ... I am not to be bought!'

And she was gone.

The lawyer was left dumbfounded, his eyes fixed on his beautiful embroidered slippers. They were a love gift; eventually the sight of them consoled him. He reflected also that such an adventure might have taken him too far.

'What a wretch! What a blackguard! ... What wickedness!' she said to herself as she fled on nervous feet beneath the aspens at the side of the road. Disappointment at failure reinforced indignation at the outrage to her modesty. It seemed that Providence was bent on persecuting her. The thought gave a fillip to her pride. Never had she felt so high an esteem for herself or so great a contempt for everybody else. She was in a fighting fury. She would have liked to hit men, to spit in their faces, to trample on them. She strode rapidly forward, pale, quivering, mad with rage, scanning the empty horizon with tear-filled eyes, gloating, almost, over the hatred that choked her.

The sight of her house paralysed her. She couldn't go on. Yet she must. Where else was there?

Félicité was waiting at the door.

'Well?'

'No,' said Emma.

For a quarter of an hour they considered together the various people in Yonville who might be willing to help her. But each name that Félicité suggested was met with: 'No! No, I'm sure they wouldn't!'

'And the doctor'll be in directly!'

'I know. ... Leave me to myself.'

She had tried everything. There was nothing else she could do. When Charles arrived she would have to say to him, 'Keep out! The carpet on which you are treading belongs to us no longer. There's not a chair or a pin or a wisp of straw in your house, that's yours. And it is I, poor man, I who have ruined you!'

There would be a great sob, many tears, and in the end, recovered from the shock, he would forgive ...

'Yes,' she muttered, gritting her teeth, 'he'll forgive me – he, whom I'd never forgive for having known me though he had a million to offer me! No, never, never!'

She felt furious at the idea of Bovary's being superior to herself. And whether she confessed or not, soon, very soon – tomorrow! – he'd know of the calamity just the same. She must await that horrible scene and bear the burden of his magnanimity.

She had an impulse to go back to Lheureux. But what was the use? To write to her father – it was too late. And she was perhaps beginning to regret that she hadn't yielded to that man, when she heard the sound of a horse trotting up the lane. It was Charles. He was opening the gate, his face whiter than the plaster on the wall. Running down the staircase, she dashed out across the square; and the mayor's wife, who was talking to Lestiboudois in front of the church, saw her go in at the tax-collector's.

This lady ran off to tell Madame Caron; together they climbed up to her attic, and under cover of some linen that was hanging out to air, took up a position commanding the interior of Binet's house.

He was alone in his garret, engaged in making a wood copy of one of those indescribable ivory carvings which are composed of crescents and spheres fitted one inside the other, the whole erect as an obelisk, and completely useless. And he was just starting on the last piece, the final touch! In the light and shade of his workshop the yellow sawdust flew off his machine like a shower of sparks from the hooves of a galloping horse. The wheels went whirring round. Binet was smiling, chin down, nostrils dilated – absorbed in one of those utter joys, belonging doubtless only to mediocre tasks, which entertain the mind with simple difficulties and satisfy it in a fulfilment where all aspiration ends.

'There she is!' said Madame Tuvache.

But they could hear scarcely anything that she said for the noise of the lathe.

At last the two ladies thought they caught the word 'pounds'.

'She's asking for time to pay her taxes,' whispered Madame Tuvache.

'Looks like it!' the other agreed.

They watched her moving about the room, examining the serviette-rings on the walls, the candlesticks and banister-knobs, while Binet sat complacently stroking his beard.

'Do you think she's gone to order something from him?' said the mayor's wife.

'He never sells anything!' her neighbour answered.

The tax-collector appeared to be listening, a blank stare of incomprehension on his face. She went on in a tender, supplicating manner. She drew closer to him. Her breast heaved. They had stopped talking.

'Is she making up to him?' exclaimed Madame Tuvache.

Binet had gone red to the roots of his hair. She took his hands in hers.

'Well, of all the ...!'

And it must indeed have been a scandalous proposition that she was putting to him, for the tax-collector – albeit a man of mettle, who had fought at Bautzen and Lutzen, taken part in the French campaign and even been recommended for a decoration – suddenly sprang back as if he had seen a snake.

'Madame!' he cried. 'How can you think of such a thing!'

'Women like that ought to be whipped!' said Madame Tuvache.

'Where's she gone?' said Madame Caron.

For she had vanished as they were speaking. When they saw her hurry along the High Street and then turn right as though making for the cemetery, they plunged into a whirl of conjecture.

'Mother Rollet,' she said as she entered the nurse's house, 'I can't breathe! Unlace me!'

She dropped on the bed, sobbing. Madame Rollet covered her with a petticoat, and stood beside her. But as she made no remark, the good woman moved away and set to work at her spinning-wheel.

'Stop!' muttered Emma, thinking she could hear Binet's lathe.

'What's troubling her?' the nurse wondered. 'Why has she come here?'

She had fled there at the urging of a kind of panic that drove her from her own house.

Lying on her back, motionless, her eyes staring, she could not see things clearly though she strained with imbecile persistency to fix her attention upon them. She gazed at the plaster flaking off the wall, at the two sticks smouldering end to end on the fire, at a large spider crawling along a crack in the beam above her head. At last she collected her thoughts. She remembered ... one day with Léon ... (how long ago!) ... the river glittering in the sun ... the scent of the clematis ... Swept headlong down the seething torrent of her memories, she soon returned to the recollection of the previous day.

'What time is it?' she asked.

Mother Rollet went outside, held up the fingers of her right hand in the direction where the sky was brightest, and came slowly in again.

'Three o'clock nearly.'

'Ah, thank you, thank you!'

For he would come. Of course he would! He would have found some money. Perhaps he'd go to her house, though,

never imagining that she'd be here. She told the nurse to run
and fetch him.

'Hurry!'

'Yes, dear lady, I'm going, I'm going!'

She was surprised now that she hadn't thought of him at
first. He had given his word yesterday; he wouldn't go back
on it. She already saw herself laying the three bank-notes on
Lheureux's desk. Then she'd have to think up some tale to
explain matters to Bovary. What should it be?

The nurse was a long time coming back. But as there was
no clock in the cottage, Emma thought that perhaps it seemed
longer than it was. She started pacing slowly round the garden.
Then she went out along the path by the hedge, and hurried
back hoping the woman might have come home a different
way. At last, tired of waiting, assailed by suspicions that she
tried to thrust from her, knowing no longer whether she had
been there an age or a minute, she sat down in a corner, shut
her eyes and stopped her ears. The gate creaked. She started
to her feet. Before she could say anything, Mother Rollet told
her, 'There's nobody come!'

'What?'

'Nobody! And your husband's crying. He keeps calling for
you. They're looking for you.'

Emma made no answer. She was panting and rolling her
eyes, and the peasant-woman, scared at the look on her face,
shrank back instinctively, thinking she had gone mad. All at
once Emma clapped her hands to her forehead and gave a cry:
like a flash of lightning on a dark night, the thought of
Rodolphe had come to her. He was so kind, so considerate, so
generous! And if he should hesitate to do her this service she
could soon make him, for a single glance would suffice to remind him of their lost love. So she set off for La Huchette,
unaware that she was hastening to expose herself to what a
little while before had so enraged her, never for a moment
suspecting prostitution.

8

'WHAT shall I say? How shall I begin?' she asked herself as she went. And as she drew nearer she recognized the shrubs and trees, the furze on the hill-side and, down in the hollow, the château. She was back among the sensations of her first love, and her poor constricted heart swelled again with the tenderness of it. A warm breeze fanned her face. The snow was melting: it fell drop by drop from the young shoots on to the grass.

She went in at the same little park-gate and came to the courtyard with the double border of bushy lime-trees. Their long branches rustled as they swayed to and fro. The dogs in the kennels all barked, but no one appeared at their clamour.

Emma climbed the straight wide staircase with the wooden banisters that led to the dusty stone corridor from which several rooms opened off in a row as in a hotel or a monastery. His was at the far end, the last one on the left. With her hand on the latch her strength suddenly deserted her. She felt afraid he wouldn't be there; she almost wished he were not; yet he was her one hope, her last chance. She waited a minute composing herself, then, re-tempering her courage in the awareness of her present need, she entered.

He was sitting in front of the fire with both feet on the fender, smoking a pipe.

'Lord! It's you!' he said, getting up hastily.

'Yes, it's me. ... Rodolphe, I want some advice. ...' But try as she might, she couldn't get another word out.

'You haven't changed. You're charming as ever!'

'Sad charms, my friend,' she answered bitterly, 'since you disdained them.'

He launched into an explanation of his conduct, offering vague excuses for want of a more plausible story.

She let herself succumb to his words, more still to the

sound of his voice and the sight of him – to the point of pretending to believe him (or perhaps she really did believe him) when he said that his motive for breaking with her was a secret on which depended the honour, even the life, of a third person.

'I've suffered, all the same,' she said, looking at him unhappily.

'Life is like that!' he answered philosophically.

'Has it, at any rate, been kind to you since we parted?'

'Oh, neither kind nor unkind.'

'It might have been better if we'd stayed together.'

'Yes. Perhaps!'

'Do you think so?' she said, going up to him.

She sighed. 'Oh, Rodolphe, if you only knew! ... I loved you so!'

And then she took his hand, and for a while they sat with fingers interwined – as on that first day at the Show. His pride struggled against his feeling; but she nestled against him and said: 'How did you expect me to live without you? Do you think it's easy to part with happiness? I was desperate. I thought I should die. I'll tell you everything. ... And you, you kept away from me!'

He had, indeed, carefully avoided her for the last three years, with that innate cowardice that characterizes the stronger sex.

Emma went on, with pretty little movements of her head, coaxing him like an amorous kitten: 'You've got other women: own up! Oh, I understand. I forgive them. You'll have fascinated them as you fascinated me. You are a man! You've everything to make a woman love you. ... But we'll start again, won't we? We'll love each other? Look, I'm laughing, I'm happy! ... Talk to me!'

And she was lovely to see, with a tear trembling in her eye like a raindrop in a blue petal.

He took her on his knees and stroked her smooth hair with

the back of his hand; on those plaited coils a last ray of sunshine gleamed like a golden arrow in the fading light. She bent her head, and at last he kissed her very gently on the eyelids, just brushing them with his lips.

'You've been crying!' he said. 'Why?'

She burst out sobbing. Rodolphe thought it was her passion finding its release. She said nothing; he took her silence for a final reserve of modesty, and exclaimed: 'Oh, forgive me! You are the only one I care for. I have been foolish and wicked! I love you and I shall always love you! ... What is it? Tell me!' And he went down on his knees.

'Very well. ... I'm ruined, Rodolphe! You've got to lend me a hundred and twenty pounds!'

'But ... but ...' said he, gradually rising to his feet, his face assuming a grave expression.

'You know,' she went on hurriedly, 'my husband had put all his money into the hands of a lawyer? He disappeared. We had to borrow. The patients didn't pay. And my father-in-law's estate isn't yet wound up. We shall have that some time. But today, unless we can get a hundred and twenty pounds, the bailiffs will be arriving—now—this very instant. ... And so, relying on your friendship, I came to you!'

'So that's it!' thought Rodolphe, going suddenly quite pale. After a pause, he said calmly: 'I haven't got it, my dear lady.'

He was not lying. If he had had it he would doubtless have given it to her, distasteful though it usually is to perform such noble deeds: a request for money being of all the icy blasts that blow upon love the coldest and most uprooting.

She kept her gaze on him for some minutes. 'You haven't got it. ... You haven't got it,' she repeated. 'I might have spared myself this last humiliation. You never loved me! You're no better than the rest!'

She was giving herself away, losing her head.

Rodolphe interrupted to say he happened to be 'a bit short' himself.

'Oh, I'm sorry for you,' said Emma. 'I *am* sorry for you.'

She let her gaze rest on a damascened rifle that glittered in a rack on the wall.

'When people are poor, they don't put silver on the butts of their guns! Or buy a clock inlaid with tortoise-shell!' she added, pointing to his Buhl timepiece, 'or silver-plated whistles for their whips' (she touched them) 'or trinkets for their watches! Oh, he wants for nothing! A liqueur-stand in his bedroom, even. You love yourself too much: you live well, you've got a country-house, farms and woods, you ride to hounds, you go up to Paris. ... Why, these alone,' she cried, picking up his cuff-links from the mantelpiece, 'the smallest of these fripperies can be turned into money! ... No, keep them, I don't want them!'

And she flung the links away from her. Their gold chain snapped as they struck against the wall.

'And I, I'd have given you everything, sold everything I had, worked with my hands, begged in the streets, just for a smile, for a glance, just to hear you say "Thank you". And you sit there quite calmly in your easy-chair, as if you hadn't made me suffer enough already! Do you know I could have been happy if I'd never known you? Why did you have to do it? Was it for a wager? No, you loved me, you told me so. Just now, even ... Oh, you'd have done better to send me away at once. My hands are still burning from your kisses. And here's the place on the carpet where you knelt at my feet and vowed me an eternity of love. And I believed you. For two years you led me on through the sweetest and most magnificent of dreams. Ha! Our plans for going away – do you remember? Oh, that letter, that letter, it tore my heart in two! And now when I come back to him, him with his money, his happiness, his freedom, to beg help that any casual stranger might give – entreating him, bringing back to him all my love – he turns me away because it'd cost him a hundred and twenty pounds!'

'I haven't got it,' Rodolphe answered with that perfect calm which is the defence of a resigned anger.

She went. The walls were quivering, the ceiling pressing down upon her. She made her way back up the long drive, stumbling among the heaps of dead leaves that were scattering in the wind. At last she reached the ditch, the gate; in her haste to get it open she tore her nails on the latch. A hundred yards farther on, breathless, tottering, she halted, turned and looked back once more at the impassive mansion, the park, the gardens, the three courtyards, all the windows of the façade.

She stood in a daze, conscious of herself only through the throbbing of her arteries, which she fancied she could hear going forth like a deafening music and filling the countryside around. The ground seemed to give beneath her like water, the furrows looked like vast brown waves breaking into foam. All the thoughts and memories in her mind came rushing out together like a thousand fireworks going off at once. She saw her father: Lheureux's office: the room at Rouen: a different landscape. Madness was laying hold on her. Terrified, she managed to pull herself together, though in some bewilderment; for the thing that had brought her to this frightful condition – her need of money – she could not recall. Only in her love did she suffer; through the thought of that she felt her soul escape from her as a wounded man in his last agony feels life flow out through his bleeding gashes.

Night was falling. Some rooks flew overhead.

All at once it seemed as if the air were bursting with little globes of fire, like bullets, flattening out as they exploded. Round and round they went and finally melted in the snow amid the branches of the trees. In the centre of each the face of Rodolphe appeared. They multiplied, clustered together, bored into her. Then everything vanished, and she saw the lights of the houses glimmering through the mist far away.

And once again the deep hopelessness of her plight came back to her. Her lungs heaved as though they would burst. Then, in a transport of heroism which made her almost gay, she ran down the hill and across the cow-plank, hurried along the path, up the lane, through the market-place, and arrived in front of the chemist's shop.

It was empty. She was about to go in; but the bell would ring and someone might come. She slipped through the side-gate holding her breath, and felt her way along the wall to the kitchen door. Inside, a candle was burning on the range. Justin, in his shirt-sleeves, was taking in a dish.

'They're at dinner. Wait.'

He returned. She tapped on the window. He came out.

'The key! The key for upstairs, where the ...'

'What?' He stared at her, astonished at the pallor of her face, which stood out white in the darkness. She looked so extraordinarily beautiful, possessed of a ghostly majesty. Without understanding what she wanted, he had a presentiment of something terrible.

She went on quickly in a low voice, a voice that was sweet and melting: 'I want it! Give it me!'

Through the thin wall came the clatter of knives and forks from the dining-room. She said she wanted to kill some rats that were keeping her awake.

'I'll have to tell the master.'

'No! Stop! ... It's not worth bothering,' she added more casually, 'I'll tell him directly. Now, show me a light!'

She went down the passage off which the laboratory opened. Hanging on the wall was a key labelled *Capharnaum*.

'Justin!' shouted the chemist, who was growing impatient.

'Upstairs!' she whispered. And he followed her.

The key turned in the lock. She went straight over to the third shelf, so well did her memory guide her. She seized the blue jar, tugged at the cork, plunged her hand inside, and drew it out full of a white powder which she proceeded to cram into her mouth.

'Stop!' he cried, hurling himself upon her.

'Be quiet! They'll come!'

He was desperate; he wanted to shout out.

'Don't say anything. All the blame will be put on your master!'

And she went away, suddenly at peace, serene as in the consciousness of duty done.

When Charles got home, overwrought at the news of the distraint, Emma had just gone. He called for her, wept, fainted away, but she did not return. Where could she be? He sent Félicité to the Homais', to Monsieur Tuvache's, to Lheureux's, to the Golden Lion, everywhere; and in the intervals of his anguish he saw his reputation lost, his money gone, Berthe's future wrecked. Through what cause? No word to tell him! He waited till six o'clock, then could stand it no longer. Fancying that she must have set off for Rouen, he walked a mile and a half along the highroad, met nobody, waited a while, turned back home again.

She had come in.

'What happened? What was it? Tell me!'

She sat down at her desk and wrote a letter, which she slowly sealed, adding the date and time.

'Read it tomorrow,' she said in a solemn voice. 'Till then, please don't ask me a single question. ... No, not one!'

'But ...'

'No, leave me alone!'

She lay down full length on the bed.

An acrid taste in her mouth awoke her. She saw Charles and closed her eyes again.

She watched with curiosity for any sign of pain. No, nothing yet. She heard the clock ticking, the fire crackling, Charles breathing as he stood beside her.

'There's not much in dying,' she thought. 'I shall go to sleep, and it will all be over.'

She gulped down some water, and turned to the wall.

That dreadful inky taste was still there.

'I'm thirsty ... I'm so thirsty!' she whispered.

'What can it be?' said Charles, handing her the glass.

'It's nothing ... Open the window ... I feel choked!'

And she vomited so suddenly that she barely had time to grab her handkerchief from under the pillow.

'Take it out! Throw it away!' she said quickly.

He started questioning her. She didn't answer. She kept quite still, afraid that the least agitation might make her sick. She began to feel an icy coldness mounting from her feet towards her heart.

'That's it, it's beginning!' she mumbled.

'What did you say?'

She rolled her head with a gentle, anguished movement, trying to open her jaws all the while as though she had a heavy weight on her tongue. At eight o'clock the vomiting began again.

Charles noticed a sort of white sediment clinging to the bottom of the basin.

'That's queer! That's funny!' he kept saying.

'No, it's nothing,' she said in a firm voice.

Very gently, almost caressingly, he passed his hand over her stomach. She gave a shriek. He started back in terror.

She began to groan, feebly at first. A violent shudder went through her shoulders, she turned whiter than the sheet she was clutching in her fingers. Her wavering pulse could hardly be felt at all now.

Drops of sweat stood on her blue-veined face, which looked as if it had been petrified by exposure to some metallic vapour. Her teeth chattered, her pupils were dilated, her eyes stared vaguely about her. To every question she responded with simply a shake of the head. Two or three times she smiled.

Little by little her groans grew louder. A muffled scream broke from her. She pretended to be feeling better and said she would soon be getting up. But then she was seized with convulsions.

'Oh, God, it's ghastly!' she cried.

He went down on his knees beside her.

'Tell me what you've eaten! For God's sake answer!' And he looked at her with such tenderness in his eyes as she had never seen before.

'All right,' she said in a faltering voice. 'There ... over there. ...'

He sprang to the desk, broke the seal and read aloud, 'No one is guilty ...' He stopped, passed his hand over his eyes, read on.

'What ... Help! Oh, help!' And he could only utter the one word, 'Poisoned! Poisoned!'

Félicité ran to get Homais, who shouted the news across the square. Madame Lefrançois heard him at the Golden Lion, several people got out of bed to tell their neighbours, and the village was awake all night.

Aghast, mouthing, hardly able to stand, Charles stumbled round the room, bumping into the furniture, tearing at his hair. Never had the chemist thought to see so appalling a sight.

He returned to his own house to write to Monsieur Canivet and Dr Larivière. He lost his head and made over a dozen rough drafts. Hippolyte set off for Neufchâtel, Justin spurred Bovary's horse so unmercifully that he had to leave it on the hill at Bois-Guillaume foundered and three parts dead.

Charles tried to turn over the pages of his medical dictionary; but he could see nothing, the lines danced.

'Keep calm!' said the chemist. 'It's only a matter of administering some powerful antidote. What poison was it?'

Charles pointed to the letter. It was arsenic.

'Right!' said Homais. 'We must analyse.'

For he knew that in all cases of poisoning it was necessary

to analyse. Charles, not understanding, answered, 'Yes, yes, go on! Save her!'

He went over to her again, sank down on the carpet and knelt with his head against the edge of the bed, sobbing.

'Don't cry!' she said. 'Soon I shall be troubling you no more.'

'Why did you? What made you?'

'It had to be, my dear,' she replied.

'Weren't you happy? Is it my fault? I did all I could ...'

'Yes ... that's true. ... You are a good man.' And she passed her hand over his hair slowly. The sweetness of that sensation overcharged his grief. He felt his whole being dissolve in despair at the thought that he must lose her, just when she was showing more love for him than ever before. And he didn't know, he couldn't think, what to do; he didn't dare do anything – the necessity of an immediate decision serving to paralyse him completely.

She had done, she was thinking, with all the treachery and the squalor and the numberless desires that had racked her. She hated no one now; a twilight confusion was descending on her mind, and of all the noises of the earth Emma could no longer hear any but the intermittent lamentation of that poor soul at her side, blurred and tender as the last echo of a symphony dying in the distance.

'Bring me Berthe!' she said, raising herself on her elbow.

'You're not feeling worse?' asked Charles.

'No, no!'

The little girl arrived in her nurse's arms, her bare feet sticking out from under her long nightdress – solemn-faced and scarcely out of her dreams. She stared with wondering eyes at the untidy room, blinked at the dazzling candles that were burning on the tables. They must have reminded her of New Year's Day or mid-Lent when, woken early like this by candle-light, she used to get into her mother's bed to be given her presents; for she at once asked: 'Where is it, Mummy?'

No one spoke.

'I can't see my stocking!'

And while Félicité held her over the bed, she kept her eyes turned towards the fireplace.

'Has nurse taken it?' she asked.

At the word 'nurse', which revived the memory of her lusts and her miseries, Madame Bovary turned her head aside as though another, stronger, poison were rising nauseously in her throat. Berthe remained perched on the bed.

'Oh, mummy, what big eyes you've got! How pale you are! You're sticky!'

Her mother looked at her.

'I'm frightened!' said the child, shrinking away.

Emma took her hand and tried to kiss it. She struggled.

'That'll do! Take her away!' cried Charles, who was sobbing in the corner.

Then for a moment the symptoms ceased. She seemed less agitated, and at every slightest word, at every quieter breath she drew, he took fresh hope. When Canivet at last walked in, Charles threw himself into his arms, weeping.

'It's you! Thank you, it is kind of you! But she's better now. Look – !'

His colleague by no means shared this opinion; and without – as he put it – beating about the bush, he prescribed an emetic to clear the stomach completely.

Not long afterwards she started vomiting blood. Her lips pressed tighter together, her limbs writhed, brown spots broke out over her body, her pulse slid between the fingers like a taut wire, like a harp-string about to snap.

She began to scream, horribly. She damned and cursed the poison, begged it to be quick, and with her stiffening arms pushed away everything that Charles, in a still worse agony than she, kept trying to make her drink. He stood with his handkerchief to his lips, croaking, crying, choked by the sobs that shook his frame. Félicité ran hither and thither about the room. Homais stood motionless, sighing deeply; Monsieur Canivet, though still preserving his swagger, had none the less begun to feel uneasy.

'Damn! ... But she's purged now, and the minute you stop the cause ...'

'You stop the effect,' said Homais. 'That's obvious.'

'Save her!' cried Bovary.

Accordingly, paying no heed to the chemist, who ventured the further hypothesis that it 'might be a salutary paroxysm', Canivet was preparing to give her an antidote, when they heard the crack of a whip outside; the window-panes rattled, and a stage-coach, whisked along by three horses, in full harness and up to their ears in mud, came hurtling round the corner of the market. It was Dr Larivière.

The advent of a god could have caused no greater commotion. Bovary lifted up his hands. Canivet stopped short. Homais removed his skull-cap long before the great man entered.

He belonged to that great line of surgeons that sprang from Bichat, that now-vanished generation of philosopher-healers who cherished their art with a fanatical love and practised it with zeal and sagacity. When Dr Larivière was angry, the whole hospital quaked. His pupils revered him to the point of trying to imitate him in everything as soon as they set up in practice themselves; consequently, every town for miles around had its replica of his long merino greatcoat and his loose black jacket, the cuffs of which hung down unbuttoned over his firm hands – beautiful hands, always ungloved, as though to be the readier to plunge to the relief of suffering. Disdaining all academic honours, titles and decorations, hospitable and generous, like a father to the poor, practising goodness without believing in it, he might almost have passed for a saint had not his mental acuity caused him to be feared as a demon. Sharper than a lancet, his eyes looked straight into your soul, piercing through all pretence and reticence to dissect the lie beneath. So he went his way, in all the easy majesty that comes of the consciousness of great talent, wealth and forty years of hard work and irreproachable living.

He closed the door behind him and his brows contracted at sight of Emma's cadaverous face, as she lay there on her back, her mouth agape. While apparently listening to Canivet, he rubbed his nostril with his forefinger and said, 'Good, good. ...' But his shoulders lifted in a slow gesture. Bovary noticed it. They looked at one another. And that man who was so accustomed to the sight of grief, could not restrain a tear; it dropped down on his shirt-front. He tried to take Canivet aside into the next room; Charles followed them.

'She's very bad, isn't she? Could we try poulticing? I don't know ... Oh, think of something! You have saved so many lives!'

Charles had pinioned the doctor with both arms and was fixing him with a gaze of terrified entreaty, half-swooning on his chest.

'Come, my poor boy. Be brave! ... There's nothing I can do.' And Dr Larivière turned away.

'Are you going?'

'I'm coming back.'

He went out as though to give orders to the coachman, and Canivet followed, being no less reluctant to have Emma die under his care.

The chemist joined them in the market-place. He was temperamentally incapable of tearing himself away from celebrities and he accordingly requested Dr Larivière to do him the signal honour of taking luncheon at his house.

Orders were hastily sent to the Golden Lion for pigeons, to the butcher's for all the cutlets he had in his shop, to Tuvache's for cream and to Lestiboudois for eggs. The chemist took a hand in the preparations himself.

'You'll excuse us, sir,' said Madame Homais, tugging at the strings of her bodice. 'In our little village, you know, unless we're warned the day before ...'

'The wine-glasses!!!' whispered Homais.

'If we lived in town, now, we'd always have stuffed trotters to fall back on. ...'

'Quiet! ... Will you take your seat, Doctor!'

After a few mouthfuls he thought fit to impart certain details of the tragedy.

'First, we had a parched feeling in the pharynx, then horrible pains in the epigastrium, superpurgation, and coma.'

'How did she poison herself?'

'I've no idea, Doctor. Neither do I know where she could have obtained that arsenious acid.'

Justin, who had just come in with a pile of plates, started trembling violently.

'What's the matter with you?' said the chemist.

So addressed, the young man let his whole load go crashing to the floor.

'Fool!' yelled Homais. 'Clumsy blockhead! Pitiable idiot!'

Suddenly regaining control of himself, he went on: 'I decided to attempt an analysis, Doctor. First, I carefully introduced into a tube ...'

'You'd have done better,' said the surgeon, 'to introduce your fingers into her throat!'

His colleague remained silent; he had just received, in private, a severe rebuke on the subject of his emetic, and in consequence, the worthy Canivet, who had been so arrogant and loquacious at the time of the club-foot operation, today sat very quiet, wearing a continuous smile of approval.

Homais expanded in his hostly pride, and the distressing thought of Bovary lent, by contrast, a certain spice to his pleasure. The presence of the doctor quite enraptured him; he showed off all his erudition, pouring out allusions to cantharides, the upas, the manchineel, the viper.

'I've even read of people becoming intoxicated – struck down, you might say – by black puddings that had been submitted to an excessively strong fumigation! At least, so we were told in an excellent report composed by one of our leading pharmacists – one of our masters, the illustrious Cadet de Gassicourt!'

Madame Homais reappeared, carrying one of those rickety contrivances that you heat with a spirit-lamp: for Homais insisted on making his coffee at table. What was more, he had previously roasted, ground and blended it himself.

'*Saccharum*, Doctor?' he said as he passed the sugar.

Then he had all his children brought downstairs to hear what the surgeon thought of their constitutions.

And then, when Monsieur Larivière was on the point of leaving, Madame Homais asked him to examine her husband. He was 'thickening his blood' by going to sleep every evening after dinner.

'Oh, it's not his *blood* that's thick.' And with a little smile at this unnoticed witticism, the doctor opened the door. The shop was thronged with people, and he had great difficulty in getting away from Monsieur Tuvache, who suspected inflammation in his wife's lungs because she was always spitting in the fire; then from Monsieur Binet, who sometimes had hunger-pangs, and from Madame Caron, who had pins and needles; from Lheureux with his vertigo, Lestiboudois with his rheumatism, and Madame Lefrançois with her heartburn. When the three horses finally trotted off, the general opinion was that he had been most unobliging.

Public attention was distracted, however, by the appearance of Monsieur Bournisien coming through the market with the holy oils.

Homais owed it to his principles to compare priests with crows attracted by the smell of the dead. The sight of an ecclesiastic was physically repugnant to him, for the cassock put him in mind of the shroud, and his abomination of the one was partly due to his dread of the other.

Nevertheless, not shrinking from what he called his 'mission', he returned to Bovary's house, together with

Canivet, whom Monsieur Larivière, before leaving, had strongly urged to remain. But for his wife's remonstrances, the chemist would have taken his two sons along with him as well, to accustom them to painful occasions and give them a lesson, an example, a solemn picture that would remain in their minds thereafter.

The bedroom, when they entered, was filled with a mournful solemnity. On the work-table, covered with a white cloth, were five or six little balls of cotton-wool in a silver dish and a large crucifix standing between a pair of lighted candles. Emma lay with her chin sunk on her breast, her eyelids unnaturally wide apart, and her poor hands trailing over the sheets in that hideous, gentle movement of the dying, who seem prematurely eager to wrap themselves in the winding-sheet. Pale as a statue, with eyes like burning coals, Charles, not weeping now, stood facing her at the foot of the bed, while the priest knelt down and mumbled under his breath.

Slowly she turned her face, and when her eyes lighted on the violet stole she seemed to be seized with a sudden joy. Doubtless she was finding again in the midst of a wondrous appeasement the lost ecstasy of her first flights of mysticism, and beginning to see visions of eternal blessedness.

The priest rose to take the crucifix. Reaching forward like one in thirst, she glued her lips to the body of the Man-God and laid upon it with all her failing strength the most mighty kiss of love she had ever given. The priest recited the *Misereatur* and the *Indulgentiam*; then he dipped his right thumb into the oil and began the unctions: first on the eyes, that had so coveted all earthly splendours; then on the nostrils, that had loved warm breezes and amorous perfumes; then on the mouth, that had opened for falsehood, had groaned with pride and cried out in lust; then on the hands, that had revelled in delicious contacts; lastly on the soles of the feet, that once had run so swiftly to the assuaging of her desires, and now would walk no more.

The *curé* wiped his fingers, threw the oily wads of cotton-wool on the fire and sat down once more beside the dying woman, to tell her that she must now unite her sufferings with those of Jesus Christ and cast herself on the Divine Mercy.

As he finished his exhortation, he tried to put into her hand a consecrated taper, symbolic of the celestial glories by which she was soon to be surrounded. Emma was too weak to close her fingers on it, and Monsieur Bournisien caught it as it fell to the floor.

However, she was less pale now and her face wore an expression of serenity, as though the sacrament had healed her.

The priest did not fail to remark on this. Indeed, he explained to Bovary that the Lord did sometimes prolong people's lives when He deemed it meet for their salvation; and Charles remembered another day when she had been near to death like this and had received the communion.

'There may still be hope,' he thought.

And just then she looked all round her, slowly, as one waking from a dream. In a clear voice she asked for her mirror, and remained bowed over it for some time, until big tears began to trickle out of her eyes. Then she threw up her head with a sigh and fell back on the pillow.

At once her lungs began to heave rapidly, the whole of her tongue protruded from her mouth, her rolling eyes turned pale like the globes of two guttering lamps: she might have been dead already but for the frightful oscillation of her ribs, that shook with furious gusts as though her soul were leaping to get free. Félicité knelt before the crucifix; even the chemist bent his knees a little; Monsieur Canivet stared vaguely out into the square. Bournisien had started praying again, his face bowed over the edge of the bed, his long black cassock trailing across the floor behind him. Charles knelt opposite, his arms stretched out towards Emma. He had taken her hands and was pressing them in his, shuddering at every beat of her heart as at the reverberation of a falling ruin. As the death-rattle grew louder, the priest hastened his orisons; they mingled with Bovary's stifled sobs, and sometimes everything seemed to be drowned in the dull murmur of the Latin syllables, that sounded like the tolling of a knell.

Suddenly there was a clumping of sabots on the pavement outside, the scraping of a stick, and a voice came up, a hoarse voice singing:

> *'When the sun shines warm above,*
> *It turns a maiden's thoughts to love.'*

Emma sat up like a corpse galvanized, her hair dishevelled, her eyes fixed, gaping.

> *'All across the furrows brown*
> *See Nanette go bending down,*
> *Gathering up with careful hand*
> *The golden harvest from the land.'*

'The blind man!' she cried.

And Emma started laughing, a ghastly, frantic, desperate laugh, fancying she could see the hideous face of the beggar rising up like a nightmare amid the eternal darkness.

> *'The wind it blew so hard one day,*
> *Her little petticoat flew away!'*

A convulsion flung her down upon the mattress. They moved nearer. She was no more.

9

THE coming of death always induces a sort of stupefaction, so hard is it to realize this advent of nothingness and to bring oneself to believe in it. Yet when he saw how still she lay, Charles threw himself upon her crying, 'Good-bye! Good-bye!'

Homais and Canivet dragged him from the room.

'Try to be calm!'

'Yes,' he said struggling, 'I'll be sensible, I won't do any harm. ... Only leave me! I must be with her! She's my wife!'

He was crying.

'Cry!' said the chemist. 'Let Nature have her way. It will bring you relief!'

Weaker than a child, Charles let himself be led downstairs into the dining-room; and Homais presently returned to his own house.

He was accosted in the square by the blind man, who had trudged all the way to Yonville in the hope of getting the anti-phlogiston ointment, and was asking everyone he met where the chemist lived.

'Goodness! As if I hadn't enough on my plate already! ... No, I can't help it, you must come back later.' And he hastily retreated into his shop.

He had two letters to write and a sedative to make up for Bovary; then he had to think out an alternative version of Emma's death for the readers of the *Beacon*; not to mention all the people who were waiting outside to ply him with questions. When all the Yonville folk had heard his story of her mistaking arsenic for sugar while making a vanilla cream, Homais went back to Bovary's once more.

He found him alone (Monsieur Canivet had just left), sitting in the armchair by the window, staring idiotically at the stone floor.

'Now,' said the chemist. 'You must fix a time for the ceremony.'

'What for? What ceremony?' Then in a frightened voice he stammered, 'Oh, no! No! I want to keep her.'

Homais covered his confusion by taking a glass jug from the dresser and watering the geraniums.

'Ah, thank you,' said Charles, 'you are kind. ...' And he could say no more; his heart was too full of the memories that this action of the chemist's recalled to him.

Homais thought a little chat about plants might do him good. Growing things, he declared, needed moisture. Charles bowed his head in assent.

'And the spring'll soon be here again.'

'Ah!' from Bovary.

The chemist, at the end of his resources, gently drew the little curtains aside. 'Hallo, there's Monsieur Tuvache going by!'

'Monsieur Tuvache going by,' Charles repeated mechanically.

Homais did not dare to mention the funeral arrangements again. It was the priest who finally persuaded him.

He shut himself up in his consulting-room, took a pen, sobbed for some time, then wrote:

'I want her to be buried in her wedding-dress, with white shoes and a wreath, and her hair spread out over her shoulders. Three coffins, one oak, one mahogany, and one lead. If no one speaks to me I shall be all right. On top of everything lay a large piece of green velvet. These are my wishes.'

Cleric and chemist were both amazed at Bovary's romantic notions, and Homais went straight in to tell him:

'This velvet seems to me a superfluity. And the expense ...'

'What's that to you?' shouted Charles. 'Leave me! You never loved her! Get out!'

The priest took him by the arm for a turn round the garden, discoursing the while on the vanity of earthly things. God was very great and very good. We ought to submit to His decrees without complaining: nay, we should be thankful to Him!

Charles burst out blaspheming. 'I hate your God!'

'The spirit of rebellion is still in you,' sighed the cleric.

Bovary had broken away from him, and was striding beside the fruit-wall, gnashing his teeth, raking the heavens with looks of imprecation. But not so much as a leaf stirred.

A fine rain was falling. Charles, whose chest was bare, at last began to shiver. He went in and sat down in the kitchen.

At six o'clock a rattle of old iron was heard in the square; the *Hirondelle* drove up. He stood with his forehead against the window and watched the passengers alighting one by one. Félicité brought down a mattress and laid it on the drawing-room floor; he threw himself upon it and fell asleep.

Thinker that he was, Monsieur Homais yet respected the dead. He therefore returned, harbouring no resentment against poor Charles, to watch beside the body during the night; he brought with him three volumes and a pocket-book for taking notes.

Bournisien was there already. Two tall tapers burned at the head of the bed, which had been moved out of the alcove.

The silence weighed on the chemist, and it was not long before he was formulating a lament for this 'luckless young woman'. The priest replied that there was nothing left now but to pray for her.

'My dear sir,' said Homais, 'you can't have it both ways. Either she died in a state of grace (as the Church puts it), in which case she has no need of our prayers; or she passed away impenitent (such is, I believe, the ecclesiastical expression), in which case ...'

Bournisien broke in surlily with the retort that it was just as necessary to pray for her.

'But,' argued the chemist, 'since God knows all our needs, what purpose can be served by prayer?'

'What!' cried the priest. 'By prayer? Do you mean to say you're not a Christian?'

'Pardon me! I admire Christianity. For one thing, it abolished slavery; it introduced into the world a morality ...'

'That is not the point! All the texts ...'

'Oh, the texts, the texts! Look up your history. Everybody knows they were falsified by the Jesuits.'

Charles entered, walked up to the bed and slowly drew the curtains.

Emma lay with her head on her right shoulder. Her mouth hung open, the corner of it showing like a black hole at the bottom of her face; her thumbs were still crushed into the palms of her hands; a sort of white dust bestrewed her lashes, and her eyes were beginning to disappear in a viscous pallor that was like a fine web, as though spiders had been spinning there.

The sheet sank down between her breasts and her knees, lifting again at the tips of her toes. It seemed to Charles that there were infinite masses, of enormous weight, pressing down upon her.

The church clock struck two. Through the darkness came the deep murmur of the river flowing by at the foot of the terrace.

From time to time Bournisien blew his nose noisily, and Homais' pen went scratching over his paper.

'Come, my friend,' said the chemist, 'you have been here long enough. This is a terrible sight for you.'

Once Charles had gone, the two gentlemen resumed their debate.

'Read Voltaire!' said the one. 'Read D'Holbach! Read the *Encyclopedia!*'

'Read the *Letters of some Portuguese Jews!*' said the other. 'Read the *Proof of Christianity*, by the ex-magistrate Nicolas!'

They were growing heated, flushed, both talking at once, neither listening to the other. Bournisien was shocked by such audacity, Homais was amazed at such stupidity; and they were near to exchanging insults, when suddenly Charles reappeared. A continual fascination kept drawing him up the stairs.

He stood where he could see her best, lost in a contemplation too deep now to be painful.

He remembered hearing about catalepsy, and the wonders of magnetism. He told himself that if only he willed it strongly enough he might succeed in bringing her back to life. Once he even leant over her and gave a low cry: 'Emma! Emma!'

His panting breath set the flames of the tapers flickering against the wall.

In the early morning his mother arrived. As he kissed her, Charles burst into another flood of tears. She tried, as the chemist had done, to say something to him about the funeral expenses; he became so angry that she shut her mouth; he even assigned her the task of going off to Rouen straight away to buy what was necessary.

Charles remained alone all the afternoon. Berthe had been taken in to Madame Homais'; Félicité stayed upstairs in the bedroom with old Mother Lefrançois.

In the evening some visitors came. He rose and shook hands with them without speaking, and each in turn took his place in a large circle round the fire. With faces lowered and legs crossed they swung their feet backwards and forwards and at intervals gave vent to deep sighs. Everyone was inordinately bored, yet none would be the first to leave.

When Homais returned at nine o'clock (for two days it had been nothing but Homais running to and fro across the square) he was loaded with a supply of camphor, benjamin and aromatic herbs. He also brought a jar of chlorine water, to sweeten the air. The maid, Madame Lefrançois and old Madame Bovary were at that moment busy about Emma, in the final stage of dressing her. They drew down the long stiff veil, which covered her to her satin shoes.

'Oh, my poor mistress, my poor mistress!' sobbed Félicité.

'Look at her!' said the landlady with a sigh. 'How pretty she is still! Wouldn't you swear she'd be on her feet again directly?'

They bent over to put on her wreath; they had to lift her head a little, and as they did so a stream of dark liquid poured from her mouth, as though she were vomiting.

'Good Lord, the dress! Watch out!' cried Madame Lefrançois. 'Here, give us a hand!' she said to the chemist. 'Are you afraid, man?'

'Me afraid?' he answered with a shrug of the shoulders. 'Is it likely, after all I saw at the hospital when I was doing my pharmacy? Why, we used to make punch in the dissecting-room. Death has no terrors for a philosopher. In fact, as I've said many a time, I intend to bequeath my body to a hospital and so be of use to science after I'm dead.'

The *curé*, arriving, asked as to the doctor's condition, and when the chemist told him, he observed: 'The shock's still fresh, you understand.'

Homais thereupon congratulated him on not being exposed, like other men, to the danger of losing a beloved helpmeet: whence ensued a discussion on the celibacy of the priesthood.

'It isn't natural,' said the chemist, 'for a man to do without women. Crimes have been known ...'

'But, bless my soul!' cried the cleric, 'how do you suppose a married man would be capable of preserving such a thing as the secrecy of the confessional?'

Homais attacked confession. Bournisien defended it, dwelling on the acts of restitution it prompted and recounting various anecdotes of thieves suddenly turned honest men. Soldiers, approaching the tribunal of penitence, had felt the scales fall from their eyes. There was a minister at Fribourg ...

His companion had dropped asleep. Feeling oppressed by the stuffy atmosphere, Bournisien opened the window, and this woke the chemist.

'Have a pinch of snuff!' said he. 'Go on, take some. It clears the head.'

An incessant barking came from somewhere in the distance.

'D'you hear that dog howling?' said the chemist.

'People say they scent the dead,' answered the priest. 'Like bees, that leave the hive and fly away when anyone dies.'

Homais did not challenge these notions, for he was asleep again. The robuster Bournisien continued to move his lips gently for some time, then, insensibly, his chin dropped, his big black book slipped from his hand and he started snoring.

They sat opposite one another, bellies protruding, faces puffy and scowling, after so much discord united at last in the same human weakness; and they stirred no more than the corpse that seemed as if it were sleeping at their side.

Charles entered without waking them. It was the last time. He had come to say good-bye.

The aromatic herbs still smoked; swirls of bluish vapour mingled with the mist drifting in at the casement.

Some stars were shining. It was a mild night.

Great tears of wax fell from the tapers on to the bedclothes. Charles watched them burn, tiring his eyes in the glow of their yellow flames.

On Emma's satin dress, white as a moonbeam, the watering shimmered. She disappeared beneath it. It seemed to him as if she were escaping from herself and melting confusedly into everything about her, into the silence, the night, the passing wind, the damp odours rising.

All at once he saw her in the garden at Tostes, on the bench against the thorn hedge; or at Rouen, in the street; on the threshold of their house; in the yard at Les Bertaux. Once more he heard the merry laughter of the lads dancing under the apple-trees; the room was filled with the scent her hair had had; he felt her dress rustling in his arms again with a sound like sparks crackling – that same dress that she was wearing now!

A long time he stood there, trying to remember all those vanished delights, her poses and gestures, the tone of her voice. After one ache of despair came another and another, inexhaustibly, like the waves of an inundating tide.

A terrible curiosity gripped him. Slowly, with the tips of his fingers, his heart pounding, he lifted her veil. His shriek of horror woke the other two; they led him down into the dining-room.

Félicité came up to say he was asking for a lock of her hair.

'Cut some off!' replied the chemist.

She hesitated, and so he stepped forward himself, scissors in hand. He was shaking so violently that he punctured the skin in several places on the forehead. Finally, bracing himself for the shock, Homais gave two or three big cuts at random, which left white patches in her beautiful black hair.

The chemist and the *curé* resumed their occupations, varying these with intervals of sleep, a weakness of which they mutually accused one another at each successive awakening. Bournisien would then sprinkle the room with holy water, while Homais poured a little chlorine on the floor.

Félicité had thought to put brandy, cheese and a large roll for each of them on the chest of drawers. At about four in the morning the chemist could hold out no longer.

'My word!' he sighed. 'I would gladly partake of a little nourishment.'

The cleric needed no persuading. He went out to say his mass, came back again, and then they fell to, chuckling gently as they ate and drank without quite knowing why, animated by that vague hilarity that seizes upon us after a long spell of gloom. Over the last glass the priest clapped the chemist on the shoulder and said: 'We'll get along fine before we've finished!'

Downstairs in the hall they met the workmen arriving. For the next two hours Charles had to endure the torture of listening to the hammer resounding on the planks. Then they brought her down in her coffin, and this they encased in the other two; the outer one being too large, they had to fill up the space between with wool from a mattress. After the three lids had been planed, nailed on and soldered, they set her down by the door. The house was thrown open and the people of Yonville began to crowd in.

Old Rouault arrived, and fainted away in the square at sight of the black cloth.

10

THE chemist's letter had not reached him until thirty-six hours after the event, and out of consideration for his feelings Homais had so worded it that it was impossible to know what to believe.

At first reading, the old fellow had dropped down as though in an apoplectic fit. Then he took it that she wasn't dead. But yet she might be. ... Finally he had slipped on his blouse, picked up his hat, fixed a spur to his boot, and set off at the gallop; and all the way, as he bounded breathlessly along, old Rouault was torn with anguish. Once he had to get down from his horse to steady himself. His eyes blurred, he began to hear voices, he felt himself going mad.

Day broke. He noticed three black hens roosting in a tree, and shuddered in panic at the omen. He promised the Blessed Virgin three chasubles for the church, and made a vow to go barefoot from the cemetery at Les Bertaux to the chapel at Vassonville.

He rode into Maromme shouting for the inn people, burst open the stable-door with his shoulder, made for the oat-sack, poured out a bottle of sweet cider in the manger, and remounted his nag, setting the sparks flying from its hooves.

He told himself she'd be certain to come through. Of course the doctors would find some treatment. He called to mind all the miraculous recoveries he had heard of.

Then he had an image of her dead – there before his eyes lying on her back in the middle of the road. He drew rein, and the hallucination vanished.

At Quincampoix he drank three coffees in succession to put some heart in him.

He thought they might have made a mistake in the name, fished in his pocket for the letter, felt it there but dared not open it.

He even imagined it might be a hoax—some practical joker's idea of revenge. Besides, if she were really dead, there'd be some sign. But no, the countryside was normal, the sky blue, the trees swaying, a flock of sheep going past. He came in sight of the village. They saw him come tearing along, bent almost double on his horse, lashing it furiously, while the blood dripped from its flanks.

When he came to, he fell weeping into Bovary's arms.

'My girl! My Emma! My child! How did it ...?'

'I don't know, I don't know, it's a curse that's on us!' answered Charles amid his sobs.

The chemist parted them. 'No use going into these frightful details! I will tell your father-in-law. Here are some people coming now. Be dignified, philosophical!'

Poor Charles was struggling to control himself.

'Yes, be brave ... be brave ...' he said over and over.

'Ay, by thunder, an' I will, then!' cried the old man. 'I'll go along with her to the end!'

The bell began to toll. Everything was ready. It was time to start.

Seated side by side in one of the choir stalls, they watched the three choristers pass and repass continually in front of them, chanting. The harmonium wheezed for all it was worth. Bournisien, in full vestments, intoned in a shrill voice, bowed to the tabernacle, raised his hands, spread out his arms. Lestiboudois moved about the church with his verger's staff. The bier lay beside the lectern, between four rows of tapers; Charles felt a strong desire to go and snuff them out.

Nevertheless, he made an effort to work up some feeling of devotion, to soar on the hope of an after-life in which he would meet her again. He tried to think of her as having gone away, gone long ago, on a distant journey. But then he remembered that she was down there beneath that pall, that everything was over, that they were about to carry her away and lay her in the earth: and he was filled with a black, sullen, desperate rage. Sometimes he seemed to be past all feeling, and then he welcomed, though with some shame, that easing of his grief.

Across the flagstones sounded the sharp, regular tap-tap of a metalled stick. It came up from the far end of the church and stopped short in the aisle. A man in a loose brown jacket knelt down with difficulty. It was Hippolyte the ostler. He was wearing his best leg.

One of the choristers came round the nave to take up the collection, and the coppers rattled one by one into the silver plate.

'Be quick! This is terrible for me!' cried Bovary, angrily throwing him a crown piece.

The churchman thanked him with a low bow.

They sang, they knelt, they stood up again, there was no end to it. He remembered how once in the early days they had attended mass together and taken their places on the far side, on the right, against the wall. ... The bell started tolling again. There was a great scraping of chairs. The bearers slid their three poles under the bier and the congregation filed out.

At that moment Justin appeared in the doorway of the chemist's shop, to withdraw again hurriedly, white-faced, faltering.

People stood at their windows to see the funeral go by. Charles walked in front, squaring his shoulders, making a brave show of it, nodding to the villagers who emerged from lanes and doorways to take their places in the crowd. The six bearers, three on each side, advanced with short steps, panting a little. The priests and cantors, with the two choir-boys, re-cited the *De Profundis*; their voices carried over the fields in an undulating rise and fall. Sometimes they were lost to view at a turn in the path; but the great silver cross still rose erect amid the trees.

The women followed in black cloaks with turned-down hoods, each carrying a tall lighted taper. Charles felt himself weakening beneath the strain of all those prayers and all those candles, amid the oppressive odours of wax and cassocks. A cool breeze was blowing; the rye and the colza were coming green; tiny dewdrops trembled on the thorn hedge by the pathway. All sorts of joyful noises filled the air – the rattle of a cart jolting in the ruts far away, a cock crowing, a foal scampering off beneath the apple-trees. The clear sky was flecked with rosy clouds, a blue haze of light hung above the iris-hidden cottages. Charles, recognizing each of the gardens as he went by, recalled mornings such as this when, after visiting a number of patients, he would come away from the last of them and ride home to her.

The black pall, strewn with beads like tears, lifted occasionally in the breeze, exposing the coffin. The bearers were tiring and slowing down now, and it moved forward in a series of jerks like a boat tossing at every wave.

They reached the cemetery and kept straight on down to the bottom, where a grave had been dug in the grass.

The mourners ranged themselves around, and all the time the priest was speaking, the red earth heaped up over the edges kept slipping down at the corners ceaselessly, noiselessly.

When the four ropes were in position, the coffin was pushed on to them. He watched it go down, down ...

At last there was a thud. The ropes came creaking up again. Bournisien took the spade from Lestiboudois, and while sprinkling holy water with his right hand, drove a vigorous spadeful with his left; and the pebbles striking on the coffin gave out that dread sound that seems to us the echo of eternity.

The priest handed the sprinkler to his neighbour. It was Homais. He shook it gravely and passed it on to Charles, who sank down, up to his knees in the earth, throwing in great handfuls, crying out 'Good-bye', sending her kisses and dragging himself to the edge that he might be swallowed up with her.

They led him away. He soon grew calmer. Perhaps, like everyone else, he felt vaguely relieved that it was all over.

On the way back old Rouault started peaceably smoking his pipe – which Homais, in his inner conscience, considered scarcely decent. He noticed likewise that Monsieur Binet had absented himself, that Tuvache had slipped away after the mass, and that Théodore, the lawyer's man, had been wearing a blue coat – 'as if he couldn't get a black one! Damn it, it *is* the custom!' And he went round from group to group imparting these observations. Emma's death was being generally lamented, by none more than Lheureux, who had not failed to attend the funeral.

'Poor little lady!' said he. 'What a sorrow for her husband!'

'If it hadn't been for me, you know,' announced the chemist, 'he'd have laid violent hands on himself!'

'Such a good woman! To think I saw her in my shop only last Saturday!'

'I'd no time to spare,' said Homais, 'or I'd have prepared a few words to say over her tomb.'

Charles changed his clothes when he got home, Rouault put on his blouse again. It was a new one, and as he had frequently wiped his eyes with his sleeve on the way along, the dye had come off on his face, which still showed where the tears had run down through the dust.

Charles' mother was with them. All three were silent until at last the good Rouault sighed: 'Do you remember me coming to Tostes once when you had lost your first wife? I comforted you then. I found something to say, then. But now ...' His chest heaved with a long groan as he went on, 'There's nothing left for me now, my boy! I've seen my wife go, my son after her – and now today it's my daughter!'

He said he wouldn't be able to sleep in that house and had better start back for Les Bertaux straight away. He even refused to see his granddaughter.

'It'd upset me too much. But give her a big kiss for me. ...

Good-bye, you're a good lad! I'll never forget this, you know,' he added, slapping his thigh; 'you'll still get your turkey, never fear!'

But when he reached the top of the hill he turned and looked back, as he had turned once before after parting from her on the St Victor road. The windows of the village were all afire in the slanting rays of the sun that was sinking behind the meadows. He shaded his eyes with his hand. Away in the distance he made out a walled enclosure with black clumps of trees set here and there among white stones. Then he went his way at an easy trot, for his nag was limping.

Weary though they were, Charles and his mother stayed up talking very late. They spoke of the old days and the future; she would come to live at Yonville now and keep house for him, they would never be parted again. She was tactful and comforting, inwardly delighted at the prospect of regaining an affection that had been slipping from her over so many years. Midnight sounded. The village was silent as ever. Charles lay awake thinking incessantly of *her*.

Rodolphe, who had been out beating the coverts all day to beguile the time, slept peacefully in his mansion. Far away, Léon was sleeping too.

There was one other who was still awake at that hour.

On the grave among the pines a boy knelt weeping. His chest, shaken with sobs, heaved in the shadows beneath the burden of a measureless sorrow that was tenderer than the moon and deeper than night. Suddenly the gate creaked. It was Lestiboudois, returning to fetch his spade which he had left behind a while before. He recognized Justin clambering over the wall and knew at last where to put his finger on the rascal who stole his potatoes.

CHARLES had the little girl fetched home next day. She asked for her mummy. They told her she had gone away and would be bringing her back some toys. Berthe spoke of her several times more, then gradually stopped thinking about her. Bovary was harrowed by that child's gaiety. He had also to endure the insufferable condolences of the chemist.

Money troubles soon began again, with Lheureux once more egging on his friend Vinçart. Charles bound himself for exorbitant sums; for he would never agree to the sale of the least of *her* possessions. This annoyed his mother. However, his anger vanquished hers. He had altogether changed. She took herself off.

Then all of them spied their chance. Mademoiselle Lempereur sent in an account for three months' lessons, though Emma had never had a single one, despite the receipt she had shown Bovary; it had been an arrangement between the two women. The lending library demanded three years' subscriptions. Old Mother Rollet claimed for the delivery of a score of letters. When Charles asked her for an explanation she had the tact to reply, 'Oh, I've no idea! It was for her affairs.'

As each debt was paid, Charles thought it must be the last; but new ones kept rolling in.

He wrote to his patients asking them to settle long-outstanding accounts, was shown the letters his wife had sent, and had to apologize.

Félicité had taken to wearing Madame's dresses: not all of them, however, for he kept some of them in her dressing-room and used to go and shut himself up in there to look at them. The maid was much of her mistress's height, and often, seeing her from behind, his fancy would get the better of him and he would cry out, 'Stay! Stay there!'

But at Whitsun she flitted from Yonville, carried off by

Théodore and taking with her the remainder of the wardrobe.

About the same time, Madame Dupuis had the honour to inform him of the 'marriage of her son Monsieur Léon Dupuis, solicitor at Yvetot, to Mademoiselle Léocadie Lebœuf of Bondeville.'

'How pleased my poor wife would have been!' wrote Charles in his letter of congratulation.

One day his aimless wanderings about the house had taken him up to the attic, where as he shuffled about he felt a little ball of thin paper under his foot. He picked it up and opened it. 'Be brave, Emma, be brave!' he read. 'I do not want to ruin your life. ...' It was Rodolphe's letter. It had fallen down between some boxes and there remained until, just now, the draught from the window had blown it towards the door. Charles stood gaping at it, on the very spot where once Emma had stood in despair, paler even than he was now, thinking to end her life. At the bottom of the second page he found a little R. What did it mean? He remembered Rodolphe's assiduous attentions, his sudden disappearance, his air of constraint when they had met on two or three occasions since. But the respectful tone of the letter still deceived him.

'Perhaps,' he said to himself, 'there was a platonic love between them.' In any case Charles was not one to go to the roots of things. He shrank from proof, and his incipient jealousy was lost in the immensity of his grief.

No one, he thought, could have helped adoring her. Of course all men had wanted her. It made her seem the more beautiful and begot in him a permanent, furious desire for her, which inflamed his despair and was boundless because it could never now be gratified.

To please her, as though she were still alive, he adopted her preferences and ideas. He bought himself patent-leather boots, took to wearing white cravats, waxed his moustache and, like her, signed notes of hand. She was corrupting him from beyond the grave.

He had to sell the silver piece by piece, and after that the drawing-room furniture. All the rooms were stripped except the bedroom – *her* room – which was left just as it had been. Charles used to go up there after dinner. He pushed the round table over to the fire, drew up her armchair and sat down facing it. A candle burned in one of the gilt candlesticks. Berthe coloured prints at his side.

It hurt him, poor man, to see the child so badly dressed, no laces in her shoes, her blouses torn from arm-hole to hip; for the woman who looked after the house gave her but scant attention. But she was so sweet and pretty, and her little head bent forward so gracefully, swinging her lovely fair hair down over her rosy cheeks, that it gave him an infinite delight to watch her: a delight all mixed up with bitterness, like those raw wines that taste of the resin. He used to mend her toys or cut out cardboard puppets for her or sew up her dolls when their bellies burst. And if his eyes lighted on the work-box, on a stray ribbon, even on a pin stuck in a crevice in the table, he would fall into a reverie and look so sad that she grew sad with him.

No one came to see them now. Justin had run away to Rouen and become a grocer's boy, and the chemist's children had less and less to do with the little girl, Monsieur Homais not being anxious for the intimacy to continue, in view of the difference in their social position.

The blind man, whom he had not succeeded in curing with his ointment, had returned to the hill at Bois-Guillaume, and was telling everybody on the road about the chemist's vain endeavour, until Homais, whenever he went into Rouen, took to hiding behind the curtains of the *Hirondelle* to avoid the encounter. He detested the creature; the interests of his own reputation demanded that he be got rid of at all costs, and to that end Homais mounted a concealed battery against him, thus revealing at once the depth of his intelligence and the ruthlessness of his vanity. For six months on end little paragraphs like this might be read in the *Beacon*:

'All who take the road for the fertile plains of Picardy will have observed on the hill at Bois-Guillaume a creature afflicted with a horrible facial sore. He importunes you, persecutes you, levies what can only be called a tax on travel. Are we still in the wilderness of the Middle Ages, when tramps were permitted to expose to the public gaze the leprous and scrofulous diseases they brought back from the Crusades?'

Or again:

'Despite the vagrancy laws the approaches to our larger towns continue to be infested by troops of beggars. Solitary vagabonds are also to be seen, and these are perhaps not the least dangerous. What are the authorities thinking of?'

He concocted anecdotes:

'Yesterday on the hill at Bois-Guillaume, a skittish horse ...' – and there followed a report of an accident occasioned by the presence of the blind man.

And in the end Homais managed to get him imprisoned. He was released again, however, and resumed activity. So did Homais. It was a tussle. Homais won, his enemy being condemned to be detained for life in an institution.

Success emboldened him, and from then on there was not a dog run over, not a barn fired, not a wife beaten in all the district, but he immediately retailed it to the public, guided always by his passion for progress and his abhorrence of priests. He drew comparisons between the Primary Schools and those of the Christian Brothers, to the disadvantage of the latter. In connexion with a five-pound grant to the church he recalled the Massacre of St Bartholomew. He denounced abuses, he was 'provocative' – his own word. Homais was laying his mines.

Soon, however, he came to feel cramped within the narrow limits of journalism. Now for a book, an opus! Accordingly he compiled a *Statistical Survey of the Canton of Yonville, with*

Climatological Observations. Statistics led him into philosophy. He turned his mind to the questions of the day, to social problems, to the 'moralization' of the lower classes, to fish-breeding, rubber, railways, and so on. He began to feel ashamed of being a bourgeois; he aped the artistic temperament; he smoked! And he bought a smart pair of Pompadour statuettes to grace his drawing-room.

Not that he gave up pharmacy; on the contrary, he kept abreast of all the latest discoveries. He followed the great chocolate movement, and was the first to bring 'cho-ca' and 'revalentia' into Seine-Inférieure; he waxed enthusiastic about Pulvermacher's hydro-electric chains, and wore one himself. When he took off his flannel vest at night, Madame Homais was quite entranced by the golden spiral that enveloped him; it redoubled the fervour of her feelings for that husband swathed like a Scythian and resplendent as any of the Magi.

He had various bright ideas for Emma's tombstone. First he suggested a broken column with draping; then a pyramid; then a Temple of Vesta, a kind of rotunda; or else a 'heap of ruins'. And in all his plans Homais clung to the weeping willow, which he regarded as the necessary symbol of grief.

Charles and he went to Rouen together to inspect some tombstones at a mason's, accompanied by one Vaufrilard, an artist friend of Bridoux's, who made puns all the time. After examining scores of designs and obtaining estimates, Charles made a second journey to Rouen and finally decided on a mausoleum, to bear on its two principal sides a 'spirit holding an extinguished torch'.

For the inscription, Homais found nothing to beat '*Sta viator ...*' – and there he stuck. He racked his brains, kept saying, '*Sta viator ... Sta viator ...*' until at last he hit upon '*... amabilem conjugem calcas*', which was adopted.

It is strange how, constantly as he thought of Emma, Bovary was beginning to forget her. It drove him frantic to feel her image fading from his memory despite all his efforts to retain it. Yet he dreamt of her every night. It was always the same dream: he came close up to her, but just as he was about to clasp her to him she crumbled to dust in his arms.

For a week he went to church every evening. Bournisien even paid him two or three visits, then gave him up. That worthy was veering – said Homais – towards intolerance and fanaticism. He began to thunder against the spirit of the age, and never failed to introduce into his fortnightly sermon the story of Voltaire, who died, as everyone knows, devouring his excrement.

For all his economizing, Bovary was far from being able to pay off his debts. Lheureux refused to renew any more bills. Distraint was imminent. He applied to his mother, who, with a wealth of recriminations against Emma, agreed to let him raise a mortgage on her property. In return for this concession she asked for a shawl that had survived the ravages of Félicité. He refused to give it to her, and they quarrelled.

She made the first overtures of reconciliation by suggesting that she should take the little girl, who would be a comfort to her in the house. Charles agreed, but when the moment for parting came his courage failed him. This time the break was final and complete.

As other attachments weakened, he became the more wrapped up in his love for his child. She was an anxiety to him, though, for she used to cough, and had a red flush on her cheeks.

Across the way the chemist, whom everything conspired to bless, exhibited his hale and hearty brood. Napoléon helped him in the laboratory, Athalie was embroidering him a smoking-cap, Irma used to cut out little paper discs to go on the jam-pots, Franklin could recite the multiplication table in one breath. Was he not the happiest of fathers and the luckiest of men?

Alas! One secret ambition gnawed his heart: Homais

coveted the Legion of Honour. His claims thereto were not
lacking:

First, for having distinguished himself by an unbounded
devotion to duty at the time of the cholera.

Secondly, for having published – 'at my own expense' –
sundry works of public utility, such as ... (here he referred to
his memorandum *Cider, its Manufacture and Operation*; to
certain observations on the woolly aphis, sent to the Academy;
to his volume of statistics, and even to his pharmaceutical
thesis).

'In addition to which, I am a member of several learned
societies.' (He belonged to one.)

'And anyhow,' cried he, pivoting on his heels, 'have I not
distinguished myself with the fire-brigade?'

So Homais began to woo Authority. He secretly rendered
valuable service to the Prefect during the elections. He sold,
he prostituted, himself. He even addressed a petition to the
Sovereign, begging him to 'see justice done', calling him 'our
good King', comparing him to Henri IV.

And every morning the chemist pounced on the paper to see
if his nomination were in. It never was. At last, in his impatience, he had a little plot marked out in his garden in the shape
of the star of the order, with two strips of grass at the top to
represent the ribbon. He walked round it with folded arms,
pondering on the ineptitude of the Government and the ingratitude of men.

Whether from respect, or from a kind of sensual satisfaction
he found in spinning out his investigations, Charles had still
not opened a certain secret drawer in an ebony writing-desk
that Emma had been in the habit of using. At last one day he
sat down in front of it, turned the key and pressed the spring.
All Léon's letters were there. ... No doubt this time! He devoured them to the last one; he rummaged in every corner,
every piece of furniture, every drawer; he searched along the
walls, sobbing, howling, distraught, frantic. He found a box

and kicked it open. Amid a heap of love-letters, Rodolphe's portrait stared him in the face.

People were astonished at his dejection. He stayed indoors and saw no one, even refusing to go out to his patients. It began to be alleged that he 'shut himself up to drink'.

However, the curious would occasionally clamber up and look over the hedge, to be dumbfounded at the spectacle of a wild, shabby, bearded man who wept aloud as he strode up and down.

In the summer evenings he used to take his daughter to the cemetery; they returned after nightfall, when the only light in the square was that from Binet's attic-window.

But with no one about him to share his sorrow he could not indulge it to the full, and he used to go and see Madame Lefrançois so as to be able to talk about *her*. The landlady listened with but half an ear, having troubles of her own nowadays, for Lheureux had succeeded in putting the 'Traders' Choice' on the road, and Hivert, who enjoyed a great reputation as a shopper, was demanding a rise and threatening to go over to the opposition.

One day Charles, reduced to selling his horse, went over to the market at Argueil; and there he met Rodolphe.

Each of them paled at sight of the other. Rodolphe, who at Emma's death had merely sent his card, at first mumbled his apologies, then grew bolder, and finally regained his assurance to the point of inviting Charles (it was August and very hot) to take a bottle of beer with him at the tavern.

Leaning across the table, he chewed at his cigar as he talked, and Charles, confronted with those features that she had loved, lapsed into a daydream. It was as though he were looking at something of her. It was a miracle. He would have liked to be that man.

Rodolphe chattered about crops and cattle and fertilizers, filling in with banalities any gap that might let through an uncomfortable allusion. But Charles was not listening, and

Rodolphe could observe the flow of his memories in the changing expressions of his face. Gradually he grew flushed, his nostrils quivered, his lips began to tremble. There was even a moment when Rodolphe broke off in a kind of terror as Charles fixed his eyes on him, full of a sombre fury. But the old look of dismal lifelessness soon returned.

'I'm not angry with you,' he said.

Rodolphe sat silent, and Charles, his head in his hands, repeated in a whisper, with the resigned accent of an infinite sorrow: 'No, I'm not angry with you any more.' And then he delivered himself of the one large utterance he ever made: 'It is the fault of Fate.'

Rodolphe, who had directed 'Fate' in this instance, thought him pretty easy-going for a man in his position, rather comic, in fact, and a bit abject.

Next day Charles went to sit out on the bench in the arbour. Sunlight streamed in through the trellis, the vine-leaves traced their shadows on the gravel, jasmine scented the air, the sky was blue. Bumble-bees buzzed round the lilies in flower, and Charles felt suffocated, like a young man, by the vague currents of love that swelled his stricken heart.

At seven o'clock, Berthe, who had not seen him all afternoon, came to fetch him in to dinner.

His head was thrown back against the wall, his eyes were closed, his mouth was open, and in his hand he held a long tress of black hair.

'Come on, Daddy!' she said. And thinking he was having a game with her, she gave him a push. He fell to the ground. He was dead.

Thirty-six hours later, in answer to the chemist's request, Monsieur Canivet arrived. He opened up the body but found nothing.

When everything had been sold up there was a balance of twelve francs and seventy-five centimes which paid for Mademoiselle Bovary's journey to her grandmother's. That good lady died within the year, and the little girl was then taken in by an aunt – old Rouault being paralysed. The aunt is poor, and sends her to earn her living in a cotton-mill.

Since Bovary's death three doctors have followed one another at Yonville without success: so rapid and determined has been Homais' onslaught upon them. His practice grows like wildfire. Authority respects and public opinion protects him.

He has just been awarded the Legion of Honour.